KU-481-838

SALMAN RUSHDIE

Grimus

PANTHER
Granada Publishing

Panther Books
Granada Publishing Ltd
8 Grafton Street, London W1X 3LA

Published by Panther Books 1977
Reprinted 1981, 1982, 1983, 1984

First published in Great Britain by
Victor Gollancz Ltd 1975

ISBN 0-586-04289-X

Printed and bound in Great Britain by
Collins, Glasgow

Set in Linotype Plantin

For Clarissa

ACKNOWLEDGEMENTS

The author would like to thank Messrs Faber
& Faber for permission to quote from *The Four
Quartets*, T. S. Eliot: *Collected Poems, 1909–
1962*, and from *Crow's Playmates*, Ted Hughes:
Crow

Go, go, go, said the bird; human kind
Cannot bear very much reality.

(T. S. ELIOT)

Come, you lost atoms, to your Centre draw,
And *be* the Eternal Mirror that you saw;
Rays that have wandered into darkness wide,
Return, and back into your sun subside.

(FARID-UD-DIN 'ATTAR,
The Conference of the Birds, trans. Fitzgerald)

Crow straggled, limply bedraggled his remnant.
He was his own leftover, the spat-out scrag.
He was what his brain could make nothing of.

(TED HUGHES,
'Crow's Playmates')

The sands of Time are steeped in new
Beginnings.

(IGNATIUS Q. GRIBB,
The All-Purpose Quotable Philosophy)

THE CHAPTERS

PART ONE

TIMES PRESENT

ONE

Mr Virgil Jones, a man devoid of friends and with a tongue rather too large for his mouth, was fond of descending this cliff-path on Tiusday mornings. (Mr Jones, something of a pedant and interested in the origins of things, referred to the days of his week as Sunday, Moonday, Tiusday, Wodensday, Thorsday, Freyday and Saturnday; it was affectations like this, among other things, that had left him friendless.) It was five a.m.; for no reason, Mr Jones habitually chose this entirely random time to indulge his liking for Calf Island's one small beach. Accordingly, he was tripping goat-fashion down the downward spiral of the path, trailing in the nimbler wake of a hunchbacked crone called Dolores O'Toole, who had an exceptionally beautiful walnut rocking-chair strapped to her back. The strap was Mr Jones' belt. Which meant he was obliged to use both his hands to hold his trousers up. This kept him fairly preoccupied.

Some more facts about Mr Jones: he was gross of body and short of sight. His eyes blinked a lot, refusing to believe in their myopia. He had three initials: V. B. C. Jones, Esq. The B was for Beauvoir and the C for Chanakya. These were historical names, names to conjure with, and Mr Jones, though no conjurer, considered himself something of an historian. Today, as he arrived at the dead greysilver sands of his chosen island, surrounded by the greysilver mists that hung forever upon the surrounding, sundering seas, he was about to make his rendezvous with a small historical event. If he had known, he would have philosophized at length about the parade of history, about the historian's inability to stand apart and watch; it was erroneous, he would have said, to look upon oneself as an Olympian chronicler; one was a member of the parade. An historian is affected by the present events that eternally recreate the past. He would have thought this earnestly, although for some time now the parade had been progressing without his help. However, because he was shortsighted, because of the mist and because he was trying to keep his trousers on, he didn't see the body of one Flapping Eagle floating in on the incoming tide; and

Dolores O'Toole was spared the trouble of being an audience.

Sometimes, people trying to commit suicide manage it in a manner that leaves them breathless with astonishment. Flapping Eagle, coming in fast now on the crest of a wave, was about to discover this fact. At present he was unconscious; he had just fallen through a hole in the sea. The sea had been the Mediterranean. It wasn't now; or not quite.

The crone Dolores placed the rocking-chair on the sands. Mr Jones supervised approvingly. The rocking-chair faced away from the sea and towards the massive forested rock of Calf Mountain, which occupied most of the island except for the small clearing, directly above the beach, where Mr Jones and Dolores lived. Mr Jones sat down and began to rock.

Dolores O'Toole was a lapsed Catholic. She sometimes took unholy pleasure in the act of stimulating herself with church, or roman, candles. She did this because she was separated from her husband but not from her desires. Her sometime spouse, Mr O'Toole, ran a drinking establishment in K, the town high on the slopes of Calf Mountain, and she disapproved of K in general, of drinkers in particular and of her husband most particularly of all. She gave vent to this disapproval by living in isolation with Virgil Jones (far from K, from Mr O'Toole's bar and from his favourite place of recreation, Madame Jocasta's notorious bawdy-house). And every Tiusday at dawn she carried Mr Jones' rocking-chair to the beach.

– Crestfallen, murmured Mr Jones to himself, with his back to the sea. Crestfallen, the sea today.

The body of Flapping Eagle touched land face upwards, which explains why he hadn't drowned. He was quite near the back of Mr Jones' rocking-chair, and the encroaching waves pushed him ever nearer and nearer. Mr Jones and Mrs O'Toole remained oblivious of his presence.

It should be pointed out that Flapping Eagle was averagely kind and good; but he would soon be responsible for a large number of deaths. He was also as sane as the next man, but then the next man was Mr Virgil Jones.

There was an extraordinary coincidence involved in the relationship of Virgil Jones and Dolores O'Toole: they loved each other and found it impossible to declare their love. It was no beautiful love, for they were extremely ugly. It was undeclared, because each had been so badly damaged by experience that

13

they preferred to nurture their feelings in the privacy of their own bosoms, rather than expose them to possible ridicule and rejection. So they would sit close, but separated by this privacy, and Dolores would sing cracked songs, toothless rimes of mourning requition; while Virgil would talk his lilting elliptical talk, exercising the thoughts and the tongue which were both too large for his head to hold, and there on the deserted beach was as close as they came to joy.

Whitebeard is all my love and whitebeard is my desire, sang Dolores dolefully, to the rhythm of the swaying rocking-chair. Virgil, lost in thought, stroked his white-grizzled chin and did not hear.

– Language, he mused, language makes concepts. Concepts make chains. I am bound, Dotty, bound and I don't know where. Not enough of the ether for the way of Grimus, not enough of the earth for the way of K, moving pingpongways in thought between them and you. Dolores O'Thule. Sorrow of the gods. My dear, I was not always as you see me now. The terror of the titties, I. Once. Then. Before.

– *Early one morning, just as the Son was borning, I a maiden crying in the valley below,* wailed Dolores.

The insensate Eagle was within a foot of the rockers.

– This island, muttered Virgil Jones firmly, but under his breath, is the most terrible place in all creation. Since we seem to survive and are not sucked into its ways, we seem to love.

He would have reflected further, on ritual, on obsession, on the neuroses and displacement activities that exile creates, on age, on entrapment, on friendship and love, on the state of his corns, on the ornithology of myth, and refined and invented thoughts in the peace of Dolores' presence; and she would have sung further, until her songs dropped a tear from her eyes; and then they would have gone home.

But at that moment the body of Flapping Eagle came to rest against the perfectly-carved rockers of the perfectly-carved rocking-chair with the perfectly-carved dancers spiralling along them. The chair, thus affronted, stopped rocking.

– Death, exclaimed Dolores in terror. Death, from the sea. . . .

Virgil Jones didn't reply, having a mouth full of the sea

14

which had lodged in Flapping Eagle's lungs. But he, too, as he breathed life back into the stranger, was alarmed.

– No, he said eventually, willing himself and Dolores to believe it. The face is too pale.

A remarkable fact about Flapping Eagle's arrival at Calf Island: the island-dwellers, who shouldn't have been too surprised at his arrival, found it highly disturbing, even unnerving. Whereas Flapping Eagle himself, once he acquired a certain piece of knowledge, rapidly came to acept his arrival as entirely unremarkable.

The piece of knowledge was this:
No-one ever came to Calf Island by accident.
The mountain drew its own kind to itself.
Or perhaps it was Grimus who did that.

TWO

The day had begun well enough. That is to say, it resembled the previous day sufficiently (in terms of weather, temperature and mood) to give the half-sleeping young man the illusion of continuity. Yet it also differed sufficiently from the recently-passed (in terms of subtle things like the direction of the wind, the cries of the swooping birds above and the squawks of the womenfolk below) to produce an equal and opposite illusion of temporal movement. The young man was basking pleasurably in these conflicting and harmonious mirages, drifting slowly up towards consciousness, which would banish both and substitute a third illusion: the present.

I was the boy. I was Joe-Sue, Axona Indian, orphan, named ambiguously at birth because my sex was uncertain until some time later, virgin, young brother of a wild female animal called Bird-Dog, who was scared of losing her beauty, which was ironic, for she was not beautiful. It was my (his) twenty-first birthday, too, and I was about to become Flapping Eagle. And cease to be a few other people.

(I was Flapping Eagle.)

The Axona aren't interested in twenty-first birthdays. They celebrate only puberty, loss of virginity, proof of bravery, marriage and death. At puberty the Old took goats' hairs and tied them like a beard round my face, while the Sham-Man anointed my newly-potent organs with the entrails of a hare, for fertility, chanting to the god Axona as he did so.

The god Axona had only two laws: he liked the Axona to chant to him as often as possible, in the field, on the toilet, while making love if concentration allowed; and he instructed the Axona to be a race apart and have no doings with the wicked world. I never had much time for the god Axona, especially after I reached puberty, because once my voice cracked it became extremely infelicitous and I gave up chanting entirely. And then there was Bird-Dog and her fondness for the outside world. If it hadn't been for this fondness, she might never have met the pedlar Sispy; and then she might never have left, and then I might never have left, and it would all have been different. Or perhaps there would inevitably have been a Sispy.

Let me explain some things. I grew up on a table-top in what is, I believe, still known as the United States, or, colloquially, Amerindia. The table-top was self-supporting: that is to say, it produced all the food the Axona required. No Axona had ever descended from this plateau to the plains beneath; and after a few battles in which the wicked world discovered how impregnable a fortress Axona was, they left us alone. Bird-Dog was the first Axona to visit the plains as far as I know; she was certainly the first to learn the language and develop a distinct taste or affinity for them.

To understand Bird-Dog, it is necessary to know that we were orphans, Bird-Dog and Joe-Sue. My mother died moments before I was born, which is why my formal given name was Born-From-Dead. Joe-Sue is what they called me to spare me hurt. Though whether it is painless to be known for twenty-one years by a hermaphrodite's name, which causes every eligible female to recoil for fear of breaking tabu, I leave others to judge.

My father died soon afterwards, leaving the thirteen-year old Bird-Dog with full responsibility for me. Bird-Dog was not her formal given name. Nobody ever told me what that was. She took it for herself, as a brave's name, at the age of sixteen.

This was not a popular move among the Axona, but Bird-Dog and I were never much loved after the death of my people. This is why: orphans in Axona are like mongrels among pedigree hounds. We were near-pariah from the moment my father passed on, and our natures exacerbated our plight.

Bird-Dog had always been a free spirit. I say this with some envy, for I never was, nor am. Conventions did not touch her, artifice never seized her. As a child she was drawn to the bow and arrow and loathed the stove and cauldron, much to the dismay of the Old. This was a stroke of luck for me. It meant she could forage food for us. It meant she was as good in the fields as most young men. Bird-Dog was a born provider. With breasts. Breasted providers were anathema to the Axona.

As I grew, the disapproval became more and more overt. Conversation would stop at the water well when I approached. Shoulders grew cold when Bird-Dog passed. Noses tilted into the air, the Axona ostracized us as far as they could. They could not expel us; we had committed no crime. But they didn't have to like us, so they didn't.

— Well, said Bird-Dog to me when I was sixteen (and a young, helpless sixteen I was), if they don't want us, we can do without them.

— Yes, I said, we can do without. I said it sadly, because though I was easily influenced by Bird-Dog, I had the adolescent's latent love of acceptability.

— We'll just have to find our friends elsewhere. She said it casually if a little defiantly. She had obviously brooded on it for years. It was a sentence which would change our present, our future, our whole lives. Of course, Joe-Sue agreed with his big, competent, manly sister.

What Bird-Dog never accused me of, what I found out only after she had gone, was that the main reason, the true cause of our detachment from our tribe, was not our orphan status, not her manliness, not her taking of a brave's name, not her general demeanour, not her at all. It was me, Joe-Sue.

For three reasons: first, my confused sex; second, the circumstances of my birth; and third, my pigmentation. To take them in order. To be a hermaphrodite among the Axona is to be very bad medicine. A monster. To mutate from that state into a 'normal' male is akin to black magic. They didn't like that. To be what I was, born from dead, was a dire omen; if I could bring death at the moment of my birth, it would sit upon my shoulder like a vulture wherever I went. As for my colouring: the Axona are a dark-skinned race and shortish. As I grew, it became apparent that I was, inexplicably, to be fair-skinned and tallish. This further genetic aberration – *whiteness* – meant they were frightened of me and shied away from contact.

Because they were frightened, they gave us a measure of respect. Because I was a freak, they gave us a measure of scorn.

It goes without saying that Bird-Dog and I were very close indeed. How much she suffered because of my deformities, she never said. It was a mark of her love.

So, unconsciously, from those early days, I was being equipped for the voyage to Calf Island. I was an exile in an isolated community, and I clung to my love for my sister as a castaway to driftwood.

That day, when Bird-Dog spoke the unspeakable, she let me into a secret.

– Before I was your age I went Down, she said. I was shocked. In those days the idea of breaking the law of Axona still shocked me.

– When I was your age I went into the town, she said, and listened at a window outside an eating-place. There was a singing machine there. It sang about a creature called a bird-dog, clever, fiendish. It feared the creature. I thought: that is the brave's name for me.

In a state of semi-shock, I asked: – What about the Demons? and my voice stuttered. How did you escape the Whirling Demons?

She tossed her head. – Easy, she said with contempt. They're nothing at all but air, they aren't.

Ever since that day, Bird-Dog made frequent journeys into town. She would return full of tales of moving pictures and fast-moving machines; of machines that gave water and food, and of such numbers and numbers of people . . . I never had the courage to accompany her. It was there, in the town, that she learnt about twenty-first birthdays. – That's the day you'll prove you're a brave, she said. You'll go into town; and what's more you'll go in alone.

It was also the day she met Mr Sispy and was given eternal life.

As I said, the day began well enough for young Joe-Sue. But once he was awake it gave the lie to its beginnings.

THREE

It was Joe-Sue's birthday: I got up and went outside. The sky was a blinding blue. The table-top dotted with red-brown tents was a deep, rich green, a green thumb sticking sorely above a rich-red, barren-brown world. If the Whirling Demons were whirling below, they couldn't catch me, and all seemed right with the world.

Bird-Dog was sitting on an outcrop of rock, a grown woman of thirty-four years, three months and four days, in rags, her hair falling blackly over the olive face. She clutched two small bottles. The one in her right hand was full of bright yellow liquid. The one in her left hand was full of bright blue liquid. Colour was rampant everywhere, except in my skin. I felt a cloud pass across the sun.

The gleam of excitement in Bird-Dog's face as she crouched eagerly over her treasures dispelled the bleak moment.

– I've been down, she said, to see if the Whirling Demons are quiet today. They're quiet. It's all right. But her voice was absent, her eyes stared fiercely at the brightly-coloured phials.

– I met a man between here and the town, she said distantly. He gave me these.

– What are they? Who was he? Why did he give you them?

– He was a pedlar. His name was Mr Sispy. Nice man. Funny name, Sispy. He gave them to me because I wanted them.

– But what do they do?

– They'll keep me young, she said, clutching them ever more tightly. Or at least this one will. She held up the yellow phial.

– For how long? I asked timorously. The shadow was back.

– Forever, she screamed triumphantly, and then burst into tears.

With my arms around her, moistened by her tears of frightened joy, I asked:

– What does the other one do, the blue one?

She didn't answer at once.

Now that I am so much older, I am not at all sure what the word *magician* means. To Joe-Sue that day, born and raised as he was in a tribe where magic intermingled continually with

19

daily life, it meant anyone apparently in possession of powers, or knowledge, which he himself lacked. Perhaps that's the only sense in which the word has meaning; and by that definition, for Joe-Sue and Bird-Dog as they were then, Mr Sispy was unquestionably a magician. This is how Bird-Dog described their encounter:

— I was sitting behind a rock watching for Whirling Demons and suddenly behind me there was this voice whispering SISPY SISPY it said and I whirled fast as any demon to find where he WAS and he knew my name. Bird-Dog he whispered and the sound sounded so harsh on his lips because he spoke so softly and sighing like the breeze in a whisper it was, his voice the whole world in a whisper such a spell it was. Bird-Dog are you beautiful he asked and since he asked it it was so and I answered yes, yes I am beautiful if you say it and he said yes you are beautiful but Bird-Dog you will die such a word it sounded harsh as my name on his lips so I cried. Sispy I cried Sispy. Such a smile it was the sun in it and the summer too he smiled and I could not cry. The world is full of secrets he said and surprises. I say Sispy behind you and here I am surprising you. With a secret in my sack. I travel he said and search for the likes of you, like seeking like, passing on my little secret. The beauty of it is: with it you will stay beautiful, you will not die, you will have the gift of time to search out all you wish to seek, to learn all you wish to know, to accomplish all you wish to do, to become all you wish to be. And the horror of it is: all who possess the secret wish in the end to give it up, it weighing them down like a last straw at last, and the camel's back bends and passes through the eye of the needle. Then he gave me the drinks, yellow for the sun and brightness and life and blue for infinity and calm and release when I want it. Life in a yellow bottle, death blue as the sky, ice-blue as steel, he said. He was so badly-dressed, a poor pedlar's dress and a large sack of patches with drawings drawn on it and he turned to go. I said I have a brother called Born-From-Dead and today is his brave's day, have you secrets for him? He had, the same for young Born-From-Dead, he said. Then before he went he said, for those who will not use the blue there is only one place I know of; I am going there now and someday if you will not use the blue you will come with me. And finally he said: tell your brother Born-From-Dead that all eagles come at last to eyrie and all sailors come at last to shore. SISPY SISPY he whispered to the breeze and shivered and then he wasn't there.

Bird-Dog was not normally a voluble woman so Joe-Sue would have found her speech strange even if it had been about the weather. As it was it was shattering. She reached into a deep pocket of her rags and brought out two more bottles, identical to her own proud possessions. They were his, mine. The yellow eternity of life and the blue eternity of death. Joe-Sue took them and ran into his tent, scrabbling in the earth to bury them under his sleeping-mat. When he came out again the yellow bottle stood empty and the blue bottle lay dashed to fragments on the rock where Bird-Dog sat. – Death, she said. Death to death.

But Joe-Sue didn't drink his. It would soon be a division between them.

After a long silence, in which distances stretched like universes in every direction, she said, with her old aggressive practicality, – Off with you now Joe-Sue, off with you to town.

So I went down the side of the Axona table-top to the plain of the Whirling Demons that I had been taught to fear; but the little whirlwinds that spring up on that barren plain soon proved, as Bird-Dog had said, to be nothing but air, so I reached the town without trouble, dancing easily out of their way. I saw automobiles and launderettes and juke-boxes and all kinds of machines and people dressed in dusty clothes with a kind of despair in their eyes; I saw it all hiding behind doors and fences and lurking in corridors and I don't think I was seen. Finally I'd seen enough; the glimpse had infected me already and entirely though I didn't know it yet, just as it had infected Bird-Dog.

And the people in the town were white.

A curious thing happened on my way up to the table-top. I saw an eagle sitting on a rock, about shoulder-height to me, looking at me. It stopped me in my tracks, I tell you. A great full-grown cruel-looking monster of an eagle. I moved slowly, slowly, closer and closer to the bird. It didn't move, showed no sign of fear, as if it were expecting me. I stretched out my hands; it came peacefully into my grasp. I was astonished yet again on this astonishing day. I held it and stroked it a moment and then, abruptly, as unexpectedly violent as it had been calm, it began to fight me. Of course I released my grip rapidly, but not before that cruel beak had scarred my chest. It flew away. I watched it go; you could say a part of me went with it.

– Flapping Eagle. The voice was Bird-Dog's. She had been watching, silently.

– That is your name. Flapping Eagle. Why else do you think the eagle came to you before attacking you? It's your brave's name, it must be.

– Flapping Eagle, said Joe-Sue aloud. Yes.

– It's a name to live up to, said Bird-Dog.

– Yes, I said.

– And now's the time to start, she said. She lay down on the rock where she had sat to watch me with the eagle, and raised her ragged skirts.

So, on one day, I was offered eternal life, broke the law of the Axona, took a brave's name from an omen and lost my virginity to my sister. It was enough to make a fellow believe there was something special about being twenty-one.

FOUR

The Sham-Man entered Flapping Eagle's tent brandishing his ju-ju stick like a sad, sadistic schoolmaster, filled with deep regret for the grief he loved to cause. The Sham-Man said he only loved bringing pain to others when it was forced on him by his duty, for he loved his work. He was a huge, shambling, beaded walrus to Flapping Eagle's tense, terse, silent oyster.

– My apologies, said the Sham-Man mournfully, for intruding. I believe we have a slightly delicate matter to discuss. (Flapping Eagle noticed his mouth; it was watering at the edges.)

– Ahem, continued the Sham-Man, I just wondered, have you any idea at all where . . . she . . . is? In common with most of the Axona, he was reluctant to concede to Bird-Dog her right to a brave's name; also in common with most of the Axona, he'd forgotten what she had been called before.

– No, said Flapping Eagle. But she's not here. Not in Axona.

– Precisely. You realize this puts us both into a rather awkward position? *Vis-à-vis* the law, you see.

It really was very simple. Bird-Dog's sudden disappearance meant Flapping Eagle, as next of kin and sole surviving family, was at last open to attack by the Axona. As the lawbreaker could not be punished, so her guilt fell upon him. There was only one punishment: exile.

All that Bird-Dog had said was: I saw Sispy again today. We're leaving. That was in the small hours of the morning. It was only later that Flapping Eagle had been struck by the thought that he was exactly as old today as Bird-Dog had been on the day she first met the pedlar. Thirty-four years, three months and four days. It was as if his future had touched her past.

It was an abrupt departure, but then the two of them had been growing away from each other ever since Flapping Eagle's refusal to drink the yellow elixir. To him, it had been faintly nauseating to watch Bird-Dog petrified at an immutable age, her cells reproducing perfectly every day, not a hair falling that wasn't replaced by a new one. And for Bird-Dog, the spectacle of her little brother growing up towards her daily was a constant rejection of herself and the decision she had made. It was the first and only important thing in which Flapping Eagle had not followed her lead.

They hadn't even made love for several years; both of them missed it. Still, thought Flapping Eagle, now she's got Sispy. A pedlar's woman: tame ending for her.

The Sham-Man was clearing his throat again. Flapping Eagle forced himself to listen to his equivocations.

– Health, you know, said the walrus pontifically, is a tricky thing. Awfully tricky. The thing is to make sure one is always one jump ahead. Craftier than the slinking germ, if you follow me. Catch the worm before it turns, eh, eh?

The Axona were obsessed with health and cleanliness. They used more metaphors deriving from this preoccupation than the wildest hypochondriac.

– At this moment (the Sham-Man's face shaped itself into a mask of tragedy) I'm afraid the corpse of opinion is dead against you, old chap.

– Corpus, said Flapping Eagle.

– Exactly. Dead against. Temperatures are rising. There is a

23

fever abroad in the land, if you take my meaning. There are those who diagnose a modicum of blood-letting (his lips curled into an expression of elegant distaste) but of course I'm not wholly in agreement with them. See their point, mind you. Just don't happen to agree. Must be my liberal upbringing.

– What is your position, asked Flapping Eagle.

– Ah. My position. Ah. Now there's a question. I quote the sayings of Axona, correct me if I get anything wrong: 'All that is Unaxona is Unclean.' I'm afraid we really can't have contamination around here, you know. Spreads like wildfire. And before you know it, poof, there's a disease. Nothing against you personally, naturally. Always thought you more sinned against and so forth. But there you are, what can one do, she's got you for the high jump, I'm afraid. After all you may already be infected.

– So what do you suggest?

– Tell you what. TELL you WHAT. Why not, this evening, under cover of darkness, you follow, why not just slip away completely? Save a lot of unpleasant scenes. That's what I suggest. Think about it. I'm really very sorry about all this.

Flapping Eagle, alone in his tent, scrabbled furiously at the floor. Then he had them: the yellow and the blue. – At least, he thought, if I am to live in the Outside, I may as well give myself one advantage. He drained the life-giving fluid. It tasted bitter-sweet. He put the blue bottle in a pocket.

I mentioned that life among the Axona prepared me in many ways for Calf Island. One of the ways was this: it taught Flapping Eagle the power of obsession.

The town was called Phoenix because it had risen from the ashes of a great fire which had completely destroyed the earlier and much larger city also called Phoenix. Nobody knew why the city had been given that name. It was a small town now.

When Livia Cramm drove through towns like Phoenix, she kept her eyes skinned, while affecting a pose of languid boredom. Mrs Cramm was a human predator; she consumed the passions of men with an entirely unwholesome glee. The unfortunate Mr Cramm, a small, bespectacled, inadequate billionaire, had long ago been drained by her of all his vital juices and expired in her crushing embrace, murmuring words of

24

endearment and leaving her all his billions in his will. He also left her his vehicles, his horses, his Amerindian and Caucasian estates, and best of all his yacht. If there was one thing that could seduce Mrs Cramm away from seduction, it was the sea. It was a love she and Mr Cramm had shared: the only love they had shared.

– Mr Cramm, Mrs Cramm was fond of saying, in the days before she refined her speech, had a favourite joke about the sea. Whenever you're sad or confused, he would declare, the thing to do is contemplate your naval. Navel, you see. Mr Cramm always did have a terrible sensayuma. He used to call me his Jungfrau, being something of a polyglot. When I asked him why he'd say quick as anything, baby, you sure ain't no Freudlein!! Oh, Jee-Zuss, that sensayuma. I like a man that makes me laugh. Especially when he's got a maritime background.

These days Mrs Cramm, being past her prime, was more refined and less choosy. She liked them young, but not too young; tall, but not too tall; fair, but with a hint of dark. Otherwise she took them as they came. She kept her eyes skinned in towns like Phoenix because they were full of youngish, tallish, fair-to-darkish, hopelessly broke possibles.

So seeing Flapping Eagle quickened her pulse noticeably. The thrill of the chase had never palled on Livia Cramm. Yoicks, she thought.

– Hey you there with the big eyes, she called. Coo-eee.

Flapping Eagle stopped mooching idly down the street. The can he had been kicking came clattering to rest.

– Like a job?

– Doing what? Flapping Eagle tried not to show his eagerness.

– Oh, you know, earning money, shouted Mrs Cramm. Odd jobs. Stuff like that.

Flapping Eagle considered for about one second. He came up to her huge car.

– Ma'am, he said, where I come from, we have a saying. A live dog is better than a dead lion, but death is preferable to poverty.

– I can see, said Mrs Cramm, we're going to have a fascinating relationship. I like a man with brains.

As the car swept them off, Flapping Eagle reflected that once

25

again he was being ruled by an older woman. Hot on the heels of this thought came the notion that he didn't mind. I was an adaptable sort of man, more a chameleon than an eagle, better at reaction than action. Whereas Mrs Cramm looked good for some action.

FIVE

Flapping Eagle never liked Nicholas Deggle. He couldn't understand, for one thing, what he was to Livia Cramm. He appeared to do little more than the occasional conjuring trick and receive large sums of money – and the odd jewel – for doing it.

– Gifts, darling, was Mrs Cramm's explanation. He's a friend of mine and a genius what's more. A real *malin* talent. Can't I give my friends presents?

Nicholas Deggle never looked like a genius in Flapping Eagle's eyes: except perhaps in that he had a genuine gift for accepting his benefactor's munificence graciously. Nor, in his dark svelte finery, ring-laden and perfumed, with a rose in his buttonhole, did he look as if he needed the gifts.

Being absolved from the depredations of age, Flapping Eagle missed the key to Livia's dependence on Deggle. As she aged, she became increasingly absorbed in the supernatural. She devoured the tarot, the scriptures, the cabbala, palmistry, anything and everything which held that the world was more than it seemed; that the physical end was not, in fact, the end. Since Deggle shared her interests and was a good deal more expert than she, Livia Cramm found him indispensable.

Deggle was in the habit of carrying around what he called his wand. This was an extraordinary object: cylindrical, some six inches long, slightly curving. The extraordinary thing was that it was made of solid stone. Flapping Eagle had never seen the like.

– Where did you find that? he once asked. Deggle looked at him quizzically and replied:

– It is the stem of a stone rose; I broke it off. Flapping Eagle felt foolish; by asking the question he had laid himself open to the ridicule of the answer.

The wand would be used in Deggle's occasional displays of

conjuring skill. He would stand, long-nosed and dark, in a black cloak, and conjure marvels from the air. Even Flapping Eagle was impressed at these displays, and disliked Deggle even more for impressing him. The conjurer never revealed his secrets, but they made Livia dote upon him.

Once, after such a display, Livia was eager to show off her own supernatural skills. She beckoned Flapping Eagle imperiously. – Come over here, she said, and let Livia read your darling hand.

Flapping Eagle approached suspiciously. Livia looked and squeezed and felt and prodded; and assumed an air of great gravity.

– Well, my Eagle, she said, What a terrible hand it is.

Flapping Eagle's heart missed an involuntary beat.

– Are you sure you want to know? asked Mrs Cramm seriously.

Flapping Eagle thought : she makes it sound as though I have a choice. He looked into her eager eyes, glistening with their dread knowledge, and nodded.

Livia Cramm closed her eyes and intoned :

– You will live long and except for one serious illness be very healthy. The illness is an illness of the mind, but you will recover from it, though it may have a profound effect upon your career. You will neither marry nor father children. You will have no profession; nor do you have great talent. Your luck is bad. It is your lot to be led by others; in the end you will accept this. But most of all you are dangerous. You will bring grief and suffering and pain to those you know. Not intentionally; you are not malicious. But you are a bringer of ill winds. Where you walk, walks Death.

Flapping Eagle had to tense his muscles to prevent his hand from quivering. Without knowing about it, Livia Cramm had reiterated the curse of his birth and his given name.

She looked up and smiled as if to comfort him.

– But you are very attractive, she said in her usual voice. Deggle smiled too.

Mrs Cramm's dependence on Deggle grew unceasingly. Whenever Flapping Eagle made a suggestion, that they should sail here, or winter there, or even eat at such and such a place, it irked him to observe the slight questioning inclination of her head in Deggle's direction before she delightedly agreed or gently demurred. There was no appeal from her decisions.

Two phrases usually formed the focal point of Flapping Eagle's irritation. One was Livia Cramm's. Whenever Deggle let drop some dark conversational flower from those saturnine lips, she would clap her hands excitedly, like a pubertal girl shown a naughty thing behind a rosebush, and exclaim (meticulously cultivated accent slipping in her transport) – *Ain't that the Deggle himself talkin' to you.* And she would look gleamingly pleased with the wickedness of the pun. At which Flapping Eagle clamped his mouth shut and stifled his thoughts.

The second phrase was Deggle's own. He came and went his unknowable way, sauntering in and out of Mrs Cramm's villa on the southern coast of Morispain, and every time he left, he would wave unsmilingly and say: – Ethiopia!

It was a complex and awful joke, arising from the archaic name of that closed, hidden, historical country (Abyssinia . . . I'll be seeing you) and it drove Flapping Eagle out of his mind every time it was said. Ethiopia. Ethiopia. Ethiopia.

Deggle made Flapping Eagle wonder if he could bear his chosen fate.

He had been with Livia Cramm now, her personal gigolo, for twenty-five years. His reasoning was very simple: He had time, more than any in the universe but he had no money. She had a great deal of money and very little time. Thus, by sacrificing a small amount of his time he could very likely acquire a large amount of her cash. It was his most cynical decision, born of desperation, born from the future of dead possibilities that stared him in the face when Mrs Cramm had noticed him in Phoenix. He would have felt a great deal of guilt about it except for one thing: he did not like Livia Cramm.

Livia had been forty-five when she first met Flapping Eagle, and was then a ruined beauty of still-considerable sexual attraction and magnetism. Now, at seventy, the sexual attraction had gone. The magnetism had become an obnoxious, claustrophobic clinging. She clutched Flapping Eagle fiercely, as though she would never let go until he died on her as the unlamented Oscar Cramm had done so many years ago. In public her bony claws of hands never released him; in private she lay, her head eternally on his lap, gripping her own legs till her knuckles stood

28

out whitely; in bed, she squeezed him with a strength so remarkable, it often left him winded. If she saw him speak to
another woman she would descend upon them and in her
cracked old tones deliver herself of a ringingly vulgar insult
which sent the unfortunate female scurrying for shelter. Then
she would apologize to Flapping Eagle, trying to look little-
girl-coy (which was a sickening sight) and say: – I'm sorry,
loveliest, did I spoil your fun then, did I?

There was no escape from Mrs Cramm.

Deggle had arrived on the scene comparatively recently: only
eighteen months or so. This had made life even less supportable
because Flapping Eagle was now no longer even the one who
helped Livia decide the next step in her trivial, perpetually-
dying life. He was just a symbol of her pulling power, male
physical beauty incarnate, and thinking was no part of his
duties. He was her refuge from the lonely blasts of antiquity.

– My Eagle never grows old, she would say proudly. Look at
him: fifty-one (Flapping Eagle had lied to her about his age
when they first met) and doesn't look a day over thirty. Wonderful what good screwing can do.

Her politer acquaintances replied: – He's not the only one,
Livia. You're incredible yourself, you know. Which had been
the point of her comment. There were less and less of these
acquaintances left.

Flapping Eagle's only permitted source of regular human
contact was, of course, Nicholas Deggle. And so cramped, so
enclosed by the engulfing Mrs Cramm did he feel, that every so
often he would make use of this source. He tried to tell himself
that he treated Deggle as a social whore, in the same way as he
was Livia's sexual whore; but Deggle got the better of their
exchanges too regularly to be so described.

Deggle reclined on a brocaded sofa.
– The issue is beyond doubt, he drawled. Livia Cramm is a
monster.

Flapping Eagle said nothing.
– La Femme-Crammpon, said Deggle, and laughed, a shrill,
falsetto noise.
– What?
– My dear Eagle, I've just realized. Do you know into whose

clutches you have fallen? He was beside himself with laughter at his incomprehensible joke.

Flapping Eagle gave him his feed-line. – Go on. Tell me who it is.

– But my dear, *c'est la Femme-Crampon*! The clutching woman. Or, as you'd say, the Old Woman of the Sea! The Vieillarde herself!

He clutched his sides in agonies of mirth. (I sat ashen-faced and silent. There were times when Deggle frightened me.)

– It's all true, he burst out between uncontrollable spasms. She's old enough. She's ugly enough. She lives for sea-travel. She picks up wandering youths like yourself, though you're not as young as you look. And now she's got you in her clutches, to squeeze and tighten and constrict until there's no breath left in your body. Livia Cramm, the terror of voyagers! Why, she's even taught you to love the sea to make it easier to rule you! Poor sailor, poor pretty-faced matelot that you are. You're no more than a walking corpse with the Old Woman on your back, her legs gripping tightly, tightly, like the knot that tightens as you wrestle with it, tightly round your, ha ha, windpipe.

I wouldn't even bother to struggle, he finished, wiping away the tears.

And this was another conversation with Nicholas Deggle:

– Have you ever wondered about old Oscar Cramm?

– Not really, said Flapping Eagle. He had had too many other things to wonder about.

– He never had a chance with that old man-eater, said Deggle. They say he passed on while making love to her, you know. I wonder if there were any bite-marks in his neck.

– Are you saying ... began Flapping Eagle.

– Possibly I am, smiled Deggle. He wasn't all that old, you know. Now if Livia were to think that you were getting on a bit yourself, she might begin to fancy a change.

– You have absolutely no reason ... began Flapping Eagle, but Deggle interrupted again. It was quite remarkable how few of his sentences Flapping Eagle ever finished when in conversation with this dark smiler.

– I merely mean, said Deggle, that for some unknown reason I feel quite attached to you, I shouldn't like to see you come to any harm, pretty-face.

After this conversation Flapping Eagle found himself watching Mrs Cramm; and when her legs constricted or her arms squeezed him, he remembered the passing of Oscar Cramm and became nervous. Which hampered his sexual duties on more than one occasion, and on these occasions he saw Livia Cramm frown thoughtfully and purse her lips before assuring him that it didn't matter. She would sip from the jug of water that always sat by her bedside, surrounded by her army of pills, and turn away from him to sleep.

One night, Flapping Eagle had a curious dream. Livia Cramm had both her attenuated hands fixed vice-like around his throat and was pushing, pushing with her thumbs. He was sleeping in his dream and awoke in it to find his life being squeezed away. He wrestled then, wrestled for his life, and as he did so she changed continually into all manner of wet, stinking, shapeless, slippery things. He could not grip her and all the time her hold was tightening. Just before he fainted he forced out these words:

— You are old, Livia. Old hag. You'll never find another.

All of a sudden (he could see nothing now: it was black inside his eyes) the hold relaxed. He heard Livia's voice say:

– Yes, my eagle, my soaring bird. Yes.

When he awoke, he found Livia Cramm dead as a stone, both hands fixed clawingly about her own neck. The jug of water was upset; her army of pills was substantially diminished.

It was only later that morning that Flapping Eagle discovered that his own precious bottle, the phial with the blue, release-giving liquid, had disappeared. He went to confront Deggle, who reclined as usual on the brocaded sofa in the drawing-room, his habitual dark clothing for once appropriate.

– Livia didn't seem the sort to commit suicide, he said.

– What sort is that, foolish boy? asked Deggle. She was old.

– You don't know about a certain bottle disappearing, do you? asked Flapping Eagle.

– You're overwrought, said Deggle. I like you, you know. What you need, my boy, is to get away from all this. Take the yacht. Sail into the, ha ha, blue.

What can you say to a man who may or may not be a murderer, who may or may not have saved your life?

– You really are remarkably well-preserved, smiled Deggle. You must have a guardian angel.

Flapping Eagle thought: *Or devil.*

The will left me the money but it left Deggle the yacht. The verdict was suicide.

Since Deggle didn't want the yacht, and since I wanted desperately to get away, I accepted his offer and set sail, alone for the first time in a quarter of a century, for ports unknown.

SIX

He was the leopard who changed his spots, he was the worm that turned. He was the shifting sands and the ebbing tide. He was moody as the sky, circular as the seasons, nameless as glass. He was Chameleon, changeling, all things to all men and nothing to any man. He had become his enemies and eaten his friends. He was all of them and none of them.

He was the eagle, prince of birds; and he was also the albatross. She clung round his neck and died, and the mariner became the albatross.

Having little option, he survived, wheeling his craft from shore to unsung shore, earning his keep, filling the empty hours of the hollow days of the vacant years. Contentment without contents, achievement without goal, these were the paradoxes that swallowed him.

He saw things most men miss in a mere lifetime. He saw:

A beach on which a maiden had been staked out naked, as giant ants moved up her thighs towards their goal; he heard her screams and sailed on by.

A man rehearsing voices on a cliff top: high whining voices, low gravelly voices, subtle insinuating voices, raucous strident voices, voices honeyed with pain, voices glinting with laughter, the voices of the birds and of the fishes. He asked the man what he was doing (as he sailed by). The man called back – and each word was the word of a different being: – I am looking for a suitable voice to speak in. As he called, he leaned forward, lost his balance and fell. The cry was in a single voice; but the rocks on the shore cut it and shredded it for him again.

A beggar shaking with starvation on a raft, and the fish that leapt from the ocean into his begging bowl and died for him.

Whales making love.

And many other things; but nowhere in the seas, for all the solace of the waters, for all the wonders beyond the curved liquid horizon, could he see or sniff or feel his own death.

Death: a blue fluid, blue like the sea, vanished down a monster's throat. All that remained was to survive. Stripped of his past, forsaking the language of his ancestors for the languages of the archipelagos of the world, forsaking the ways of his ancestors for those of the places he drifted to, forsaking any hope of ideals in the face of the changing and contradicting ideals he encountered, he lived, doing what he was given to do, thinking what he was instructed to think, being what it was most desirable to be, hoping only for what was permitted, and doing it so skilfully, with such natural aptitude, that the men he encountered thought he was thus of his own free will and liked him for it. He loved many women – being so easily able to adapt to the needs and pleasures of any woman.

Several times he changed the name he gave to people. His face was such, his skin was such, that in many places he could pass for local; and pass he did, using what had once been his curse to his advantage. The change of name was necessary, if his immortality was not to be noticed. This immortality kept him moving, too: always seeking out places where he was unknown or forgotten.

For a tyrant, he slew rebels; in a free state, he denounced tyranny.

Among carnivores, he praised the strength-giving virtues of animal flesh; among vegetarians he spoke of the spiritual purity that abstinence from such flesh brought; among cannibals, he devoured a companion.

Though he was kind by nature, he worked for a time as an executioner, perfecting the arts of axe and knife. Though he believed himself to be good, he betrayed many women. Few left him: he always moved on first.

And after a while, he realized he had learnt nothing at all. The many, many experiences, the multitude of people and the myriad crimes had left him empty; a grin without a face. He was no more now than a nod of agreement, a bow of acquiescence.

*His body continued to keep itself perfectly; his mind never
grew dimmer. He lived the same physiological day over and
over again. His body: an empire on which there was no sun to
set.*

One day, afloat and nowhere, he said aloud:
– I want to grow old. Not to die: to grow old.
A gull screeched its ridicule.

Flapping Eagle began his search for Sispy and Bird-Dog as
methodically as he could. He sailed back to Amerindia and
made his way inland to Axona and Phoenix, where the whole
cold trail began. But that led him nowhere. Sispy and Bird-
Dog didn't seem to have travelled anywhere at all. They had
simply vanished.

– Sispy? said people in Phoenix. That some kind of a pree-
vert foreign name?

After that, Flapping Eagle gave up any pretence of method.
He sailed on through seas, channels, rivers, lakes, oceans,
wherever his craft took him, asking, wherever he stopped, if
anyone knew of the pedlar, or his sister.

He knew it was almost certainly hopeless; they might be
anywhere on the globe; they might use different names; they
might have drowned, or died some other violent death; they
might no longer be together.

Only two things kept him going: the first was the knowledge
that only Sispy would know if there was a way, not of dying,
but of restoring his body to the normal, vulnerable state of
human bodies: to allow him to grow old.

The second was the message Sispy had sent him through
Bird-Dog on his first appearance:

*Tell your brother Born-From-Dead that all eagles come at
last to eyrie and all sailors come at last to shore.*

Sispy had said that before Joe-Sue had even become Flapping Eagle; and years before he had any notion of going to sea.
Perhaps, thought Flapping Eagle, sailor, Sispy divined something of my future.

It wasn't much grounds for optimism, but it was something.

He remembered another sentence of Sispy's: *For those who
will not use the blue there is only one place I know of.*

Flapping Eagle told himself firmly, over and over again:
there is such a place; it's only a matter of time before you find

34

it; and you'll know when you do, because its inhabitants will be like you. Young or old, they cannot disguise their eyes from me. Eyes like mine, which have seen everything and know nothing. The eyes of the survivor.

But the years passed. And more years. And more years.

Flapping Eagle was beginning to wonder if he was sane. Perhaps there never was a Sispy, never a Bird-Dog or Sham-Man or Phoenix: perhaps not even a Livia Cramm or a Deggle. Yes. Madness explained everything. He was mad.

So when his boat sailed into its home port, the port of X on the Moorish coast of Morispain, his eyes were glazed and distant.

He was contemplating killing himself.

SEVEN

Nicholas Deggle sat on a bollard on the jetty, long and black, with an inordinately wicked smile playing about his lips.

— I trust you had a nice sail, pretty-face, he said. Wind all right? Not too high? Not too low? I'm afraid I'm not an expert in these matters.

Flapping Eagle raised his head slowly. Now he knew he was mad.

— Deggle, he said .

— The same. None other. Accept no substitute, said Deggle. But a word in your shell-like orifice: I'm not called by that name any more. Time flies, you know, and names with it.

— Yes, said Flapping Eagle, bemused.

— I'm called Lokki, actually. The Great Lokki at your service. Phenomenal Pheats of Prestidigitation Phantastically Performed. Dear me, how one does fall upon hard times. Straitened circumstances. I've become my own descendant, as a matter of fact, or my own ancestor, depending on your historical perspective. The legal problems were enormous. Anyway, I've been careful to keep leaving myself my own boat, so thank you for returning it.

— Not at all, mouthed Flapping Eagle.

— Lokki, said Deggle, rolling the L. It's a good name, don't you think? Echoes of the old Norse and so forth. Gives one's act a kind of artistic respectability. Shame about Livia, wasn't it? I'm sure you did the right thing, going off like that. It must have been a great shock for you, all that money at once. You're quite better now, I hope?

The eyes.

Deggle's eyes: the eyes of the survivor, filled with an ageless twinkle.

– Deggle, if you . . .

Deggle was still a master of interruption. He waved a ringed hand.

– Please, my dear. I did tell you. Do call me Lokki. People might *hear*.

– Lokki. If you're still here after all this time, *you must know about Sispy.*

Deggle cocked his head and looked puzzled.

– Sispy, he mused, Siss-pee. What is it, old eagle? Soup? It sounds awfully familiar.

– You know very well. Sispy. Sispy the pedlar. With the bottles, Lokki. The blue bottle. You remember Livia.

Flapping Eagle tried to make it sound like a threat, but Deggle laughed happily.

– Mmm, he said. Of course, Livia – by which I take it you mean Mrs Livia Cramm, widow of Oscar Cramm, the tin-tack king – has been dead for such a very long time. Long before my time, of course. Now if only my illustrious ancestor Nicholas Deggle were still alive, I'm sure he'd know exactly what you mean.

He smiled beautifully. Like the Deggle himself, Flapping Eagle remembered.

– Now, he said, may I offer you a drink?

The Great Lokki lived in a caravan just outside X. There was a horse between the shafts and an extremely beautiful and very stupid conjurer's assistant between the sheets.

– Lotti, explained Deggle, looking embarrassed. Lokki and Lotti, you see.

Frustration was building within Flapping Eagle, the frustration of centuries.

– Deggle, he said, ignoring the Great Lokki's anguished protest, I think it's time you stopped trying to make a fool of me.

– But my dear, said Deggle and his eyes were not twinkling, that's so easy.

Flapping Eagle was on the verge of committing an act of physical violence when, abruptly, Deggle said: – Piss off, Lotti. His language seemed to have acquired occasional lapses, its quality reduced to suit his reduced way of life. There couldn't have been a Livia Cramm for a very long time. At any rate, Lotti pissed off outside to chat to the horse, which was therefore able to feel intellectually superior to at least one human being.

Deggle said: – I think you're just about ready for Calf Island.

Flapping Eagle didn't entirely understand or believe what Deggle told him, about 'making a gate' to the island. It had apparently taken centuries of trying, and even now might be dangerous. But despite his bewilderment, he didn't care. This was undoubtedly the haven of which Sispy had spoken, so it was undoubtedly the place for which he was destined.

Mrs Cramm had said it was his lot to be led; and he was filled with something approaching hate for Sispy, who had distorted his entire life in one casual stroke so very long ago. He found himself wanting not only his freedom from the chains of immortality, but some kind of satisfaction as well.

He went for a walk alone the next morning, in the hills above X. He was saying goodbye to the world, since, if half of what Deggle had said was true, there was a good chance he would never see it again.

In the afternoon he went down to the jetty and prepared the boat for departure. Deggle still disclaimed any need for it.

In the evening, Deggle and Lotti came to see him off. – The evening is the best time to try and get through, Deggle had said. They waved.

– Deggle, Flapping Eagle said as he pushed off, I'd love to know what motivates you.

– Oh, well, shrugged the wickedly-smiling conjurer, perhaps I don't like your friend Sispy very much either. But then, perhaps I do.

– Byeee, squeaked Lotti.

– Ethiopia, said Deggle.

Flapping Eagle no longer knew whether he was mad, whether he had accepted Deggle's story so unquestioningly, been so willing to follow his instructions despite the warnings of physical danger, just as an excuse for doing away with himself. He was, he told himself, doing the only thing he could do.

– They go there, Deggle had said, from choice, because they chose immortality. Whereas you are after something quite different: old age. Physical decay. And, presumably, death. You should set the cat among the pigeons, pretty-face. Not to mention old Livia's prophecy.

The Deggle giggle lasted for a long while after that.

The Mediterranean was calm, dark and calm. No wind. A clear sky. Stars. Flapping Eagle dozed for a moment. When he awoke, it was to feel a gale rushing at his face, a cloud rushing over his head, a crackle of electricity in the air. He was standing erect now, fighting to keep his craft from breaking under the force of the holocaust, when quite unaccountably dizziness swept over him and he fell from his yacht, Deggle's yacht, into the angry sea. The last thing he heard was a loud drumming noise . . . like the beating of mighty wings.

A few seconds later he fell through the hole in the Mediterranean into that other sea, that not-quite-Mediterranean, and was carried towards the misty beach in the first light of dawn as Mr Virgil Jones rocked in his chair.

When Flapping Eagle arrived at Calf Island his body was thirty-four years, three months and four days old. He had lived for a total of seven hundred and seventy-seven years, seven months and seven days. By a swift calculation, we see that he had stopped ageing seven hundred and forty-three years, four months and three days ago.

He was a tired man.

EIGHT

– Introductions would be proper, said Virgil Jones, at a time like the present. Would you care for a nice steaming bowl of Mrs O'Toole's very own root-tea, as it is the hour? Never let it be said the decencies were not observed in the Maison O'Toole.

– I'm wearing a frock, said Flapping Eagle in astonishment.

– Certainly you are, certainly, said Virgil Jones. Allow me to explain. Always a rational explanation, as they say, or, that is to say, as they said.

– Please do, said Flapping Eagle, feeling his throbbing head.

– Ah yes, said Virgil Jones, the head. I expect it hurts, not entirely unexpectedly, if I might be momentarily tautologous. Half-drowned heads have a way of protesting, you might even say bellyaching, although obviously we are not speaking of your belly. You have, sir, my unrestrained sympathy and the offer of root-tea. Mrs O'Toole swears by the arrowroot for such malaises. It flies straight and true to the heart of the affliction and thunk! one is cured.

– About the frock, said Flapping Eagle, raising himself from the prone position until he was jack-knifed, legs lying along the rush mat, torso and head leaning upwards into the room inquiringly, supported on a rubbery arm.

– Now, now, said Mr Jones, if I were you I wouldn't attempt the vertical just yet. The horizontal is a far more suitable position for recuperation. I have often wondered if those tragic cases of people buried alive did not spring from this: the horizontal helping them to recover, you understand. Possibly one should be buried standing up, if you'll excuse the brief foray into necrology. Merely a small pleasantry, no morbidity intended, nor I hope taken.

– The frock, said Flapping Eagle.

– O, my sincere apologies, said Virgil Jones, if it seems I was ducking your inquiry. Far from it, sir, far from it. Nothing could give me greater pleasure than to elucidate the matter of the frock. The fact of the matter is one's conversational partners have been rather limited of late and the opportunity is well-nigh irresistible. The affair of the frock is a trifle. Merely that when we fished you from the sea your garments were a little moist, not to say damp, not to say positively sodden. And the fact of the matter is my own wardrobe is somewhat limited; so on the whole we thought it best, if you take my meaning, to employ one of Mrs O'Toole's garments. You have our unreserved apologies if it brings you any embarrassment, but I assure you all proper decencies were observed, Mrs O'Toole leaving the room during the process of disinvestiture.

– I'm sure they were, said Flapping Eagle, trying to put the voluble, excited man at his ease; and, remembering his manners, went on: I owe you my thanks, sir, for saving my life. My name is Flapping Eagle.

– Virgil Beauvoir Chanakya Jones at your service, said Mr Jones, approximating a bow from the waist, which he did with some difficulty, there being so much of his own flesh to impede him. – Mrs O'Toole will be here presently, he confided. She is at the beach retrieving my rocking-chair, which she was unable to carry back with us, owing to having yourself strapped across her shoulders.

Flapping Eagle must have failed to conceal his puzzlement, for Mr Jones added hastily: – As you will observe, I am sitting down. Were I to stand, you would see why I am unable to carry the chair myself. My belt, you follow. It serves as a strap; but tragically, when doing so, the efficiency of my trousers is somewhat impaired.

It didn't sound like a very good explanation, but then it was none of Flapping Eagle's business. – Quite so, he said, and noticed in himself, not for the first time, a tendency to adopt the speaking style and speech patterns of others.

His head reminded him of its existence; he lay back on the mat. – I think I would like that root-tea, he said.

Mr Jones stood up laboriously, clutching at his trousers. He moved across the room, blinking in the direction of the fire-place, where a small pot hung above the winking embers. – Keeps it warm, he said; then added: Damnation. He had just knocked over a low, rickety table. The pieces of a large jigsaw puzzle dispersed themselves informally around the accident.

– Fornication, Mr Jones swore further. It was a black day for mankind when my glasses broke. Your pardon for my foul-mouthed speech, Mr Eagle; one's bodily inadequacies are a constant affliction, are they not?

– You do jigsaw puzzles, then.

– Do them? Mr Eagle, I construct them. In these solitary years they have provided my one stimulation. One day, I expect, I shall be some good at the things. At the moment my skill in construction far surpasses my talents at reconstruction. And myopia does nothing to assist. O for a qualified grinder of lenses.

He poured out a bowl of root-tea and carried it back, nearly slipping on the scattered jigsaw, and sat down by Flapping Eagle once more.

How unlikely, thought Flapping Eagle, that surroundings as

meagre as these should exude so comfortable, so friendly an atmosphere. The room in which he lay was little more than the interior of a hovel; two rush mats some distance apart, one of which currently bore his weakened frame, lying on a dirt floor – although it was a meticulously swept floor. The broom, a bundle of twigs, rested indolently against a wall. The walls were logs covered in caked mud, the roof as well. A fireplace and the upturned rickety low table. A few pots. In a far corner, an old trunk. Nothing on the walls; no decoration anywhere. It was as distant from the sumptuous residence of, say, Livia Cramm as was China. And yet it was friendly.

Noises off : the twitterings of birds. A rustle of thick shrubbery. The occasional distant howl of a wild dog. No footsteps, no concourse of humanity. One window, with a piece of sacking drawn across it, flapping in the breeze; one door, covered in the same manner. It was the dwelling of a savage, or a castaway. Virgil Jones fitted into it about as easily as an elephant in a pepperpot.

He sat solicitously on the floor, wearing a dark and aged suit. There was a bowler hat upon his head and a gold chain traversed his waistcoat. (There was no gold watch at the end of it.) Somehow, thought Flapping Eagle, in these unsavoury surroundings, he preserves an air of dignity. Short-sighted, clumsy, loquacious, large-tongued, slobbering dignity, the injured hauteur of the impoverished. He reminded Flapping Eagle of an old railway engine he had once seen, a giant of steam in its day, rusting in a siding. The form of power denied its content. A stranded hulk. Puffing Billy. Flapping Eagle finished his root-tea, put the bowl down and fell fast asleep.

– That's right, murmured Virgil Jones. Build your strength. The birds sang their agreement from the trees.

When he awoke it was to find a different face staring down at him : the crinkled monkey folds of Dolores O'Toole's physiognomy. At first he leapt in alarm, but then as wakefulness came subsided again, realizing that what he had taken for a snarl of hate was in fact a smile. Dolores O'Toole was the ugliest woman he had ever seen.

He gathered himself. – May I ask an obvious question, he said. Where am I?

– That's a good question, approved Virgil Jones.

– Among friends, soothed Dolores O'Toole, snarling her sympathy.

Flapping Eagle felt highly confused.

NINE

– You are at the foot of a mountain, said Virgil Jones. This is Calf Island, and the mountain is Calf Mountain. The mountain is really the whole island.

– Are you alone here? asked Flapping Eagle.

– Here, yes. Yes, here we are alone. Relatively speaking, said Virgil Jones. There are the birds, of course, and the chickens, and a few harmless wild animals.

– Do you mean there are no other human beings on the island at all?

– O, said Virgil Jones, no, I can't truthfully say that.

– No, agreed Dolores, not truthfully.

Flapping Eagle had the distinct impression that they spoke with reluctance.

– Where are they then? he pressed.

– Ah, said Virgil.

– A long distance away, said Dolores.

Flapping Eagle's head hurt; he felt ill. Scarcely strong enough to force information out of the lip-biting pair.

– Please, he said, tell me where.

Virgil Jones appeared to make a decision. – The slopes of the mountain, he said, are mainly covered in forestation. I believe there are a few people wandering around in the woods, but we rather keep ourselves to ourselves, so I couldn't truthfully say where.

– And that's all? asked Flapping Eagle.

– N...n...no, admitted Virgil.

– There are others, yielded Dolores.

– Are you going to tell me about them? asked Flapping Eagle, his skull giving a fair impression of splintering into a million tiny shards.

– O, you don't want to know about them, said Virgil Jones hopefully.

– They are completely uninteresting, assured Dolores.

Flapping Eagle closed his eyes.
– *Please*, he said.
– He asks so politely, said Dolores despairingly.
So they told him.

From Dolores, he learned that K was a town of reprobates
and degraded types; selfish, decadent people that no decent
woman would want to be near; but then Flapping Eagle was no
decent woman. From Virgil Jones he learned what he had hoped
to learn. This was the place Sispy had spoken of. An island of
immortals who had found their longevity too burdensome in
the outside world, yet had been unwilling to give it up; with
Sispy's guidance they had come to Calf Mountain to be with
their own kind.
– Does the name Bird-Dog mean anything to you? he asked.
– Bird-Dog, said Virgil Jones. (Was that alarm or concentration on his face?) Is the lady a friend of yours?
– My sister, said Flapping Eagle.
– No, said Virgil Jones. No, it doesn't.
Later that night Flapping Eagle suddenly realized it must
have been a lie. How had Mr Jones known the name Bird-Dog
was a woman's name?
And more importantly: why had he denied knowing her?

He pressed the point the next morning.
– My dear Mr Eagle, said Virgil Jones, I feel very strongly
you should bend all your energies to the recovery of your
health. You have been greatly weakened by your misadventure.
When you are well, you have my word that Mrs O'Toole and I
will answer all your questions. It's a complex matter; I would
be happier if you were in as fit a condition as possible.
– All I want, said Flapping Eagle, is an answer to one question: are my sister and Mr Sispy on this island? The answer to
that will not strain my health, I assure you.
– Very well, sighed Mr Jones, the answer is Yes; yes, they
are. After a fashion. And now I'll say no more. Do get well soon,
dear Mr Eagle.
Flapping Eagle let the subject drop and drank another bowl
of root-tea.

Dolores O'Toole had hobbled off to collect fruits and berries.

43

Virgil sat by Flapping Eagle's bedside watching with ill-concealed jealousy as the convalescent man worked at the jigsaw puzzle.

– You astonish me with your skill, he said, with as good grace as he could muster.

– Beginners' luck, disclaimed Flapping Eagle. He really was doing very well.

– Dolores and I are very anxious to hear all about you, now that you're so much better. You must have had quite a time on your way here. But upon consideration perhaps it would be polite if I told you a little about ourselves first, so as to put you at your ease. If you'd like to hear about us, that is.

– Please, said Flapping Eagle and fitted three more pieces into the puzzle.

Virgil Jones frowned. – I think that one goes at the top, he said, a shade abruptly. Flapping Eagle tried; it didn't.

– O, I see, said Flapping Eagle; it fits here. The piece slid into place at the bottom of the puzzle.

– I always wanted to be an archaeologist, you know, said Virgil Jones, changing the subject. Unfortunately life has a way of sidetracking one's greatest ambitions. Painters, would-be artists, end up whitewashing walls. Sculptors are forced to design toilets. Writers become critics or publicists. Archaeologists, like myself, can become gravediggers.

– You were a gravedigger? asked Flapping Eagle in genuine surprise. But it fitted: Mr Jones' habitual lugubrious expression went well with that profession.

– For a time, said Mr Jones. For a time. Before events conspired to bring me here. It was pleasant enough work; the most pleasing aspect being that everyone one met was happy. The corpses were content enough, and so, usually, were the mourners. It was a source of lasting comfort to me, the sight of so many tears of joy, so freely shed.

– That's a very cynical statement, said Flapping Eagle.

– Alas, poor Yorick, said Virgil Jones; the worms long ago gnawed his romanticism to shreds.

In the ensuing silence, Flapping Eagle fitted together all but three of the remaining pieces.

– There's not much for a gravedigger to do on Calf Mountain, said Virgil Jones; so I have retired into my true love – contemplation.

– And Dolores? asked Flapping Eagle.

– Ah, Dolores; there is a sad tale. To love life so much under such a physical burden . . . it is my belief she lives alone, or, that is to say, with me, because she finds she can only love human beings in their absence.

– This last piece, said Flapping Eagle, doesn't fit.

Virgil Jones smiled in satisfaction. – That's my little joke, he said. The jigsaw cannot be completed.

TEN

As Virgil Jones and Dolores O'Toole prepared the evening meal, Flapping Eagle could not help observe what a good team they made in their distorted way. They seemed to work at different planes of the room – Dolores low and stooping, Virgil gross but erect. For a moment Flapping Eagle had the illusion that they actually stood at different ground levels. Then it passed, and he smiled. Despite their secrecy, their unwillingness to talk about the island, he could not help liking them. He wondered if they made love.

He had told them his own story earlier in the afternoon; they had listened with the rapt silence of children, nodding and gasping. Mr Jones had spoken only once, when Flapping Eagle first mentioned Nicholas Deggle. Then the eyebrows had lifted high into the fleshy forehead and Mr Jones had said : – So, so. When he finished, they sat in respectful silence for a moment; then Virgil Jones had said :

– By the heavens, Mr Eagle, you do seem to have led a rather epic life. I'm afraid we can offer you no stories to match yours. We live wholly in the microcosm, you see; the state of my corns and the state of nations are to me of equal concern. I don't want at all to preach but I would recommend that you adapt yourself to minutiae; they are so much less confusing.

– There is the end of my search to be achieved, said Flapping Eagle.

– I'm afraid, to be honest, said Virgil Jones apologetically, I've ceased to see the merit in achievement or heroism. One tries by one's life and actions to bring a little sense into an inane universe; to attempt more is to be sucked into the whirlpool.

Flapping Eagle thought: they seem very anxious for me to abandon my intentions. But he thought he had heard a subsidiary note in Virgil Jones' voice: a note of uncertainty. Perhaps he didn't quite believe what he was saying. He also thought Dolores O'Toole was the more tense of the two; and when he had spoken of his desire to continue his search, her glance had not been wholly neighbourly.

– Concentrate on the *here*, Mr Eagle, that's my advice to you, finished Virgil Jones. Don't worry about the *there*. Or the past. Or the future. Worry about dinner and your corns. Those are things you can affect.

– You said you would answer my questions when I was well, said Flapping Eagle. I am well now.

– Tomorrow morning, said Dolores hastily. After a good night's sleep.

– There's no time like the present, said Flapping Eagle.

– Tomorrow, pleaded Dolores O'Toole.

Flapping Eagle drew a breath.

– Since I am living on your kindness, he said, I am naturally at your mercy. Tomorrow will be quite soon enough.

Virgil Jones assumed a hearty air. – Let us celebrate your recovery, he said. I think we might slay a chicken tonight. In fact, Mr Eagle, since the peeling and so forth of vegetables rather preoccupies Mrs O'Toole and myself at present, perhaps you would be so kind?

Flapping Eagle could not very well refuse; he took the proffered knife and went out into the yard. It struck him that this was his first conscious sally into Calf Island.

When he was outside, Dolores came hesitantly to stand by Mr Jones' side.

– You won't . . . you won't go with him? Her eyes were filled with fear.

Virgil Jones silently took her hand; she squeezed it violently. It was, for both of them an irreversible declaration, forced at last from an eternity of concealment.

– I could not bear to lose you, she said.

Flapping Eagle looked up at Calf Mountain in the failing light. It climbed steeply away into lost forests, forbidding, green, which cleared somewhere up there to make room for the town of K. Calf Mountain: as alien to him as it was to the world he had known; and yet there was a similarity: a likeness of self and mountain, of mist-isolated island and much-travelled continents. It was there in the gloom and he couldn't see it. Just the faces of his sister and the unknown pedlar in the darkness, waiting to be found, or forgotten.

– Chicken, he said to the chicken, shall I kill you?

The knife was in his hand, and the fowl at his mercy; but he hesitated, an old conflict reopening within him. He had never been an outsider by choice, and the desire to be acceptable, to please, which he knew to be within him, created a warring sensation inside. If only for this reason, he would not mind, in some ways, if he did stay awhile with Mr Jones and Mrs O'Toole. It would give pleasure, perhaps; it would, for once, unite him with other human beings, a welcome change from his accustomed separateness. And it would be peaceful. But to give up his search altogether . . .

He killed the chicken, because it was there to be killed.

Dinner was a silent meal for long stretches. Dolores O'Toole was lost in nervous broodings; she would snap out of the reverie to offer Mr Jones and Flapping Eagle further helpings of chicken. Flapping Eagle saw in her eyes a new light; he didn't know what it meant, but it was new. He himself was preoccupied with the mountain, cloud-topped and unknown.

Virgil Jones made fitful attempts at conversation.

– Would you agree, Mr Eagle, he said, that what the human race fears most is the workings of its own mind?

– Yes and no, said Flapping Eagle distantly. Mr Jones frowned; he knew he should find a less serious topic, but none presented itself in the candle-lit murkiness. They squatted round the rickety, low table, Flapping Eagle once again unfrocked, Virgil hatless, and thought their separate thoughts.

– The mountain is really irresistible at this time of evening, offered Virgil Jones, and received only a few syllables in reply.

– Yes, yes it is, said Flapping Eagle, and was rewarded with a fierce glare from Mrs O'Toole.

– You cannot have failed to hear the birds, Mr Jones tried again. They are legion. Has it ever struck you how often one uses birds as analogies of human attributes and behaviour?

– No, said Flapping Eagle.

– Ah. Consider. The bird-kingdom is remarkably suitable

47

for myth-makers. It occupies a different medium, yet it is in many ways an excellent parallel – having languages, courtship, family ties and so forth. Distant enough in appearance to be a safely abstract analogue, birds are near enough to be interesting. Consider the lark. Or the hawk. Or the nightingale. Or the vulture. The names are more than descriptions; they have become symbols. Consider too, the profusion of bird-gods in Antiquity. The Phoenix. The Roc. The Homa. The Garuda. The Bennu. The Bar Yuchre. The Hathilinga with the strength of five elephants. The Kerkes. The Gryphon. The Norka. The Sacred Dragon. The Pheng. The Kirni. The Orosch. The Saëna. The Anqa. And of course, the master of them all, Simurg himself. Quite a number. Quite a number.

There was no reply.

– If I am not very much mistaken, Mr Eagle, Mr Jones added, the Eagle has an interesting significance in Amerindian mythology. Am I not right in saying that it is the symbol of the Destroyer? Its destruction being terrible and swift. I was fascinated by your choice of the name.

– I did not choose the name, said Flapping Eagle. It chose me.

– Quite, said Virgil Jones, and crossed his fingers.

ELEVEN

Midnight, or thereabouts. In the small house in the small clearing by the grey cliffs above the grey beach, silence. In the dark forests on the dark slopes of the magic mountain, silence. Even the sea and sky were hushed.

Flapping Eagle was asleep; but the worried, ugly woman on the mat across the floor was wide awake.

Virgil Jones sat, an ample mound of flesh partly concealed by a less-than-simple blanket, in his rocking-chair. Its irregular movements betrayed that he, too, was some way from dreams. His eyes closed for a moment; when, inexorably, they inched open again, he saw that Dolores stood in front of him, a bent body in a crude shift, spindleshanked and shaking slightly. The invitation in her eyes was unmistakable. They remained thus for a long instant, obesity and attenuation linked by the naked expression of desire. Then Virgil's mouth twitched briefly in an unconvincing attempt at a smile; and he hauled himself from the chair, his nerves crying outrage in his tired frame. He walked to the door and drew back the sackcloth, standing with stiff gallantry as Mrs O'Toole hobbled out.

In the clearing, amid the sleeping chickens, they came to a halt again, uncertainty, paralysing their half-willing limbs. Virgil's tongue licked its outsize way around his lips; Dolores O'Toole's hands fluttered limply at her sides, like a sparrow with a broken wing.

– Virgil.

His name floated discreetly across the paralysis; Dolores had voiced it with the care of a woman revealing a secret treasure. It lanced its way into him through the old night-shirt, and abruptly he felt less ridiculous.

– O, Virgil.

A second call; his eyes moved until they were looking at Dolores' eyes, and saw the shine. He found himself full of the charm of those eyes, so alive, so fond.

– Madam, he said, as fright coursed once more through his body, Madam, I fear I may not be . . .

– Dolores, she said. Not Madam. Dolores.

He opened his mouth; the name emerged to cleanse him.

– Dolores, he said.

– Virgil.

And again the hiatus; now it was the woman who waited upon the man, unwilling to move further without his support.

Virgil Jones thought: We are like two frightened, ugly virgins. He found the power of his limbs returning and moved the few steps to Dolores' side.

– My arm, he offered. She made a brief bob.

– I thank you, sir, she said, and took it.

– This way, I think, said Virgil Jones; there is a soft hollow of grass adjacent to the well.

She inclined her head in agreement. They walked to the edge of the clearing in a formal, deliberate gait, and then the trees moved around them.

Virgil Jones sat down heavily in the hollow, exhaling air in a gush. He was at a loss to know what Dolores might do now, and equally at a loss in himself. Alas, poor Yorick.

Dolores remained standing, her eyes fixed upon him in a

glassy, cocked glance; her hands moved slowly to her shoulders, where rough bows held her shift in place. Something near panic flooded through Virgil as he realized their purpose; but she was fixed now, determination set in her chin. The hands reached their goal and tugged; the shift fell.

– It is a warm night, thankfully, essayed Mr Jones. The mist is all but cleared. The words sounded idiotic as he said them, but Dolores showed no sign of disapproval, standing before him shyly, one hand half-accidentally poised at the joining of her thighs. In the dark, she seemed less wrinkled, her hunched body less broken.

Virgil extended an arm, and she came to him, jerking her way to the ground, to lie motionless, yet expectant.

He kissed her.

Their hands were slow at first, slow and unsure, learning once more the touches of skin and skin, weaving inelegant patterns upon the fellow-bodies. But slowly they found their purpose, kneading away the knots of tension in necks and shoulders and backs, finding a natural rhythm, glad hands.

So now the hands remembered, and the lips, lips feverishly seeking each other out, parting and joining, tongues twisting in the elation of rediscovery.

– Not bad for a pair of youngsters, said Virgil Jones, and Dolores O'Toole laughed. It was so long since he had heard her laugh; it was to him a delightful thing, and he laughed too.

It was the laughter that did it; the floodgates opened and drowned their hesitations. Their bodies assaulted each other.

Dolores cried out at some time: – My hump! Hold my hump!

And Virgil's hands had grasped the forbidden deformity, to stroke and scratch and grasp; she shuddered with the pleasure of it, of feeling disfiguration transmute into sexuality.

She lay beside him for a moment; then sprang up to straddle him, her hands grasping great folds of his flesh, to squeeze and twist them in a child's delight. Again they laughed; Virgil, too, was freed from the disadvantages of his shape. – It's like making bread, she giggled, pretending to work his belly into a loaf.

*   *   *

He came only once, and she not at all. All organs atrophy through disuse. But their limitations were important to neither of them; their achievement was what concerned and satisfied them. For a long time he simply lay over her, spilling over her on both sides, enveloping her in himself, feeling her bones, hard and near the surface of her as they lay covered in his flesh, and they were one beast, four-handed, four-legged, two-headed and wreathed in a smile.

Her breasts were as small as pendulous dried figs, while his were as fleshy as watermelons. His penis lay short and fat in the hard hollow of her hand.

– Don't be thin, she said. Don't ever be thin. Stay fat. Stay Virgil.

– I scarcely have any option, he replied, having a Condition as I do. The thyroid gland does not respond to dieting.

– Good, she said.

– By the same token, said Virgil Jones, I couldn't imagine you being overweight.

– Nothing will change, she said. We shall still sit upon the beach and feed the chickens and listen to the birds and dust the house and . . .

The expression on his face stopped her.

– Virgil, she cried. Nothing will change! Nothing!

The expression on his face did not change.

Perhaps it was wrong to lie with him. Now I have given him what he wanted. Now I have nothing for him, nothing held back, nothing to hold him.

Perhaps it was wrong to lie with her. Another duty, another obligation, another potential source of guilt. Was I lying to her in lying with her?

Perhaps it was right to lie with him. Now there is no secrecy, all of it out in the open and fixed and unchanging. Now he will know that he loves me.

Perhaps it was right to lie with her . . .

– I love you, said Dolores O'Toole.

– I love you, said Virgil Jones.

They both felt very, very sad.

– It was *him*, said Dolores fiercely.

– Who?

– Flapping Eagle, she said. If he were not here, we would not be. Here.

– We have much to thank him for, then, said Virgil Jones.

– Yes, said Dolores, unhappily. We have everything to thank him for.

But the risk of grief, thought Virgil, and the risk of guilt: could one not lay that, very properly, at the door of Grimus?

Dolores stared at the mountain with a possessed intensity.

– Nothing will change, she said, between clenched teeth.

TWELVE

It was the tremor that woke Flapping Eagle early. It shook at him through the thin mat; it upset the room's single low table to send the jigsaw crashing. He came awake fast, and leapt to his feet at the same instant; but it was over, too slight to cause any damage.

He had been dreaming: a nightmare. He stood on a black rock, in full warpaint, clutching a tomahawk, slashing vainly at the eagle that swooped endlessly down at him, scarring his body, biting at his flesh, while on the ground below stood a faceless figure, long and black and very smooth, with jewelled rings on every finger, laughing and laughing and laughing: the laugh of Deggle.

The room was still dark, sackcloth barring the first faint light. He stood gulping breath for a nervous instant, and saw that Dolores O'Toole's mat was unused, and Virgil Jones' rocking-chair was rocking emptily. He went outside.

Mr Jones and Mrs O'Toole stood in the clearing; chickens squawked with alarm and birds screeched, interrupted in their sleep. The ill-assorted pair stood still. Virgil's tongue was working unconsciously; Dolores' eyes looked vague and distant. They did not focus on Flapping Eagle.

– Earthquake, she said.

– What? said Flapping Eagle. Dolores appeared not to hear.

– The Great Turtle moved, she said to Virgil and cackled.

Virgil looked at her worriedly, as she broke off and said gravely:

– No, no, I was mistaken. Nothing happened. Nothing changes.

– Is Mrs O'Toole all right? asked Flapping Eagle.

– Yes, yes, said Mr Jones, shepherding her into the room. A little overwrought, he said in an aside to Flapping Eagle. Rest is what she needs. I suggest you and I go for a walk. Have our little chat. Let her rest, wouldn't you agree?

– Of course, said Flapping Eagle.

So they left her in the hut and walked towards Virgil and Dolores' night-hollow. When they were gone, Dolores moved jerkily towards the old trunk that lay unopened in the corner. This is where the past sat locked, her past, unchanged, un-changeable. She sat on the ground and embraced the trunk, whispering to it.

– It is yesterday, she whispered. Every day is yesterday, so every day is fixed.

THIRTEEN

Flapping Eagle, sensitive to changes in atmosphere, knew that the Virgil Jones of this morning was a different man from the Virgil Jones of the previous night. He also felt that Dolores O'Toole's antagonism to him, so imperceptible at first, was hardening fast. But this morning he had deliberately closed his mind to both these facts; he wanted information from Mr Jones. The sooner he knew the nature of Calf Island and its mountain, not to mention the whereabouts of Bird-Dog and Sispy, the sooner he could leave the outcast couple to their devices and move on down his solitary road.

Virgil Jones led him away from the hut and into the fringes of the wood. They sat beside a deep well. Or, rather, a deep hole that had been meant for a well, but was quite dry. Virgil Jones was making a valiant attempt to conceal some strong emotion behind a schoolmasterly façade.

– Very well, he said. Might I begin by reminding you of your own adventures . . . and indeed misadventures. By your own account you have had at least one or two experiences which would normally be classed as supernatural. Your very accept-ance of immortality, for instance: most human beings would classify that as sorcery. So, then. You must accept that the world in which you lived was no simple, matter-of-fact place.

Flapping Eagle nodded.

— Chanakya, said Virgil Jones. By which I do not mean myself but an ancient philosopher-king of that name, used to say that the world was neither what it seemed, nor what it did not seem, nor more, nor less, but all those things. Both what it appears to be and not what it appears to be. That is to say, I think it was Chanakya who said that. It was such a long time ago, you follow. But for the sake of argument, let us accept it as a genuine quote.

His eyes flickered momentarily to a hollow in the ground nearby and then dragged themselves away again.

— Let me put it another way, he said. When you look at me, you perceive that I am solid. By contrast, when you look at the well-shaft, you perceive that it is empty. Now would you agree that the reason for those two descriptions has a great deal less to do with the nature, either of the well or myself, than it has to do with the *way* you see us both?

Flapping Eagle frowned.

— Forgive me, said Mr Jones. I see you are confused, and why not? But observe: I myself am composed of matter, which, in its turn, is composed of tinier particles and so on into the ultra-microcosm. The fact is that the spaces between the particles of matter which compose me are just as great as the spaces between the particles of matter composing the air in that well-shaft. So that, with a different set of tools of perception – I mean other than eyes – one could conclude say, either that I am as 'empty' as the air in the shaft, or that it is as 'full' or 'solid' as I.

— I suppose so . . . said Flapping Eagle doubtfully.

— What I am driving at, said Virgil Jones, in my rather indirect fashion, is that the limitations we place upon the world are imposed by ourselves rather than the world. And, should we meet things which do not conform to our structure of reality, we place them outside it. Ghosts. Unidentified flying objects. Visions. We suspect the sanity of those who claim to see or sense them. An interesting point: a man is sane only to the extent that he subscribes to a previously-agreed construction of reality.

— Mm, said Flapping Eagle.

– 'Go, go, go, said the bird,' intoned Virgil Jones.

– What?

– A literary reference, said Virgil Jones. A whim. A piece of self-indulgence. Let us continue, and accept my apologies for the digression.

Perhaps I might make a highly inexact analogy to demonstrate my thesis. Here we all are, a world of living beings and inanimate objects and gusts of breeze, all of us composed of infinitely more empty space than solid matter. Is it not a conceptual possibility that here, in our midst, permeating all of us and all that surrounds us, is a completely other world, composed of different kinds of solids, different kinds of empty spaces, with different perceptual tools which make us as non-existent to its inhabitants as they are to ours? In a word, another dimension.

– I don't know, said Flapping Eagle. What if there were?

– If you concede that conceptual possibility, said Mr Jones, you must also concede that there may well be more than one. In fact, that an infinity of dimensions might exist, as palimpsests, upon and within and around our own, without our being in any wise able to perceive them.

And further : there is no reason why those dimensions should operate solely on our scale. The infinity could range from the tiniest micro-particle, the smallest sub-atom, to the universe. Is it not fascinating to speculate that we might all exist within the spaces of a few sub-atomic particles in some other, unknowably vast universe?

Flapping Eagle felt irritated. – It might well be interesting, he said brusquely, but I don't see its relevance to the whereabouts of my sister.

– My dear Eagle, said Mr Jones, I have simply been striving, as it were, to widen your eyes. There is no other manner in which I can explain to you the location of Calf Island.

Flapping Eagle's thoughts fell into a dizzy spin. He could not speak.

– Perhaps you have come across the theory of potential existences, continued Virgil Jones affably. So suppose there were, say, merely four potential pasts and futures for the Mediterranean Sea. In one of them, there never was nor will be an island such as this. In another the island existed but no longer does. In a third the island does not exist but will at some time

55

in the future. And in the fourth . . . he gestured around him . . . it has existed; and continues to do so.

He allowed a brief dramatic pause.

– The dimensions come in several varieties, you see, he said. There are a million possible Earths with a million possible histories, all of which actually exist simultaneously. In the course of one's daily life, one weaves a course between them, if you like, but that does not destroy the existence of pasts or futures we choose not to enter. What has happened to you is that you have fallen into a different historical continuum, in which Calf Island, and all of us, have our being. The place you came from knows nothing of us.

– So you are all ghosts, said Flapping Eagle, and I am mad. Is that what you are saying? I'm seeing things, places, that do not exist.

– That is really too depressing a notion, said Virgil Jones. Because it has this obverse: perhaps it is you who is the ghost. And your sister Bird-Dog.

– Where is she? asked Flapping Eagle viciously, as though seeing her would resolve all his confusions.

– I'm not sure, said Virgil. Up there somewhere. I assure you that the chances of finding her are remote; even if your arrival here proves you to be highly sensitive to the existence of the Dimensions.

– It's not that big an island, cried Flapping Eagle.

Virgil Jones said nothing for a moment, and then: – Please think about it, Mr Eagle. You see why we wished to wait until you were well.

– I'll find her, said Flapping Eagle.

– Touch wood, said Virgil Jones. He walked to a tree and did so.

– In a structure of reality where anything is possible, he said shamefacedly, I find it better to be safe than sorry. Hence my somewhat ridiculous predilection for superstition. There might be an evil spirit in that tree, after all. There might be an avenging god. It might be possible to conjure demons. The lines on one's palm might speak the truth. Symbols might be as real as people. One theory has it that in this dimension, as indeed in yours, we overlay our symbolic natures with this vast, obscurantist weight of personality. Thus making it very difficult for us to know the true forces that move us. Given this never-ending stream of possibilities, I find my little foibles a comfort.

Flapping Eagle was sitting very still, his knuckles white, his fists locked shut, his mouth a thin, tight line.

– Come, come, Mr Eagle, said Virgil Jones. I had thought you were a more flexible soul than this.

– I'm going up the mountain today, said Flapping Eagle. I want to find Bird-Dog and Sispy and get myself out of this whole vile mess.

– O, but you mustn't, said Virgil Jones.

– Why not? shouted Flapping Eagle.

– It's the Grimus Effect, said Virgil Jones. It gets more powerful all the time. To tell the truth, it's just a question of waiting until its power reaches down here. I really wouldn't advise you to climb.

Flapping Eagle felt ill again.

– What Effect? he asked, wearily.

– Grimus. The Grimus Effect.

– What the hell is that?

– Ah, said Virgil, I think you've had enough for one day. Suffice to say this: the slopes of Calf Mountain are full of monsters, Mr Eagle. You'd never survive without a guide. Possibly not even then.

Flapping Eagle shook his head, an utterly bewildered man, and buried his face in his hands. Virgil Jones came over to him and put a hand on his shoulder.

– I'm very sorry, he said. I'm very, very sorry.

– No. It's my turn to apologize, said Flapping Eagle. I'm behaving like a bad-tempered child.

– Entirely understandable, my dear fellow, said Virgil Jones, good-naturedly.

– Perhaps you could explain about the monsters?

Virgil Jones nodded sadly.

– You are quite resolved, are you not? he said.

– Yes, said Flapping Eagle. For better or worse.

– What I have been describing are the Outer Dimensions, said Mr Jones. There are Inner Dimensions as well. One never knows what universes may lie locked within one's mind. The Effect can work upon the mind with devastating effects.

He fell silent. Flapping Eagle pressed him for more, but he would only say:

– There are some things about Calf Mountain which cannot

be explained, only experienced. I hope you never experience them, Mr Eagle. I have grown fond of you. There is a great deal of spirit in that questing frame, is there not?

Flapping Eagle smiled uncertainly.

– Consider this well, gestured Virgil quickly to cover his embarrassment. It is physical proof that not all superstitions are effective. It was, as a matter-of-fact, the use of a divining-rod that settled me on this spot; and as you see it is bone-dry. But one does not have the heart to fill it up; one hopes against hope that water will begin to seep through those parched walls.

– But you didn't need a well, said Flapping Eagle. There's the stream. He pointed at the freshwater rivulet that ran through the trees.

Virgil Jones snorted. – It was something to do, he said, even if it was a bad idea.

– It's a sad ambition you have, Mr Eagle, said Virgil Jones. To grow old, to die; how is it that someone like you, so young in mind and body, can have such an ambition?

Flapping Eagle replied, with a bitter tone in his voice which surprised him : – I want to return to the human race.

A dark look flashed across Mr Jones' face : shock first, then something more like . . . apology? He seemed to apologize a lot, thought Flapping Eagle.

– Interesting, said Virgil, that you should think of death as such a humanizing force.

Flapping Eagle's confusions had settled into a slough of unwanted depression; Virgil Jones appeared to be no merrier. He stood up, shook himself, straightened his hat, dusted his trousers, and attempted to lighten the atmosphere.

– Calf Mountain, I've always thought, is rather like a giant *lingam* weltering in the *yoni* that is the Sea, he offered, and was forced to explain to the uncomprehending Flapping Eagle : A Sanskrit circumlocution, my dear Eagle. Small pleasantry. I fear I have a rather obscure sense of humour.

Then the gloom descended on him again, and he went on :
– Though why I should see this wretched place as so overtly phallic, I cannot think. After all the one thing we have in common on the island is . . . He broke off.

– What? asked Flapping Eagle.

– But you must know, sir, said Virgil Jones, retreating behind a shell of formality. Sterility. Sterility. That is what I left unsaid. A tragic side-effect of the Drink of Life. You will find no children on this rock, godforsaken as it is. Sterile, every manjack of us.

Including you.

Bitterness had now entered the voice of Virgil Jones.

Flapping Eagle walked away towards the hut. He left Virgil Jones deep in thought, absentmindedly snapping twigs in half.

FOURTEEN

In normal circumstances, Flapping Eagle would have felt an instinctive sympathy for Mrs O'Toole, physically distorted as she was. He himself had suffered the social darts that fly at the freak; they should have had much in common. He now knew why they did not. If Virgil Jones was right in saying that Calf Mountain could not, should not be climbed without an experienced guide, it was obvious who that guide had to be. Flapping Eagle realized that he was impatient to set off, catching himself in the act of wondering how to persuade Mr Jones to accompany him. No wonder Dolores was distraught; no wonder she had turned against him after that polite, friendly beginning.

Could she be persuaded to come as well? That would be the neatest solution, he thought. If she would not come, then it had to be admitted that she and Flapping Eagle must now be enemies. The admission did nothing to lessen his depression.

FIFTEEN

O, it was a certain thing, the trunk, so ponderous, so cob-webbed, so comforting, the trunk with its long-broken locks, never opened, captor of her life. O, it was a wondrous thing to be so sure, to hold her memories so fast. Open it now and let them flood her, washing her in certainties of days and griefs that could not change a jot. The moving finger writes and having writ moves on. Nor all your tears wash out a word of it. Nor tears nor the ghost of an eagle. Sure, sure, sure, as fixed in the fluid of the years as her immortal body, immortal now as souls, replenished daily, neither growing old nor young, static. The present is tomorrow's past, as fixed, as sure, the trunk would tell her so. There, the creak, the weight of the lid lifted, the open gape of time. There, the candles, devoted servants of god, immortal invisible godonlywise, in light inaccessible hidfromoureyes. O thou who changest not abide with me. No, no, they can't take this away from me. O, the candles, how did I lapse, how misuse them so, stark white pure candles? Look, the photographs, yellow as dust and half as crumbling, ashes to ashes, into the grave the great queen dashes. Grave Virgil, named for a poet, photograph him if only there were a camera and fix him there, yellow and crumbling, for evermore. Her eyes, better than any camera, conjure him now before them, hold him there, not yellow, not crumbling, warm flesh as she felt it in the night, folds enfolding her to make her safe and send the time away, nothing can change beneath the folds. There, the photographs. The little girl, poor dear thing said Auntie to have the hump. The hump, the hump, the cameeelious hump. She, La Belle Dame Aux Camelious. Or sans mercy. Merciful heavens that do not alter, there, see the uniform, the little nunkit, conventpure little girl, say seven ave marias and he won't go away. There, the past. Put him in the trunk, dear gravedigger poet, put him there to stay unaltered, put him in the trunk and keep him, folded, enfolded, the same for ever and ever, world without end, our men. Fix me jesus, fix him in a song, the fat greekname, virgil virgil give me your answer do. I'm half crazy all for the love of you. And how could he leave, how returned to all that pain? The wounds are closed here, the hurt half-healed, here he is safe and I to make him so, safe in the unchanging daytoday. No eagle can snatch him away, no eagle take him back to his past, the past is sure, it cannot be re-entered, fixed and yellow and crumbling, the past. The moving finger having writ. Close the trunk, put away childish things, it is done and he stays and nothing will change nothing nothing nothing there is nothing to change it and we shall stay virgil and dolores fixed and unchanging in the glue of love. Poor dear gravedigger jones, so much to remain forgotten in him, the weight of the past and its doings ensures the present will not change. Virgil, virgil, give me your answer do. There, the trunk, shut, sure, certain, fixed.

Pat it so and be grateful. Now might I do it, pat. Pat, it is done.

She swept the room and tidied the table, rolled the rushmats and dusted the rocking-chair, stoked the embers and filled the pot with water and roots, and began to prepare food for two. There were only the two of them, solid as a rock, immutable as the room, Dolores O'Toole and Virgil Jones, Virgil O'Toole and Dolores Jones, Virgil Dolores and Jones O'Toole, Virgil O'Dolores and Dolores O'Virgil. Like the two queers: William Fitzhenry and Henry Fitzwilliam. She cackled as she worked.

She did not see the ghost at first. It stood, tallish and fairish in the doorway looking worried, trying to decide how to express its problems to her. Eventually, since she continued to ignore it, it coughed.

She turned to the doorway, the word *Virgil!* forming on her lips, and froze. Her mouth opened and worked noiselessly, a scream without a sound. She backed slowly away from it until she stumbled against the trunk.

– Mrs O'Toole, it said. Are you ill? You look like death.

Terror entered her. She hauled open the lid of the trunk and jumped in. Rummaging feverishly, she found what she was looking for. She held it up: a small crucifix, carved in wood, crumbling with the work of maggots.

She said: – *Apage me, Satanas.*

– Dolores, said the ghost. It's all right. Dolores.

– Go away, said Dolores O'Toole. You aren't there. We live alone. Virgil Jones and Dolores O'Toole. There is no-one else. Look: there are only two mats. I am cooking for two. There are only two of us. That doesn't change.

– Do you recognize me? said the ghost, slowly. Do you know who I am?

– Go away, said Mrs O'Toole, cowering behind the edge of the trunk. Don't come closer. Go back where you came from. Go back where you belong. Go back to Grimus. Spectre of the Stone Rose, begone! I don't believe in you.

– The Stone Rose, repeated the ghost. Grimus. What . . .

– *Apage me!* shrieked Dolores O'Toole and pulled the lid of the trunk shut over her head.

The ghost stood in the centre of the room, wondering what to do. Finally, since he wished to speak to Dolores in private, he decided against summoning Virgil Jones just yet. He approached the trunk.

– God protect me, came from within as he lifted the lid.

– Mrs O'Toole . . . Dolores . . . said the ghost, I've a proposition for you.

– No, no, said Dolores. You're not here.

– I know you'd rather I left, said the ghost; I know you're worried I'll try and persuade Virgil to come with me. But what I'm suggesting is this : would you come, too? Would you?

– You cannot tempt me up the mountain, said Dolores, her eyes gleaming. Up there is the past. We left it behind. The past cannot be re-entered. Nothing changes. The past is fixed. Go away.

The ghost sighed.

– Then I must be your enemy, it said. Dear Mrs O'Toole, I am sorry, believe me; especially since I see you are ill. I'll go and get Virgil . . . Mr Jones.

– Leave him alone! cried Dolores. Go away and leave him alone!

The ghost left her.

Flapping Eagle, running to find Virgil Jones, remembered overhearing, when he was still young, two women of the Axona talking.

One of them had said : – We must be careful with Born-From-Dead.

And the second woman, the older of the two, had replied, – Yes. To be born thus is to have death sitting always behind the eyes.

And Livia Cramm had said the same.

And Virgil Jones had named him Destroyer.

And yet he had wanted none of it.

So who did?

And who or what was Grimus?

And the Stone Rose?

And would Virgil Jones agree to accompany him? Or would Mrs O'Toole's illness be the deciding factor?

He ran, panting, to the hollow by the well.

SIXTEEN

It was the well that finally helped Virgil Jones to decide; but before he reached that point, he had snapped almost every twig he could find. When he broke them, he threw the pieces into the well.

This is how he persuaded himself:

Nicholas Deggle could not have known that Flapping Eagle would meet old Virgil.

Snap.

Ergo, he *could* have sent the Axona to Calf Mountain purely as an experiment, to see if the Gate he had built would hold.

Snap.

Which meant he intended to follow.

Snap.

If Nicholas Deggle returned, life would be insupportable anyway. After Grimus, Virgil Jones must rank as his main enemy. Ever since he was expelled from the island.

Snap.

If he did not return, life would scarcely be better. The effect was spreading. Dolores had made experimental forays a little way up the slopes and she had felt it. Once it reached their little hovel, it would be no better than K. For Dolores, at any rate.

Snap.

But Nicholas Deggle must have known (Flapping Eagle must not know, not yet) what Flapping Eagle, wanting what he wanted, *being what he was*, would do to the island. What he would in all probability do.

Snap.

Still, there was little merit left in staying put.

Snap.

Except for Dolores, of course: she would never climb the mountain again. But then, it was possible to argue that should he agree to guide Flapping Eagle – *the irrevocable choice* – he would be doing so for Dolores' sake.

Snap.

Then again, what if Deggle arrived once he had left? Could

Dolores cope? He thought about that for a moment; then he concluded that, if he did go, he would have to assume that she could.

Snap.

A crucial question: would he be any use as a guide, damaged as he was by past experience of the dimensions? Again, a bleak answer: he would have to hope for the best.

Snap.

Another crucial question: Could he influence Flapping Eagle sufficiently to make the whole plan work? Yet again, uncertainty: it all depended on how Flapping Eagle reacted to what he encountered on the mountain.

Snap.

And yet, was there an alternative? What with the growth of the effect, and the increased frequency of the admittedly minor earth-tremors, the island was deteriorating, and not at all slowly.

Snap.

It was at this point that the well helped. He threw the broken twig into it and reflected upon the similarity between the well and the island. An idea that didn't work. Did one abandon it, set oneself apart from it as he had done from the life of the island? Did one attempt to save it? Or did one agree to destroy it, in the same way as one would fill up a dry well . . .?

Like Flapping Eagle, who had already chosen ascent instead of stasis; like Dolores O'Toole, who, last night, had chosen to speak her love rather than keep silent any more; in the same way, Virgil Jones decided upon action rather than prolonged inaction. Because it was there to be done, as the chicken had been there for Flapping Eagle to kill, as Dolores' love had been there to be declared, and as the well was there to fill. One does, in the end, what there is to do, he told himself, and stood up, straightening his bowler hat, blinking.

He snapped a last twig, and then Flapping Eagle arrived at a run.

Virgil Jones took his courage in both hands and said:
— Mr Eagle, are you still set upon climbing the mountain?
Flapping Eagle stopped, out of breath.
— Yes, he said, and was about to continue when Virgil said:
— In that case, you must permit me to be your guide.

64

Flapping Eagle was struck dumb by the unexpectedness of the statement.

– Mrs O'Toole, he said at last. I don't think she's very well.

Dolores O'Toole was still in the trunk when Virgil went into the hut – alone, on Flapping Eagle's suggestion.

She stood up with a cry of pleasure as he came in.

– Virgil, she said. I was so afraid.

– Now, now, Dolores, he said helplessly, feeling grossly hypocritical.

She climbed out of the trunk and came to him, standing in front of him like a vulnerable chimpanzee.

– Nothing will change, will it, Virgil? she repeated.

Virgil Jones closed his eyes.

– Dolores, he said. Please try to understand. I must go up the mountain with Mr Eagle. I must.

– O good, she cried all at once, clapping her hands. I knew it would be all right.

He looked at her. – Dolores, he said. Did you hear? We are going to leave in the morning. *Leave.*

– Yes, she said, early in the morning. We'll go down to the beach as usual, and I'll carry your chair for you, clumsy and shortsighted as you are. My love.

– O god, said Virgil Jones.

– It's not your fault, he said outside, to Flapping Eagle. Please ascribe no blame to yourself. It is my responsibility. Mea culpa.

– You'll stay with her, of course, said Flapping Eagle.

– No, said Mr Jones. If acceptable to you, we leave to-morrow morning.

Flapping Eagle had to ask: – Why, Mr Jones? Why choose me?

Mr Jones smiled crookedly. – My dear fellow, he said, never look a gift horse in the mouth. Do you know Latin?

– No, said Flapping Eagle. Or just a few words.

– *Timere Danaos et dona ferentes,* said Mr Jones. Do you follow me?

– No, said Flapping Eagle.

– Perhaps it's just as well, said Virgil Jones, if we are to be friends.

SEVENTEEN

To keep Dolores calm, Flapping Eagle had dinner alone that night, by the well; Virgil Jones brought it out to him. He was puzzled; there was a whole set of facts that didn't add up: some awful history of which he was unaware, and which had brought Mr Jones to his surprising decision. He tried to work it out and failed; so he tried to go to sleep instead, and eventually succeeded.

Meanwhile, Virgil Jones was making a despairing attempt to break through the barrier in Dolores' mind.

— You remember Nicholas Deggle, he said.

— O yes, said Dolores, quite normally. I never took to him. Good riddance, I thought, when he disappeared.

— He didn't disappear, Dolores. He was thrown out. So listen: if he should arrive, don't mention you knew me. All right?

— Very well, darling, she said equably, but you're being foolish. Why, he'll *see* you, for heaven's sake.

— Dolores, exclaimed Virgil Jones, I'm going away!

— I love you too, said Mrs O'Toole.

Virgil shook his head in a gesture of impotence.

— Listen, Dolores, he tried again. Nicholas Deggle has a grudge against me. So don't let him know I loved you . . . love you. For your own sake.

— Darling, said Mrs O'Toole, I want to tell the whole world about our love. I want to shout it out all over the island. I want . . .

— Dolores, said Virgil Jones. Stop. Stop.

— I'm so glad you're staying, she said. And I'm proud of you, too.

— Proud, echoed Mr Jones.

— O yes, she said. For chasing away that spectre from Grimus. That was well done. Now nothing can happen.

— No, said Mr Jones, admitting defeat. Nothing.

That night, Virgil Jones dreamt of Liv. Tall, beautiful, deadly Liv, who had been the breaking of him so long ago. She was the centre of the whirlpool and he was falling towards her as her mouth opened in a smile of welcome and opened further and wider and opened and opened and he fell towards her and the water rushed up over his head and he broke, like a twig.

Flapping Eagle woke several times during the night, since the bare ground was both hard and lumpy. There was an itching on his chest. He scratched at it sleepily, and thought as he drifted off again: *That damn scar.*

That damn scar played him up sometimes.

Tiusday morning again. Misty.
Virgil Jones was shaken gently awake. He found Mrs O'Toole smiling at him, saying: – Time to get up, my love.
He got up. Methodically, he took an old bag from its peg on the wall, filling it with fruit and vegetables.
– Why ever do you need all that for the beach, dear? asked Dolores. He didn't reply.
– I'll need your belt now, my love, she said, attempting a dulcet tone. He dressed in silence: the black suit, the bowler hat.
– Dolores, he said, I need the belt myself today.
– O, she pouted. Well, if you're going to be like that, I'll manage without it.
She hoisted the chair on to her hump. – Come on, she cooed. Time to be off.
– I'm not coming with you, he said.
– All right, dear, she said; you come on behind as usual. I'll see you down there.
– Goodbye, Dolores, he said.
She hobbled out of the hut with the rocking-chair on her back.

He collected Flapping Eagle from the wellside. The Axona had tied a cloth around his forehead and stuck a feather in at the back.
– Ceremonial dress, he joked; Virgil Jones didn't smile.
– Let's go, he said.

The rocking-chair sat upon the beach, with its back to the

sea. Beside it, on the greysilver sands, Dolores O'Toole sat and sang her songs of mourning and requition.

O, Virgil, she said. I'm so, so happy.

Waiting in the forests on the slopes of Calf Mountain, silent, invisible, as the fat, stumbling man and his tallish feathered companion, feather bobbing beside bowler, made their progress up the overgrown paths, watching over them and waiting, was a Gorf.

EIGHTEEN

The Gorfic planet is sometimes called Thera. It winds its way around the star Nus in the Yawy Klim galaxy of the Gorfic Nirveesu. This area is the major component of the zone sometimes termed the Gorfic Endimions.

The Gorfic obsession with anagram-making ranges from simple rearrangement of word-forms to the exalted level of the Divine Game of Order. The Game extends far beyond mere letter-puzzling; the vast mental powers of the Gorfs make it possible for them anagrammatically to alter their very environment and indeed their own physical make-up – in the latter case within the severe limits imposed by their somewhat grotesque given material. The Rules of the Game are known as Anagrammar; and to hold the title of Magister Anagrammari is the highest desire of any living Gorf.

'Living' is a troublesome term, for Gorfs are not life-forms as we know them. They need no food, no water, no atmosphere, and possess only one intangible sensory tool which serves for sight, sound, touch, taste, smell and quite a lot besides: a sort of aura or emanation surrounding their huge, hard, useless bodies.

To be explicit: the Gorfs look like nothing so much as enormous sightless frogs, with one important peculiarity. They are made entirely out of rock.

Their origins are lost in mystery; some radiation, perhaps, blasting their now-barren planet, formed the rock into these masterpieces of intelligence and at the same time trapped them in the tragic irony of near-immobility and total isolation. For this is the tragedy of the Gorfs: not only Thera itself, but the entire Endimions, is totally devoid of any other life-form. No animals bound, no plants wave, nor is there any breeze to wave them.

This irony prevented the Gorfs, for several millennia, from being able to determine how advanced a culture they actually were, having no standards of measurement. The result was a certain philosophical paranoia. The supreme Master of the Game, Dota himself, asked in the celebrated Questions of Dota: *And are we actually to be the least intelligent race in our Endimions?* – a philosophy of despair: he who is unique *is* both largest and smallest. Our own Gorf, the one now eagerly overseeing the progress of Flapping Eagle and Mr Virgil Jones, took especial pride in his Ordering of this last and most famous of the Questions. He had altered it to make quite a different question, thus: *Determine how catalytic an elite is; use our talent and learning-lobe.* This is a perfect use of Anagrammar; for not only does it contain all the letters of the Chiefest Question and only those letters, but moreover, it enriches the Question itself, adding to it the concept of elitism and its desirability, the concept of catalysis and its origins, and instructions about how the question is to be answered. 'Talent' to the Gorfs means only one thing: skill at Ordering. Thus the very skill that caused the Chiefest Question to be asked must be used in its solution, with the aid of the 'Learning-lobe', that inexhaustible memory-vault locked within each Gorf, giving the species absolute recall of anything that has ever befallen any Gorf.

The title of Magister Anagrammari, and the modest acclaim that resulted, (the Gorfs not being an excitable race) now came the way of our Gorf, and may fairly be said to have turned his head (though properly speaking, he had none).

It should be pointed out that the Gorfs had developed no orthodox technology; the Divine Game sufficed them for science and art. Their philosophy, as may be observed from the above example, preferred questions to answers; even though our Gorf's Ordering of Dota's Question hinted at the source of an answer, he was well aware that further Orderings might make its examination impossible. However, our Gorf, filled with his triumph, now moved towards heresy. He developed a minor branch of the Divine Game to such a point that it threatened the Game itself. It also gave the Gorfs the chance, at last, of measuring the extent of their brilliance or mediocrity against other civilizations.

The minor branch was called Conceptualism. It is perhaps best defined in one of the rare Statements of Dota: '*I think, therefore it is.*' It was our Gorf who first saw the tremendous implications of this statement. Dota had intended it to mean simply that nothing could exist without the presence of a cognitive intellect to perceive its existence; our Gorf reversed this to postulate that anything of which such an intellect could conceive *must therefore exist.* He followed this by conceiving the possibility of other Endimions: other Endimions containing accessible life-forms. The Gorfs were not sure whether to cheer or throw brickbats. Suddenly they felt exposed. The comfortable, if melancholy, period of isolation was being brought to a rapid close . . .

To pacify the fears of his fellow-beings, our Gorf then conceptualized an Object. An Object would exist in every single conceivable Endimions, and it was only through contact with Objects that movement between the Endimions would be possible. This would give the Gorfs a measure of control over their new Idea.

It was through such an Object that our Gorf came into contact with Grimus. And Calf Island. In order to observe it without being himself involved, he Ordered his own vile body in such a way as to make him invisible. And watched.

As he watched over the stumbling ascent of Mr Jones and Flapping Eagle, he felt a mounting excitement. His aura positively quivered with pleasure. This was why: ever since he arrived at Calf Island he had sensed a missing link, an absence of some vital ingredient that would stabilize the structure of the place. Any Gorf would have spotted that: it was one of the elementary stages of the Divine Game to be sure of one's components. This sureness became, in the hands of a Master, a kind of instinct; so that the Gorf *knew*, when he saw Flapping Eagle, that this man was the link. That this journey, if completed, would also complete the Ordering of the island and the mountain. He longed to know what that Order would be like.

If our Gorf had a fault, it was that he was a meddler. Long years of Ordering had given him a consuming passion for it. So far, on Calf Island, he had resisted the temptation; but now,

now that the great final events for which the island had (unconsciously) been waiting were in train, he found a reason for meddling.

He argued:

Only if you were Grimus would you be fully conscious of what was happening on Calf Island.

Unless, that is, you were a Gorf.

Now, since consciousness is a dynamic condition (that is, you have to choose whether to act or not to act upon your knowledge, and even a decision to remain inactive is an action) it becomes the privilege, not to say duty, of conscious beings to move, and possibly alter the flow of their times.

Thus it was perfectly proper for a Gorf on Calf Island, knowing what he knew, being what he was, to act as he saw fit.

The Gorf nodded gleefully to himself. He was almost hoping for one especial treat before the Final Ordering: almost hoping that Flapping Eagle would fall under the terrifying and often fatal spell of Endimions-Fever.

Of course, he told himself, he would have to be very careful.

NINETEEN

Thick forest, dark as the tomb. Behind them the broken, isolated mind of Dolores O'Toole, abandoned by love at the very moment at which she had allowed it to possess her; ahead of them, K and whatever it held. Between the two, the inhospitable slopes and Forest of Calf. All that spurred Flapping Eagle on was the phantasm of Bird-Dog in his mind's eye, walking away from him hand-in-hand with the faceless Mr Sispy. He wished he knew what spurred Virgil Jones.

A faint whine in the corners of his head. He had the impression it was growing louder as they climbed the mountain tracks. Virgil Jones gave no sign of hearing it; he wore the lost air of a man trying to recall old habits. – Yes, yes, he would mutter to himself every so often and plunge heavily through this or that thicket. Drat, he would swear on occasion and bury his head in his hands, lost in memories or recriminations – and then he would jerk up again, ploughing forward like a wounded buffalo.

Flapping Eagle followed; and so they forged their erratic way through the undergrowth and up the Mountain.

The whine was still there; were his ears playing tricks? Did it seem to be getting louder only because he was thinking about it? He struck the side of his head with the flat of his hand, in exasperation. For an instant, he had the impression that the forest was a solid impenetrable mass, surrounding, enclosing. He blinked, and it passed; there was the faint track again.

Virgil Jones was staring at him.

– Why did you cry out? he asked.

– Whatever do you mean? asked Flapping Eagle.

– You didn't hear yourself?

– I most certainly did not, said Flapping Eagle, annoyed. Is this a joke?

– No, no, I assure you, said Mr Jones. Tell me, can you hear anything at all? A kind of high-pitched whistle?

– Yes . . . said Flapping Eagle, alarm growing.

– Right, said Virgil Jones. I'm afraid my hearing, like my eyesight, is somewhat diminished, particularly in the upper registers. The fact is, we are entering the zone of the Effect. It now becomes of vital importance that we talk to each other.

– What Effect? asked Flapping Eagle. And why talk?

– About anything except the Effect, said Virgil Jones. Now is no time for explanations. Please do as I say. Silence could prove very dangerous.

Flapping Eagle bit back a flurry of questions and decided to go along with Mr Jones' advice.

– Dolores, he said. Will she be all right?

– I hope so, said Mr Jones. I surely hope so.

A brief silence : then Mr Jones burst into speech.

– Did you ever hear the story of how a prostitute once started a civil war in your country? Polly Adams was her name . . .

But Flapping Eagle's mind had wandered. He was thinking of Bird-Dog, of Mr Jones' motives, of the dense wood in which they were lost, of the whine in his ears, the whine in his ears, the whine in his ears, and it grew louder and louder . . .

Virgil Jones was shouting into his ear :

– A riddle, Mr Eagle. Think about this : Why does an Irishman wear three prophylactics?

Weakness, illness. Both alien things to Flapping Eagle, both now rushing towards and over him like the wave that brought him to Calf Island. That same sensation of puzzled abstraction which he'd felt before passing out on his boat was creeping upon him once more. His legs wobbled; standing became harder and harder, climbing impossible. He came to a halt. His forehead blazed. The whine grew louder still and louder.

– I don't know, Mr Jones, he said feebly. Why does an Irishman wear three ...

Something was distorting his sight. Virgil seemed a mile away; his arm came stretching across light-years like a long, snaking tentacle. Flapping Eagle shied away, instinctively, and fell over. He felt a chill in his bones. His forehead was icy now. The whine now practically deafened him to Virgil's bellowing voice.

– Don't worry, Virgil was shouting. Just a touch of Dimension-fever, that's all. We'll soon get you better ... the words echoed and faded.

Dimension-fever: what was that? Flapping Eagle felt a rage at having been kept in ignorance, and his eyes seemed to clear. He saw a solicitous Virgil Jones leaning over him.

– It's worse in the dark, Virgil was shouting. I'll get you to a clearing. Try and concentrate on my voice. I'll talk all the way. Daylight helps: chases away the monsters.

– Monsters ... said Flapping Eagle faintly.

– They come from inside you, said Virgil Jones. Inside you ... (His voice, fading, diminishing.)

Confusion returned to Flapping Eagle. Again the distorted vision.

– Can't explain, Virgil yelled down a long tunnel. To live through it is to understand it. Listen to my voice. Listen only to my voice.

Fear enveloped Flapping Eagle, the fear of a healthy man for an inexplicable disease. He felt his convictions slipping from him; what was he doing here, anyway? What kind of devilry had seized him? Why had he not simply killed himself when he had the chance? Perhaps, after all, he was dead. Yes, he was dead. He had drowned in the boat and this was hell and Virgil Jones was a demon and this was some infernal torture. Yes, he was dead.

O, I remember, I remember: I was Flapping Eagle. As the unknowable swept over me, I went all but mad. Hallucinations

73

. . . I thought they were hallucinations at first, but gradually they gained the certitude of absolute reality and it was the voice of Virgil Jones that came drifting to me like a dream. The world had turned upside down; I was climbing a mountain into the depths of an inferno, plunging deep into myself.

The scene I saw seemed to freeze; it went through a myriad transmutations, in which colours altered, the trees became moving creatures, the ground became liquid and the sky solid, grass spoke and flowers played music. In some of these transformations Virgil Jones was not there at all; in others he was a huge suppurating monster. In others he was dead. In others I could hear his voice speaking to me, pouring words of comfort and advice into my ear. It was a baptism of fire.

Virgil Jones and I: a strange pair of bedfellows. He a burnt-out man, the shell of his past, secure in the knowledge of some great failure; I an incomplete man, looking for the knowledge of dying which would finish me, seeking my face in the eye of death. For a reason I did not understand until much later, he loved me like a son, like the last of his living sons; and once I recovered from the fever, I loved him too, though I loved him badly and not enough. He nursed me then, dragging me to a clearing, rubbery and sluggish as I was, talking, talking to distract my mind from the depredations of the Effect. In the dark, before we reached the clearing, he was lost to me. In the clearing, his voice gave me some strength. Until he came to get me.

Virgil Jones: a soul without a future helping me to mine, leaving behind him Dolores, his sorrow and love, heading for places long-since fled. A brave man.

To live through the fever of the Dimensions is to abandon the question Why? And yet, before the end, I had an answer to all the unanswered whys, and a few unasked ones as well.

As Virgil Jones dragged Flapping Eagle to the clearing he said :

– O dear, my friend. I wish it didn't have to be you. Grimus used to say a man would either lose or find himself in these woods. That is the difference between myself and yourself. I can only lose.

Mr Eagle, you are not a realized man. That is your weakness and also your power. Before one realizes oneself one has the optimism of ignorance. It can be the saving of one's life. Once

74

realized, one faces the terror of knowing what it is you are and have done . . . the realized man can have a profound effect on the world about him; he must bear the consequences, and guilt, of that as well . . .

Finally, in the clearing, he sat down, placed Flapping Eagle's head on his lap, and answered his own riddle, abstractedly:

– An Irishman wears three prophylactics to be sure, to be sure, to be sure.

To himself he thought:

Now, Mr Jones, we shall see if you are capable of being a guide.

TWENTY

Bird-Dog said, brandishing a bone:

– Look, little brother. Look. Here's a bone for you. Good dog. It's a very special bone. The Bone of K. Take it. Come and bury it.

– Bird-Dog, said Flapping Eagle, slowly. Is it you?

She stood mockingly upon a rock, stamping her right foot as she turned in a slow circle. She tossed him the bone. It fell unerringly into his hand; a rose grew from a crack in it. He stuffed it into his trousers.

She was lying mockingly upon the rock, pulling her raggedy skirt up to her waist and spreading her legs, arching her back.

– Come in, little brother, she said. Come and bury it.

He crawled towards her, weakly, and the nearer he came, the larger she grew. A hundred yards away and she was already as large as a horse. The hole between her legs yawned; its hairs were like ropes. Ten yards away. She was a house, a cavern lying red and palpitating before him, the curtain of hair parting. He heard her booming voice.

– Why resist, she was saying. Give up, little brother. Come in. Give up. Come in. Give up.

He crawled into the cavern. The curtain fell into place behind him, cutting off all light.

Inside . . . a dark reddish glow. There she was again, fleet Bird-Dog, racing away into her own depths, squealing with childish delight.

—Silly little brother, can't catch me, she cried and vanished around a corner. He was not yet strong enough to chase. He stood up.

And heard the voice of Virgil Jones.

— The trouble with Grimus, the voice said, is he can't control the Effect. Its field grows stronger and stronger. You'll have to get used to it gradually. Control your thoughts. Slowly. Softlee softlee catchee monkee. The inner dimensions are lonely places. We create our own, so to speak. Frightening, that: each man his own universe. Imagine the effect. Men go mad. That's the tragedy of K. They're all scared of their own minds. I was, myself, once, but there's not much of it left now. Like old Father William, eh? Small pleasantry. May I interest you in a theory? Fellow in K, you'll meet him, calls himself a philosopher, Ignatius Gribb, Ignatius Q. Gribb. Q for Quasimodo. I. Q. Gribb, you see, never knew if it was his idea of a joke or his parents', the initials. He used to say: — there are no human beings alive. What we all are is Shells, and hovering around in the ether are what he called Forms. Things like emotions, reasons and so forth. They occupy one of us for a while, then another one moves in. It's pretty in its fashion. Explains the illogicality of some human actions. Shifts of character and so forth. It's completely exploded by the dimensions, of course. The one thing that stays constant in the shifts between the dimensions is one's own consciousness. But then Mr Gribb tries very hard to ignore the dimensions. They're a frightening thing. Cultivate your consciousness, Mr Eagle, that's the way out. There's always a way. Where there's a will. Only control you have.

The voice faded away again.

Flapping Eagle took a deep breath, closed his eyes, opened his eyes and tried to establish his whereabouts. It was like standing in foam. Springy, his feet subsided into it. Soft wet reddish foam.

Red: that meant light. If there was colour, there was light, but he could see no light-source. Yet there was light, dim, diffuse, but light. He gave up the search.

He turned to look behind him, at the entrance. It was no longer there. A brief moment of claustrophobia, then calm, despite the ancient saying that grew in his head and took words for itself: *Jonah in the belly of the whale.*

The survival instinct lies buried deep in soft civilizations; in the peripatetic Flapping Eagle, it lay very near the surface, if somewhat weakened by his knowledge of his immortality. Now, when he was plunged into a world his senses told him could not exist, but which they also told him did exist, this instinct took him over. It did so in a very physical way. He could perceive a thing which was entirely himself but also not-himself assuming command of his faculties and gritting his teeth for him. It was a simple but overwhelming self-command to survive this. He was astonished and a little pleased at the strength of his own will. *In extremis veritas.*

WHERE THERE'S A WILL. The realization of his own power, of Virgil Jones' meaning, dawned on him. Here was his way out, if his resolve was strong enough.

He began to practise. At his first attempt, a rose grew from the floor of the Place. (He could not think of it as his sister's insides, especially as he had seen her disappearing down the fleshy corridor.) The rose died almost at once. He thought about this, and a second rose grew. It showed no signs of dying.

He looked at the floor, and it became solid. A carpet covered it, hand-woven in silk, with an Eye embroidered into the very centre. He used the eye to make windows. It glared at the red walls and they fell into order.

It was really quite an elegant room, even if the walls were a livid red. He felt almost proud of himself.

Outside the windows, Calf Mountain was beginning to form. He got as far as seeing the clearing, the forest around it, and even caught a glimpse of Virgil Jones, who seemed to come right up to one of the windows until his fleshy face filled it. There was a door in the wall, ebony-handled; all he had to do was open it and walk out and he would be well. Controlling the Dimensions was easy, if you knew what you were doing, he told himself cockily. He rather fancied he saw a look of respect in Mr Jones' eyes.

The Gorf was feeling disappointed. He had locked himself to Flapping Eagle's *self*, using the parasitic technique by which Gorfs communicated, and had fully expected a long, delectable time of Endimions-shuffling, which was the next best thing he knew to the Divine Game. But here was Flapping Eagle displaying an exceptional capacity for controlling the Endimions.

The Gorf decided to take a hand. After all, the Final Ordering of the island could wait a little longer ... Flapping Eagle found the room dissolving as he reached for the door-handle. The shock wrecked his new-found confidence. The darkness descended. He was, for a moment, blind and giddy. The world seemed to spin rapidly. When his head cleared, the Abyssinians were squatting in front of him.

TWENTY-ONE

The dance has had many functions. It has been a social ice-breaker and a ritual cloudbreaker. It has been a mark of passion and a sign of hate. Stars have danced in young girls' eyes and death has danced with its unwilling family. Today, in the hollow of a wood, with the green light of the leaves playing about his face, stark naked, a grim-faced fat man called Virgil Jones was dancing for the life of his new friend.

— Friend: he had repeated the word to himself a million times, he had whispered it into the ear of the unconscious Eagle to give him strength.

— You are the straw, Flapping Eagle, he had said, and I am the drowning man.

Last chances, like first chances, come only once. Virgil Jones was convinced that his last chance was upon him. A last chance to do, to help, to expiate the guilt and the uselessness that lay within him, rusting his insides; a chance to save instead of ruining.

A man who lives in tolerable comfort amidst extreme poverty learns in the end not to see the quagmire of hopelessness. It is a survival mechanism. In just the same way, Virgil Jones had shut out his past from his mind. He had come down the mountain and forgotten the blank terrors he had fled. They were still there, locked in his head, but he did not see them.

Now, for Flapping Eagle's sake, he unlocked the prison and like Pandora's uncontrollable sprites his memory came flooding out, grating painfully upon him as it emerged. He had forgotten the pain. So much had been numb for so long.

78

At first he had thought Flapping Eagle might have been strong enough, had been hardened enough by his long journeys to survive the Dimensions unaided. (But then he had forgotten their devastating power.) And for a moment Flapping Eagle's eyes had sparked – he had almost pulled his mind away from itself. But he hadn't been strong enough; and now there was only one thing to do.

Virgil Jones had to go in there, into the dimensions of another man's mind, more dangerous even than one's own, and guide him out. The alternative was a foregone conclusion. Flapping Eagle's mind would overheat and in the end it would burn out, perhaps beyond all saving. As Virgil Jones' mind had nearly destroyed itself. The worm biting its own tail would finally swallow itself.

Because the worlds that Calf Mountain and its Effect unleashed inside the head were not phantoms. They were solid. They could hit and hurt.

Virgil Jones had sat for an age, running his thoughts over the agonies of his past, when he had travelled the Dimensions, before the Effect had become too huge for him to handle, trying to clutch at the knowledge he needed. He knew that he had known it; that somewhere on his travels he had met – who? – someone – that knew the technique for locking on to the mind of another living being.

Virgil Jones had not told Flapping Eagle about his own travels. In his day he had rejoiced in those interdimensional trips. There had been the voyages to the real, physical, alternative space-time continua. So close, yet such an eternity away. And there had been his own annihilating journey into the Inner Dimensions, like the internal inferno which now clutched Flapping Eagle, which had left him hollow and impotent and lucky to be alive. And there was the third kind.

The bridge between the first two kinds.

With sufficient imagination, Virgil Jones had found, one could *create* worlds, physical, external worlds, neither aspects of oneself nor a palimpsest-universe.

Fictions where a man could live.

In those days, Mr Jones had been a highly imaginative man.

He fought his way past the unbearable memory of his breakdown, when the power became a monster which turned upon him and seared his mind, and came to the good times. He smiled. What worlds he had visited! What things he had learned! He recalled with admiration the sexual techniques of the Ydjac, the instinct-logic of the plant-geniuses of Poli XI, the tonal sculpture of the Aurelions. The pain was gone now; he was past the block, excavating his own history with the pleasure of the genuine archaeologist. And so he came, eventually, to the time he visited the Spiral Dancers.

Certain kinds of science aspire to the condition of poetry; and on the planet of the Spiral Dancers, a long tradition of scientist-poets had elevated a branch of physics until it became a high symbolist religion. They had probed matter, dividing it into ever-smaller units, until they found at its very roots the pure, beautiful dance of life. This was a harmony of the infinitesimal, where energy and matter moved like fluids. Energy forces came gracefully together to create at their point of union a *pinch* which was matter. The pinches came together into larger pinches; or else fell away again into pure energy, according to the rules of a highly formal, spiral rhythm. When they came together, they were dancing the Strongdance. When they fell back into the Primal, they were dancing the Weakdance.

From this discovery came the religion of Spiral Unity. If everything was energy, everything was the same. A thinking being and a table were only aspects of the same force. It had been proven scientifically.

The main ritual of the religion, which was only established after generations of poet-scientists worked on applications of the Theory, was the Spiral Dance. It was a physical exercise based on the primal rhythms, and its purpose was to enable every humble, imperfect living thing to aspire to that fundamental perfection. Dance the Dance, and you would commune with the Oneness surrounding you on all sides.

Virgil Jones stood up.

He removed his old dark jacket. And his old dark trousers. And his old dark waistcoat with the watchless gold chain.

He removed his bowler from his head; and placed all these things, with his undergarments, neatly on Flapping Eagle's prone form, where they wouldn't get in the way.

And ignoring his protesting corns, he danced.

The Gorf, already locked into the mind of Flapping Eagle

(which was a good deal easier for him than for Mr Jones) was
about to receive a surprise.

Mr Jones circled the body of Flapping Eagle slowly, humming a low-pitched note. As he did this, he turned round and
round, stamping his feet at regular intervals. After a while, he
stopped feeling giddy. After a longer while, he no longer had to
think about what he was doing. His body took over and guided
him on his looping path by remote control. After a much longer
while he ceased to be conscious of anything – surroundings,
body, anything – except the hum, which hung around him like a
curtain. Then that died away (though his vocal cords continued
to produce the noise) and for a brief second he was not conscious even of being. It was during that instant that the *ripples*
of Flapping Eagle lapped over his own; and Virgil Jones became attuned to the ailing mind.

If you'd been in the right Dimension, you would have seen
a thin veil-like mist encasing the two bodies.

Virgil Jones had gone to the rescue.

TWENTY-TWO

The Gorf was pleased with the puzzle he had set Flapping
Eagle. Having come to the conclusion that the Amerindian's
near-immunity to Dimension-fever sprang from a temporary
paralysis of the imagination, the Master of Ordering had decided to fill the gap with his own. The puzzle he constructed
was especially satisfying since all its elements, as well as the
way out, had been built from Flapping Eagle's memories; so
that it was a perfectly passable counterfeit of a dimension that
a more freely-thinking Flapping Eagle might have entered. The
Gorf relaxed and prepared to enjoy Flapping Eagle's attempts
to solve it.

These were the elements of the puzzle:

A place called Abyssinia. Its characteristics sprang from the
name the Gorf had taken from Flapping Eagle's mind. It was
a huge abyss, a narrow canyon with stone walls reaching up to
the sky. And, just to add an intriguing time-factor, it was get-

ting slowly narrower. The cliffs were encroaching on both sides; they even seemed to be coming together overhead, so that in time they would form a tomb of constricting rock.

At the bottom of the canyon with Flapping Eagle were two Abyssinians. They looked like Deggle, creator of the memory. Both of them were long and saturnine. They wore black cloaks and emerald necklaces. But there the resemblance to Deggle ended. (Even so, it served its purpose; Flapping Eagle was utterly unnerved by the spectacle of twin Deggles standing before him, and forgot about Bird-Dog and his own powers long enough to enable the dimension to 'set' firmly, like concrete.)

The Two Abyssinians were called Khallit and Mallit. They were engaged in an eternal argument without beginning or end, its very lack of purpose or decision undermining Flapping Eagle's ability to think clearly.

One more thing: Flapping Eagle was tied hand and foot. He lay beside the two Abyssinians as they squatted around a campfire. They seemed oblivious of his presence, and did not answer when he spoke to them.

A very pleasing puzzle indeed.

Between them, Khallit and Mallit placed a gold coin. Every so often one of them would flip it; it was the only way they ever decided on any element of their eternal wrangle.

At the present moment, they seemed indirectly to be discussing Flapping Eagle.

– There are two sides to every question, Mallit, are there not?

– Well . . . said Mallit doubtfully. He flipped the coin – Yes, he said.

Khallit breathed a sigh of relief.

– Then if good is on one side of the coin, bad is on the other. If peace is on one side, war is on the other.

– Arguable, said Mallit.

– For the sake of argument, pleaded Khallit.

– For the sake of argument, agreed Mallit, after tossing the coin.

– Then if life is on one side, death must be on the other, said Khallit.

– Only if, said Mallit.

– For the sake of argument, they said in unison, and smiled at each other.

The walls of the canyon moved in a fraction.

– But here's a paradox, said Khallit. Suppose a man deprived of death. Suppose him wandering through all eternity, a beginning without an end. Does the absence of death in him mean that life is also absent?

– Debatable, said Mallit. He flipped the coin. Yes, he said.

– So he is, in fact, no more than the living dead?

– Or no less.

– Would you agree that the major difference between the living and the dead is the power to act?

– For the sake of argument, said Mallit.

– So that such a man would be impotent. Helpless.

– Impotent. Helpless, echoed Mallit.

– Incapable of influencing his own life.

– Incapable of influencing his own life.

– Flung eternally between his doubts and his fears.

– Flung.

Their voices were melodious. Flapping Eagle found himself listening raptly. He had never realized the beauty of speech, the appeal of simply speaking and arguing for ever and ever ... he felt his mind slipping away and tried to force it back. It was unconscionably difficult.

He suddenly realized what was happening to the canyon. Because there was a great deal less room in it than when he had first arrived. He struggled desperately against his ropes. To no avail. He screamed at Khallit and Mallit.

– Can the dead speak? asked Khallit.

– Doubtful, said Mallit and tossed the coin. – No, he said.

– No, echoed Khallit.

Flapping Eagle realized bleakly that there was no way out. He remembered Virgil Jones' whisper: there is always a way out. He no longer believed it. He would lie here, listening to the eternal indecision of these two extrapolations of himself until the rock claimed them.

Flapping Eagle closed his eyes.

The Gorf was feeling irritated this time. What good was such a simple, beautiful puzzle if the man wouldn't make any attempt to solve it? Of course there was a way out. Very simple it was, too. All the man had to do was work it out. The Gorf had a suspicion that Flapping Eagle would never be any good at the Game of Order.

And then his irritation vanished, to be replaced by wonderment, as something happened for which he had made no provision.

A whirlwind suddenly appeared at one end of the canyon.

Khallit looked up and became highly agitated.
– Mallit, he said. Mallit, is that a whirlwind?
Mallit spun a coin without looking up. – No, he said. It is not.
– Mallit, cried Khallit, it is. It is a whirlwind.
Mallit looked up. – It can't be, he said.
– But it is, it is, cried Khallit.
The whirlwind came closer and closer.
– Fascinating paradox, said Mallit.
– Fascinating, said Khallit doubtfully.
Then the whirlwind was upon them. Like the mere notions they were, the less-than-human constructs of an alien imagination, the force of Virgil Jones' arrival dispersed them. They returned to the shreds of energy they had once been. On the planet of the Spiral Dancers, people would have said: – they danced the Weakdance to the end.

Flapping Eagle had opened his eyes. The whirlwind stood in front of him and slowed down. It began to look like a man.
– The Whirling Demon! cried Flapping Eagle, using the phrase after seven centuries.
– Hullo, said Virgil Jones.

A few questions from Virgil Jones, and Flapping Eagle was talking about Deggle and mentioned the word 'Ethiopia'. The instant he said the word, the Gorf's puzzle dissolved. Because that was the key, the way out. Ethiopia . . . Abyssinia . . . I'll be seeing you . . . Goodbye. All he had to do was say Goodbye and the puzzle was solved.

It was easy, the Gorf thought sulkily. It was. The people looked like Deggle. The place was named after one half of his favourite phrase. Even an idiot could have guessed that escape lay through the other half. Even an idiot. That was the trouble with most people. They were so bad at games.

TWENTY-THREE

The sea felt pure beneath them, its spray salting their cheeks, stinging, refreshing; a sea of mists and clouds, grey curling waves hidden behind the veils; a sea to be lost on, a drifting, unchanged sea.

Flapping Eagle lay breathless on the raft's rough boards, half-dazed, uncomprehending; Virgil Jones, a naked speck on another man's horizons, stood by the tattered sail, on guard, the juices of excitement flowing renewed in his veins. The tableau held and was fixed.

— May I call you Virgil? Flapping Eagle's voice was hesitant. Virgil Jones felt inordinately pleased.

— Certainly, certainly. Certainly, call me Virgil.

A long silence, in which a bond was sealed.

— What may I call you? Virgil broke the stillness.

Flapping Eagle didn't answer.

— Mr Eagle? Virgil Jones turned to look at the Axona.

But Flapping Eagle was asleep.

Virgil lumbered across the raft and sat by the sleeping form.

— Don't thank me for your life, he said to it. I'm grateful to you, more than I can say. Don't thank me for coming here; it was a debt paid, a world remembered. Don't thank me for anything; and don't be afraid.

The sea curled over the edges of their frail craft, and fell away; curled, and fell away, as the old bull elephant watched over the body of the young-old buck.

— I have some food, said Flapping Eagle, in some surprise. He had reached into the pocket of his ragged trousers and found two old sea-biscuits. He passed one to Virgil Jones, who hid his nakedness behind Flapping Eagle's old coat. They ate slowly.

— Just call me Flapping Eagle, said Flapping Eagle, and then added: Virgil.

They looked at each other as they munched.

— Everything you've ever done, said Virgil, has been a preparation for Calf Mountain, in a way.

Flapping Eagle noticed a difference in Virgil; he was calm rather than stagnant. There seemed to be a surge of strength in him which was very reassuring. Flapping Eagle realized how mutually dependent they had become, and it was a pleasurable realization.

– Everything I ever did, said Virgil, was just the same, in a way.

– What sort of thing, asked Flapping Eagle.

– O, said Virgil, I travelled, like you.

The sea whispered secrets to the raft.

– A life, said Virgil, always contains a peak. A moment, you follow, that makes it all worthwhile. Justifies it. At any rate, that's what I find. You're either moving towards it or away from it. Or for an instant you're at it and you're . . . full.

They were becalmed. Flapping Eagle sat up, looking at the stillness with equanimity. Virgil's large tongue licked contentedly at the outskirts of his mouth: patrolling the frontiers.

– Have you ever thought about the phrase: *petrified with fear*? asked Virgil. Turned to stone, you see.

Flapping Eagle half-turned, half-spoke, but Virgil was far away in a train of thought.

–That's what they're like in K, you see, he continued. Petrified. And why? He heaved his shoulders, tossing the weight from them. Why, because of the damned dimensions. (He frowned.) You remember my saying you should fix your mind on one thing, like Bird-Dog. It's the only defence. The effect is much stronger in K, you know. Much nearer to Grimus. It drove them out of their wits . . . they found the only way to keep the bloody thing at bay was to be single-minded. To a fault. Obsessive. That's the word. Obsessions close the mind to dimensions. That's what K's like. Obsessive. You can probably understand why. Petrified with fear. It's a fearful thing to be a stranger within oneself. People don't like their own complexities. Tragic, really.

Flapping Eagle asked: What about? Obsessive. What about?

– O, said Virgil, anything. Doesn't matter. Cleaning the floor, whatever. Carry it to its extreme and it serves to protect. Mrs O'Toole's obsession with constancy may well be her best protection. As I said, the Effect is spreading, you know. It spreads.

· He was silent.

– Often they fix themselves a time in their lives to mull over. Live the same day over and over again. Displaced persons are like that, you know. Always counterfeiting roots. Still. If a false front's thick enough, it serves. To protect.

There was no time; they sat, stood, moved, slept. At some point, Flapping Eagle had asked:

– What about yourself, Virgil?

– What about me? replied Virgil.

– You were saying every life has a peak . . . what about you?

– O yes, said Virgil. Long past it.

The silence settled again. Then Virgil said:

– Once. Then. Before. The terror of the titties, eh?

Flapping Eagle asked: – Were you married?

– O, said Virgil, yes. Eventually. Roughly. Temporarily.

There was a wind. The rudimentary sail was full; they moved from anywhere to nowhere across the infinite sea.

– Towards infinity, said Virgil Jones, where all paradoxes are resolved.

– Virgil, asked Flapping Eagle, am I getting better?

– Better?

– The Dimension-fever, said Flapping Eagle. Everything seems to be smooth just at the moment. Am I mending? ·

– I don't know, said Virgil. Perhaps. Perhaps not. Usually one meets a few monsters. You know the sort of thing.

– No, said Flapping Eagle.

– At any rate, said Virgil, trying to sound confident, between us, we should be able to handle them.

The Gorf had made a decision. No more meddling. But he might speed things up a bit; he was getting bored. Though Mr Jones' presence was very interesting.

TWENTY-FOUR

Land rose up from the sea to meet them, but it was unlike any soil or earth either of them had ever seen. It was not so much solid as not-liquid, a viscous, glutinous stuff. At one second it seemed insubstantial as air, at another it acquired the consistency of treacle, at another it lay smooth as glass. It seemed to smoke, or steam, a little.

Virgil Jones knew where they were. It was the nearest they would get to escape, and also the most dangerous of the Inner Dimensions. They stood at the very fringes of Flapping Eagle's awareness. close to the point at which his senses merged with the void. This was unmade ground, the raw materials of the mind. If they bent it right, it would lead them wherever they wished to go; if they failed to master it, they could drift on its wisps out of Flapping Eagle's existence. To put it another way, they would die.

The raft had lodged – or *stuck* – in the land. Gingerly, they placed feet upon the colourless, formless substance. Flapping Eagle looked nervous.

– We're in very deep, said Virgil and explained.

– Now then, he said, we'll need to concentrate as hard as we can. Try and imagine the topography of this Dimension, since it seems to be topographic. It's a series of concentric circles.

– A series of concentric circles, repeated Flapping Eagle.

– We're on the outermost circle. We need to get to the centre.

– We need to get to the centre, repeated Flapping Eagle.

– Once we're in the centre, we'll need to climb. The waking state lies directly above the centre. Do you understand?

– Yes, said Flapping Eagle.

– If we concentrate hard enough we can use this stuff to make a passage. We'll be able to move through it to the centre without being affected by the Dimensions.

Virgil Jones had taken on a new dimension himself. He was crisp, authoritative. Flapping Eagle settled down to shape the stuff of his mind.

The passage, or tunnel, took shape around them. It was dark

grey, suffused with dirty yellow light. In mounting excitement, Flapping Eagle realized that he was shaping it into a passable facsimile of the red tunnel down which Bird-Dog had fled at the beginning of the fever. His strength began to flood back; the malleable not-land stretched into a longer and longer tunnel. Virgil Jones, watching, felt an enormous relief. And finally at the very far end of the tunnel they saw a tiny beckoning pin-prick of light.

– Time to go, said Virgil Jones.

Flapping Eagle didn't speak. All his efforts were plunged into holding the tunnel, preserving its existence until it *set*. So Virgil Jones, ever co-operative, concentrated on creating a means of transport. A moment later (he derived a sizeable pleasure from the speed) they were the proud possessors of two bicycles.

– I'm sorry, he apologized, the mysteries of the internal combustion engine have always been beyond me.

The tunnel had *set*. They mounted their anachronistic steeds and headed into its depths, towards the siren light.

For all his recent achievements, for all his new-found confidence, Virgil seemed to Flapping Eagle to be a worried man.

– Virgil, he asked, you wouldn't hold anything back from me, would you?

– My dear fellow, admonished Virgil Jones. My dear fellow.

– Well, then. You wouldn't know what's at the other end of this tunnel, would you?

– My dear fellow, repeated Virgil Jones; and then, after a pause, he added quietly: That depends entirely on you.

– Explain?

– In all probability, said Virgil, there will be nothing at all.

– And that's what worries you?

Virgil Jones coughed. – You seem to be an unusual fellow, he said. Perhaps you won't need . . . He stopped.

– What? asked Flapping Eagle.

– The monsters, said Virgil Jones.

When he had explained, Flapping Eagle knew what had to happen.

The cure for Dimension-fever is a complex thing. It involves more than mere survival, more than just the ability to find one's way through the labyrinth. If that is all a sufferer has to offer, the fever can recur and recur. Once exposed to it, the sufferer's resistance is lowered; he can expect further and perhaps worse attacks to set in without warning. Even the cure is sometimes not total; it does, however, insulate the sufferer from the worst the Effect can produce. That is, if it doesn't kill him.

Lurking in the Inner Dimensions of every victim of the fever is his own particular set of monsters. His own devils burning in his own inner fires. His own worms gnawing at his strength. These are the obstacles he must leap, if he can. Often, sadly, they are stronger than he is; and then he dies. Or lives on, a working body encasing a ruined mind.

Flapping Eagle thought: all he had ever done was survive. To have been so much and done so little. Searching, always searching for the path through the maze that led to Bird-Dog, and Sispy, and his way out. It had left him half a man, unfound even by himself. It was this lack in himself that was now reaching a time of crisis. And, added to it, the cross it seemed he was always to bear, was his responsibility for the life of Virgil, his rescuer, guide and friend. Why, he thought in anguish, why is it that I place the lives, the happinesses of all I touch in danger? I never wished it.

As if reading his thoughts, Virgil said:
– Don't worry about me. Glad to have been of service. Might even be able to render some assistance.

He knew this to be untrue. It was Flapping Eagle's fight that must wait at the growing circle of light. No-one could help without hampering his own chances of success.

Flapping Eagle set his jaw.

Bird-Dog: his search: all of it. A gigantic blind alley. A voyage through the waste land that had destroyed his appetite for his greatest treasure: life. He resolved that if he emerged from this tunnel, he would abandon his search. He would go to K and make his home. The discovery and befriending of other human beings was enough, more than enough, even for a man with eternity at his fingertips. If Calf Mountain was not perfect (and it was no Utopia), then what matter? Perfection was a curse, a stultifying finality. He would seek out and grow rich in the glorious fallibility of human beings, dirty, wartish, magnificent creatures that they were.

Virgil half-guessed the thoughts going through his friend's

mind, and his eyes clouded. They had good reason to. He was
thinking about his own fate, which was entirely out of his control. Now that Flapping Eagle had set his mind on the contest,
it would be waiting as sure as eggs were eggs. Everything hung
on the battle. Virgil ordered his mind into something approaching resignation.

The Gorf woke, roused by some mental alarm-system, and
immediately began to take an acute interest in events. This was
better he thought. This was something like it. If he had had
hands, he would have rubbed them.

On their rickety bicycles, dressed in their forlorn garments,
Flapping Eagle and Virgil Jones, Don Quixote and Sancho,
rode to their tryst.

TWENTY-FIVE

The colours were all wrong. The sky was red, the grass mauve,
the water a virulent green. Flapping Eagle blinked, but they
didn't change. He looked at the unearthly scene for a long
moment and then, gradually, as his eyes accustomed themselves
to full light, normality did return.

They were on a river-bank. Behind them was a thickly-
wooded hill and the mouth of their tunnel. The river filled the
gap between it and the next hill, then emptied itself into what
had been a bright green lake. Hills circled them, silent captors
and judges. In the centre of the lake stood a stone building, tall
and circular. A high-pitched voice chanted words which were,
at first, as meaningless to Flapping Eagle as the crazy colours
had been; and then his ears, like his eyes before them, found
the key to the sounds. His heart missed a beat.

It was a chant he had not heard for over seven centuries: a
hymn of praise to the great god Axona. He bit his lip. Virgil
Jones looked at him, but said nothing.

They were standing by their bicycles at the water's edge
when Flapping Eagle saw the boat. A crude coracle with this
name painted on a board tied to its side: *Skid-Blade*. Flapping
Eagle, the master of the knife, felt his spirits sink still lower,
and realized that he had read an omen into the name. *Where
the blade skids, there skid I.* He climbed into the boat, motion-

ing Virgil Jones to stay behind; and helplessly, weightily, Mr Jones subsided to the ground as Flapping Eagle paddled out to the stone shrine which was the voice of his past, claiming him. Their bicycles lay crookedly, uselessly, beside Virgil on the empty shore.

It was the votary flame that produced the second illusion. When Flapping Eagle, on his guard, passed through the open door of the shrine, he saw, in light once again dirty and yellow, the forms of two giants shadowed on the far wall. Vast forms: an Axona chieftain in his full headdress sitting in erect profile on a ceremonial stool as a supplicant knelt chanting at his feet; the whole tableau some twenty feet high.

It was, however, the votary flame that had done it. It burned in its stone bowl immediately below the small platform where the scene was actually taking place and cast huge shadows on the distant wall. But even when he deciphered the trick his eyes had played, Flapping Eagle found no relief; partly because, now twice-bitten by illusion, he expected a third; but mostly because he felt in himself both an absolute certainty and a crippling fear that this old, dark, hawknosed, feathered chief was the incarnation of the god Axona himself. And, the dimension being what it was, the truth was as he believed it to be.

The god Axona rose from his stool; his devotee continued his chanting until the chief cut it short with a gesture. He was quite a small man, but the glare in his fierce, heavy-lidded eyes pierced even the temple's stygian gloom.

– So Born-From-Dead has come at last to his god, said Axona, and the words struck a new chill into Flapping Eagle's heart, because they revealed what the darkness and ceremonial garments had hidden.

The god Axona was an old, dark, hawknosed, feathered woman.

– Born-From-Dead.

The god mouthed his name (ignoring his self-given brave's name in calculated insult) in tones of overweening disgust.

– All that is Unaxona is Unclean, said the god. Unclean. Had you forgotten, miserable defiled whelp that you are, what that commandment means? Is it to commit sacrilege upon this holy place that you come, whiteskin, paleface, mongrel among the pure, traitor to your race, is it to commit your supreme act of defilement that you come? Born-From-Dead has no patience with Axona; he cannot have come to worship. In death you were born and destruction is your doom. Whatsoever you touch, is soiled; whatsoever you grasp, you break; any person you love is stifled by your love; any person you hate is purified by your loathing. Is it the god Axona herself you seek to destroy? Is it this far that the worm in you has stretched?

She had touched the roots of Flapping Eagle's own self-doubts; he could barely speak, yet he forced the words from his dry lips. They rustled weakly in the half-light.

— If I can, said Flapping Eagle. I will break you if I can.

Axona laughed, and her cachinnation rang around the room.

— From your own mouth you are condemned, Born-From-Dead, she cried; and it is by your own hand you shall die.

As she sat down once more upon her stool, the devotee, who had lain silent while they spoke, whirled round and cast off his cloak. Again Flapping Eagle's self-control received a body-blow.

He was gazing into his own eyes.

His own eyes: but a vilely altered representation of himself. The body was the same; and, like Flapping Eagle, the creature wore a single feather in its hair; but the rest of its garnishings were utterly different. He wore a striped single-breasted jacket over a bare chest. The skin was deathly white. Around his waist was a string of beads, from which hung two squares of cloth, a yellow square covering his genitals, a blue square flapping at his buttocks. Otherwise he was quite naked. There were women's earrings in his ears, women's redness in his cheeks, women's lipstick on his lips. His eyebrows were plucked into slender arches and his eyelashes were long and drooping.

And that voice: the unbroken, high, eunuch's voice, a travesty of his own.

— Come, Born-From-Dead, it said. Come.

In the creature's right hand was a light axe, or tomahawk. In its left hand was a rifle. Flapping Eagle had no doubt that it was loaded. He also knew that he was helplessly unarmed.

— Come, Born-From-Dead, mocked the voice of Axona, Will you not face my champion? They say you are a great warrior. Come.

93

Flapping Eagle sighed and came slowly forward.

He was gambling on his surrogate behaving as he would in such a situation, and using the tomahawk before falling back on the simplicity of the rifle. He had always been more at home with the throwing, infighting instruments. So he sauntered in, almost insolently, and thrust his hands into his pockets casually, to irritate his opponent.

His right hand closed over a hard, rounded object. He pulled it out, wondering. It was the *Bone of K*! The very same Bone that Bird-Dog had flung to him before she disappeared down the tunnel of herself.

The Bone of K: Flapping Eagle lost no time in speculation. He could have thought: where did that come from after all this time? Would it not have been noticed before now? But none of that mattered. He had a weapon, and that changed the nature of the contest. It was now probable that his surrogate would decide on safety and use the rifle. So he had only a few seconds, the brief 'freeze' his opponent would undergo when he saw the unexpected object.

Flapping Eagle hurled the Bone, in a single, fluid movement, like throwing a large, ungainly dart. It hit the rifle at the point where his enemy's hand gripped it. A shriek of pain and the rifle fell to the floor. So did the Bone; it shattered, with results that froze both Flapping Eagle and his alter ego in their tracks.

It was only afterwards that Virgil Jones decoded for Flapping Eagle the secret meaning of the name. It was a cypher whose key was the sound of its secret name:

Os, a bone. K, a place. Hence K-os, the Bone of K. Or, alternatively: Chaos.

At the time Flapping Eagle saw only the terrifying effect of the breaking of the Bone.

The shards and splinters rose like a spinning mist from the floor where they shattered and formed a cloud in the centre of the arena of combat. The rifle disappeared completely. It simply ceased to be. So did everything else.

What was left was a hole. A turbulent disarrangement in the structure of the dimension. Chaos.

Flapping Eagle came out of shock a fraction faster than his alter ego; probably because he was further from the hole. He rushed at his adversary head-first and hit him full-tilt in the belly. The surrogate Flapping Eagle staggered, stepped backwards and sideways.

And was gone in the hole, decomposed into chaos, into notbeing.

Axona was on her feet, eyes blazing with wrath; but Flapping Eagle knew that behind that anger she was afraid. The Bone, the random element, had foiled her perfect plan; and now she was at his mercy. He advanced upon her with slow deliberation.

– Stay where you are, Unclean, she said, but her voice betrayed her.

– I don't know what you are, said Flapping Eagle as he walked forward, but when I defile you, I am cleansed of my past. Cleansed of the guilt and shame that possessed some hidden part of my mind, of which your presence is the proof. To free myself, I must render Axona unclean. Do you understand?

He spoke the words with a gentle astonishment, like truths he had just understood.

Then he raped her.

When Skid-Blade returned to the shore where Virgil waited, it carried a new Flapping Eagle. Virgil listened to his account, then said: – You really must do something about your imagination, you know. It's so awfully lurid.

With the help of Virgil Jones, it wasn't difficult for Flapping Eagle to extricate himself from the web of Dimension-fever. They constructed their escape simply: Flapping Eagle closed his eyes and, while Virgil danced the Strongdance, willed himself to awake. It was, in the end, as anticlimactic as that, now that the battle was over, Flapping Eagle had become stronger than the inner dimensions.

Long experience, however, adds to strength a certain sensitivity to nuance and *wrongnesses*; so that as they neared consciousness (as their separate consciousnesses drew closer and closer together, almost touching for an instant, before separating) it was not Flapping Eagle, but Virgil Jones who became aware of a third presence, a third consciousness, also rising.

An instant before the blackout that spanned the fragment of time in which he was restored to himself, Virgil touched the intruder and knew it.

Wakefulness. He was naked, his clothes piled where he left

them, on Flapping Eagle's chest, the greenwood surrounding them, his body still describing the methodical, circular perambulations of the Strongdance. He felt the dead weight of exhaustion in his limbs, but forgot it in his anger.

– Where are you? he shouted. Where?

The 'voice' of the unseen Gorf came calm from the woods.

– Greetings, Mr Jones.

Virgil dressed rapidly.

Flapping Eagle awoke with a splitting headache. The words *where am I?* formed on his lips for the second time on Calf Island; he dismissed them with a wry twist of the mouth. Where is anywhere? he asked himself.

Nevertheless, it was Calf Mountain; the slope of the forested ground told him so. And the cry of the dimensions, for the Effect remained, even though he had mastered it . . . a nagging in the corners of the eyes, ears and mind. Soon it would become like a mild tintinabulatory infection of the ear; he would become unaware of its presence except in moments of utter stillness. Now, it remained an irritant, niggling at him, a whining reminder of the world's infinite cavities.

He stood up and found himself alone. A moment of panic; he shouted Virgil's name into the clearing. Then, collecting himself, he heard the voice in the forest. Virgil's voice, low and angry. He crept towards the sound with the stealth of his childhood.

In the forest, Virgil Jones was remonstrating with an old acquaintance.

TWENTY-SIX

– As you perceive, said the 'voice' of the Gorf, I stayed.

– The hand of the born interferer, said Virgil, can never resist a superfluous gesture or two.

– Pot and kettle, replied the voice. Mote and beam.

– The acquisition of rudimentary idiom, said Virgil, confers no freedoms. Any intellect which confines itself to mere structuralism is bound to rest trapped in its own webs. Your words serve only to spin cocoons around your own irrelevance.

96

A thing that happened to Virgil Jones when he was angry: his speech became involuted and obscure. It came of a horror of displaying his loss of self-control. When he was angry, he felt weakest, most easily outwitted; so his speech wound around itself those very cocoons he ascribed to the Gorf.

He was more angry than he could remember. Much of it, he told himself, was reaction. He had put himself through a rigorous physical and mental examination; his very survival had been at risk; it was reasonable, he argued inwardly, for any human being to react overmuch to provocation after all that.

He knew, also, of another thorn. He had felt good on his recent travels; he had felt as he had once felt. Then. Ago. Before. To be plunged from that high confidence into his present weakening choler was intolerable. Which thought only served to make him more angry. The circle was vicious.

The overlarge tongue played about his mouth; a bead of saliva worked its way down to the cleft in his chin; his hands, in the pockets of his crumpled coat, worked feverishly. He sat on a fallen branch of an unknown conifer; it felt rough beneath him. He kicked morosely at a cone, glaring at the invisible creature, as if to scald him with a look.

Silently, crouched behind a clump of trees, Flapping Eagle listened to his guide talking into the void and apparently receiving answers. (The 'voice' of the Gorf is only audible to the being it addresses.) He thought: Virgil Jones, there is more to you than meets the eye. And since there was a large quantity of Virgil for any eye to meet, that was a compliment.

The third protagonist sat equably, ten yards or so from Virgil, resting against a tree, his sensory aura quivering slightly. He had had no fears of this confrontation; it had amused him to meet Mr Jones again, and had given him a clue to the final Ordering he was now anxious to discover; but Virgil's last words rankled, as they were meant to. Irrelevance, indeed.

— Are you aware, Mr Jones, he said haughtily, of my status as an Orderer?

Mr Jones said nothing.

— I see you are, continued the peevish voice. In which case you will no doubt recall the Prime Rule of that noble calling.

Mr Jones looked innocent. Now that he had penetrated the Gorf's (thick) hide, he felt his own anger cooling.

— Possibly I should remind you, snapped the Gorf. Possibly

it will induce you to refrain from these allusions.

– If memory serves, interposed Virgil Jones, the Prime Rule of Order is to eschew all irrelevance. Please correct me if wrong.

There was a brief pause. Then: – You are not wrong, came the reply.

– So, said Virgil Jones, may I be permitted to accuse the Master of a cardinal infringement of his own rules?

This time the silence was aghast.

– Grounds, said the Gorf tersely. Your grounds, please.

– First: that by your intrusion into the personal dimensions of another being, inviolable except in dire emergency, you committed an act not merely irrelevant to those dimensions, but actually dangerous. Even the most skilled of the Masters cannot toy with another's dimensions without risk. In this case the risk was enormous.

The Gorf said: – If you believe I meant him harm, you underestimate my skill. Having intuited his role, as a participant in the Final Ordering, it would be grossly bad play to distort that Ordering by a wilful act. I merely set him a puzzle to deepen his knowledge of the dimensions. Consider: if I had not done so, if he had fought off the fever instantly, he would never have conquered his monsters. How can this be irrelevance?

Virgil considered.

– There's some truth in that, he said. But we don't know if he needed to overcome those monsters. Now that it has happened as it happened, even he will say he did. But he might not have, had it been otherwise. Your defence rests on an unproveable first principle.

– The onus of proof rests with you, came the answer.

Virgil returned to the attack.

– Second: that, having no place whatsoever in the Final Ordering of the Island, you have been irrelevant ever since you perceived that fact, and stayed. There is no reason for you being here; the Island did not include you in its conception, so by your own rules it would be a distortion if it were to use you in any Ordering process. Nor do we have any need of observers. What do you say to that?

The silence lasted for several minutes. (Flapping Eagle, eavesdropping on half the eerie debate, half-thought it was over). Then the Gorf's voice sounded, slow and heavy.

— That was the correct move, Mr Jones. You should not have let your irritation get the better of your judgement at first. The first was a wasted move, which deprives you of perfection. Nevertheless, a score is a score. A score is a score. A score is a score. A score is a score. A score is a score.

The phrase, monotonously repeated, was burdened with a world of defeat. Virgil, suddenly sympathetic, asked:

— Master, if you knew, why did you stay?

— You must not call me Master. A Master would not have done it.

— A Master did, said Virgil. I should like to know his reasons. Simply, the Gorf replied:

— I liked it here.

Virgil thought of the planet Thera. Bleak. Empty. He understood how this hugely intelligent being would prefer the complex order of Calf Island.

— Master, he said finally, I must ask you to leave now.

The Gorf's voice was fierce. Defiant.

— I will not leave. I will stay.

— Then, said Virgil tiredly, his body aching with fatigue, I shall have to Order you away.

Something like a hollow laugh came from the void. — I am not that far gone, said the Gorf. You scored only because of my perverse infringement of the rules. You could not win an Ordering contest.

Flapping Eagle saw Virgil stand up. He covered his face with his hands, and an extraordinary thing happened: he seemed to *grow*. Not in height. Not in width.

In depth.

The only phrase that seemed to fit had a curious second meaning.

He added several dimensions to himself.

Flapping Eagle thought: it seems we each must fight a battle; but I was ready and Virgil is weak. And his opponent has chosen the ground.

Virgil was thinking along similar lines; but was very pleased at his continuing reawakening. The dimensions seemed his to visit again, after all this time, after all. That. Pain.

He turned to face the Gorf.

– Mr Jones, said the Gorf. A word of warning before the contest. In case you should win.

– Yes? said Virgil. (Was this a delaying tactic?)

– I am not the only irrelevance on the island, Mr Jones. I fear you are another.

Virgil said nothing, but he knew the Gorf had succeeded in wounding him. This renaissance of his was a fragile thing. Doubts assailed it easily.

– Just an intuition, Mr Jones, said the disembodied voice. I rather fancy you will take little part in the final Ordering. Truly. It gives a certain symmetry to this contest, wouldn't you say?

– Let's get on with it, barked Virgil Jones.

To the watching Flapping Eagle, it appeared that there followed a period of complete inactivity. Not being versed in the Outer Dimensions, he could not enter the battlefield. Virgil Jones stood frozenly, head bowed, arms outstretched, hands splayed, like a man pushing against a very heavy door. Then, without warning, he collapsed. Inert matter in a heap on the forest floor.

Flapping Eagle rushed forward.

Virgil Jones came round slowly.

– Shouldn't have bothered, he said. No contest, really. Not a hope. Flea trying to rape an elephant. Couldn't Order him back. Not in a million years. It's his game.

– Where is he? asked Flapping Eagle, looking around.

– Who knows, said Virgil. Doesn't matter. Won't trouble us again. I won that point, anyway. And then, in a brave attempt at lightheartedness, he said: – Who will rid me of this meddlesome Gorf?

Something had gone out of Virgil Jones' face. His defeat had drained him of a great deal more than energy. He seemed to Flapping Eagle now as he had first seemed: shambling, bumbling, ineffectual. The decisive figure of the Inner Dimensions had gone, nursed once more behind a skin of failure.

– Virgil, said Flapping Eagle. Virgil. Thank you.

Virgil Jones snorted.

And fainted.

The roles of nurse and patient were reversed.

TWENTY-SEVEN

Once. Then. Ago. Before. The terror of the titties, I. They came easily into my hands. They came. Easily. Gently does it, though some like it rough. Gently to the peaks of pleasure. Softly to the peaks of pain. Breasts like twin peaks, they had then, mountains yielding to the touch. Mine. Sweet things. What things they are. A randy bugger, then. All organs decay through disuse. Pulled out all the stops, then. *Let me have it, Virgie!* Give and take, give and take, pingpong of bodies possessed. *O, Virgil, you know how to please.* Please ... pleas, they pleaded and I kneaded their soft volcanoes. I needed their soft. A virgin, eh? My name's Virgil. What's one consonant between friends? That worked once. Then. Birds. The coo of a turtle-dove in my ear as it nibbled and the quake of the great turtle itself as we came. Then. Before. Ah, a bird-fancier, I, no fancier bird than I. Ornithology's no substitute for sex. Feathers go best in a bed, in a pillow, under the bouncing bodies. All I could wish for, more wishing for me than I wished for, squeeze me, please, me! Once. Then. Ago. Go anywhere, inside, outside, fornication never changes. Odd. The pleasure principle transcends all boundaries. Contraception stretches into a million different places, different worlds, different techniques, vive la différence, I was there, where the pill was, my skill was, where the coil, my toil, and they came. Easily. In my hand. Once. Then. Ago. Before. Liv.

> *Drink this, Virgil. Water from the stream.*
> *Eat this, Virgil, berries from the tree.*
> *Rest now, Virgil, don't talk, rest. Sleep. It heals.*

Guilt. My fault. Mea maxima. Sorry I spoke. Sorry I moved. Sorry I lived. Sorry. On my knees. Forgive me. Liv. Forgive. It rhymes. Or accurately. Leev. Relieve. She was always Liv to me, her name married to sieve and give as she was wife to me. Ah the terror of her titties. Terrible beautiful white. I scaled them and fell. The strong do not forgive the weak. Their. Lesness. Brightly we burned like any star, brighter than brightest, my moth to her flame, I was scalded and fell. The heat is cruel to the luke. Warm. Toad, she said and I croaked. Go, she said and I went. In terror of the titties. Then. But. Before. Daughter of the Rising Son, I thought she loved me. In the house of pleasure and I paid in kindness. *So kind*, she said, *so kind*, I thought she loved me. Love grows and swallows its love, digests and spits it out. Seared by the gastric juices of her loving. Sorry. Liv. From the house of rising suns to the black hole, hole-black house, your rise and partial fall. Bitterness succeeding your pride, I'm sorry. She'd ruffle my hair, one day she tore a handful from the root. Dark lady with the fair skin fair hair fair eyes so fair and so unfair and yet so fair. Fire in her to burn a man, ice in her to heal him. I was not the man. For. Her. Liv, ice-peak of perfection, how she cast me off, how sorry I . . . mea, maxima, thing. Then. Ago. Before. The strong do not forgive. The weak their lessness.

TWENTY-EIGHT

— Liv was my wife, said Virgil, sitting up at the edge of the clearing, propped against a tree. She should have had a stronger man.

Flapping Eagle had already decided never to pry further into Virgil than he was willing to reveal; he had no wish to bring him pain. So he asked no questions about Liv.

— I remember K, mused Virgil absently, when they first came. To settle, to marry, to whore. And one or two . . . went a bit further.

— Like Grimus? asked Flapping Eagle sharply.

— Well, said Virgil, pursing his lips, I don't know if I do.

— What?

— Like Grimus.

Even in his frustration, Flapping Eagle had to laugh.

— You're certainly well again, he said, if you can perpetrate jokes like that.

— My dear fellow, said Virgil. It was no joke.

— I know, said Flapping Eagle, still laughing. *Small pleasantry.*

Virgil shrugged.

– Virgil, repeated Flapping Eagle, who or what is he?
Grimus.

– Yes, said Virgil Jones.

– A sad fact, said Virgil Jones as they climbed. One's environment is a great deal more epic than oneself. Events may be epic: people rarely are. Which is why they find such an environment appalling. I once mentioned to you that I was superstitious because this was a place where anything could happen; I'm sure you understand what I meant now. But there's another reaction. It is this: *if anything can happen, we'd better make damn sure it never does.*

– You mean like Dolores, said Flapping Eagle.

Virgil did not answer.

TWENTY-NINE

– Bugger, said Nicholas Deggle.

He was standing on Calf Beach, having arrived through the 'gate' he had despatched Flapping Eagle through two weeks earlier; and he was feeling very angry with himself, and, therefore, with the universe. He had made a mistake so elementary it was mind-defying: he had failed to consider where on Calf Island the gate would deposit him, and as a result, here he was, the wrong side of the Forest, with a mountainful of climbing to do.

Of course he should have worked it out: since the gate was at sea-level that would have been its logical exit-point. Except that in all the *setting* he had done with his wand, the Stem, he had aimed at a point above K; and he had blithely assumed that that must have been where Flapping Eagle had gone, once the passage of the days had made it clear that the gate had worked. He was, he told himself bitterly, an unadulterated fool; and then he put the thought from him; too much had to be done to waste time on self-criticism.

No point in trying to use the gate the other way, back to X, and then re-angling it; it was clear that the Stem was an unreliable *setter*, and it had taken him years to get this far. Besides, the gate was only a one-way affair: again a function of time. No point, either, in attempting to use the Stem to move him up the mountain; again, its unreliability might land him anywhere, perhaps in a worse situation than he was. There was nothing for it: he'd have to climb.

– Bugger, he repeated. His long, willowy frame was not meant for such physical labour; the very thought of it led his tongue forcibly into profanity.

He cheered himself up with a vision of the reaction of Grimus – and indeed Jones – when they discovered that he was back. Back, he said aloud to the beach. Back to do what he should have done so long ago, and what they had prevented him from doing. This time he'd make sure they didn't.

Now he noticed that he was not alone on the beach. A woman sat some way from him, on the sands, beside an empty rocking-chair, gazing fixedly at the cliffs. He knew that rocking-chair; it belonged to Virgil Jones. He knew the woman, too: there could not be two women on Calf Island as ugly as O'Toole's wife. Here was a mystery, then. He sauntered over to Dolores; she sang on, toothlessly, ignoring him.

– Mrs O'Toole? he asked.

Dolores stopped singing and turned slowly to look at him.

– Darling, she said, do sit down.

Darling? thought Deggle; but he was feeling tired, so he did seat himself in Jones' chair.

Virgil, thought Dolores. The lilting voice in the baggy face. The soaring heart in the sagging body. Virgil, who took her from the soulless church-wax and gave her flesh. How lucky she was to have him.

– Virgil, she said aloud, taking pleasure in his name. Virgil Jones.

Deggle was watching her. – Is he here? he said, eyes piercing her.

– As always, she said, clutching at his hand. Virgil is here.

Deggle disengaged his hand with delicate loathing.

– Are you . . . his woman? he asked.

She looked up at him adoringly and sang in her awful voice:
– *Till all the seas run dry, my love.*

Deggle found the cracked old woman's rendition of the song unaccountably hilarious. Between giggles he said: – Quite a change from Liv, aren't you, Mrs O'Toole?

– Nothing changes, said Dolores O'Toole. Does it, darling?

– I suppose not, said Deggle, to fill the expectant silence. She smiled happily.

– O Virgil, she said to the recoiling Deggle, I do, do love you. Deggle made a quick decision.

– I love you too, he said, and fought back a wave of nausea.

– Let's go home, she said. Time for breakfast. Give me your belt.

– My belt? Deggle almost squeaked.

– O, you are fussy, she said. Come on, now.

Blankly, Deggle handed her his belt. Unlike Virgil, he didn't need it to hold his trousers up. Also unlike Virgil, he wasn't fat; so his belt wasn't long enough.

– I think I'll manage without it today, said Dolores O'Toole composedly.

Nicholas Deggle, half-amused, half-frightened by the old madwoman, followed her up the cliff-path to the little hovel. I wonder what happened to Virgil Jones, he asked himself.

Later that day.

Dolores O'Toole was boiling up some arrowroot tea when Deggle came in, looking dishevelled, and even gloomier than he had when he arrived.

– Wherever have you been, my love? she asked. Have some root-tea.

He had been up the mountain a small way. Then he had heard it: the deadly whine. At first he had ignored it; then it became increasingly intrusive, and the dizziness came, and the sense of detachment. Fortunately for himself, Nicholas Deggle was a man of some presence of mind and had staggered and rolled down the mountain, out of the danger zone. Then (for he could recognize an effect of the Rose when he experienced it) he cursed Grimus silently and long.

– Root-tea, said Dolores O'Toole, giving him a bowl. It was revolting; in his anger he hurled the bowl to the floor, where it shattered.

– Tch, tch, said Dolores. Accidents will happen. She began to mop up the mess, uncomplaining.

When she had finished, she came to him and sat at his feet. He was in the rocking-chair again. – We'll sit like this, she said, every tea-time, for ever.

– You know, said Nicholas Deggle, you could easily be quite right.

– You were clever to chase away the ghost, she said, full of admiration.

– What ghost? asked Deggle.

– O, don't be falsely modest. You know. That Spectre of Grimus with the scar on its chest.

– Ah, said Deggle, that ghost.

Jones had obviously gone somewhere with Flapping Eagle; but where? Had they killed each other? Had they been mad enough to try and get through the Effect?

– One thing is certain, he told himself, if Flapping Eagle doesn't get to Bird-Dog and then do what I was going to do, I'm stuck here for life. With a hag who loves me because she thinks I'm Virgil Jones. He wondered if Virgil Jones would see the joke.

He doubted it; because he didn't see it, either.

He was asleep on the rush-mat carefully laid down for him by Mrs O'Toole, when a nudge jerked him fully awake. There was Dolores O'Toole, in the nude, her hump looming up behind her, her withered breasts swaying with her breathing, her face lit by a ghastly invitation, her lips snarling a smile.

– O God, said Deggle, and closed his eyes to think of the Empire. He opened them; she was still there, leering at him.

– Not tonight, Josephine, he begged.

– Dolores, she corrected affectionately and went back to bed.

Nicholas Deggle was perspiring heavily.

THIRTY

– Valhalla, said Virgil Jones.

Valhalla: where dead warriors live on in stark splendour, fighting their past battles daily, reliving the hour of glory in which they fell, falling bloodied once more to the gleaming floors and being renewed the next morning to resume the eternal combat. Valhalla, the hall of fame, the living museum of the heroism of the past. Valhalla, close to the pool of knowledge where Odin drank, shaded by the Great Ash Yggdrasil, the World-Tree. When the ash falls, so does Valhalla.

With a slyly amused flick of the tongue, Virgil was pointing at the town of K.

The ascent of the mountain had posed no problems once Virgil had regained his strength (though not his vigour); and now Flapping Eagle stood beside his guide at the very fringe of the forested slopes, looking across a surprisingly large plain.

It was as though a vast step had been cut into the side of Calf Mountain. Flapping Eagle, appreciating the mountain's true shape for the first time, found himself imagining a giant, using the island as a step up from sea to sky. On the flat horizontal of the step lay the town of K, hard up against the renewed mountain-wall. Fields took up the rest of the plain, some with herds of cattle, others of sheep; still others grew wheat and other crops. But it was night now and the fields were still. Farmhouses dotted the plain, glowing like worms in a garden.

Above the town, on an outcrop of the mountain, stood a single house. Its walls, in direct opposition to the whitewash uniform worn by the rest of the town, were black as jet. It was invisible now, showing no lights; but Virgil Jones knew it was there. It was Liv's house.

Above it, the mountain's peak was hidden in a wall of cloud.
– It never lifts, said Virgil Jones, and then silence resumed.

Flapping Eagle had not forgotten his vow to himself in that inner dimension; he would abandon his search and make his life here, if he could. So here was an end to centuries of wandering, a methuselah age of following blindly where the moving finger led. He should have felt relief; but only tension came. For any man, it is a hard thing to empty the mind of all its aims and substitute a new set, cleanly, just so; for Flapping Eagle, whose aims had been *set*, like one of those inner dimensions, for seven hundred years, it was an herculean task.

Virgil Jones, too, was making plans, and plans which involved Flapping Eagle at that. For now, now that he had brought Flapping Eagle to K, was the crucial time. If he should react to it (and it to him) as Virgil hoped, he would be ready for the task Virgil wished him to perform. If not, then there was nothing to be done. Virgil no longer had the strength to approach Grimus. He had had a glimpse of it, there in the forest; but it had been ruined once more, in his struggle with the Gorf. Now it was up to Flapping Eagle. Virgil derived some dark amusement from the fact that he was planning exactly what Deggle would have wished; that would amuse Master Nicholas, too, if he knew. If there were no god, we should have to invent one, remembered Virgil, and made this reversal of that aphorism: since there is a Grimus, he must be destroyed.

This, then, was a return to a long-lost war. There would be O'Toole to face, and possibly even Liv. But there was no going back.

– Flapping Eagle, he said, I'd like to tell you this: we are all most vulnerable to the ones we love.

Flapping Eagle was only half-listening. Virgil went on, gazing into the night-mist lying lightly over the plain, giving the town itself a shimmering, insubstantial air.

– I mean yourself, said Virgil. I hope you will not end by causing me pain. I really am very vulnerable to any wounds you may care to inflict. That, it appears to me, is what a friendship means.

Flapping Eagle was listening now. Virgil had spoken haltingly; the words had been hard to say. They were a plea for help, a cry of need from a man who had now saved his life twice.

– Agreed, he said. Virgil nodded briefly.

They had been at the woods' end for some time now. Night was well under way.

– Well, said Virgil Jones, shall we?

On an impulse, Flapping Eagle linked his left arm around Virgil's right; and they marched, in step, comrades-in-arms, towards their separate dooms.

The moon, filtering faintly through the mist, shed white flecks on their moving heads.

PART TWO

TIMES PAST

THIRTY-ONE

K by night: houses huddling together as though clustered for protection, drawing warmth from each other. Rough exteriors, stained by damp and mist and time, dirty-whitewash crudities, architectural cripples, surviving defiantly for all their crooked tiles and ill-fitting doors.

Around the houses, the streets. Lifelines of dust, eddying and swirling among the deformed homes, coming from nowhere, circling aimlessly, existence itself their only purpose. A place must have streets; blank spaces between the filled-up holes.

One street, and only one, could hold its head high. An avenue of cobbles bifurcating the eddies of dust, it stalked through the night town from end to end, proclaiming its seniority, a roman among barbarians.

A man, decrepit as his clothes, stained as the houses, dusty as the streets, on all fours, crawling the length of this majestic thoroughfare, a pilgrim on the road to Rome, engaged for all appearances in an act of worship.

This was Stone; he answered to no other name and rarely enough to his chosen soubriquet. Silence was his way, the road his hill and the stones the stones of Sisyphus. He counted them daily, one by one, enumerating the cobbles for posterity. A task without end for a man with a poor memory, an infinite series of numbers without a sum. At first, so long ago that he had forgotten, he had tried; his parched tongue would stumble over the large, ungainly figures; they would slip his mind; and patiently he would return to the beginning. Now the counting was only an excuse; his real purpose was the constant renewal of his friendship with each single stone. He greeted them like old friends, coming with pleasure across a favourite cracked cobble here, a particularly round and pleasing one there. To some of them he gave names; others were the scenes of great adventures in his dreams. The street was his microcosm and afforded him all his delights and pains. Small and attenuated, he was as much a part of the road as any of his stones. In one of his rare sorties into the spoken word he had said earnestly to Elfrida Gribb, wife of Ignatius Q. Gribb, the town thinker, – If it weren't for me the road would crumble. Stones need love as much as you. And in a practical sense he did protect the road, guarding it zealously against the onslaughts of dust from the side-streets, and against the injuries of animals on its progress through the fields. He washed it and nurtured it. It was his. In return for this labour of love, he was fed by whomever he was nearest to when hungry and housed by whomever he was nearest to when tired. It was his road along which Virgil Jones and Flapping Eagle made their way into the ill-made community.

As they passed the occasional farmhouse, Flapping Eagle felt his pulse quicken. Lights glowed in windows through thin curtains, warm islands where a traveller might shelter. He glanced eagerly at Virgil and was about to voice his new-found exhilaration; but his companion's face was clouded and immobile. It was a time to keep one's peace: Flapping Eagle restrained the bubbling enthusiasm within him.

Home: that was the word that had done it. It crept into his head as he stood looking at the town from the breaking waves of the forest. It had come announced, filtering into him on a shaft of light from the distant windows. Home is the sailor, home from the sea, and the hunter home from the hill. Flapping Eagle was coming home, to a town where he had never lived. He saw home in the mist lying softly over the fields; he scented it in the perfume-laden night; he felt it in the cobbles; but most of all it was the windows that were home, the closed eyes of a protected life, glowing with contentment, the closed windows.

Flapping Eagle stopped for a moment. Virgil looked at him curiously, and then, unknowingly, returned his compliment: restraining his words, which would have been an intrusion.

The farmhouse stood at the side of the road. It was long and low and white. No doubt animals were sleeping in the shed; it was the closed window that had transfixed Flapping Eagle. People were moving behind it, lives were being led. Abruptly, he vaulted the gate and crept up to the yellow light. Virgil Jones stood in the road, watching.

Slowly, Flapping Eagle raised himself from the ground to look through the glass; and found himself staring into an unblinking granite face. The farmer must have drawn back the curtains just as Flapping Eagle looked in. It was a face filled with crevices; deep valleys and pocks scarred it, but the eyes were strong and showed no anger or astonishment. They stared through Flapping Eagle as though he wasn't there. Shaken, mumbling wordless apologies, he backed away to the gate, the road and Virgil, who fell into step beside him. They walked away from the stone face in the window and Flapping Eagle discovered that his hands were quivering. The eyes had done it: they had told him that he was still pariah. The untouchable.

Pariah. That word rose from his past to increase his discomfiture.

– Virgil, he hesitated, where shall we stay?

Virgil shrugged. – We'll find somewhere, he said. Or other. His tongue slobbered in the corner of his mouth.

On the very outskirts of the town itself stood its tallest building, the only one Flapping Eagle had seen that stood two storeys high. It was in immaculate condition, which fact alone set it apart from the rest. Its walls rose straight and true, gleaming white in the blue-mist dark, a spotless sentinel and guardian of the town. It was a brothel. Madame Jocasta's House of the Rising Son, a discreet wooden plate by the door proclaimed. And by the plate someone had scrawled an inexplicable phrase. Tomorrow, no doubt, a new coat of whitewash would expunge it, but tonight it stood, blemishing the whitewalled purity of the house of pleasure. *A Rushian Generals Welcom*, it said.

Virgil saw the phrase and muttered to himself: – Alex got out tonight, then.

– What does it mean? asked Flapping Eagle.

– Childish joke, said Virgil. Product of a child-mind.

Flapping Eagle was forced to repeat his question, since Virgil offered no more.

– The Russian Generals, said Virgil, are called Pissov, Sodov, Bugrov and Phukov. Childish.

But Flapping Eagle, already disconcerted by the stone eyes in the granite face, felt even more uneasy for knowing the meaning of the jejune phrase.

In the town now; flurries of activity around them, sporadic because the hour was late. A glimpse through another window: an old woman gazing at a photograph album, immersed in her past. It is the natural condition of the exile – putting down roots in memories. Flapping Eagle knew he would have to learn these pasts, make them his own, so that the community could make him theirs. He entered K in search of a history.

They saw ahead of them on the street the crawling form of the man called Stone, greeting the cobbles. Flapping Eagle could also hear a clip-clop of hooves, somewhere near at hand, hidden by the clustering houses; and every so often the noise of laughter came to them on the breeze, muffled by the mist.

At the far end of the cobbled road, the opposite axis from Madame Jocasta's stood the source of the laughter. This was the moment Virgil had been dreading and which he knew must be faced. This was the Elbaroom, home of the drinking community of K, centre of village information. According to his plans, they would have to go in, not just to find a place to stay, but to show Flapping Eagle to K; so they would have to meet its keeper.

His name was O'Toole.

– Able was I ere I saw Elba, murmured Virgil Jones. Apart from the language called Malayalam, it was the only palindrome he could ever remember.

THIRTY-TWO

Flapping Eagle saw her first; and an eerie shape she made, half-woman, half-quadruped, coming at them through the circling mist. As she drew nearer, it struck him that she was one of the most palely beautiful women he had ever seen.

Elfrida Gribb suffered, albeit infrequently, from insomnia. When it struck, leaving her dry-eyed and awake in the midnight hours, she would get up, don her warmest shawl and ride through K on a small velvet donkey. Wrapped up well to spite the mist and damp, she found it a soothing thing to do. One had to keep oneself occupied, after all.

Elfrida: the name suited her, and she abhorred all diminutives. – A name is a name, she said. Elfin-faced and elf-boned, there could have been no other name for Mrs Gribb. She was delicately roseate skin fitting perfectly over soft rises and falls of flesh; her mouth small and softly-pursed and her eyes like sparkling water. Her clothes were old lace, her shawl embroidered with lilies, her hats as wide-brimmed as her wide green eyes, drooping across her face like long quiet lashes. Often she wore a veil. Mostly she was happy, her lightness of spirit infecting all around her; and when she was sad she kept it to herself. Other people had their own worries to fret at, she told herself stoically. She could cope with herself perfectly well.

Thanks to Ignatius. Ignatius Gribb provided her with a secure, immovable centre for her being. Her entire life and all her delight revolved around him. I thank whatever brought us together, she would tell him. If marriages are made in the heavens, then ours was made in the seventh. And he would grunt and nod and she would sniff his reassuring new-socks smell and be comforted and whole. A woman needed a love like this in a place like K. It kept away the darkness.

Shored up by the strength of this love, she felt it her duty to do her level best to impart something of her strength to the weak. To nurse the halt and feed the hungry was to her a privilege and a debt paid. This zeal made her as many enemies as friends. Not everyone likes to be helped; not everyone in K responded to her cosy goodwill. And the obverse of her sunny life was that Elfrida Gribb was something of a prig.

She was, however, beautiful, even through a veil; and Flapping Eagle stood entranced for a moment at the entrance to the Elbaroom, framed with Virgil in the filtering yellow light of the doorway and the flicker of the lamp above their heads, silhouettes watching the pale, lovely ghost on its night ride.

An instant when their eyes met; and at that instant, the universe went out for an instant, freezing the inhabitants of the town in a series of characteristic positions, a tableau fixed in the aspic of a blink in time.

The most unlikely duo in the Elbaroom sat at a low round table about halfway down the long, narrow hostelry. One of them was enormous, a bear of a man, an impression he heightened by wearing a bearskin coat practically all the time, for all that it was rarely very cold in K. Perhaps it was the coat that gave his face its bright red colouring. It was a face like a craggy tomato. Beads of sweat stood excitedly on its brow. Its eyebrows beetled inwards and downwards towards the rough peak of his nose, spilling over gleaming eyes on their way. He spoke rapidly; his hands swung in huge, dangerous, clawing arcs. His companion was as slim as he was wide, as slight and elegant as he was cumbersome; a dainty man with a young face and Calf Island's traditional ancient eyes. At present, these eyes held a look of infinite boredom – held it, moreover as though accustomed to doing so. They were discreetly downcast, watching his tapered hands pulling the legs off a spider, sharply, cleanly.

The dainty man was called Hunter. His full name was Anthony St Clair Peyrefitte Hunter, but his companion called him *The Two-Time Kid*. The name had stuck, not particularly because of the insult latent in it, but thanks to Hunter's frequent avowal that he would 'try anything twice'. The bear-like man, with his unerring gift for the obvious, had asked, why twice? and Mr Hunter had replied, with the slight disdain of centuries of good inbreeding:

– Once to see if one likes it; twice to see if one was right.

– Wal, guffawed the bear, you little two-timer! His bellow had effectively overpowered Hunter's dainty sneer.

The bear was called Peckenpaw. K knew him as 'One-Track' Peckenpaw. He told stories no man questioned; he was too big to be accused of telling tall tales. His stories were full of the legends of the Old West; the time he stood up against old Wild Bill and stared him down; the time he bent William Bonney's rifle into a knot with his bare hands; gold rush tales of mining towns where men were men and women were grateful. But at the time of the blink he was boring Mr Hunter with his favourite story, told a thousand times before, that was one reason for the title of 'One-Track'. His repetitive, compulsive tale-telling was the other.

One-Track Peckenpaw had once spent centuries of his life hunting the North American counterpart of the Yeti: Bigfoot. He had never caught him. His tales were full of the aggressive melancholia of failure, sterile inventions about how the big one got away. It was to catch Bigfoot that he had accepted the burden of immortality; it was the grudging certainty that he never would which eventually made him a Candidate for Calf Mountain.

– There was this time, he was saying, I got sure he was a woman. It was the cunning of him, the way he played me along, the bastard. I got to thinking, if he'd been a human-been he'd've been a woman for sure and a cockteaser to boot. It was a fool idea, him being a female, but it climbed in my head and wouldn't get out. Once I dreamed I fucked him . . . her. Jesus that was a wrestling match. Woulda broken you in two at the least, Mister Two-Time.

— I'll try anything . . . began Hunter mildly.

— Twice, bellowed One-Track Peckenpaw, drowning his audience's voice. Yeah. Anyway. It was a pleasure to track him. Like being on the heels of a wilful woman needing taming. I'd think how a woman would behave when I saw his footprint near a stream. Was it a bluff or a double-bluff? Which way was he really going? I've always trusted to instinct. You get a feel of your quarry stronger than any scent. If the signs don't add up with the feel you ignore the signs. That's the difference between a lousy tracker and a great one.

— You never caught it, though, interposed Two-Time sweetly.

— Saw him twice, said Peckenpaw from a distance. This shape, huge like a mountain, going through thick forest growth like it wasn't there. When I got to the spot it was like a tank had gone through. It gives a man respect seeing a thing like that.

He was silent for a moment.

— The second time, he went on, was the time he came to visit me. Sleeping's a risky business in Bigfoot land. I used to put an alarm system round my campfire – tripwires everywhere to ring bells and clatter my pans. One night I wake up and there he is, just standing there, looking down at me. Walked through all the alarms as neat as you please just to take a good look. That's when I stopped thinking he was a woman. I lay there still as the grave and he nodded and walked away so then I turn to grab my rifle. IT WASN'T THERE. He moved it to the other side of the fire. O he was clever all right. And I'll tell you something else, Mr sophisticated Hunter. I may not have caught the motherfucker but he made me more of a man than you'll ever be. COME AND GET ME, he meant when he gave me that stare. CATCH AS CATCH CAN. You see: he showed me a point of no return. Didn't matter that I was the best tracker that ever lived with ten lifetimes' experience. He had a *million* years' practice at running away. So now? Now I respect his privacy.

One-Track Peckenpaw leapt to his feet suddenly, his arms windmilling as he shouted : – COME AND GET ME, YOU BASTARD! CATCH AS CATCH CAN! and burst into convulsive laughter, great gulping laughs that shook his eyebrows; while Two-Time

116

Hunter pulled the last leg off his spider, leaving it a round, wriggling, dying core.

Blink.

Elfrida Gribb had always thought the trouble with Flann O'Toole had to do with two things: his preoccupation with being such a disgustingly uproarious broth of a boy, and the fact that his middle name was Napoleon. An Irish Napoleon was a concept so grotesque it had to end up like O'Toole.

O'Toole made potato whisky in a back room and seduction attempts upon the person of every female who entered the Elbaroom; he swore oaths regularly and broke promises unfeelingly; he was prone to fits of violent temper, but thought himself a reasonable man; he was likely at any moment of the day or night to keel over in an alcoholic stupor, but he considered himself a man of power; he was carried to his bed every night in a haze of obscenity and vomit, but was convinced he was a leader in the community; he quoted poetry as he did ugly things. To Elfrida, his presence darkened a room and denied the beauty of life; to himself, he was a lightning-rod, conductor of electricity, Prometheus unchained, raw, carnal man in his prime, the very vitality of life. There was, too, a strong religious streak left in him; on mornings-after he could be seen mortifying his flesh with a cane, or heard crying in agony through the door of Mlle de Sade's chambers at the House of the Rising Son. It was one of the reasons Dolores had left him; those who undergo physical suffering or mutilation involuntarily naturally loathe those who inflict it upon themselves in the name of God. Her only possible reaction had been flight.

— Holy Mary, cried O'Toole to a farmer's wife, who had shrunk away in fear, you look about ready for it, me darlin. What wouldn't you say now to a large dose of O'Toole's hot cock, eh? There, don't shrink away. 'Tis the Organ O'Toole I offer, you Protestant whore. And that's no mean gift I can tell you surely with the stops pulled out and all.

The farmer sat bridling by his wife, but made no attempt to defend her; a bellyful of potato whisky makes a mean fighter.

— There now, observe your husband, lurched O'Toole, if he isn't being more sensible than yourself, then I don't know what. Compliance is a virtue; resistance is an act o' violence and me

I'm a hater of all that. Come now, up with your skirts, down with your underwear and Napoleon O'Toole will give you an evening to remember him by. 'Twould be an act of true pacifism. For which I believe the Sanskrit word is Ahimsa. Mr Gandy himself'd be proud of you.

The woman shook her head imploringly at her husband.

– Now then, he said, half-rising from his seat. O'Toole shoved him back.

– Would you deny me my due, sir, would you? This place is my land and a seigneur on his land has droits. Do not cross me. Do not. In the morning no doubt I shall chastise meself as once I chastised meself for years upon years through a holy union with a broken hag of a wife. That was a religious thing to do if you like, to pleasure the crippled and suffer agonies in the doing. Have you ever screwed a hunchback, farmer? Then do not deny me my freedom. My time is served.

– I will not go with you, said the woman.

– Will you not? roared O'Toole. Will you not now? You come to the Elbaroom and will not go with its master? Is that manners, woman, to treat your host so? The name itself gives you fair warning, El Barooom! The blast of the rocket and the prick of Napoleon. Have you no wish to roll with emperors? I would give you children of genius. If I could.

– I will not go, insisted the woman tearfully.

– Then go to the devil, cried O'Toole, and raised the small table that sat between the peasant couple over his head, scattering glasses and drinks. He made to throw it across the room.

Blink.

(In O'Toole's version of the breakdown of his marriage to Dolores, he held that when he had suffered long enough, been tortured long enough by her deformity and ungratefulness, he had thrown her out. The truth was a different matter. Dolores O'Toole had left her husband because he could not satisfy her. Flann Napoleon O'Toole had only half a testicle, having lost the rest in a fight with a dog; his limp penis was but an inch long and, owing to the depredations of the demon drink, he could only rarely stiffen it to twice that size. These circumstances are offered in extenuation of his behaviour.)

When Jocasta had replaced Liv as Madame of the town's

brothel, it was Virgil Jones who had suggested the ironic play on words that was now its name. But though she insisted on keeping a spotless house, it possessed none of the expansive, trellised, wrought-iron elegance of the city that New Orleans had once been; nor did the Madame resemble the tragic queen, wife and mother to the oedipal Rex, in any wise but their shared name. Thus both arms of the pun were somewhat truncated, and the House of the Rising Son forged its own style.

One of the first innovations she had made, once she felt strong enough to move out of the all-encompassing shadow of Liv, was to increase the specialization of her employees' functions. Liv had thought it enough that they should all be dedicated exponents of the horizontal arts *in general*; Jocasta had always disagreed, perhaps because she was herself best at being an all-rounder, jack-of-all-trades, and had always felt a nagging dissatisfaction with herself. So she gave her employees new names on the same day as the brothel; and with the new names went extremely precise sexual functions. She believed the change had paid dividends; people said the House of the Rising Son was an altogether lighter, more open, less embarrassing, more rewarding place to visit than Liv's ménage. (It is easier to ask for the services of a lady whom you know to be an expert in your favourite variations than to ask an anonymous whore to indulge your whims.) And Jocasta had the feeling that her girls took a greater pride in their work these days.

The one employee who gave her cause for concern was the single male whore, Gilles Priape. He was lazy for his size; she knew men needed longer rest-periods than women, but she suspected Monsieur Gilles of malingering. Specialization again, you see: he was the only one practising the male arts and was therefore forced into versatility. Still, his customers seemed content enough. *Speciality of the House,* they called him, much to the irritation of the girls. Especially when his customers were men.

Jocasta was walking the corridors of her empire. Behind closed doors, the staff were busy. Jocasta liked nothing better that these muffled sounds, the grunts of real ecstasy mingling with the far more expert sighs of simulation. She sometimes thought she preferred this aural stimulation to the act itself . . . but then she put the unprofessional thought firmly in its place.

Certainly she was a desirable woman; she knew that all right.

Not, perhaps, in the same visual class as some of the girls, but definitely a class lady. Her features were as classically Grecian as her name; and if her breasts were a trifle too heavy, she had stopped worrying about them aeons ago. They looked well enough, swelling through her long, floor-length, white lace nightgown, shadowed by the light from the candle she held as she toured the building. She enjoyed dressing like this. It made her feel pure.

Whereas, as every one of her staff was fully aware, anything they could do, Madame Jocasta could perform twice as erotically. She was the best; and if she undervalued her all-round gifts, her cohorts did not. On the rare occasions when she performed herself, they would crowd to the observation-holes in the walls of her room, and learn.

The sound of the whip was unmistakable. It came from the door behind which 'Boom-Boom' de Sade was in full cry. Her hungry voice drawled something about a red-hot poker and Jocasta moved on contentedly.

Boom-Boom was a great favourite of Flann O'Toole's, since she made him positively enjoy his self-mortifications; but Flann O'Toole was no favourite of Jocasta's. He was too liable to turn sadist himself and damage the staff.

The next door yielded only silence. This was Mlle Florence Nightingale's chamber. She exuded a comfortable homely sexuality, so peaceful as she displayed an accidental nipple, so demure as she undressed. Florence always *did it*, never screwed or fucked or shafted or banged; did it with grace and in the dark. As Jocasta paused, a tuneful hum welled up from within. Florence was singing her client to sleep with a soft lullaby.

From Gilles' room came the sound of music. It could be that he was trying to conceal his lack of effort; but Madame Jocasta decided not to interfere tonight. She would, however, have to speak to Gilles soon.

The Indian girl, Kamala, was not in her room. Madame Jocasta remembered the presence next door, in the bed of the Chinese contortionist Lee Kok Fook, of a very special guest. Count Cherkassov had requested the company of his two favourite ladies, and while Madame the Countess Cherkassova slept unknowing in her bed, the two mistresses of the arts of the East were persuading the amiably stupid Count's aristocratic blood to flow somewhat faster than usual. Lee Kok Fook and Kamala Sutra made a perfect team.

– Come in, Madame.

Media's voice brought a glow of pleasure to Jocasta's face. This one was her favourite; the only one who truly understood her. Media was the talent nearest Jocasta's own. To avoid competing with her protégée, Jocasta had allotted her the task of pleasing only women; which she did with great zest. – I like women, she said. I get on well with them.

Jocasta entered her lieutenant's room.

– It would appear we're both free tonight, said Media. She was standing with her back to the window, naked, displaying herself to the night.

– Shut the window, Media. The mist. You'll catch something. Media obeyed unquestioningly. Madame knew best.

– Since we have this little time on our hands, she suggested, I was wondering if you felt like a little practice, Madame?

– That's what I like, Media, said Madame Jocasta, letting her nightgown fall to the floor. Devotion.

– It's a pleasure, Madame, replied Media, coming to her. Blink.

Mr Norbert Page was a small man.

He wore small silver-rimmed bifocals.

He took small steps.

He drank small drinks.

His hands made small movements of nervousness as they discovered that the door to the shed was unlocked. Alex was getting far too good with his golden toothpick. He pushed the door open, and Alex grinned up at him, all innocence and childish charm.

– Alex, said Norbert Page, wagging as stern a finger as he could muster, you haven't been out, have you? It was a forlorn question; Alex nodded the answer happily : – *Yes*.

– Did anyone see you?

Alex shook his head, still smiling beatifically.

– Alexy, said Mr Page in great relief, you'll be the death of me, you will. If you'd been seen . . . if your mother had found out I went to have a little drinkie . . .

He gave up; Alex's grin widened. – Play, he commanded. Play game.

Norbert Page loved indoor games; his armchair athleticism had earned him the title of 'Sports' Page. This love made him Alex's ideal guardian.

They played draughts on a chessboard, with chessmen. This enabled Mr Page to add a secret level of difficulty for himself. When the draughts reached the queening square, he would replace a pawn by a major chess piece. To Alex, these signified no more than a normal doubled draught; but Sports Page meticulously observed the seniority of Queen over Rook, Rook over Bishop and so forth, never permitting himself to take a great piece with a lesser. It made the game more interesting for him and gave Alex a chance of winning.

– Your move, said Mr Page.

Blink.

There were, of course, some who slept through the blink. Irina Cherkassova for instance lay unmoved in her large, if crude, four-poster, oblivious to this as she was to her husband's nocturnal retreat.

If the Rising Son was the tallest house in K, the Cherkassov residence, somewhat distant from the main body of the town, was the most sprawling. It also had a fine, large garden. In fact, it was as near to an old dacha as they could make it; but since the family was not nearly large enough to fill it, they were obliged to share it with one P. S. Moonshy, about whom the standing joke was that he had been an afterthought on the part of his parents – hence his initials. P. S. Moonshy was the town quartermaster, and the continual battle that raged between him and the Cherkassovs was one of the wonders and hilarities of the town. – 'Tis a happy irony, O'Toole had been heard to say in a sober moment, that the nest of gentility should be afflicted with so potent a viper of levelling.

P. S. Moonshy slept every night with Marx under the pillow. It was uncomfortable, but he did it, as a mark of respect. He was sleeping now. Badly.

So, in the neighbouring house, was that other possessor of meaningful initials, Ignatius Quasimodo Gribb.

Elfrida Gribb, being a prig, was filled with a faint nausea as she turned on to the Cobble-way and approached the Elbaroom. She could tolerate it no more than she could Madame Jocasta's hell-hole; and if she had a complaint to level at her sleeping husband, it was that in his all-embracing love for the town where he had made his home, he could find no place for a condemnation of those two mansions of corruption.

It was, then, an ill-assorted quartet that found itself outside the Elbaroom . . . Virgil Jones, all of a shamble, slouching beside Flapping Eagle, squinting into the mist; the man called Stone crouching up the cobbled way; and the pale woman astride her pliant donkey.

Elfrida's eyes met Flapping Eagle's. She caught her breath. Blink.

THIRTY-THREE

How long is an interlude in being? The blink had gone — or so it felt to those who experienced it — almost before it had had time to happen; and yet it had happened, and Elfrida shivered with the chill. She found herself thinking hard about Ignatius, holding his face in her mind's eye, making him solid enough to clutch. Elsewhere, Jocasta and Media continued their practice with unwonted ferocity; and in the Elbaroon, Flann O'Toole put down the table he had been about to hurl and retreated behind his bar, where his Alsatian bitch stared up at him in confused silence.

— Virgil? asked Flapping Eagle; but Virgil Jones shook his head, uncomprehending. — Some sort of blackout, he said. We must be tired.

— But both of us, Virgil? At the same time?

Virgil shook his head again. — I don't know, he said, his voice grating on Flapping Eagle's jangled nerves.

— Let's go in, said Flapping Eagle. We may as well try and find beds.

Elfrida had heard the name Virgil. Surely not, she thought, surely Mr Jones has not returned? And yet one of the figures in the doorway had a distinct air of Virgil Jones about it. The other . . . his companion . . . the one who had stared at her . . . the face . . . no, it was the mist and her imagination. He was a stranger. The feather, that proved it. He was a stranger.

One thing is now certain, Elfrida told herself. Whatever

hopes of sleep I entertained are in utter disarray. Perhaps the night would be best used in arriving at a solution of this mystery.

Flapping Eagle and Virgil had gone into the Elbaroom.

Elfrida dismounted, and pulling her shawl tightly about her, she stole to the wall of the Elbaroom, to stand between the door and window.

For the first time in her life, Mrs Gribb was deliberately eavesdropping.

THIRTY-FOUR

The silence spread with them as they walked through the long, narrow room. It was as though they exuded some invisible, deadening substance to kill words on people's lips and stifle movements at their source. It was also a magnetic substance, since the eyes of the numbed were capable only of following the two walking men. Quiet was an alien condition here; the entry of Virgil and Flapping Eagle had somehow altered the element in which these late revellers habitually had their being. Under the shock, too, Flapping Eagle sensed the presence of something more slippery, more dangerous, less predictable in its effects: the emotion of the prison guard whose escaped charge has just returned to his captors of his own free will, or that of the lion faced with a suicidal christian. Puzzlingly, this emotion seemed to be directed at both of them. Not for the first or last time, Flapping Eagle was consumed with curiosity about his companion's past. Moreover, though, he was shocked by the looks, almost of *recognition*, he was receiving himself. And subsequently he found himself – equally confusingly – utterly ignored. As though he shouldn't have been there, and all present wished he weren't.

Once they know me, he reassured himself, they will not be hostile. In the face of the blank hush of the Elbaroom, it was perhaps an overly optimistic thought.

Noise returned to the bar as abruptly as it had left; and with it, every eye snapped away from the two newcomers. It was an unnerving reversal; they might not have existed as the denizens of the drinking-house exploded into an effusion of speech.

Hunter was gazing at One-Track Peckenpaw with a desperate interest.

— Tell me, he said, a shade too earnestly, about your hunting techniques.

Peckenpaw burst into a voluble speech about trap-laying, stalking, shooting and survival in the wild. All trace of boredom was gone from the Two-Time Kid's features, replaced by a new-found passion for the hunt. One-Track himself had rarely been so passionate; he spoke of his past as though his life depended on it.

Meanwhile Flann O'Toole seemed to have collapsed completely. He stood, eyes squeezed shut, fists drumming on the bar-top, repeating monotonously: — Holy Mary Mother of God I swear I'll never drink again. Holy Mary Mother of God I swear I'll never . . .

He broke off to be sick into a bucket under the bar.

— Jesu Maria, he groaned.

It was at this point that O'Toole's Alsatian did an unexpected thing. Worming her way past her vomiting master and under the bar, she launched herself at Virgil Jones, tail wagging, tongue licking, to give the returning man his first taste of welcome. O'Toole looked up, grey-faced; his eyes widened.

— Certainly I don't believe it, he said. But then the dog always liked him; being closer to animals than human beings he always had a way with 'em. 'Tis Virgil Jones himself an' no miasma. Jones the Dig. The grave fool is returned.

Eyes slowly drifted back across the room to Virgil and Flapping Eagle and the big friendly animal leaping about them as they stood stock-still halfway along the bar, next to Peckenpaw and the Two-Time Kid. Flapping Eagle watched the eyes and saw them run through a fast series of expressions. Disbelief first, to echo O'Toole; then wonderment; and finally relief.

— *Wal*, said Peckenpaw. Jones and a *stranger*. He gave the word a heavy emphasis.

— Well, well, said Two-Time, two times. Jones and a stranger.

And there were other similar exclamations along the length of the room. Gradually, joviality returned to the night.

Flann O'Toole came out from behind the bar, recovering fast, his ebullience already restored. There was a smile on his face that looked friendly. *Looked* friendly, Flapping Eagle warned himself. Looking isn't being.

— His friend, bellowed One-Track Peckenpaw obviously, got

a feather in his hair. Reminds me when I scalped an Indian chief. (Laughs, cheers, boos.)

And that sparked a memory in Flapping Eagle. Not of an experience, but of a history. He knew what their arrival reminded him of: old films in the fleapit at Phoenix, illicitly visited. The Redskin enters the Saloon. The boys make fun of him before shooting him. *We don't dig Redskins in this town. We dig holes.*

– Dog, said Flann O'Toole to the bitch, be in order. The rebuke heightened Flapping Eagle's growing qualms, but there was still that pleasant-looking smile carving its way across O'Toole's face. The Alsatian skulked away behind the bar.

Flann O'Toole's hands: great hams hanging at the ends of his arms. *Strangler's hands*, thought Flapping Eagle. He would remember that thought at another time and place. At the moment they were spread in a gesture of friendship.

– Virgil, boomed O'Toole. Virgil me lad. Is it you it is?

His left hand flashed forward and pinched Virgil mightily on the arm. He had been standing immobile for some time now. Flapping Eagle saw the pain fly across his face and vanish again. His eyes were vacant.

Flann O'Toole was roaring with laughter at his trick. – It's either a fool or brilliant you are, Mr Jones, he said. Only a fool would let a thing like that go unpunished. A fool or a man who knows his weakness. At least I'm sure of this now, you're flesh and blood. Come now and let me make amends. Have a drink on me.

Virgil did not move.

– Come on, come on, chuckled O'Toole, now fully himself again and enjoying his needling of the fat, blinking man, I was merciful enough; I could have used the right. After all we have to be sure, eh? Come and drink with O'Toole and introduce your baleful friend while you're at it. Drinks on O'Toole! he shouted to the room at large. Cluster round and welcome home the wandering soul!

Virgil spoke.

– Before I drink with you, O'Toole, I must talk to you.

– Ridiculous, cried O'Toole. Why, we'll talk as we drink.

– Privately, said Virgil.

Flann O'Toole assumed an air of mock-seriousness. *He treats Virgil like the village idiot*, thought Flapping Eagle, and wondered why that was Virgil's chosen rôle here. Perhaps, he guessed, it was not choice that had allotted him the part.

– Hoomph, exhaled O'Toole. Serious is it? But these are my friends here, my close and valued comrades. I'll have no secrets from them. So spill it, man. I'm thirsty with the thrill of seeing you again.

– Your wife Dolores, said Virgil Jones, who left you. With good reason, I might add. She and I are lovers. I cannot drink with you. Everything she said about you was true. It was true then, before she fled. It is true now. We're not here to drink with you. Just looking for rooms, you follow. So if you'll excuse me . . .

The rumble began low in Flann O'Toole's chest and swelled slowly to a wild, shaking noise. His eyes grew red and large in his head. He stood thus for a moment, roaring and reddening, and then his hands lunged for Virgil Jones. Before Virgil could move, he was held in a constricting grip around the throat. He wheezed for breath.

– Excuse you indeed! yelled O'Toole. O you're a fine fool all right, Mr Virgil Casanova. Saints spare me if I don't strangle you here and now, choke you slowly to your well-deserved death. To come into the house of O'Toole himself and accuse him of being a cuckold, 'tis the true folly of the madman you are. Seduce my wife! Lucky you are I don't believe you. You could not seduce a sausage, which saves your life.

– I thought you said your wife was a trial to you, said Two-Time Hunter with interest.

– You'll keep out of this, said O'Toole. My wife is my wife and I'll not have her name insulted for it insults me in the association. It's time Mr Jones acquired some manners. Even idiots are not spared that.

His hands released Virgil who staggered back a step, drawing lungsful of air into himself. Flapping Eagle saw the big right hand clench and begin to travel. He found he was rooted to the spot. In slow-motion he saw the fist glide through the air towards the gasping Virgil; and the noise of impact seemed less than it should have been. Virgil folded from the knees, wordlessly, and fell to the floor.

Still Flapping Eagle stood stock-still. O'Toole turned, a bull after his second matador. – Aren't you going to help your friend, what'syourname? he said, still speaking at maximum

volume. Flapping Eagle felt his head nodding from side to side :
– No. O'Toole laughed.
– Virgil never did make close friends, he said. You're a wise
man to keep your distance. Flapping Eagle felt a sickness in
the pit of his stomach.
– Give him the rush, called a voice from the back of the
room. The bum's rush for him.
O'Toole grinned. – One-Track, he called. Your assistance,
if you please. They hoisted Virgil Jones between them and
dragged him towards the door. Flapping Eagle watched them
go.
One.
Two.
Three.
And Virgil had gone to clatter on the cobbles.
Elfrida Gribb, alarmed, rushed to him and cradled his head
in her lap; but when he gained his consciousness he stood
shakily, replaced his hat and, without thanking her, made his
way down to the far end of the Cobble-way, falling once, over
the crouching Stone.
Elfrida pursed her lips, full of the injury of the unappre-
ciated helper. Ignatius had always said Virgil Jones was out of
his mind. He had evidently been right.

It was the voice in his head that had paralysed him. It had
been as persuasive as it ever had been, and it left Flapping
Eagle disgusted with himself. This is what it had told him :
He was already a suspected outsider in the town where he
had resolved to settle. He needed the people in the Elbaroom –
needed their trust and help if he was even to find a bed for the
night, let alone a place in the town's life. To ally himself with
Virgil Jones now would be to kiss goodbye to his hopes of
reaching, at last, the end of his road; of finding his haven. It
nauseated him as he thought it : for he was already allied to
Virgil and in his debt to the tune of two lives. And yet the voice
was persuasive. He knew himself now; knew that the urge to
fit in, to be accepted, had taken over as the spirit of adventure
and the passion for his long-time search waned in him.
– Tomorrow, he told himself. Or later tonight, maybe. I'll
go and find Virgil and apologize. Yes, that's it. Tomorrow.
He could hear Virgil's plea, made only hour ago : – *I really*

am very vulnerable to any wounds you may care to inflict. Already the fears under those words had been realized. Flapping Eagle knew that he had hit his friend a great deal harder than Flann O'Toole, and in a more sensitive spot. The guilt was there; but it seemed he did not wish to atone. Not yet. He had to introduce himself first.

Guilt. My fault. Mea maxima.

He shook himself into awareness of his surroundings. All around him, unsmiling faces; except for O'Toole's, which was grinning its violent grin.

– Where will he go? asked Flapping Eagle.

– O, Jocasta's, where else? said a beetling-browed, red face. She's the only one'll have him.

– I suppose, said a narrow, elegantly-boned face, we'll have to accustom ourselves to him once more.

– Not in here, said Flann O'Toole, he'll not enter Napoleon's Empire.

– May I sit down? asked Flapping Eagle.

– You may, said Flann O'Toole. And you'll answer some questions as well.

Cynicism in the elegant face, violence in O'Toole's. O'Toole: the conscious face of violence, brute strength revelling in itself, a masturbation of power. God, thought Flapping Eagle, where have I come?

– I should be happy to answer, he said, and bit his tongue in shame.

– What's your name? asked O'Toole.

– Flapping Eagle. I am an Axona Amerindian. (Rank and serial number. He could feel blood on his mouth. And Virgil's on his hands. Another human being damaged by contact with him.)

– Never heard of them, said Peckenpaw, shaking his head slowly.

– Age, said O'Toole.

– Seven hundred and seventy-seven. (How ridiculous it sounded; how divorced he was from all his life before these last days. And here on Calf Island he had already suffered this change: his immortality was no longer important, no longer even a subject for thought or discussion, let alone sadness. Strange to think it had once driven him near suicide. Among geniuses intelligence loses its currency; they vie with each other at cooking or sex. So with immortals. When age becomes a constant, it becomes irrelevant.)

– Profession?

– Sailor . . . I was a sailor. (That, too, seemed now to be a description of some other Flapping Eagle.)

– Prime interest?

– I . . . excuse me?

– Prime interest, repeated O'Toole.

– I don't quite understand, said Flapping Eagle.

– Will you do the explaining, Two-Time, sighed O'Toole, and I'll get meself some liquid nourishment.

The elegant face replaced O'Toole's. – We in K, it said in a voice heavy with cynicism, like to think of ourselves as complete men. Most, or actually all of us have a special area of interest to call our own. I don't think we could accept anyone who thought otherwise. It's the difference, you see, between casual sex and love. The more you love, the more closely you get to know, the more profoundly you see, the more you are enriched. We like to think of ourselves as being enriched. We'd like to think you agreed.

– Yes, said Flapping Eagle, I agree. (. . . *to any wounds you may care to inflict*, Virgil had said. – *Agreed*, Flapping Eagle had answered.)

O'Toole was back. – Now then, he said, let's try again, why don't we? Prime interest?

The faces waited.

Flapping Eagle, dizzy and confused, and without knowing the origins of the thought, said: – Grimus. It's Grimus.

Ah, said O'Toole, at a loss for words.

– Tsk, tsk, said Hunter. You have, unhappily, a gift for touching nerves. We don't say too much about that . . . about that here.

The faces looked sullen. If O'Toole were to advocate violence now, there would be no chance.

It was One-Track Peckenpaw who sided unexpectedly with the 'Redskin'.

– Hell, he said, live and let live. Don't see why it shouldn't be allowed just on account of he's a queer looking Indian. Some of my best buddies was Indians. There's no reason for objecting, right? He's different, right? It fills a gap, right? So why the shit not?

Peckenpaw was the one man who could stand up to Flann O'Toole on his own patch. O'Toole's glazed expression relaxed into that two-way grin.

— O.K., he said, we'll let it be for the good Count to say. I don't mind if we do speak of Grimus. I like fairy-tales.

— They say he couldn't hold his drink, said a voice seriously. Everyone laughed.

— They say he was good at games, said another voice, and the laughter redoubled.

— They say he was a mighty hunter, said Peckenpaw, and led the third gale of laughter.

Flapping Eagle said: — Gentlemen, it really isn't necessary to make fun of me. I am in good faith; I wish to settle here.

— At least you're in better company now, said O'Toole. Have a drink, Mr Flapping Eagle. 'Tis Count Cherkassov's province to decide, not ours. You'll see him tomorrow. In the meanwhile I'll find you a place to sleep right here.

Relief flooded into Flapping Eagle, but it was tempered with caution.

— I'd like to ask . . . he began.

— Fire away, said O'Toole.

— Well, then, what day is it?

This time O'Toole's laugh was good-natured. — You see what comes of hanging about with the likes of Jones, he said. A man loses all track of time. Tuesday is what it is, though 'tis more likely Wednesday a.m. by now. You have any more of these brain-teasers?

— Yes, said Flapping Eagle. Who is Virgil Jones?

Flann O'Toole gaped for a moment and then shattered Flapping Eagle's eardrums with his guffaw. — Well, there's a joke if you like. He's your friend, that's what he is, and the more fool you. Drink up, Mr Eagle, drink up now.

Perhaps it was the potato whisky or fatigue, but Flapping Eagle felt a surge of nausea and giddiness. — I'll just go and get a breath of fresh air, he said and made his way to the door, a dirty tramp with a skewed feather in his hair, at the end of his tether. The faces parted to let him through. The room was full of mist.

Flann O'Toole and Dolores O'Toole in bed. He sodden-drunk, she wide-eyed, reaching for him. Flann Napoleon O'Toole grunted in his sleep:

– Not tonight, Josephine.

– Dolores, she corrected him coldly and went to sleep.

O'Toole, remembering, crushed a glass in his hand.

THIRTY-FIVE

The listening Elfrida Gribb had made a decision; her delicate jaw was firmly set. She waited, anxious but resolved, for the emerging Flapping Eagle.

He dragged himself out of the bar and immediately fell against the wall. His head rolled slightly; for all the world to see he was a man in the last stages of physical and mental exhaustion. And so badly dressed, too, thought Elfrida. So dirty.

– Sir, she said as firmly as she could.

Flapping Eagle's head rolled in her direction. The woman . . . it was the beautiful woman . . . yes, there, the donkey . . . He couldn't understand what she wanted.

– Sir, persisted Elfrida, you cannot stay here.

– Uh? he asked.

– You must come with me, said Elfrida categorically. If you are indeed in earnest about wishing to settle in K, you could not have made a worse start. First Mr Virgil Jones and now this . . . this unruly, wanton rabble. No, sir, you come away with me. My husband and I have a guest room where you can sleep. Does the thought of clean linen please you? And good meals, too, though I say it myself. Do come, sir. The Cherkassovs are our friends and neighbours. Count Cherkassov values my husband's advice highly. I assure you it is quite the best thing you can do. Only do make haste, please, or they will come for you.

Flapping Eagle understood that this beautiful woman was offering him her hospitality. Not knowing her addiction to good works, he had no idea why, and was too tired to think. What he was quite clear about was that she was a great deal prettier than Flann O'Toole, so his choice was clear. Even if he had heard the word 'husband'.

He attempted to draw himself up. – Flapping Eagle, he mumbled.

She laughed under her breath. – You do look comic, Mr Eagle, if you'll forgive my saying so; but a night's rest will work wonders. I am Elfrida Gribb. My husband is Mr Ignatius Gribb, the philosopher.

– And I, attempted Flapping Eagle, am the philosopher's millstone. He lurched.

– What, she said, can this be wit? I'm sure that in your condition you could do no more than transmute base metals into fool's gold. Now hurry, do.

– I . . . I'll need your help.

Half-leaning on her he made his way to where the donkey stood; after some more trouble they were both astride her, Mrs Gribb in front; and they moved off down the Cobble-way to that place which had haunted Flapping Eagle earlier in the evening: home.

By the time they passed the House of the Rising Son, Flapping Eagle was asleep, one arm round Mrs Gribb's waist to hold himself on to their mount, his head resting against the back of her neck.

My, my, thought Elfrida Gribb, this is an adventure.

The long night was nearly over.

THIRTY-SIX

There was a gnome at the foot of the bed. – Remarkable, it said. Remarkable. It was a very clean gnome and it hopped up and down with an air of insatiable curiosity exacerbated by acute impatience. It wore, spotlessly, a silk shirt and cravat, a smoking-jacket, a rather incongruous pair of very aged (but immaculately hygienic) cord trousers and carpet slippers. Its eyes lit up, bright and violet, when it saw that Flapping Eagle was awake. – Ah, it said, Mr Eagle. Be the well-arrived, as they used to say in La Belle France. Permit me to shake you by the thumb.

Flapping Eagle decided he was either still asleep, or else had misheard.

— By the thumb?

— Yes, yes, yes, yes, yes, rushed the gnome. Like this, you see?

He skipped round to Flapping Eagle's side and stuck out his hand. Flapping Eagle's own hand went out in automatic politeness. The gnome locked thumbs with him and folded his fingers around the hand. — There, he said. Local usage is terribly important, you know. Be in command of local usage and doors will open. Ignatius Quasimodo Gribb at your service, sir. Sometime professor of philosophy at, ah, but it's unimportant. Unlike, as I was mentioning, local customs. Which are. I trust you are quite recovered? . . . His mouth hung open and his eyes glistened as he hopped from foot to foot awaiting Flapping Eagle's answer.

— Thank you, Mr Gribb, said Flapping Eagle. You and your wife have been most generous.

— Nonsense, nonsense, nonsense, nonsense! Now you have a bath and we'll find you some clothes that haven't been shredded by angry savages. Smart and spic it, that's the ticket. Spic and span makes the man. Eh, eh?

— Yes, said Flapping Eagle dubiously. But I'm not sure if your clothes would fit . . . He stopped; Mr Gribb was waving him down violently.

— Not mine, not mine, not mine, he said. Courtesy of the good Count Cherkassov. A neighbourly act, wouldn't you agree? Bodes well, too. No harm in wearing a man's clothes when asking his consent, eh, eh? He nudged Flapping Eagle sharply in the ribs with one violet eye closed.

— No, indeed, said Flapping Eagle hastily.

Elfrida Gribb came into the room. She looked none the worse for her sleepless night; if anything, the surroundings of her own home and the misty daylight only served to heighten her ethereal loveliness.

— You must forgive my husband, she said. It's so exciting for him to have you here; I'm afraid he gets a trifle frenetic. You two must have a long talk. As for me, I shall be pottering about if you need me.

She kissed her husband on the dome of his balding head (or

rather, a head petrified for ever in a state of moulting), bending over him to do so; and left.

— So this was where the new life began, thought Flapping Eagle as he bathed. A night between expensive linen on a feather mattress. *He had to make it work.* One thing, at least: the Gribbs lived a great deal better than his last benefactors, Virgil Jones and Dolores O'Toole.

The bath-water was black. He must have been absolutely filthy. His hair had been a tangled, matted wilderness. He decided to have a second bath; this time the water ran cold, but no matter. He blackened the water again. Only after a third bathful did he declare himself clean. When he emerged, Ignatius Gribb was waiting with a selection of clothes laid out on the bed. Flapping Eagle chose a modest dark suit and tie; they fitted tolerably well. He refused a hat: — I hope I didn't use too much water, he said.

— Nonsense, nonsense, said Gribb. We have a large tank on the roof. Now come and display your shining self to Elfrida. She'll be transfixed.

They went out of the bedroom into a perfectly neat chamber. Elfrida lay with her petit-point on a chaise-longue. As they entered, she sat up and clapped.

— My, my, she said, now we see you in your true colours, Mr Eagle.

— Thanks to you, Madame, he said and bowed.

She allowed a touch of crimson pleasure to creep into her cheeks. — Off with you both now, she said. I'm awfully busy.

There was an old, even antique, wind-up phonograph by her side; and she placed the needle on a record. Music played. Music, which Flapping Eagle had not heard in an age. Flutes and violins: an interlude of almost forgotten peace. He stumbled upon a lump in his throat.

— My study, Mr Eagle, said Ignatius Gribb. Will you join me for a drink?

Tearing his eyes with difficulty from the enchanted scene, Flapping Eagle followed the small, bright, wrinkled man.

— You are evidently a man of much worldly experience, Mr Eagle, said Ignatius Gribb. It sings from your every action.

— Your home reminds me constantly of the past, said Flapping Eagle. Of its sweetest moments. This sherry, for instance. I have not tasted sherry in over a century.

– Elfrida, among her many virtues, is a prudent woman, said Gribb. When we decided to make the journey to Calf Island, she insisted that every perquisite of a civilized household should accompany us. So we have a small cellar, you understand, for use on occasions as rare as this is. For the most part we drink the local wine. A bit underweight, perhaps, but better so than obese.

Flapping Eagle choked back his laugh: Mr Gribb was looking delighted with his critique.

– As I was saying, the philosopher continued, I have found it possible to determine the extent and nature of a man's experience from his eyes. A man whom life has beaten will have narrow slits of eyes; his opposite, the conquering hero, perhaps, will hold his eyes wide and proud. I am pleased to see your eyes so wide, Mr Eagle. It means we may be friends.

In confusion. Flapping Eagle stammered a word of thanks. To himself, he thought: the man's a fool, and dogmatic with it; but no doubt that would prove tolerable in return for the unstinted hospitality.

Mr Gribb was just getting into his stride, and when Flapping Eagle asked, – To what school of philosophy do you belong, sir? Gribb needed no further encouragement.

– Many years ago, he said, I became engrossed in the notion of race-memory: the sediment of highly-concentrated knowledge that passes down the ages, constantly being added to and subtracted from. It struck me that the source-material of this body of knowledge must be the stuff itself of philosophy. In a word, sir, I have achieved the ultimate harmony: the combination of the most profound thoughts of the race, tested by time, and the cadences that give those thoughts coherence and, even more important, popularity. I am taking the intellect back to the people.

– I don't quite . . . began Flapping Eagle.

– But don't you see, my dear fellow? The cadence, the structure, the style: it's all there to use, in old wives' tales, in tall stories, and most of all . . . (he flourished his right hand dramatically and raised a manuscript aloft from his desk) . . . in the cliché!

O my God, thought Flapping Eagle.

– This, said Gribb, jabbing a finger at the pages, is my great endeavour. The All-Purpose Quotable Philosophy. A quote for all seasons to make life both supportable and comprehensible. A framework of phrases to live within, pregnant with a truly universal meaning. As for instance, my very first entry, perhaps the most perfectly all-purpose quote of all:

The sands of time are steeped in new

Beginnings.

– That's incredible, said Flapping Eagle.

– You think so, you think so? Yes, yes, yes: consider this. An old aunt at a wedding seeks a phrase to put it into perspective. She would use this phrase and the ceremony would gain a new and deeper context. The same woman cooks a disastrous meal; she uses – with stoic fortitude – the same quote and immediately she has linked two quite disparate events. In this way the all-purpose quote increases our awareness of the interrelations of life. It shows us precisely how a wedding is like having to cook a second meal. Thus illuminating both events.

– Remarkable, said Flapping Eagle.

– Dear, dear, dear, said Ignatius Gribb. I can tell we shall be the best of friends. Cherkassov will like you, be in no doubt of that. I shall instruct him that he must.

– There may be some trouble, said Flapping Eagle, over my choice of prime interest.

– Pooh, said Gribb. Tchah. Cherkassov's never turned one down yet.

– It created quite a stir at the Elbaroom when I mentioned it.

Gribb grunted dismissively. – Well, well, well, what is this dangerous interest of yours, eh, eh?

– Grimus, said Flapping Eagle. Ignatius Gribb sat down and was silent. A grandfather clock ticked off the pause. A fly buzzed in conspicuous intrusion.

– Elfrida mentioned something of the sort, said Gribb. Nevertheless. Don't you fret yourself. And he nodded his head as if to reassure. Flapping Eagle didn't feel entirely calmed.

Elfrida sat on the chaise-longue; Ignatius was beside her; the petit-point lay carelessly on the ground, the one jarring note of untidiness in the meticulous room. The phonograph played an old, old song.

It was afternoon and the mist had turned from the morning's gold to the post-meridian yellow. *Yellow for life,* remembered Flapping Eagle, sitting opposite them in a rather-too-upright wicker chair. A slow haze lay over the room. Time is passing more slowly now, thought Flapping Eagle, and felt very nearly happy. To be in K was to return to a consciousness of history, of good times, even of nationhood: O'Toole, Cherkassov . . . like them or not, the names conjured a past world back to life. Here in the womb of the Gribb drawing-room he felt – and found – comfort.

Here, the trappings of the past were jealously guarded. It made a big difference to the home-seeking man.

He watched Elfrida as with downcast eyes she listened to her husband's voice. That was a further source of pleasure. Her long fingers wound a piece of thread slowly and elaborately in and out between themselves. It was a hypnotic sight.

Ignatius was saying:

– The one aspect of K I love above all else is the absence of scientists. I always found it shameful that mere technologists should have arrogated to themselves the right to be called that, scientists, men of knowledge. In their absence, science is returned to its true guardians; scholars, thinkers, abstract theoreticians like myself.

However, the absence of the technocrat does not mean a relapse into superstition, my dear Flapping Eagle; on the contrary, it places upon us an even greater duty to be rational. The world is as we see it, you know; no more, no less. Empirical data are the only true grounds for philosophy. I am no reactionary; in my childhood I would have laughed at the idea of immortality, but now that I know it can be bestowed I accept it. For that at least I thank the technologists; credit where it is due. To have eternity to study one's subject is a grace and a blessing; to have the sure environment of this town about one is what I would call a miracle if I were a superstitious man. Here one may indulge one's prime interest and want for nothing; one has a home, and food and company. With that and the eternal interplay of thesis and antithesis a man must be happy. I am a happy man, Mr Eagle; and do you know why? Permit me to tell you in a roundabout way.

We, too, are relatively recent arrivals, you see, Mr Eagle; I say relatively, for it is a matter of some centuries now. When I arrived I found a certain number of unfortunate myths in the process of forming; myths which I have made it my business to expunge from the minds of the townspeople. It is, incidentally, an interesting corollary study to my work on race-memory: the growth of a mythology in a single, long-lived generation. At any rate, Mr Eagle, I do not know what line you propose to take in your chosen field; may I simply hope you will do nothing to perpetuate that particular myth?

Flapping Eagle suddenly felt on very thin ice.

— Are you saying sir, he asked, that Grimus does not exist?

Ignatius Gribb looked annoyed.

— Yes, yes, yes, yes, yes, he said. Naturally that is what I say. And nor do his precious machine, nor his supposed dimensions, nor any of it. It's all the babbling of an idiot like Jones; sound and fury, signifying nothing.

— I am astonished, Mr Gribb, said Flapping Eagle; and I can't agree.

— You've spent too long with that trickster . . . that charlatan. He has no place in this town. Gribb was now definitely angry. A red dwarf.

— Darling, said Elfrida, I'm sure it might be interesting for you to have a man of Mr Eagle's undoubted experience investigate the matter.

Gribb collected himself. — Yes, of course, he said. Dear, dear, dear. It would be . . . most amusing.

Flapping Eagle was thinking hard: certainly it seemed no-one in K ever succumbed to dimension-fever; and since his own experience of it, the dimensions no longer intruded into his own consciousness. And he had been ill in Virgil's company. He wished passionately that he knew more about Virgil.

He was now sure of one thing: he intended, if permitted, to find out as much as possible about Grimus, whether he was fact or fiction. It was the only way to understand what had happened to him.

And where was Virgil Jones now?

To Mr Gribb, he said formally: — Please rest assured, sir, that I shall be the soul of impartiality in my studies. It is a debt of honour to you for housing me. Scholasticism breeds a scholarly attitude.

– Well, well, well, well, well, said Mr Gribb, mollified.

– Heavens, said Elfrida, if we are indeed dining with the Cherkassovs, I must fly and dress.

THIRTY-SEVEN

A bruised man in a torn suit knocks at the door of a brothel, seven times. Exactly on the seventh stroke, the door flies open. A hollow noise as it strikes against a darkened wall. Candle-light: a woman in a long lace nightgown, her dark hair a cascade upon her shoulders, her face glowing. The man stumbles inside; the door closes. There is no wilderness without an oasis.

The man lies in the lap of a lady with a lamp, sleeping as she sings. Behind her stands a girl, naked and motionless; at their feet the woman in the long lace nightgown lies watching. These are some of the words of the song:

> *And shall ye attempt to climb*
> *The inaccessible mountain of Kâf?*
> *It bruises all men in its time*
> *It shatters the strongest staff*
> *It brings an end to all rhyme*
> *And crushes the lightest laugh*
> *O do not attempt then to climb*
> *The inaccessible mountain of Kâf.*
> *In time all must climb it, in time.*

Awaking, the man asks for refuge; and since a brothel is a place of refuge, asylum is given. And food and new clothing.

– Your namesake Chanakya, whispered Kamala Sutra to Virgil Jones, could place his right hand upon a brazier of coals and his left hand upon the cool breast of a young girl, feeling neither the pain of the fire nor the pleasure of her skin. Ask yourself if it is your luck or your misfortune that you could feel both. And now that the fires have scalded you, allow the woman to heal you.

She lay beside him; from her throat came low clucking noises. She drew her hands over her eyes to close them and held them, fingers spread, at the corners of the sloe-shaped lids. When Virgil made no move, she took his hand in hers and put it on her breast. Slowly, it began to move.

– Be comforted, she said.

And he was.

– If you fix your eyes upon a black dot at the centre of a sheet of white paper, said Lee Kok Fook, it will either disappear or grow until it gives the illusion of filling the page. In the ancient symbol of yin and yang, the yin hemisphere contains a yang dot, and the yang hemisphere a yin dot, to show how each half contains the seeds of its opposite. If you fix your eyes upon the dot, it will grow into a cloud, and create an imbalance in the mind, such as the desolation you feel now. I will help you to avert your eyes from the cloud; by our love-making the harmony can perhaps be restored.

She wound around him like a snake, her legs and arms seemingly spiralling around his, until they were irretrievably interlocked; and he could do nothing but respond.

That night, Florence Nightingale sang him to sleep once more; and again the naked Media stood behind them silently while Madame Jocasta reclined at their feet. It was a rippling song, full of clear waters and quickly-running streams, fresh and soothing. He slept better.

– There are some men, said Lee Kok Fook, whose curse it is to be different from the rest. Among thinkers, they see only a lack of practicality; among men of action, they mourn the absence of thought. When they are at one extreme, they yearn for the other side. Such men are habitually alone, unloved by most others, incapable of making a friend, since to make a friend would be to accept the other's way of thinking. But perhaps it is not such a curse to be alone; wisdom is very rarely found in crowds. And then, she added, melting around him, there are always times when even such men are not wholly alone.

Madame Jocasta raised the flap of an observation-hole. Kamala Sutra was showing Virgil an exercise in *yoga tantra*.

He sat naked and cross-legged on her bed; she sat on his lap, her legs locked about his waist, their sexes conjoined, their eyes closed. Jocasta nodded her head in satisfaction.

Virgil Jones lay peacefully on Florence Nightingale's bed. On the bedside table stood a gleaming bronze pitcher of wine. Jocasta, Media, Kamala and Lee stood in a semi-circle around the two people on the bed.

— Welcome home, Virgil, said Madame Jocasta.

— I propose a toast, said Virgil Jones, to the House of the Rising Son and its resident angels of mercy.

— And we shall drink to your renewed good spirits, said Jocasta.

Virgil drained his glass. Florence refilled it instantly.

— Shall I play, Madame Jocasta? she asked.

— Yes, please, said Virgil. Play and sing.

Florence picked up her lute and began to sing. Looking at her, Virgil remembered a verse from another poem:

A damsel with a dulcimer
In a vision once I saw

He watched the black-skinned Nightingale sing and forgot all other songs and poems.

She was an Abyssinian maid.
And on her dulcimer she played
Singing of Mount Abora.

They lay in bed, Greek-named gravedigger and Greek-faced whore.

— At first, said Virgil, I was wounded by Flapping Eagle's desertion. But now I really don't care.

— You must stay, Virgil, said Jocasta. Stay with us and look after us. You've been wandering far too long, up and down this wretched mountain, and done quite enough. Nobody can carry the guilt for an entire island. It's time you rested. Let your Flapping Eagle travel on if he must; you've taken him as far as you can.

— Or as far as I want to, said Virgil. At the moment his mind is full of settling down. Settling down! But who knows, perhaps that's all there is to it, all there is to do, all there is to him. It's just that I thought . . .

He fell silent.

– You thought he was the one to do what you can't, said Jocasta. Virgil didn't reply.

– Revenge isn't a very worthy emotion, said Jocasta softly. You know as well as I do that nobody can touch Grimus now.

Virgil shrugged. – Probably, he said. Most probably not.

– What is it in Liv, asked Jocasta bitterly, that leaves such a cancer in people? You would never have hated Grimus if Liv hadn't made you do so.

– Probably not, repeated Virgil.

– Liv, spat Jocasta. You'll have to forget her, Virgil. Her, and Grimus, and Flapping Eagle. I can't go to bed with your ghosts.

Virgil laughed.

– You're a tolerant woman, Jocasta, he said. Give me some wine; there's absolution in it. I'd love to stay.

– Jocasta?

She stirred in her sleep.

– Jocasta, listen.

Virgil was sitting bolt-upright in bed. He could see himself, blurrily, in the dark, reflected in the mirror on the far wall.

Jocasta raised herself on one elbow. – Whatever have you thought of now? she asked. For the last few nights, this had been a regular occurrence; Virgil would be brought abruptly awake by his dreams. – It takes longer to exorcize the unconscious, he had apologized.

– I've just remembered, he said. Night I came here. Do you recall . . . something happening? Something odd.

– Lord, she said, I forgot. The jolt.

– Yes. What the devil was it?

– It's never happened before, she said.

Virgil stared out of the window at the dark bulk of Calf Mountain above them, clouds enveloping its summit. – What the hell is that fool up to now? he said angrily.

– Perhaps he can't control it, said Jocasta quietly.

– It was like . . . began Virgil, and stopped.

– Like a flash of death, finished Jocasta.

Neither of them slept again that night.

*　　*　　*

– On the way back here, said Virgil, I regained the gift, you know? And then I lost it again. Just once, I travelled.

– You shouldn't have tried, said Jocasta. The rest of us are lucky; being immune, I mean.

– Like the king who took poison regularly to make sure it couldn't kill him, Virgil said with heavy irony.

– Yes, said Jocasta seriously, exactly like that.

Virgil fell back on his pillow. – That's one thing you'll never understand, he said. There's nothing like travelling. Nothing ever invented.

– Forget it, Virgil, said Madame Jocasta. Come here.

THIRTY-EIGHT

Irina Cherkassova floated down upon Elfrida, garnishing each of her cheeks with a kiss. – But my dear, she cried, how can you manage to be so good and also so lovely? It is unfair of you to monopolize *all* the virtues. It leaves the rest of us with nothing but the vices.

Elfrida blushed. – Such nonsense, Irina, she said. You must not overpraise me; Mr Eagle will soon see through that and think me vain.

– Mr Eagle, said Irina Cherkassova, extending a long hand. We have already heard so much about you. How lucky you are that Elfrida has befriended you. She is a saint.

– If appearances are anything to judge by, said Flapping Eagle, bending over the outstretched limb, I am doubly lucky this evening.

Irina Cherkassova laughed merrily, but her eyes, as they caught and held Flapping Eagle's gaze, were examining, mysterious and grey, holding perhaps the flicker of a promise. To Elfrida she said:

– Two saints, my dear. Two saints together: what may we not accomplish? Her eyes continued to dizzy Flapping Eagle. They were eyes that knew their power. A tiny frown appeared between Elfrida Gribb's eyebrows.

– Come in, come in then, exclaimed Irina and linking arms with Elfrida led them into the *salon*. Ignatius Gribb muttered to Flapping Eagle as they followed her:

– A word of advice, Mr Eagle. Be careful.

Irina and Elfrida, two pale, exquisite, china mannequins, sailed on ahead of them. Flapping Eagle pondered on the rapid shift of his circumstances since arriving in K, from the simmering violence of the Elbaroom to the equally simmering beauty of the world of these two women; and wondered if there was, after all, much intrinsic difference between the two worlds.

Count Aleksandr Cherkassov perspired a great deal for a handsome man. He kept a handkerchief tucked in each cuff; one was already sodden, the other was catching up fast. He dabbed often and feverishly at his forehead, that high dome that gave him the appearance of a sensuous genius, an illusion fostered by his curling shock of blond hair and his curling upper lip. But it was an illusion; Aleksandr Cherkassov was a weak, stultified, barren, empty-headed fool, and his beautiful wife was keenly aware of the fact. She held it constantly against him, as a taunt and a humiliation. He never found a riposte: there was none to find.

He stood by the unused fireplace as the quartet entered, in the immemorial pose of indolent aristocracy, lounging with one elbow against the wall. Beside him stood a low table bearing a decanter of wine and a silver cigarette-case. The cigarettes contained no tobacco; but Indian hemp grew on the plains of K in sufficient quantity to make tobacco unnecessary. Cherkassov spent most of his life with a surfeit of marijuana coursing through his bloodstream, accentuating his natural glazed expression. It opened no doors in his lazy mind, serving only to sink him more deeply into the series of anachronistic gestures that made up his life. Aleksandr Cherkassov had never really left his Russian estates.

He discharged his functions in K with an absolute minimum of effort; there was little enough crime in the community, so he rarely performed as a magistrate, and until Flapping Eagle's arrrival, it had been a long time since he had had a prime interest to approve. Mostly he slept, or smoked, or walked around his garden, or ate. Life held few excitements for him, few ambitions; he was the peacock, and was content to strut. He wouldn't have minded dying in the normal way; it was Irina's fear of age and need of companionship that led him to take up the offered immortality; and when the society they knew had begun to crumble, Calf Island, where time stood still, had seemed an enticing alternative. And Madame Jocasta's whores compensated for the sleek antagonism and sexual antipathy his weakness frequently roused in Irina.

He greeted Elfrida with a kiss, Gribb with a faint mock-salute and Flapping Eagle with a limp-wristed thumbshake.

– So, Ignatius, he murmured, you've found a protégé, and such . . . such an attractive one, too. I shall have to look to my laurels, eh?

– The competitive spirit, said Gribb, not quite you, is it, Count?

– You're probably right, said Cherkassov. Yes. Probably you are.

– Be that as it may, continued Gribb, it is I who should feel ill-at-ease, the one ugly duckling in a gathering of swans.

Cherkassov laughed and *patted Gribb on the head*. – You're worth more than the lot of us, Ignatius, he said casually.

Flapping Eagle found their relationship puzzling, the more so since both Irina and Elfrida instantly murmured their agreement, like a reflex response. There was a curious dichotomy between Cherkassov's respectful words and condescending action, as though Gribb was to him a figure who should be kept on a pedestal – but also at a distance. He forgot this thought as Irina swooped towards him, grey eyes luminous as ever.

– A drink, Mr Eagle, she offered, and handed him a glass of wine, but only after cupping it in her hands for a moment. – There, she said brightly, now I've warmed it for you.

– What better place to chamber a wine? said Flapping Eagle, smiling, and again the tiny frown burgeoned between Elfrida's brows.

– I'm ravenous, announced Count Cherkassov. Shall we finish our wine as we eat? It was Irina's turn to look fleetingly irritated; then she dazzled her husband with a huge smile and said: – But naturally, my darling. Excuse me for a moment while I check things. (And, turning to Flapping Eagle:) I make do without a staff nowadays; it creates certain lapses of gentility.

Then she was gone.

Count Aleksandr dominated the conversation. His habitually vacant eyes were at this moment more distant than void. He spoke solely to his wife; the others might have vanished upon entering the dining-room. Irina sat tense and tight-lipped as he spoke, but did not attempt to interrupt, or to involve her guests in what seemed to Flapping Eagle to be some sort of private ritual.

– Good times, Cherkassov was saying. Cavalry charges the morning after the ball. Hunting down Cossacks across the wide plains. The salons of Petersburg, the wit of the men, the beauty of the women, the free flow of wine and intercourse – and not all of it social, eh?

He laughed: shrilly, nervily.

– Aleksandr, said Irina at last; but what had been meant as a reproof sounded more like concern. He ignored her.

– Intercourse, he repeated. It was all we had left. The rabble grew, its cries grew louder, its weapons grew in power. What were we, after all, but dogs who had had their day? Night and the executioner awaited us all.

His voice had acquired a disturbing, rhythmic, pounding quality.

– They hanged us, or shot us, or spilt our guts; a last drink, a last cigarette, a last laugh was all they allowed. But this they could not disallow: that we were friends. That remains for always. This room holds that memory. Let us drink to it.

Eight places had been laid at the large round table. Flapping Eagle sat at Irina's right. On his right was an empty chair. Then came Ignatius Gribb: an island between two unoccupied seats: another sign, perhaps, of his place in the Cherkassovs' social pecking-order, since he alone had no immediate neighbour with whom to converse. The sequence around the table was completed by Cherkassov, then Elfrida and finally, between her and Irina, the third vacant place.

Flapping Eagle, listening to Cherkassov's elegy, wondered whom the Count saw in this room, wondered who filled the empty chairs, what ghosts sat where he himself was sitting; but at that moment Cherkassov started slightly, and his eyes changed; still glazed, they were no longer distant. He smiled around the table a little sheepishly, and Irina visibly relaxed.

– A toast, he said. A toast to the evening and our friendship, which all the tides of history cannot sweep away.

The five of them stood and drank.

Flapping Eagle, sitting down again, remembered Virgil

Jones' description of K: *Valhalla.* He felt a pressure on his thigh. Looking down, he saw a scrap of paper. Without lifting it above the level of the table, he read the Countess's message.

DO NOT ASK QUESTIONS NOW.

FOLLOW ME TO THE GARDEN LATER.

I.

Irina and Elfrida were making a brave attempt to start a flow of inconsequential chatter when their hopes were dashed by a terrible din, pounding its way through the dining-room wall. It was as though an army of cans, pans and other hollow objects had hurled itself simultaneously to the floor. The horrible crash was followed by the sound of a thin voice raised in incantation – or even song – to the insistent, clamorous accompaniment of a rhythmically-struck gong. The voice said: SVO – BO – DA! SVO – BO – DA!

– Moonshy, said Irina Cherkassova with some resignation.

– How awful for you, said Elfrida automatically. Flapping Eagle once more had the impression that he was watching some ill-understood ritual, unfolding tonight as it had done for all time and would continue to do for all time to come. Perhaps it was the total absence of surprise that created the impression, but it was swiftly confirmed by the countess, who explained:

– Mr Moonshy shares this house with us, Mr Eagle. Not content with being the town quartermaster, a powerful enough platform for enforcing his ridiculously egalitarian views, he feels the need to disrupt our evenings with his clamourings. I believe the intent is to make us understand that we belong to the oppressor-classes. We tolerate his outbursts: they are harmless if somewhat *ennuyeux.*

Count Cherkassov was standing now. – Excuse me, he said, I'd better go to the door. Please continue with your meal.

– It's the inevitable next stage, said Irina. He'll come to the door and deliver his harangue. I sometimes think he raids his wine-stores. Don't you think that would be a true poetic irony, the demogague given dutch courage by breaking his own principles? She essayed a laugh.

– But what was he shouting? asked Flapping Eagle.

– SVOBODA, said Irina Cherkassova. In Russian, it means LIBERTY. A ludicrously unnecessary request, in the circumstances.

Mr Moonshy's thin but penetrating voice made its presence felt at the door.

– Liberty, it cried. Liberty is herself in chains!

– Good evening, said the voice of Aleksandr Cherkassov.

– It is the eve of liberation, said Moonshy. The twilight-time of the bosses. For that reason alone it is a good evening.

– Would you like a glass of wine? asked the Count.

– Thank you, said Moonshy normally and then burst out: Too many martyrs have spilt too much blood! The transgressors shall face a terrible vengeance! It is the eve, I tell you. The eve of destruction!

Irina whispered to Flapping Eagle: – It has been for several centuries. Then she continued, a shade too loud: – I was reading a fascinating story only the other day. Would you like to hear it?

Elfrida said: – Oh, *please*.

Irina pursed her lips and placed the tips of her fingers against each other in a pose of great concentration. – It's rather a serious tale, she said. It is about the Angel of Death. In the story, he is sent out by God to collect the dead souls; but he finds a frightening thing happening to him, for as he swallows each soul it becomes a part of him. And so Death is changed, metamorphosed as it were, by each dying creature. The poor Angel finds it a bigger and bigger strain, and also begins to have doubts about whether he even exists as an independent being with all these people inside him; so he returns to God and asks to be relieved of his function. And what do you think he finds? This: that God too, is tired of his job, and wants to die. God asks the Angel to swallow him and of course the Angel cannot refuse. So he does, and God dies; but the effort of swallowing him breaks the heart of the Angel. And there is a very sad ending, when he realizes that Death cannot die, for there is no-one to swallow him. Don't you think that a very pretty, neat tale?

Ignatius Gribb spoke after a silence. – My dear Irina, he said, for such a bright exterior, your mind is very dark.

But Elfrida was looking absorbed. Flapping Eagle, immersed in the two strange, pale women, forgot the harangue in the next room.

– I don't like it, said Elfrida. It's too pretty, too neat. I do not care for stories that are so, so tight. Stories should be like life, slightly frayed at the edges, full of loose ends and lives juxtaposed by accident rather than some grand design. Most of life has no meaning – so it must surely be a distortion of life to tell tales in which every single element is meaningful? And for a story to distort life is nothing short of criminal, for it may then distort one's own view of life. How terrible to have to see a meaning or a great import in everything around one, everything one does, everything that happens to one!

She paused, looking slightly ashamed of her speech which was after all, a direct antithesis to the neatness of her own life. Irina answered, with a mischievous smile:

– Darling, you put too much store by my tale. It's only a tale, after all. Tales are really very unimportant things. So why should they not bring us a little innocent pleasure by being well-shaped? Give me shapeliness over the *lumpen* face of life, every time. What do you say, Mr Eagle?

– I'm not sure, said Flapping Eagle. It depends whether you believe that all the small circles of the world are linked together in some way, or not.

– No, no, no, no, no, expostulated Gribb. You miss the point entirely. The crux is this: the word importance means 'having import'. That is to say, having meaning. Now Elfrida, who believes tales to be important things, says she would prefer them to be less full of meaning, that is to say, less important. Whereas the Countess, for whom these same tales are very unimportant things, likes them to be well-made, that is to say, meaningful selections from the 'lumpen face of life', that is to say, importful selections, or important. Thus both ladies contradict themselves. A simple matter of semantics, you follow. If tales are important, they must be well-shaped. If they are not, they cannot be. And vice versa.

He subsided into silence. Flapping Eagle had lost the thread of his argument early in his outburst; he suspected Elfrida and Irina had, too. He looked up to find Cherkassov and Moonshy standing in the doorway. Moonshy's appearance surprised him; he was quite unlike his voice, a stocky bearded man of middle height.

– Mr Moonshy has come to pay his respects, said Cherkassov. He's just leaving.

Moonshy said: – I have come to say I am leaving, not to pay my respects. Particularly not to *him*, he said, nodding towards Ignatius Gribb. Self-important hypocrite that he is. It is your ideas, Mr Gribb, that are chiefly responsible for our bondage. I am leaving now, he said sharply, turned on his heel, and marched out.

— *Well*, said Elfrida.

— What could he mean? asked Irina. Surely he cannot be saying that Ignatius' rejection of the, the myths of Calf Island is in some way wrong?

— I'd always thought, said Ignatius, that it was superstition that was supposed to provide the opiate of the masses.

Flapping Eagle was watching Irina and Elfrida. Neither of them seemed at their ease. Cherkassov was mopping his brow even more feverishly than usual.

— Ignore him, said Cherkassov hurriedly. He's a confused man.

Flapping Eagle thought: *Unless the superstitions are grounded in fact. In which case, to deny them would indeed be a form of bondage.*

The clattering began again next door.

Irina Cherkassova rose to her feet. — If we have all finished, she said, I think we may be more comfortable next door. Elfrida? The two ladies retired. Ignatius, Count Cherkassov and Flapping Eagle moved into a third room, which doubled as Cherkassov's library and bedroom. The dining-room, deserted by the diners, was filled by the cacophony which clamoured through the wall.

Flapping Eagle had given careful thought to the question of how he should best position his choice of prime interest; and this, together with Gribb's support, helped to make the discussion little more than a formality: especially, Flapping Eagle suspected, since Aleksandr Cherkassov wasn't really interested in being more than a rubber-stamp.

— I think of it, said Flapping Eagle, as a way of exploring the history of Calf Island. You must understand that I have been rootless for a very long time now; and if I am to put down roots here it would be a great help to me to find out as much as possible about the town, and the island, and the mountain.

— Quite, quite, said Cherkassov.

— Besides, added Flapping Eagle, I'm good with my hands, you know. Mending things, building things. One picks up a lot of knowledge while travelling. So I'd be glad to offer my services to anyone in K who might need anything built or repaired. For one thing it would help me get to know people.

– Fine, fine, said Cherkassov.

He conferred briefly in a corner with Ignatius Gribb. In these matters Gribb did carry some weight, even if he was rather slighted socially by the Russian aristocrats.

– Mr Eagle, said Cherkassov, I approve. If Ignatius feels the exercise would do no harm, then I concur. We owe him a great deal, you know. He has helped us set up a ... bearable ... community. Thanks to his acute, demystifying intelligence.

– Thank you both, said Flapping Eagle.

– Welcome to K, said Aleksandr Cherkassov, extending his thumb.

Flapping Eagle thought: I've arrived.

They had rejoined the ladies. Elfrida came across to her husband and said:

– Ignatius, I was just telling Irina about this curious thing last night. Were you awake? Did you feel it?

– What, my dear, asked Ignatius, with an air of patient tolerance.

– Why, the ... the sort of blink. As though for a moment one wasn't there.

– Ridiculous, said Gribb.

– No, said Flapping Eagle, Mrs Gribb is quite right. It was like a hiatus ... a break in time.

– Look, look, look, said Gribb impatiently, the thing is a logical impossibility. If you're saying there was a moment when everything ceased to be, you're contradicting yourselves. When everything ceases to be, so does time; thus there cannot be a moment of non-existence, or indeed any time-period of non-being.

– Well, there was, said Elfrida obstinately.

– My darling, said Gribb irritably, how can you claim that everything ceased to be for an instant, and at the same time say that it *was* so? The term being relates to existence; non-being cannot exist, and therefore that moment cannot have been.

He looked smugly satisfied with his argument. Flapping Eagle decided to let it slide; Gribb was not a man with whom discussion was possible. Elfrida, too, appeared to accept his rationale, but was probably a little rattled.

Irina sent her grey gaze towards Flapping Eagle as she said: — Forgive me, everyone; I'm just going into the garden for a moment; I forgot something there this afternoon and I don't want the mist and dew to get at it.

She left. A moment later, Flapping Eagle asked to be directed to the lavatory. Count Cherkassov showed him the way and left him there. Flapping Eagle noted with approval that it would be possible for him to climb through the window and thus join Irina in the garden without attracting any attention. He bolted the door behind him.

He cast a brief gaze at the mirror hanging on the wall and said aloud to his image: — Now that you're in, you'd better go and make your peace with Virgil Jones. You've been forgetting your old friends.

Then impossibly, *behind his own image*, a movement. In the mirror, as he finished speaking, *he saw the door opening*. But it's locked, he thought frantically, and turned rapidly.

The door was still firmly shut and bolted. In confusion he looked back at the mirror. There, in the reflected image, the door was still, slowly, opening. Someone was coming in.

He heard a voice, bitter but recognizable:

— Hello, little brother.

The figure of Bird-Dog came into the mirrored room. Flapping Eagle felt the cold sweat breaking out all over him.

Bird-Dog's spectre came a little way into the 'room' and repeated:

— Hello, little brother.

Then it retreated back through the mirrored door and everything was sane once more. Flapping Eagle had to lean against a shelf to support himself.

Irina Cherkassova stood by a shed at the bottom of the garden. It had no windows and the doors were padlocked. Her grey eyes were impassive as the shaken Flapping Eagle made his way towards her.

— Mr Eagle, she said. I thought you had forgotten.

— I was delayed, he said. My apologies, Countess.

— Irina, she said quietly.

— Irina, he corrected himself.

– I wanted to explain, she said. My husband lives too much in the past; we all do, I suppose. You must not think him mad. He is quite sane. So is Elfrida, despite her obsession with purity and cleanliness and Gribb. And so, I suppose, is Gribb, despite . . . the rush of words dried up. Flapping Eagle felt too disturbed to press the point.

– I hear you came to K with Virgil Jones, she said quickly. Now there is a madman, if you like. And his ex-wife, too, madam Liv. We give her food out of sympathy for her illness. We are not mad, Mr Eagle! Her voice was fierce.

– I never believed you were, he said. It must be an awful thing to have to remake one's life like this.

– I knew it, she said excitedly. I knew you were a man to confide in. I shall make you my friend, Mr Eagle.

– Flapping Eagle, he said.

– There, she said. Irina and Flapping Eagle. Now we are friends; and now I will show you how the past hangs around my neck, and what a weight it is.

She unlocked the shed and opened the door.

In the gloom Flapping Eagle could make out two men, both fully-grown, playing draughts with chessmen. One of them was Mr Page; he leapt to his feet in alarm and stood between them and the other man, until he recognized Irina.

– It's all right, Mr Page, she said. This is Mr Page, Flapping Eagle. He helps us with our difficulty. I believe the correct medical term is allopathy: the treatment of a disease by inducing a different tendency. Mr Page, you see, loves games; he comes here to play with Alexei, in the hope of stirring something within him. A forlorn hope, I fear. My son lives here, in this shed; he prefers it to the house; so we keep him here, to avoid embarrassment. We think it best.

Alexei Cherkassov grinned foolishly up at them, a large, strapping sixteen-year-old in appearance. The looseness of his movements and facial muscles revealed that all was not well.

– A moron, said Irina venomously. His brain has the age of a child of four. Do you wonder I hold my husband's stupidity against him? He has bred me an idiot for a son.

– Ma-ma, said Alexei Cherkassov, happily, and sucked his thumb.

Flapping Eagle followed Irina out of the shed. She locked

the door, sealing her skeleton once more into its cupboard.
– Mr Page has a key to the door on the far side, she said. He comes when he can. She leant against the shed, as though exhausted. Then she jerked herself erect, setting her jaw.

– Now I am going to tell you something else, Flapping Eagle, new friend, she said, grey eyes boring into him. – Touch my stomach, she ordered; and when he hesitated she grasped his hand roughly and placed it there. – Do you feel anything? she asked.

– No, he said. It is a stomach.

– Well, then, she said angrily, feel my breasts. He shook his head, uncomprehending. Was she drunk? Was this a seduction attempt?

– Feel my breasts, she repeated, dragging his hand upwards. – Well? she demanded. Again he shook his head.

– Why should you, after all, she sighed. I always think it must be glaringly obvious. This is what I mean, Flapping Eagle: soon after drinking the elixir of life I found I was three months pregnant. The elixir, as you know, arrests all growth and physical development. So that, all these centuries later, I am still with child. Still. Can you understand, Flapping Eagle, how that feels? What it is to have a second life stagnant within one's womb, perhaps a genius, perhaps a second idiot, perhaps a monster, as frozen within me as the lovers on the grecian urn? What it does to a woman to be with child, heavy-breasted with the juices of maternity for so many eternities? Do you understand that?

– Yes, said Flapping Eagle. I can understand. But there are ways . . .

– You don't understand at all, she cried. It is a life. A living thing. Innocent. Sacred. It was because I thought life was sacred that I drank the elixir. One cannot take life.

Perhaps you are not the man you look, she added, catching her breath. He would have . . . She bit off her words once again, said: – We must go in, and was gone. Flapping Eagle lingered a moment before returning to the window at the side of the house.

Irina's unfinished sentences worried him. So, slightly, did the effortlessness with which he had been accepted. After the initial hostility of the Elbaroom, he had not expected it: Cherkassov and Ignatius seemed to be positively anxious to admit him to their company. He shrugged inwardly; perhaps it was enough that he *was* accepted. No doubt the rest would be made clear in time. Even Bird-Dog ...

In the presence of the two pale ladies, his worries evaporated. He sat drinking the wine of K, desultory conversation idling between Cherkassov and Gribb, half-listening, half-dreaming, as the two of them circled the room in a hypnotic, aimless promenade. The white witches weaving their spell, binding him in silken cords. They made K real for him, despite Gribb's theorizing, despite Moonshy, and, yes, despite Virgil. Acceptance may have come from Cherkassov, but the attraction, the first holds of K upon him sprang from these two women, circling, circling, moths to his candle. The green gaze and the grey, blurring together as they drifted. Pure Elfrida, tarnished Irina, tired Eagle. A spell was being woven which none of them understood, which they would all understand too late, as the pale sorceresses circled and smiled.

– I fear I feel a little faint, said Elfrida Gribb. I think we shall have to take our leave. She looked at Irina with a glance not quite affectionate; but Irina was all solicitude as she saw the trio to the door.

Elfrida found herself disapproving of the length of time the Countess allowed her hand to rest in Flapping Eagle's, and of the expression (gratitude? remorse?) in her eyes – and then hastily corrected herself.

It was of no importance to her. She loved her husband. He loved her. The Cherkassov marriage was well known to be a hollow thing, maintained only by their joint abhorrence of scandal. What did it matter what Irina Cherkassova thought of Flapping Eagle, or he of her?

She was in an unusually bad temper as they walked home. Flapping Eagle felt almost as debilitated by his second night in K as he had by the first.

Small insects, the creatures of the night, fluttered at their faces. The stage was set.

THIRTY-NINE

The Gribbs' donkey, perhaps the most obedient, least mulish donkey that ever was, jogged demurely along the Cobble-way with a divided Flapping Eagle upon its back. He had spent most of the day exploring his new home, and his mind was filled with a struggle between his desire to get to the bottom of the contradictions and anomalies he had already found, and his desire to stay, uncomplaining, in the bosom of his new circle of friends. The two were, it seemed, mutually exclusive. To accept his own recent experience and Virgil Jones' explanation of it was to put himself outside the ethos of K, which denied Grimus and his Effect; to accept the authorized Gospel according to Gribb was to deny the evidence of his own senses, or else to view Virgil Jones as both mad and evil; Flapping Eagle could not quite do that, nor understand how, if he did, he could explain his inner voyage. Perhaps a drug? But then, how to explain the vision of Bird-Dog? Had Cherkassov laced the wine with something more narcotic? The battle raged and fluctuated within him; he felt as ignorant, as stupid as his uncomplaining donkey, and wished his horizons were as narrow.

– How do you refute the Grimus myth? he had asked Gribb.

– Tchah, had been the reply. I have no time for creation myths. I must impress upon you that this preoccupation with simplistic explanations of origins – which is all creation myths are – is a very counterproductive business.

– Perhaps you could tell me, asked Flapping Eagle, as politely as he could, how you and Mrs Gribb – and for that matter the rest of the townspeople – came to Calf Island?

Gribb said : – At times, Mr Eagle, you show a degree of perversity . . . as I just said, origins, beginnings, are valueless. Valueless. Study how we live, by all means. But leave, for goodness' sake, this womb-obsession of yours, this inquiry into birth. Surely maturity is of greater interest than birth? Please excuse me now : I must collate a few more clichés before lunch.

The donkey jogged along the Cobble-way.

More puzzles came into Flapping Eagle's bursting head.

There had been no unit of currency on the Axona Plateau;

but that had been a society born and bred to communal living. It was extraordinary that so motley a collection as the K-dwellers, so separate from each other, should find it possible to accept a similar form of commune with such apparent ease. Could a man like Flann O'Toole, aggressive, competitive, ever agree with the notion that he was worth no more and no less than any other member of the community? And, though the Cherkassovs had acquired a nominal pre-eminence, the concept was surely alien to them as well. To dispense with rewards, to distribute the produce of K's fertile farmland according to need rather than rank or status or wealth ... it must have been hard to swallow. Talking to a farmer here, a butcher there (and often struck by the incongruity of man and job), Flapping Eagle gathered that Jocasta's whores were unpaid; so was Peckenpaw the ex-trapper, now the village blacksmith. They did their work and in return were free to use the services of any other resident, and to collect generous rations of food from Quartermaster Moonshy. The town provided services, the farms provided food, and the two were freely given and taken. In a sense it was utopian; but how on earth had it become workable? The Cherkassovs were still aristocrats, Gribb was still Gribb. Only in the matter of social organization did K display this out-of-place fellow-feeling; for the rest it was a place divided into small groups, even of isolated individuals, with few of the festivities and group activities usually associated with tightly-knit communities. *And no crime.* Flapping Eagle could not help feeling that such a system, for such people, could only work in the presence of some overwhelmingly powerful enemy force, something they all feared so much that differences were sunk in the common search for a means of survival. Which led back to Virgil Jones' explanations – and to Grimus. The whine was still there when he thought about it, there in the corners of his head. He had argued himself into thinking that the absence of Dimension-fever in K could be taken as a final disproof of Virgil's theories; but the alternative was even more probable. Obsessionalism, 'single-mindedness', the process of turning human beings into the petrified, Simplified Men of K, was a defence against the Effect, Virgil had said: – concentrate on the forms of things, the material business of living, and on 'prime interests', and the inner and outer universes would be blocked out. It all fitted: that was why Gribb and the rest resolutely refused to discuss origins – to do so would be to admit the presence of the enemy which they had driven from their minds. That was why Cherkassov had treated Gribb with that mixture of respect and insult: Gribb, as perpetrator of the Grimus-denying school of thought, had to be respected; but since all of K knew it to be a convenient sham, the respect was only external; probably they despised him for his pomposity. Flapping Eagle wondered how Elfrida felt. Probably she simply adored him for his cleverness.

Elfrida, Irina: there were the two most powerful weights in favour of K. No town which contained them could be easily dismissed. And perhaps two days was too short a time in which to decide to break his vow to himself. Yes, perhaps.

But while he was reassuring himself, the face of Bird-Dog crept back into his head and refused to leave. It was not easy to be an ostrich, even in a town full of them.

The donkey paused, by habit, outside Moonshy's Stores. P. S. Moonshy had struck Flapping Eagle as a man worth talking to, if only because he had questioned the sovereignty of Gribb's ideas. But when they sat in the spartan back room of the Stores, which was Moonshy's retreat, he became less certain. Yellowing posters clung to the walls, screaming defiance at long-gone tyrannies. The clenched fist of solidarity was much in evidence. Moonshy differed from the rest only in choice of obsession. He was Opposition Man. That was what gave him the strength to question the shaky edifice on which rested the sanity of K. He questioned, but he was a part of it; so that when Flapping Eagle raised the crucial question of origins – and Grimus – he received only a stony stare and the official doctrine.

– These things, pah! said Moonshy. They do not matter. I spit upon them. What is of importance is Cherkassov's privileges, is Gribb's indolent scribblings, which the deprived workers are obliged to support, is the sinecure given to the woman Liv in consideration of her mental state. She is not deranged, nor is she talented. She is a passenger. These things are important.

– But you continue to work within the system?

– The time is not yet ripe, declaimed Moonshy. When the workers become politicized, the time will come.

His accents betrayed his words. He was secure in his attitudes, as he would never have to carry them to their logical

159

conclusion. Flapping Eagle made an excuse and left, feeling disappointed.

Evening was drawing on when Flapping Eagle saw Bird-Dog again. And this was no hallucination, nothing which could be explained away as a trick of the eyesight. It was her, his sibling and mother-substitute, Bird-Dog herself, large as life and just as plain.

Nothing was out of the ordinary in K; Mr Stone was busy at his counting, the cloud hung over the mountain-top, the mist hung over the plain. Flapping Eagle dismounted from his donkey to one side of the House of the Rising Son. He wanted to see Virgil again. Leaving the donkey tethered there, off the Cobble-way, he walked round to the front door. There was a woman leaning against it, her face in shadow. He called to her:
– Is Virgil Jones in?

The woman moved into the street. – Come, little brother, she said. Come catch me. And she was off, running as fast as ever she did, around the brothel, away from the parked donkey. The surprise rooted Flapping Eagle to the spot for a vital moment and then he was after her. But she turned each corner as he turned the previous one, holding her lead easily, calling:
– *Next time, little brother. Maybe next time.* He raced round the back of the house after her and then returned to the side where his donkey stood bellowing – but Bird-Dog was nowhere.

The donkey was bellowing because the Two-Time Kid, Anthony St Clair Peyrefitte Hunter, was in the process of sodomizing it, and even for a docile donkey, there are limits.

Fighting back anger and nausea, Flapping Eagle asked:
– Did you see her?
– Who? asked Hunter conversationally. The donkey bellowed louder.

A woman leaned out of a window of the House.
– Get away from here, she shouted. Hooligans!
– For pity's sake stop that, shouted Flapping Eagle, hauling Hunter off the tethered donkey.
– All right, said Hunter mildly, it's disgustingly unpleasant anyway.
– Then why ...
– I'll try anything twice, said Hunter as if by rote, dusting himself down fastidiously. Last time the beast kicked me. Broke my leg, damn nearly. At least I shan't have to do it again.

Flapping Eagle forced his thoughts away from this lunacy. Bird-Dog had disappeared again; but, more importantly, she had appeared again. Where did she come from? Was it some kind of taunt? It was as though she – or someone – was reluctant to allow him to settle in K. He felt a surge of contrariness. If that was so, perhaps he just would.

Hunter had gone now, but more explicably, through the mist towards the Elbaroom. Flapping Eagle patted his poor, confused donkey. – Poor donkey, he said, and mounted. Enough had happened this evening; he didn't feel up to his intended confrontation with Virgil Jones. In a way, he felt as sodomized by events as his unfortunate steed.

In the Elbaroom, Hunter said to Peckenpaw: – Benighted town, this. If you want to try something new you're reduced to raping donkeys. Thus survival doth make cowards of us all.
Peckenpaw said: – Eh?
– It shouldn't have been like this, said Hunter.
– Eh? said Peckenpaw.
– One-Track, said Hunter. Why did you come to the island?
Peckenpaw considered the question, gravely. He said:
– I got used to being alive.

FORTY

The swing. Elfrida on it, Flapping Eagle behind it, Irina leaning against the great ash which bore it. Elfrida's parasol leaning beside Irina's, closed and unnecessary in the soothing shadow of the tree. Elfrida smiling in innocent child-pleasure, Flapping Eagle half-smiling to keep her company, Irina unsmiling, eyes grey behind closed lids, halfway between dreams and waking. The swing, swaying in restful sweeps, queenly as the tree. Not even in the garden of the Cherkassovs was there a tree to match the ash, nor a swing to compare with this. The mist was light today, the sun warm and the air humming with bees about their business. There: a butterfly, glinting wings and flutters in the shafting shaded light. An elegiac day, graceful as the arcing swing, fresh and clean as new-baked bread, delicate as lace or a pale woman's skin, a day to match the beauty of the women at the swing. Flapping Eagle woke at dawn, wide-eyed and re-freshed; he had slept well and remembered no dreams. The dawn, like the succeeding day, had been a cheering thing, blinding him to his concerns. On a day, by a tree, at a swing, with two women like this spirits could not help but rise. Flapping Eagle's were high.

Elfrida on the swing. – Higher! she commanded. Flapping Eagle pushed harder, the swing soared. Irina's lids, closed like her parasol, censored the scene from her sight. Such ostentatious innocence held little attraction for her. Elfrida Gribb was her constant companion and her neighbour; and yet, she thought, the two of them had few enough common attributes, excepting their beauty. It had been a long time since Irina had thought this; a long time since Elfrida's act of child-woman had irritated her. Today, it did. No-one could be so pure, no innocence so well-protected, no action as lacking in calculation as Elfrida's claimed to be. Hers was the artifice that concealed artifice, thought Irina, and the subterfuge annoyed. She laughed, ate, slept, wondered like a child – and Irina Cherkassova was no lover of children. So she closed her eyes and let them play.

The soaring Elfrida had quite a different effect on Flapping Eagle. She had been awake early as well; and before the arrival of the Countess for a surprise breakfast visit, they had talked for a long time. Flapping Eagle had found that to look into those green eyes was to agree with their thoughts, just as Irina Cherkassova's grey eyes could hypnotize him to their will. Talking to Elfrida, he had found himself willing to dismiss all his qualms of the previous night, all his doubts, and regain the courage of his conviction that K was the place for him. There were worse fates than that of spending an eternity with those eyes. And listening to Elfrida he even felt a certain sympathy with Ignatius Gribb. In her eyes, he was a considerate, loving man, and the eyes were unanswerable. But flickeringly they grew shadowed, as though her certainty wavered . . . and then the shadow was banished, and they sparkled again. Even her dislike of Jocasta and her house failed to arouse any objection; Flapping Eagle had distasteful memories of his own whoring past and embraced her dislike with the zeal of the convert. He found himself thinking less of Virgil Jones for staying there. Which was, of course, a convenient salve for his conscience. The chameleon adaptability within him, the symbiotic expertise had taken control once again, stimulated by the gaze of Elfrida Gribb.

— Irina, said Elfrida. Come, it's your turn.

— No, no, said Irina Cherkassova. I'll forgo it.

— Nonsense, said Flapping Eagle. We'll have no spectators here.

And Irina submitted. She took Elfrida's place. Elfrida sat on the grass and hummed.

The thought struck Flapping Eagle that it had been too long since he had had a woman. And in the same instant he wondered about Irina Cherkassova, with her weak husband and idiot son and petrified pregnancy. Elfrida Gribb was attractive in spite of (because of?) her innocent airs; Irina Cherkassova's charms were more freely displayed. She was the more likely of the two. *But second best*, he told himself, and was surprised by the thought. Surprised and then worried by its implications for himself, a guest in her husband's house. Unconsciously he pushed the swing too hard.

— Mr Eagle, reproved Irina, kindly take care. *Mr Eagle:* public decorum or a rejection of the intimacy of the other night?

— Sorry, he said.

Elfrida, too, was finding her neighbour a trial today. Again, it was an unusual feeling; and again, like Irina, she failed to put her finger on its source. Or perhaps she avoided doing so, as she had banished her jealousy of the night before last by thoughts of her dear Ignatius. She forced herself to picture him now, poring over his books and minute handwriting, sitting poised as a stone for hours and then darting a line down upon the elderly exercise-book he filled so entirely, not liking to waste a blank millimetre of paper, since his stocks were not inexhaustible. The picture made her smile; and then it dissolved, and the tallish, firm figure of Flapping Eagle filled it once more. — He is certainly beautiful, she thought.

Irina dismounted from the swing. — And now, Mr Eagle, she said firmly, since you dislike spectators so, Elfrida and I shall have to make sure you take your turn.

— O, yes, cried Elfrida, jumping up. On you go, Mr Eagle.

Then he was in their hands, flying up and down and back, whistling through the almost-clear air, at the mercy of the two pale mannequins. At their mercy, because he too was gradually becoming obsessed, and they were to be the objects of his obsession.

There was nothing for it. He must see Virgil today. He had put it off too long already, and it had to be done. Perhaps his gradual introduction into the ways of K would mean seeing little of his erstwhile guide, but that was no excuse for ingratitude. And perhaps K was not the place . . . there were still those unanswered questions, that ostrich-view of things.

— I must go into town, he said.

— I'll accompany you to the Cobble-way, said Irina. I was thinking of a short walk myself.

They left Elfrida feeling ill-humoured again, and angry with herself.

Out of sight of the Gribb house, trees obscuring it from view, Irina Cherkassova said: — Are we still friends, Flapping Eagle?

— Yes, he replied. If you like.

She put her arms around his neck and kissed him on the mouth.

— Then that cements our friendship, she said, and walked away from him without looking back.

There were too many fluctuations within him — between his feelings for Virgil and his feelings for the new life to which Elfrida had introduced him; and now an emotional wavering between Elfrida and Irina, brought on by that kiss. He had to start settling things irrevocably, he told himself, and walked purposefully towards the House of the Rising Son.

FORTY-ONE

The House of the Rising Son rose gleaming from the roadside. Outside it, stationary on the cobbled way, a figure on a donkey. As he drew closer, Flapping Eagle saw that the figure wore a flowing black garment, covering it from head to toe, with a kind of grille arrangement at eye-level, criss-cross woven bars across this one window. He could not tell whether it was male or

female and felt a shiver of fear as he commanded it silently to
be anything other than a third vision of Bird-Dog. Then it
spoke to him and he relaxed slightly; the voice was a woman's,
low and toneless, and certainly not his sister's.

– Who are you? it asked.

He introduced himself, seeing no reason not to; the hidden
woman did not return the compliment. So he spoke more curtly
when he said:

– Are you from the House?

– Yes, after a fashion, said the voice; and now it seemed
amused.

– Then tell me, please, if Virgil Jones is here.

The figure nodded slowly, continuing to stare at the brothel
as it had done all the while.

– Where else? it said tonelessly.

– Good, said Flapping Eagle shortly and walked up to the
door.

– Flapping Eagle, the figure said.

– What? He stopped at the door and turned; the woman
remained impassive.

– Nothing, she said. I was just accustoming myself to your
name. But since you're going to see Virgil, you can tell him I
called.

– Who shall I say? said Flapping Eagle, curious now. The
figure contemplated for a moment, then pointed with her right
arm.

– I live there, she said.

The black house sat on the outcrop of rock above the town
and beneath the wall of cloud, black as the concealing garments
of its owner.

– I expect to see·you soon, she said and kicked her donkey
into motion.

– What is your name? said Flapping Eagle.

The donkey was moving away at a sedate walk.

– Mrs Virgil Jones, said Liv, and scornful amusement had
once again replaced tonelessness in her voice.

FORTY-TWO

Mr Virgil Jones no longer needed his trouser-belt. He was not wearing any trousers.

He wore a towel around his waist, a necklace of beads around his neck, and a bowler hat upon his head. In his right hand was a pitcher of wine. In his left hand was a quantity of the bottom of Kamala Sutra. On his lap was a bowl of fruit. A thin line of red dribbled from his tongue into the newly-shaven cleft of his chin. He sat upon a low bed; Kamala Sutra lay beside him and Madame Jocasta's head was on his knee. He was drunk as a lord.

Flapping Eagle stood in the doorway, speechless at the spectacle. Virgil Jones removed his left hand from Mlle Kamala, doffed his hat and replaced the hand. – Ah, he said, my old friend, my old bucko, so eager, so enthusiastic. Flapping Eager, I presume. Greetings, salutations, felicitations, immigrations to you. Have a drink. Take your clothes off. Relax. Don't you think I look smart? In the pink, you follow, in the proverbial pink. The pink djinn is what I am. Small pleasantry.

Flapping Eagle took a step forward, and stopped again. Kamala Sutra leapt up from the bed. She put her left foot on his right foot and wound her right leg around his waist. Then she put her right arm on his left shoulder and her left arm around his neck. Then she inclined her face up towards his and made cooing noises.

Virgil Jones spluttered gleefully, thumping his thigh with his emptied left hand, the rolls of his stomach oscillating happily.

– Look at that, he said. The climbing-up-the-mountain position! How singularly apposite, or appositely singular. Do you see, do you see, Flapping Eagle? You are the mountain and she is climbing up the mountain to beg for a kiss. Cooing noises and all. A genuine no-nonsense Kama Sutra technique.

– Cucucucucu, said Kamala Sutra.

Madame Jocasta pouted. – He seems not to like the offer much, she said. Shall we send for Gilles? Kamala Sutra detached herself and returned to the bed.

– O, do, said Virgil Jones, redoubling his laughter, drinking from the pitcher and choking. A fine spray of wine spread over the bedsheet. And over Madame Jocasta.

Madame Jocasta got up and walked by Flapping Eagle to the door, where she pulled a sash. On her way back to Virgil, she said dryly:

– How nice to see what you look like at last.

Flapping Eagle said: – I came to ... to apologize ...

Madame Jocasta interrupted: – To Virgil? Why, how perfectly *sweet* of you. She smiled stunningly and hit him as hard as she could in the face. – You took your time, she said, and the smile did not waver as she unleashed her other hand upon his other cheek. – There, that's better, she said.

The door burst open behind them. There entered the most beautiful man Flapping Eagle had ever seen. Gilles Priape sidled in languidly stroking the preternaturally generous tool of his trade. It rose equally casually to a reasonably erect angle as he sized up Flapping Eagle.

– This one? he asked Madame Jocasta, pointing.

– That one, said Madame Jocasta, returning to Virgil's knee.

– Here? asked Gilles Priape, making a superb professional moue at Flapping Eagle.

– Here, instructed Madame Jocasta.

– Would you like me to undress you? Gilles Priape asked Flapping Eagle. From his exhausted tone, it was evidently a question expecting the answer No.

– Don't be so goddam lazy, said Jocasta. Do it. To Flapping Eagle she added apologetically: – He's only slow until he begins.

Flapping Eagle shook off Gilles Priape's resigned, limp hands and spoke to Virgil Jones, attempting to ignore the rest of the whole unexpected scene.

– Virgil, he said, and his voice faltered slightly, betraying his lack of success, I am very sorry about what happened at the Elbaroom. I should not have let them treat you like that. May I speak to you alone?

– O, my, flounced Jocasta, aren't we starchy? Aren't we severe? What right do you suppose you have to ask anything at all of Mr Jones?

Virgil hiccuped and then giggled. Flapping Eagle thought he looked totally pathetic, and anger mingled with his shame and disgust, making restraint impossible.

– Very well, he said, I don't really know why I came here at all. From a sense of friendship, I suppose, a sense of obligation and, I admit it, of guilt. I had also thought you could help me . . . I wanted to ask you things, to ask your guidance . . . I see now there's no point in any of that. Don't you find it sad, Virgil, that you of all people should have sunk so low? You, who told me how you valued your dignity. 'One tries by one's life and actions to bring a little sense into an inane universe' . . . is this what you meant . . . this . . . this rag-bag of lascivious impotence? Have they persuaded you to wallow so completely in self-pity? Have they persuaded you to forget why you left Dolores? I wanted to ask you why, a dozen times, but I waited until you were ready. Now it seems I've missed my chance. You are ruined and I am settled .You're more than ruined . . . you're being embalmed, here. With a brothel for a pyramid. With . . .

Madame Jocasta said : – Shut up.

Flapping Eagle, the pent-up frustrations and guilt released, stammered to a halt and stood foolishly in the musky room as Virgil giggled, Gilles Priape looked unconcerned, Kamala Sutra kissed Virgil's feet and Madame Jocasta blazed with fury, not realizing how much that fury had done to widen the rift between the two travellers.

– You, she said with stinging scorn, are a completely selfish man. You could see that Mr Jones was a good, giving person, so you extracted service from him like a tooth. Never mind the pain it brought him; never mind what he left behind; never mind what he returned to. You still want help, advice, guidance. Because you want these things, you resent the fact that he has at last found comfort. What does he owe you, Mr Eagle? It is you who owe him everything. There is no honour in a man who returns treachery for love. Virgil has come to his place of sanctuary; let him be.

.– He owes me an explanation, said Flapping Eagle dully. An explanation of his motives in bringing me here.

– But my dear, exclaimed Virgil Jones, it was you who brought me here.

– But why? cried Flapping Eagle, helplessly. Why?

– Mr Eagle is leaving, Gilles, said Madame Jocasta. Will you show him the way?

Gilles Priape, showing an unprecedented burst of speed,

grasped Flapping Eagle's right arm and twisted it behind his back.

– No, said Virgil Jones in his old, sober voice. I'll tell him.

– Nicholas Deggle was expelled from Calf Island by myself and Grimus, said Virgil Jones, because he believed that the power in Grimus' possession should be destroyed. At the time I agreed with Grimus that the new knowledge was precious, that the forces of reaction that Deggle represented should be fought. Now, I don't. The Effect grows in strength ... I'm not sure Grimus can control it any more. I wanted the source of the Effect destroyed.

– So you were using me, said Flapping Eagle. So much for Madame's righteousness.

– If you like, I was using you, said Virgil Jones. I no longer have the ability to approach Grimus. You have, since you conquered the inner dimensions so well. I also believed you had the will, the drive, because of your urge to find your sister.

– She is with him? asked Flapping Eagle.

– Of course she is, said Virgil tiredly. Where else could she be?

– I've seen her, said Flapping Eagle, here. In K.

– So, said Virgil Jones, and his eyes gleamed for a moment, then faded once more. So now you know what poor Dolores meant by a Spectre of the Stone Rose.

– What is the stone rose? asked Flapping Eagle. And where is Grimus to be found? Higher up the mountain, presumably?

– It doesn't matter now, said Virgil Jones. You have made your decision and I mine. So the road ends here. For both of us. Goodbye, Mr Eagle.

Flapping Eagle had experienced so many emotions since entering this room that he had been forced to take refuge in anger.

– I'm glad, he said brusquely, that I haven't ended exactly here, surrounded by whores and madness.

– Haven't you? asked Virgil Jones.

– No, shouted Flapping Eagle. I damn well haven't. I may not be sure of much but I am sure of that. I've done better than you.

– I disapprove of certainties, said Virgil Jones. They limit one's range of vision. Doubt is one aspect of width.

Flapping Eagle left the room without the assistance of Gilles Priape, who was, to him, a grotesque nightmare of his own past . . . and in doing so, performed his most K-like act so far. He resolved to close his mind to the past, to close it to any guilt or humiliation, to close it to any pangs of truth he may have experienced under Madame Jocasta's fierce, despising stare. Virgil was right : the decision was made.

He also decided that he disliked Virgil Jones.

All of which helped him to render his choice supportable.

He passed two people on his way out. The first was a beautiful, dark-haired and naked woman – Media hated wearing clothes within the walls of the House. She stopped dead, staring as he passsed, immobilized. He went down the stairs without really having seen her; his eyes were looking far away. She went upstairs, into the room where Jocasta and Kamala were looking serious, though Virgil was laughing quite a lot. Gilles Priape had left, seeking a place to lounge in private.

– Mr Jones, she said, was *that* your friend?

– No, said Madame Jocasta sharply.

– Yes, said Virgil Jones. He was.

– You must tell me all about him, said Media.

Madame Jocasta felt impotence replacing her fury. It seemed Flapping Eagle was now to come between her and her favourite. Life could be very unfair sometimes.

The second person he met was Flann O'Toole, on his way from a session with Boom-Boom de Sade to the Elbaroom. They met at the door.

– Oho, boomed O'Toole. So there you are. I hear 'tis a great success you've had with the Cherkassovs and the Gribbs. Shouldn't you be drinking to celebrate your arrival amongst us? Sort of a welcome to the fold, eh?

– Lead me to it, said Flapping Eagle.

They left together; and it was only when they arrived at the Elbaroom that Flapping Eagle remembered the message he should have given Virgil Jones – the message from Liv.

FORTY-THREE

— How many geniuses have you ever heard of who were in no way obsessive? declaimed Ignatius Gribb. Obsession is the path to self-realization. The only path, Mr Eagle, the only path.

— Virgil Jones says it reflects a fear of the workings of the mind, said Flapping Eagle. He was sufficiently drunk not to care what he said, and the Gribbs sufficiently proper to pretend he wasn't drunk at all; though Elfrida sat in distressed silence at the lunch-table.

— Virgil Jones is a human wreck, said Ignatius Gribb. A living testimony of the idiocy of what he is pleased to call his ideas. I am glad you have dissociated yourself from him, Mr Eagle, very glad indeed. You must now detach yourself from his ramblings, too.

— Virgil Jones says that doubts are preferable to certainties, mumbled Flapping Eagle.

Ignatius Gribb drew a deep breath. — Hamlet's disease, he said. Doubt, I mean. It got him killed. The old story of Doubting Thomas is another case in point. Where there are certainties it is laughable to doubt. Don't you agree?

— Er . . . said Flapping Eagle, the mists of alcohol settling upon him, but Ignatius Gribb was not to be denied.

— The crucial distinction to draw, he said, is between obsession and possession. The possessed man is out of control of himself; it is a form of insanity. Possession leads to tyrannies and vile crimes. Obsession leads to the reverse. It composes symphonies and creates paintings. It writes novels and moves mountains. It is the supreme gift of the human race. To deny it is to deny our humanity. What purpose is there in immortality if it is not to be used to explore in depth one's deepest preoccupations? What purpose is there in Calf Island?

— Virgil Jones says, said Flapping Eagle, that the boot is on the other foot. He says the island creates the need . . . he says the Grimus Effect can only be survived by obsessed minds.

— And that, said Ignatius Gribb, is the myth your prime interest is intended to explode.

Elfrida Gribb spoke for the first time.

– Flapping Eagle, she said. You don't mind if I call you that, since we are all friends now? . . . I think you are too easily influenced by others. This Mr Jones should not prey so on your mind. Forget him and his lunacies . . . you do not need him now.

Again, the note of desperation in her voice.

– Forget him, said Flapping Eagle, and passed out into the soup.

FORTY-FOUR

– Elfrida, said Flapping Eagle, did you know my sister Bird-Dog?

Elfrida's eyes widened; eventually she stammered: – I . . . I know the name . . . your *sister*?

Flapping Eagle nodded, and saw a steely composure return to Elfrida as she said:

– I'm afraid I have bad news for you. Bird-Dog is dead.

Flapping Eagle said in a quiet voice: – How do you know?

– Ignatius, she said. Ignatius said . . . she disappeared . . . she must be dead. I'm sorry.

She fled from his worried stare, dropping her needlework.

– Come over this afternoon and play croquet, said Irina Cherkassova.

– I don't know the game, replied Flapping Eagle.

– Then it will be instructive, she smiled. When you play a game you don't understand, it teaches you a great deal about yourself. And your limitations.

– I'm sure Flapping Eagle knows his limitations. (Elfrida, sharply.)

Irina cocked an eyebrow. – It was only a joke, she said gaily.

– I'd love to play, said Flapping Eagle.

Elfrida said nothing.

Elfrida and Irina formed a large proportion of Flapping Eagle's life during the next few days. Gribb's studies and Cherkassov's indolence had always thrown the two women upon each other's resources; they seemed glad of his company, both of them rejuvenated by his presence. In a way, they were as much a sanctuary for him, a sanctuary from his thoughts and fears, as the House of the Rising Son was for Virgil. While in their company, he found it both possible and pleasant to play the ostrich.

The attractions of the flesh were, naturally, prominent in his thoughts. Flapping Eagle knew he was not unattractive. He also knew he was some distance from being irresistible. If he was in the enviable position of heading a triangle whose two other corners were occupied by these women, there must be other reasons. He guessed his novelty value had much to do with it. He was the Stranger, the unknown, a new life to explore.

In Irina's case, her explicit desire for him was relatively easy to understand. She obviously despised her husband; Flapping Eagle was probably a way out of the trap for her, a way of expressing her scorn for Cherkassov and escaping the tiresome monogamy of her marriage. A simple, classic case of a bored, unhappy wife given a new stimulus.

Flapping Eagle's private judgement of her was that she almost enjoyed her unhappiness, that the double grief of her motherhood and the emptiness of her marriage had become emotional crutches, platforms from which to elicit sympathy and admiration. If he were to become involved with her, he would have to bear the weight of her woes. She was a siren, too: and a siren is a devourer of men. But for all that she was a beautiful, desirable woman and she had intimated already that she, too, desired him.

He found this willingness a small drawback. The unattainable held for him a greater fascination, and Elfrida, with her frequently-voiced attachment to her canting gnome, Elfrida was a great deal closer to being unattainable. He was not even sure if she was attracted to him. Nothing had been said; he based his hopes solely on a few glances, a few brushes of skin against skin, a few hesitations when speaking of her love for Ignatius, a few sharpnesses in her voice when Irina flirted openly with him. He might be imagining all of it.

If he was not, another worrying area opened up. Perhaps she did not love Gribb as much as she had convinced herself she did. If so, why was her dedication to him so intense? Was her seemingly natural, all-consuming love simply another of the necessary exaggerations of the Way of K? And if she, too, desired him, why did she? As a rebellion against Ignatius, a parallel to Irina and Cherkassov? He shook his head. Perhaps he should give himself more credit.

Of course, Flapping Eagle did not know the real reason why his arrival had unsettled the two pale beauties so; and so his musings encompassed only a part of the truth.

The mysteries of Calf Island intruded only once during these days, but, when they did, they answered the question of whether or not Elfrida was drawn to Flapping Eagle. For the rest no Bird-Dog appeared, and the whine in Flapping Eagle's ears seemed to have faded for the time being. It was as though the island were biding its time. In retrospect it seemed to Flapping Eagle that he had been given enough rope to hang himself and several others besides.

This was how the one intrusion occurred:

Ignatius Gribb was having his afternoon nap, and thus managed once again to sleep through an important event. Elfrida and Flapping Eagle were at the swing. More precisely, they sat on the grass under the ash from which it hung. They were drowsy with food and wine; but the second blink jolted them wide awake.

It hit them like an electric shock. No living being can be removed from existence and then returned to it without feeling the effects.

It passed; Elfrida looked at Flapping Eagle, a helpless child filled with fear. He took her into his arms and they hung on to each other tightly, proving to themselves it was all right, they were there, solid, alive.

It seemed only natural that they should kiss.

Inside, in his study, Ignatius Gribb snored on.

FORTY-FIVE

Earlier, at the House of the Rising Son.

Media was saying: — Madame Jocasta, might you not have been too hard on Flapping Eagle? People do get confused. Good people can do bad things under stress.

Madame Jocasta said: — You don't even know the man.

174

Media tossed her head. — I'm just giving him the benefit of the doubt. Virgil's always encouraging people to doubt.

Jocasta said: — Flapping Eagle is not welcome here. And remember, Media, your own speciality excludes him from your bed.

— Yes, Madame, she said. And added, after a pause: I like women.

— Don't be sad, said Media.
— No, my dear, said Virgil absently.
— I'm sorry I asked about him, she said, full of contrition.
— It's not that, he said.

The Gorf had warned him: he was irrelevant, redundant; he would take no further part in the story of Calf Mountain. The Gorf had warned him; and since Flapping Eagle had chosen the Way of K, it looked as if the Gorf was right.

— People sometimes get depressed in retirement, he said to Media.

FORTY-SIX

No-one to guide him; no sister to forage, no sham-man to expel, no livia to command, no deggle to direct, no virgil to instruct. He had to choose — which of them? Either of them? And then to gamble on their choice. And to know what he wanted.

The white witches weaving their spell, binding him in silken cords.

Perhaps any choice, even the wrong one, was better than these agonizing, fluctuating self-examinations and inner debates.

Without being conscious of it, Flapping Eagle was falling into the natural thought-patterns of his adopted town.

The pale sorceresses circled and smiled.

— I know I'm a guest in his house, he said. But it's yours, too. I know he's been kind and generous to me. But it was you who brought me here. I don't expect you to love me; I'm not sure if I love you. But I want you. I know it would be easier, more comfortable if I didn't. But I do.

There: it was done.

– I love my husband, said Elfrida Gribb in a voice seized with panic.

Night. Irina Cherkassova lay awake in her bed, thinking about the blink. A spider crawled unseen along the hangings over her head, the rude canopy of her inelegant four-poster. Bats hung from the eaves outside her closed window.

For her, it had been the first blink, and the first time is the worst. She bit her lip and tasted the salty blood. Tonight she needed companionship, even if it was only Aleksandr. But how to go to him, proud Irina, how to crawl into his bedroom after this age of partitioned nights, how to ask his warmth and protection in the face of her history of icy hauteur. No: she could not. No. Yes. Yes. She could. She got out of bed and drew her dressing-gown around her.

There was no answer when she knocked at his door. Sleeping, obviously; he probably doesn't even remember it happened, addlebrained fool. She opened the door.

At that moment, at the House of the Rising Son, Lee Kok Fook licked Aleksandr Cherkassov on the ear-lobe.

She knew it, of course; in fact she expected that he should spend nights at the brothel. Having banned him from her bed, she would be naïve to think otherwise. Besides, a sated halfwit was preferable to a frustrated husband demanding his rights. But tonight, it hurt. Tonight, when she had been willing to come to him, to humble herself before him for the sake of his company. It is most galling for the sensitive to be spurned by the brutish. Irina Cherkassova returned to her own bed, now cold, and lay stroking the half-formed thing inside her and considered masturbation. The face of Flapping Eagle formed in her mind's eye and she rejected self-help. It was so much nicer to be helped, and it was time she was. Her decision comforted her into sleep.

After their single kiss, Elfrida resisted Flapping Eagle with a passion so intense it gave him hope. She would explain to him at great length why it was impossible, why they could never repeat what they had done, and certainly never progress beyond that point; but she never said the kiss had been anything but a pleasure. – It's just that there's Ignatius, she said, and though she hastened to add that it was her love for him that made her suitor's proposition unacceptable, Flapping Eagle gained the distinct impression that she had meant, perhaps just for the fraction of a second, perhaps just for the time it took her to say the words, that her husband was in the way.

He began to ask her to accompany him on long walks around the fields of K; and though she promised him fiercely after each walk that she would refuse his next invitation, she never did.

They stopped, on the first day, by a well. An ox circled it slowly, attached to a long beam of wood that worked a system of pulleys which hauled water out of the well in a continual circle of buckets, water for irrigation, flowing into the field. Elfrida, watching the animal, said:

– Animals are the luckiest of us.

Flapping Eagle waited. She patted the beast on its flank as it passed them and continued: – They die.

– You're unhappy here, said Flapping Eagle, and knew it was true.

– Rubbish, said Elfrida briskly. I'm perfectly happy. And, for the first time, she thought those words seemed hollow and untrue. She turned, abruptly, and walked away from the well. – I'm going home now, she said, as if a return to familiar surroundings would be accompanied by a return to familiar feelings.

The white witches weaving their spell, binding him in silken cords, circling, circling, moths to his candle.

The croquet lawn was a long way from being flat and the balls some way from being round, but Irina played with the concentration of a professional. Flapping Eagle found concentration difficult, but avoided disgracing himself.

– You learn quickly, she said. It must be the sadist in you taking over.

– I'm not nearly as good as you, he said.

– Practice makes perfect. She used her mallet to line up a daring long shot.

– You'll never hit it, said Flapping Eagle. The lawn's too bumpy.

She hit it.

– It's just a question of allowing for the slope, she said. I have an unfair advantage: I know every inch of this ground.

She despatched his ball into the bushes.

– O dear, she said in open hypocrisy, I've gone and lost it for you.

He went to find it, and was hunting in the thick shrubbery that ruled the bottom of the Cherkassov garden when he heard the rustling behind him. He turned to find Irina stepping out of her dress.

– It might catch on something and tear, she said. I'm better off without it.

– Are you sure you know what you're doing, Irina? he said.

– I'm helping you look for your ball, she said. You didn't seem to be doing very well on your own.

Despite Flapping Eagle's earlier qualms, their love-making was a consolation to them both.

Norbert Page, in the shed at the far side of the garden, thought he heard a cry. He came out to look, but saw nothing.

On their next walk, Elfrida allowed him to hold her hand. On the next she suffered it to be kissed. And on the next, amid a loud buzzing of bees, she permitted him – and herself – a second kiss. She wouldn't go further for a while; but eventually she let him fondle her, his hands caressing her at first through her clothes and then snaking beneath them to raise her to unbearable pitches of desire.

But there she stopped him, driving him to distraction.

– What's the point of stopping now? he cried. You've been quite unfaithful enough . . . why not enjoy it, at least?

–As you say, she replied unhappily, I've been quite unfaithful enough.

She wasn't teasing him; she was just as frustrated as he was. But she would not take the final step, would not make the final betrayal. Something stronger than Elfrida prevented that. Flapping Eagle refused to believe it was morality.

– I love *him*, I love *him*, I love *him*, she repeated over and over again, through clenched teeth.

– No, you don't, said Flapping Eagle. You were comfortable with him. You never found him attractive. You don't love him.

– I do, she cried. I know I do.

Then he watched her as the self-control returned and the tears dried in their ducts.

*　　　*　　　*

The swing, Elfrida on it, Irina watching. There are moments, thought Flapping Eagle, when they could be identical twins. So alike, so unalike.

Irina Cherkassova, who found it easy to despise, found herself despising Elfrida. Foolish, giggling woman. Elfrida Gribb, in the meanwhile, was gripped by the beginnings of a more powerful emotion: jealousy.

They smiled at each other through their veils.

It was the night of the great ball at her own home and Irina was refusing to cry. Downstairs, the music and the braided gallants; upstairs, she lay dry-eyed and fevered. To be ill on this of all nights, in this of all years, when she had budded and blossomed out of childhood and had stood for hours upon end before a mirror naked with a book on her head pulling in her stomach and pushing out her chest. There would have been no pats on the head this year, no understanding mock-adult chatter, no tolerant amusement when she flounced irritatedly to her room before midnight on her mother's command. This year she would have danced till dawn and beyond and breakfasted by the willows on the river with some adoring swain ... she thought of fat, pimply Masha downstairs, glowing with triumph, the ugly sister become the belle of the ball, whirling round the dance-floor with bored young men wondering where pretty Irina was, and the anger drove away the tears.

– May I come in?

Patashin. Grigor Patashin, *éminence grise* of her mother's salon. A large man, bearing what must have been nearly seventy years carelessly on his broad shoulders, so square he scarcely had a neck. Patashin with the wart on the point of his nose and the voice like a crushing of gravel. Patashin whose notoriety had increased with age.

– Come.

– Irina Natalyevna, he said, hitching up his ill-fitting trousers as he entered. The evening is absolutely ruined by your absence.

– Sit down, Grigor, she said, patting the bed, deliberately eschewing the title of 'Uncle' which she had given him all her life. Sit and tell me about it. Is Masha very beautiful tonight?

– Can Masha ever look beautiful, I wonder, said Patashin, eyes twinkling.

– Old grizzly, said Irina, you are a master of tact.

– And you, Irina, he said, holding her chin gently in his hand, you are too wise and composed for your own good. I look into your eyes and see knowledge. I look at your body and see anticipation. You must learn to dissimulate, to show less worldly wisdom in your eyes and more of it in your limbs.

– And die an old maid, laughed Irina. I act as I am.

– Yes, mused Patashin. His hand still rested against her chin; he moved it to her cheek. She leant against it. It was cold.

– They wouldn't miss you, she whispered. Not for a little while.

Patashin laughed out loud. – No chance of seducing you, Irina Natalyevna, he said. If you want a man, you'll make sure. If not . . . he grimaced.

– Turn the key in the door, she commanded.

Watching a great man undress is a depressing undertaking; Patashin left his genius with his wing-collar and waistcoat, draped over a chair, and stood before her, white hairs on his chest, leering. She closed her eyes, wishing fervently never to be old.

– I hope it wasn't painful, he said later.

– No, she said without concern. One of the advantages of riding.

– I must go, he fretted and she watched him regain the stature of his clothes. As he straightened his hair and combed his beard, she said:

– Ravished by genius. What a beginning!

Grigor Patashin said as he left: – Which of us was ravished, I wonder?

That evening with Grigor Patashin did more than give Irina a hatred of old age; it led her directly into the arms of young, beautiful, stupid, young Aleksandr Cherkassov. Thus Patashin was to blame for the disasters of her children. She had married his opposite, and it was his fault. Perhaps, too, on another tack, there was something of her feelings for Masha in her present attitude towards Elfrida. Except for one thing: Elfrida Gribb was beautiful.

One more thing about Grigor Patashin. He left her with a

passion for the illicit, because the illicit reminded her of that night, and therefore of being young. . . .

Flapping Eagle was definitely illicit.

Elfrida Edge, she was then. Mrs Edge's little girl. Dear Elfrida, such a darling one. Her father jumped off a roof, you know, and she saw him falling, past her bedroom window and she thought he was a chimneypot. So well-balanced, it hasn't damaged her a bit. Lucky with money, of course, rolling in it, that's what comes of ancestors with cattlefarms down under and worldfamous stamp-collections. Little penny black he called her, pale as a sheet as she is; mad, but the money's a comfort isn't it? So poised and self-possessed, little miss snowflake, butter wouldn't melt, without wishing to be uncharitable, only little girls of nine should *cry* more. No, Mrs Edge doesn't live here any more, she's off somewhere in foreign parts getting done by natives, and why not, she's still got her looks, you won't hear a word against merry widows in this neighbourhood. Not since Elfrida grew up, such a treasure, helps the old folks, babysits the young marrieds' howlers, reads a lot, sews a lot, cooks a lot, but young ladies of eighteen should *gad* more.

> *Elfrida Edge*
> *Under the hedge*
> *Plays with herself*
> *Or she plays with Reg.*

– O, Elfrida, come down the lane with me.
– No, I don't think so, thank you.
– I'll show you my thing if you do.
– I am entirely uninterested in your thing.
– Bet you've never seen one.
– Yes I have.
– No you haven't.
– Yes I have.
– Well your ma has, that's for sure. Black ones and brown ones and yellow ones and blue ones from those ayrabs who dye themselves.
– Leave Mama out of this.
– If it's good enough for her it's good enough for you.
– Reggie Smith, you have the filthiest tongue in the school.

– And you've got the cleanest knickers.

. . . the big dirty man with the one-foot prick and an artist to boot lived with bohemian types on a sea-coast so probably very good at It there in bed with her and grunting so she said Why not you never know what you're missing till you try so he said okay doll and unscrewed it there was a thread in the hole where his prick used to be and he screwed it into hers which had a thread too and she woke up feeling disappointed with the sheets all soaked in sweat . . .

> *Just because*
> *Mother does it*
> *Doesn't mean I have to.*
> *Just because*
> *Daddy did it*
> *Doesn't mean I want to.*
> (E.E. aged 16)

When Ignatius Gribb wrote refusing her a place, she knew it was the end of the line. If she couldn't get into that college, she couldn't get into college, and that was that. Studious, gadless Elfrida, education ends here. His letter had said: '. . . if that seems harsh to you, may I attempt to alleviate the hurt by saying how charmingly presentable I found you, and adding that in the event of your failing to secure a University place I should be pleased to offer you the post of secretary in my Faculty Office. Please think about this seriously.'

They were a lost couple, the unfulfilled of the world. It was inevitable that they would marry. With her as his wife, her beauty dazzling the seedy campus, he was treated as a little less of a laughing-stock. With him as her husband, she could believe herself clever – if she could bring herself to believe in him. They knew their limitations and husbanded and wifed each other against the darts and gibes of the world. So Calf Island came as a happy revelation; here he found his self-respect and she nurtured her love. Ignatius, named for the darknighted saint, her centre and love. Love was the thing, to be in love. That was the thing.

> The sands of time
> Are steeped in new
> Beginnings.

Elfrida and Irina, both bruised by youth, the one seeking to retain it by immersing herself in its innocent airs, the other by plunging into thoughts – and sometimes acts – of wickedness. Like and yet unlike. As like, as unlike, as Axona and K.

He had been living for the moment for several days, allowing events to take their course, following the dictates of his uncontrolled emotions, and being in their clutches had put all thoughts of Grimus and Bird-Dog and Virgil from him. Sufficient unto the day . . .

Living for the moment, a curiously apt phrase. Later he would recall Virgil saying: – A life always contains a peak. A moment that makes it all worthwhile.

For Flapping Eagle, that moment arrived the seventh time he made love to Irina Cherkassova.

They were in her bed for the first time, Cherkassov was at the Rising Son again, and Irina had seized the opportunity to be comfortable. A single candle provided the only light in the room. Irina was hungry, demanding as an absolute monarch; and Flapping Eagle was in just the mood to fulfil those demands. It was a violent, frenzied thing that night, the two-backed beast; and in the midst of their battle Flapping Eagle saw his vision.

Her face in the candlelight, the face of Elfrida, elfbone pale; her writhing body the body of Elfrida; her moans, Elfrida's moans. It was as though for that flash the two women had become one, joined by the intercession of his love. Then the vision faded, but the truth of it remained; and when their lovemaking was over Flapping Eagle lay in the yellow light amazed by the miracle.

Because it was so: in the unfettered lusts of Irina he looked for the elegance – yes, the primness – of Elfrida, the saintliness which gave her the edge in beauty over the Countess; and at the same time he longed for Irina's freedom of the senses to infiltrate Elfrida's self-denying morality. They were opposite and the same, Elfrida as innocent as Irina was not, Irina as free as Elfrida was trapped. In their relations to their husbands they were opposites. The unifying bond was Flapping Eagle himself. As Elfrida loved him, but would not consummate that love, so Irina lusted after him and acted upon her lust. In themselves, neither was complete; through him, they both attained completion. Their faces, bodies, even souls, super-imposed and one in his sight. To make love to Irina was to remove Elfrida's frustrations; to kiss Elfrida's cheek was to release Irina's lust. Elfrina, Irida, Elfrida, Irina.

And the converse, their completion of him, held true also. He lay in Irina's bed, balanced between love of innocence and lust for experience, between denial and consummation, stand-ing at the peak, from which the only direction was down. Elfrina Eagle. The triangle was not three points but one thing.

Then the moment was lost forever, because in his reverie he spoke a name.

— Elfrina, he said.

Irina Cherkassova stiffened beside him. *Elfrida* was the name she heard.

— Get out, she said.

Flapping Eagle came out of his mind and back into the candlelight to find his new-found perfection lying in ruins.

— Get out, said Irina Cherkassova.

The moment of perfection had spawned its own destruction.

It was after midnight as Flapping Eagle crept back into the Gribb residence, but Elfrida Gribb sat drawn and pale in the front room, and the glow of a single candle echoed the bed-room he had left.

— Good evening, Flapping Eagle, she said.

He shook his head wordlessly and sat down in a chair, opposite her.

— Irina? she asked, knowing the answer.

— What can you expect? he said and heard his words cheapen the memory of his vision.

— Ignatius is the soundest sleeper in the world, she said bitterly. So you might as well make love to me here and now.

— You don't mean it, he said.

— Make love to me, she said. Damn you.

But again it happened; in his hands, filled with the wanting of him, she froze.

— I'm sorry, she said, it seems the flesh is weak.

— Or strong, said Flapping Eagle quietly.

Count Aleksandr Cherkassov, Countess Irina Cherkassova, Alexei Cherkassov and Norbert Page were having tea together in the *salon*. Irina fanned herself frequently, though it was not really very hot.

– Ma-ma, said Alexei happily.

– Mama's here, Alexei, said Irina. Mama's always here.

– Irina, said Cherkassov, you are a very strong woman.

– Yes, she said. Yes, I am. I know how to deny myself. And when.

Mr Page caught none of the undertones; he thought they were both rather marvellous.

– It's a great gift, he said nervously, feeling he should offer some sort of conversation. A great gift. To know when to stop.

One word had thrown away the chance. He could have given Elfrida back her peace and contented himself with her soul. He could have given Irina the companionship she lacked and never worried about where her affections lay. Elfrina Eagle, they would have been, and it would have lasted into infinity. Instead of which they were three points again, no longer a triangular one. A single word, changing the course of history.

The farmhouse stood at the side of the road. It was long and low and white. Flapping Eagle felt the shock of recognition: here on his first journey into K he had vaulted this gate and peered through that window into that granite face; here he had been reminded he was pariah. He was different now; he was a part of the place of which the farmhouse was also a part, and so he was a part of the farmhouse. At least, he was today.

Elfrida Gribb was with him; this was the furthest they had walked, but neither of them had noticed the distance, walking in absorbed silence. Now Flapping Eagle told the story of the granite farmer with the face full of crevices and the basilisk eyes.

– Like a man who knew a hundred secrets and wasn't going to reveal even one, he said. Elfrida smiled wanly. Her thoughts were elsewhere.

– Which is rather like everyone I've met in K, said Flapping Eagle. I wouldn't say they keep their secrets to themselves – they simply behave as if they had never known them. There's too much left unsaid. Too much.

Elfrida replied, without looking at him:

– Yes. I believe there is.

– Glad to have you aboard, Flapping Eagle, said Ignatius
Gribb that evening. You're doing Elfrida a power of good. I'm
afraid I'm rather a recluse during the day. It must be difficult
for her to fill her day, eh, darling?
Elfrida forced a smile.
Ignatius Gribb leant quasi-confidentially towards Flapping
Eagle.
– Until you turned up, old chap, she wouldn't have known
what to do without me.
– Really, Ignatius . . . said Elfrida, but Gribb waved her
down cheerily.
– Which is only proper, he went on. Because I wouldn't know
what to do without her.
– A happy marriage is a wonderful thing, said Flapping
Eagle, feeling like a gargantuan bastard.
Elfrida Gribb left the room.

– One look and I knew, Irina was saying. He's a bad influence
on poor, innocent Elfrida. You've only got to look at him.
– Appearances are deceptive, hedged Aleksandr Cherkassov.
– I'm sure there's something between those two, said Irina.
In my opinion, you ought to have a word with Ignatius.
– Whatever for?
– Why, to warn him, of course. To warn him about his guest.
– I don't think one . . .
– If you don't, I will, she snapped.
– I tell you what, said Aleksandr Cherkassov worriedly. I'll
speak to Flapping Eagle. Straighten him out. You know.
– You stupid, stupid man, said Irina Cherkassova angrily.
Events, however, were to move faster than her anger.

*For all that it is over, Flapping Eagle told the mirror, and
despite the tragedies surrounding it, and whatever dark horrors
may come, that was a supreme moment, a moment of clarity, a
moment of light.*

– No, said Elfrida Gribb, I don't feel like a walk this morning. You go. I have one or two things to attend to here.
He left her reclining on the chaise-longue, as quiet music
played.

FORTY-SEVEN

When death came to Calf Island, it came anticlimactically, without any warning, wearing soft shoes; it was even a beginning rather than an end. It came matter-of-factly, as though it had been there all the time and had merely decided to make its presence felt; but the consternation it created was entirely undiminished by its manner of arrival.

Flapping Eagle returned from his walk to find a small crowd gathered outside the Gribb home. Norbert Page was there, and Quartermaster Moonshy. Irina Cherkassova stood still at the front door, as though mummified at the moment of entry. She moved mechanically to let him through. No-one spoke to answer his questions.

Count Aleksandr Cherkassov sat perspiring on the chaise-longue; he had picked up Elfrida's petit-point and his hands toyed with it absently.

– What has happened? asked Flapping Eagle.

– We heard a scream, said the Count. One long scream. Flapping Eagle looked around at the silent, empty room.

– WHAT HAPPENED? he shouted. Where is Elfrida?

Cherkassov nodded towards the study. – One long scream, he repeated.

Flapping Eagle lunged at the closed door and into the study. In the silence he imagined he could hear a whine in the corners of his mind.

The shutters on the window were closed, so that the only light in the room entered with Flapping Eagle through the door. There was Ignatius Gribb's desk, littered with papers and files, quills and home-made ink. There were his books, scattered on desk-top, chair, floor, falling out of shelves and off ledges. The untidiness alone was a scandal to the eye in this house.

The bed was immediately beneath the window. A figure lay upon it, still, dead, shadowed in the shuttered gloom. Another figure stood by the bed, still, alive, also shadowed. An unlit candle stood at a table by the bedside.

The figure on the bed was the short, bent corpse of Ignatius

Quasimodo Gribb, sometime professor of philosophy, bigot and sage.

The standing figure was his newly-widowed wife, Elfrida Gribb, who had been Elfrida Edge, who had thought her falling father was a chimneypot.

— I killed him, she said. It was me.

> 'Frida Gribb
> 'Frida Gribb
> Killed her hubby
> That's no fib.

Flapping Eagle closed the door behind him. The room darkened; he moved to the bedside. There were old coins on Ignatius Gribb's closed eyelids.

— His eyes were open, said Elfrida. I had to close his eyes.

He held her shoulders in his hands. — Look at me, he said. She continued to hang her head. — Elfrida! he said sharply and it lifted slowly.

— One less secret, she said. I love you.

He was looking at Ignatius Gribb's body. It wore, spotlessly, a silk shirt and cravat, a smoking-jacket, a rather incongruous pair of very aged cord trousers and carpet slippers. Its mouth was puckered and slightly open, like a fish.

— Death with dishonour, said Elfrida. He didn't just lose his life.

— There are no wounds on the body, said Flapping Eagle. No marks.

— Not his body, she said dully. I killed him in the head. I had to close his eyes. After opening them.

She broke down; the glacial control slipped; the tears flowed. She clutched at Flapping Eagle. — I love you, she said. I love you, I love you, I love you.

— You told him, didn't you? said Flapping Eagle, understanding.

— Yes, she said, in a tiny whisper. I killed him.

It was not hard to reconstruct what had happened. Elfrida, goaded by jealousy, had taken the plunge she had fought so unwillingly but so effectively for so long. But, being Elfrida, the plunge had to be as final, as irrevocable as her previous dedication to Ignatius. So she had refused to accompany Flapping Eagle on his walk and while he was safely out of the way had bearded her husband in his lair and told him she no longer loved him. In Virgil's terms, she had transferred obsessions from Ignatius to Flapping Eagle. Who thought: guess whose fault that makes it.

It had transfixed Ignatius like a thunderbolt. Even away from Calf Island it might well have broken him. These two had survived by their mutual interdependence, shielding each other from the wounds and calumnies of the world, two vulnerable people lying back to back in a marriage bed, for safety. No doubt her love had been the entire foundation of his arrogant air of self-certainty. The love of a beautiful woman can easily provide such a support for a stunted man. He had drawn from her the strength and courage which enabled him to form and hold, not just his theories and opinions, but his entire personality. She was his peace of mind, his alienable crutch, his perfect match, and she had withdrawn. Men had done away with themselves for less.

But this was Calf Mountain; and in the field of the Grimus Effect, suicide had been unnecessary. Flapping Eagle could almost see the gutted brain within the coined head. Because Elfrida's words had done more than upset Ignatius. They had broken through the unconscious, ingrained defence mechanism, the mental barrier he had built for almost every member of the community of K. Elfrida's withdrawal had removed the cornerstone of the persona he had built; and in that instant, when everything which had seemed sure was suddenly flung into a state of flux, the fever of the Inner Dimensions had swarmed over him.

What must he have felt like, Flapping Eagle asked himself, at that second, as he felt that inner multiplicity seizing him, soft and unprepared and unable to control it as he was behind those broken defences? What must it have been like to be possessed and annihilated by the very force whose denial he had made his primary contribution to the town. Death with dishonour indeed.

And what of K itself, K which rested on Gribb's theories, on his technique of Prime Interest and on his preoccupation with the here-and-now of life? Ignatius' death had shown that there was a Something, an invisible force at work upon them, and it had destroyed its arch-opponent with terrifying swiftness. Could their minds remain shut in the face of his death? Flapping Eagle was certain that some at least would not be able to remain so.

Guilt descended upon him like a soft dark avalanche, breaking the pale magical spell Irina and Elfrida had woven. He flagellated himself more cruelly than O'Toole could ever have managed. He, who had fallen so willingly into the way of K, subscribing to the illusion of permanence, betraying his own experience for the sake of a home and a triangular love. He, who had despised the man who had shown him the true nature of the island and helped him to survive it. Was social acceptability and the companionship of two beautiful women worth the damage he had wrought? Patently not; and even that was lost. Flung out by Irina, faced with a changed Elfrida, he was probably also in danger of his life. He shrugged. He could not find it in him to value his life very highly, not now that his ability to bring disaster upon those around him had reached this new peak. Selfish, Jocasta had said. That was the understatement of all time.

– I'll look after you, Elfrida was saying. I promise. I'll look after you for ever. If you will look after me.

– Elfrida . . . he said helplessly, but his voice trailed off into silence; he could think of nothing to say.

– I love you, you see, she said. You don't need anyone else. You don't, do you?

Light came into the room. Count Aleksandr Cherkassov stood in the doorway. There was a curl of distaste on his lips, overlying the shock in his eyes.

– It's not murder, said Flapping Eagle. She didn't murder him. There was no violence.

– Was there not, said Cherkassov and left the house.

Elfrida Gribb clung to Flapping Eagle as if her life depended on it. Which, in a sense, it did.

He held her there, and they stood for a long time by the corpse of the Way of K.

FORTY-EIGHT

Four graves, void sentinels at the forest's edge, fresh-made holes in Valhalla, stood at the spot where Flapping Eagle and Virgil Jones had looked across the plain an emotional age ago. It was a still morning, the light mists swirling, the mountain remaining impenetrable behind discreet clouds. Virgil, wet with fatigue, his feet complaining, his tongue licking feverishly at his lips, his eyes peering, watched the approaching procession. His limbs gathered their forces; soon they would have to undo their work. Piles of earth, dark and slightly moist, stood in attendance by the tombs.

Femme fatale. If the cap fits, wear it. One by one they fall around me; dead men around me, unborn life within. Poor, stupid count, lanced in his feeble head. I watched him die, leaving the house of death, so silent, so distant, passing without a word, into the garden, I behind, he ahead, looking ahead. A giggle from Alexei, idiot, offspring laughing at bemused parent, a chess piece falling to the ground, and back, back to the house, to sit and stare. Poor hidebound anachronism that he was, finding comfort in the arms of whores, finding none in mine, and now, when I wished to, I could give him none. Staring and smoking, as if death would waft away on the fumes. There, in the past, pinching little Sophie Lermontov's little rump, gallant he was at balls and in war, but the past was receding now, present horror ousting past pleasure, as he sat and stared and smoked. The triviality of it, to die for the death of a Gribb, his frail mind stabbed by the death of a Gribb. I watched him die, his eyes turned to some other world, his hands and lips as they moved in an unseen, unheard life, I watched it all: as he came to his feet, stiffly to his feet, erect and handsome, my idiot adonis, crumpling then before his ghostly executioners, no, no, no blindfold please, a cheroot before you shoot. The ghostly executioners – I did not see or hear them, the ghosts of his assassins, but it was them. I was not surprised to find him dead. But Page, little worshipping Norbert, last of the serfs, who wanted only to serve us, so good with Alexei he was; small man that he was, good innocent Page, he would not die for a Gribb, yet for a Cherkassov to die so broke him. While the Cherkassov stood firm in the Way of K, all the Gribbs on earth could perish without harming him. But if the trunk of the tree should fall, there is little hope for the branches. He died when he knew, when he knew the Cherkassov had fallen, invaded by Grimus, there, I have said it, died as Alexei laughed and played.

Femme fatale. It is my lot. I accept it. The grief, accepted. The pain, accepted. Let them fall around me. I shall not fall, I shall bear the burden. But not the blame. Let blame fall where it belongs, upon the living occupants of the house of death, upon her, mealy-mouthed whited sepulchre, and him, the murderous eagle. The Countess Irina shoulders no blame.

Anthony St Clair Peyrefitte Hunter was in the Elbaroom when the news of Gribb's death arrived. His first reaction had been a savage delight. – Now we'll see, he said. Now perhaps we can stop lying.

One-Track Peckenpaw gave him an uninterested glance. So Gribb was dead. So what? Peckenpaw could do without Gribb. A man did what a man had to do to stay alive. A man believed what a man had to believe to survive. One Gribb wasn't going to change that.

The uninterested glance turned to alarm as the Two-Time Kid clutched his head suddenly and fell against the bar. His expression was one of total disbelief.

Self-deception operates at different levels, and Hunter was certainly unaware of the extent to which he had come to depend on his posture. He had become the Two-Time Kid, and an elegant, cynical disenchantment with K was a part of that role. Beneath it, he was just as afraid, just as unwilling to admit the reality of Grimus and his Effect, as Gribb or Aleksandr Cherkassov. The Dimensions took him unawares and gripped him with their fever only because his self-deception ran even deeper than the rest; he had convinced himself that it did not exist, that his mind was not closed to the implications of Grimus. The storm the Inner Dimensions unleashed upon him, scalding his nerve-centres, burning out the synapses of a brain which could not accommodate the new realities invading it, proved otherwise.

Peckenpaw saw him fall forwards, saw his head strike the

floor; and ho amount of shouting and shaking did any good. Hunter's end was the quickest of all.

One-Track Peckenpaw was beside himself, in the grip of some great emotion. He would not let Hunter be dead. He would not.

— Come on, little bastard, he cajoled. Come on, you little two-timer, it's okay, it's okay, it's okay. He shook the body like a limp rag.

— It's no use, said Flann O'Toole, with unnatural gentleness. Leave him, One-Track, it's no use. He put a hand on the giant bear's shoulder.

Peckenpaw rose, taking Hunter's body into his arms.

— Someone's to blame, he said to the room at large. Some-one's paying for this, *soon.*

He carried the body to the door, then spoke to the room again.

— I'm taking him home now. The Two-Time Kid. He died with his boots on.

There were no coffins. Ignatius Gribb, Norbert Page and the Two-Time Kid had been wrapped in rough woollen blankets from the stores. Count Aleksandr Cherkassov had been swaddled in a sheet embroidered with his coat-of-arms. Each body was carried in a simple hammock, strung between two poles, a pall-bearer at each corner. Most of K followed the Chief Mourners in a tearful crocodile. The chief mourners were Elfrida, accompanied by Flapping Eagle, Irina Cherkassova and One-Track Peckenpaw.

Count Aleksandr Cherkassov had become titular head of K by default. Even Flann Napoleon O'Toole preferred to limit his empire to the alcoholic environment of the Elbaroom. But titular head he was, and now that he was dead, his duties passed naturally and without question to his son.

Leading the procession, smiling with the happiness of a child learning a new game, was Count Alexei Aleksandrovich Cher-kassov.

The funeral service was short and simple, eschewing any pretence at religiosity. The chief mourners said a few words, earth was scattered, and that was that. Alexei Cherkassov, a fool at the head of the blind, stood smiling silently in the light mist, an epitaph incarnate.

– My husband, said Elfrida Gribb, was a man more sinned against than sinning. He was the salt of the earth, the flower of his generation, the rock on which we stood. He was a good man and a loving husband.

It was appropriate that the author of the All-Purpose Quotable Philosophy should be commemorated by a string of clichés. Elfrida moved away from the head of the grave to grasp Flapping Eagle's arms. Irina Cherkassova glared.

One-Track Peckenpaw loomed hugely over the grave of Two-Time Hunter, a tragic goliath mourning the loss of his david. He could not have formed words to express what he felt but he had become aware that amid the gibes and insults the two of them had habitually hurled at each other had been an important bond, the mutual need of opposites.

He said: – The Two-Time Kid was one of the best.

Irina Cherkassova had two speeches to make. She stood in the stillness with her chin tilted up behind her veil, the very archetype of bereaved pride. She spoke briefly of the loyalty and selflessness of Norbert Page, and Alexei Cherkassov clapped his hands as she spoke his name. Then, moving to her husband's grave, she said:

– It would be a slur upon my husband's memory if his death were to break down what we have built. The Way of K is a good Way. Nothing will change.

Flapping Eagle, listening to the defiant sentences, heard in them an echo of Dolores O'Toole; but he also heard a clue, a reason for the continued survival of most of K, which he had feared would fall under the spell of the Dimensions to the last man. Those who had survived the shock were those (like Irina) for whom the Way of K had become, not just a means of defence, but an end in itself, a way of life which preserved them in the cocoon of the past and the minutiae of the present. That was what they *wanted*. Thus Irina had simply assimilated her losses into her tragic self-image, and Peckenpaw had made Hunter a part of his own, often-told legends. For these people, the Grimus Effect was resistible. They had built an alternative to it, from necessity, and the alternative had become an independent thing. The Effect could not invade them: they had sunk too deeply into themselves.

– Fill the graves, gravedigger, said Flann O'Toole, and the ceremony was over.

Three things happened before the gathering dispersed which showed that despite Irina's funeral speech, K would not remain entirely unaltered. The first of these occurred when Elfrida went up to Irina and said:

– I'm so sorry.

Irina looked at her with the practised contempt of generations and said:

– I do not speak to whores.

Elfrida, already pale, turned white as the Countess walked away.

The second event, offsetting this sharp estrangement of old friends, was a reconciliation. P. S. Moonshy approached Irina haltingly, avoiding her eyes, playing with a coat-button.

– Countess, he said, if Count Alexei should lack a games companion, I . . . I would be willing to . . . when time permits . . .

– Thank you, Mr Moonshy, said Irina.

K was closing ranks instinctively, reaffirming its unity against its resurgent enemy.

The third thing that happened was this:

One-Track Peckenpaw and Flann O'Toole had been murmuring together. They now approached the departing Flapping Eagle and Elfrida Gribb.

Peckenpaw said: – I got something to say to you.

Flapping Eagle and Elfrida stopped.

– Seems to us, said Peckenpaw, this all began when you hit town. Folks are saying the two of you been screwing each other, too. We don't care for that kind of thing in this town.

– What are you saying, Mr Peckenpaw? said Elfrida coolly. Please be explicit.

– What I'm saying, *Mrs Gribb*, said Peckenpaw, accentuating the title with heavy scorn, is it's maybe time certain people got the hell out.

– You do understand, said Flann O'Toole.

– I love you, said Elfrida Gribb, because I've stopped being a child. I don't need protection now. I need you. You made me see what I was clinging to in Ignatius: more a father than a lover. Whereas you, my love, will be a lover. I know it. We shall look after each other and make love. You've forced me to grow up and I'm glad. I don't want to be good any more.

– Glad? said Flapping Eagle. Glad, when it killed the man who loved you?

– You love me, said Elfrida, attacking his clothes. Show me.

– It's imposible, said Flapping Eagle. We've just buried him.

– I love you, now, said Elfrida. Now. This minute. This second.

– Not now, said Flapping Eagle.

She broke away from his embrace; and her love increased the burden of his guilt.

FORTY-NINE

Flapping Eagle went into K the next day, to collect food and a few other things from Moonshy's stores. From the moment he entered the town, he knew that Peckenpaw had not been making empty threats. People stopped and stared as he passed, as though aghast at his temerity. The flavour of those old films seen in the fleapit at Phoenix filled the streets; K had become Peckenpaw-land, a small town of the Old West; and Flapping Eagle was, after all, a Red Indian. He half-expected a sheriff to emerge through swing-doors and gun him down then and there.

P. S. Moonshy was busy behind a counter, weighing things on scales. There was only one other customer in the room, but Moonshy ignored Flapping Eagle completely. When the woman left, Flapping Eagle said : – It's my turn, I think.

– Think again, said P. S. Moonshy.

– Look, just give me the food and I'll go, said Flapping Eagle, offering his list.

– No food, said P. S. Moonshy.

One-Track Peckenpaw was in the street when Flapping Eagle emerged empty-handed. – Wal, he said, if it ain't the Indian. He placed himself between Flapping Eagle and his donkey.

Flapping Eagle resolved on a policy of polite firmness. – If you'll excuse me, he said, I'd like to get back to Mrs Gribb and tell her we're to be starved out of town.

– Sure, said Peckenpaw. Wouldn't dream of standing in your way. He didn't move. Flapping Eagle tried to get round him to the waiting donkey; but Peckenpaw shot out one huge, clawing hand and grabbed Flapping Eagle by the neck. It was useless to struggle, so Flapping Eagle went limp. Peckenpaw glared at him.

– Now don't get me wrong, he said. I ain't prejudiced. But if you're still around tomorrow, I'll be coming looking.

With his free hand, he delivered a devastating rabbit-punch. Flapping Eagle was sick on the cobbles. Peckenpaw threw him down into the mess and walked away.

Flapping Eagle crawled on to the donkey and made his way home.

– We've got to leave here, he said to Elfrida.

– Why? she asked. It's my house now. Our house.

– Look, they won't feed us if we stay and they'll probably try and force us out anyway. You can't resist a whole town.

– If you go, my love, she said, I shall of course accompany you. Her face was reposed and calm, her manner collected if subservient.

– We'll go, then, he said.

– Where will you take me? she asked.

Where, indeed. She had the strength of obsession to survive the journey down the mountain again – if she could survive the effect in K, she could certainly do so where it was less strong. But Elfrida Gribb had not been made for rough journeys; and Dolores O'Toole would scarcely welcome the 'Spectre of Grimus' back into her home. Besides, it smacked of deserting the scene of the crime. His crime. They could not go back. There was no going back for him. And if he was to go on, up the mountain, into the unknown clouds, what would he do there? Even worse, what would *she* do there? He shook his head. He needed guidance.

Guidance. Virgil Jones sweating at the graveside. Flapping Eagle had thought Virgil had winked at him, once, during the ceremony. Was it possible he bore no grudge? Virgil, whom he had slighted so callously?

– We'll have to go to Madame Jocasta's, he said, thinking aloud. I can't think of anywhere else.

– I scarcely think she will welcome *me*, said Elfrida.

– We'll both have to, um, eat a quantity of crow, said Flapping Eagle. I didn't go down too well with her either.

– She probably didn't like your face, said Elfrida enigmatically.

– There's nothing for it, said Flapping Eagle. I must talk to Virgil again. And I don't think they'll come for us there, somehow.

– The brothel, murmured Elfrida. Why not, why not.

He had on his old, worn, travelling clothes. Ignatius Gribb, tidy as Elfrida until his last rage, had even preserved his head-scarf and feather. Smiling wryly, he put those on as well. If he was to be in a bad Western, he might as well wear the full uniform.

He had to see Irina Cherkassova, since he had to return the late Count's clothes. She took them from him in the doorway, making no move to invite him in.

– Don't think I didn't see through you, she said. Even in his clothes.

– What do you mean? asked Flapping Eagle. You made me your friend.

– I told the Count, she said. I saw it in your face. The evil.

She shut the door, and he never saw her again.

Exactly on the seventh knock, the door was opened. Madame Jocasta looked at the pair of them in amazement. Elfrida returned her gaze calmly, twirling her parasol. She was dressed entirely in white lace.

– Is there something you want? asked Jocasta, discouragingly.

– Yes, said Flapping Eagle. This was no time to stand upon one's pride. We seek sanctuary.

Jocasta smiled without humour. – No, she said and began to close the door.

– What do you want me to say? cried Flapping Eagle. That I've seen the error of my ways? I have. That I was an inhumanly selfish bastard? I was. That I treated Virgil badly, and with every reason for treating him well? It's true. I accept all of it. Will you not accept a genuine admission of guilt? How do you think it feels to be even indirectly responsible for four deaths?

– Murderous, I expect, said Jocasta, unrelenting.

– If you don't let us in, said Flapping Eagle, you'll be responsible for two more. They won't let us have any food.

– O hello, said a voice. Media was looking over Jocasta's shoulder in open pleasure.

– Media, go and fetch Virgil, said Jocasta. It's up to him.

Virgil Jones came downstairs looking delighted.

– My dear Flapping Eagle, he said. My dear Mrs Gribb. How very nice.

– Virgil, said Flapping Eagle. You may think I'm only saying this because I'm in trouble, because I made a choice that didn't work out, but it's not so. I was very wrong. My behaviour towards you was morally indefensible. I can only say I know it, and I am sorry.

Virgil listened to this speech solemnly, but his eyes were not serious.

– Rubbish, he cried gaily when Flapping Eagle had finished. We all have to make our mistakes. Welcome to the fold.

– You want me to let him in? asked Jocasta, dubiously.

– Of course, said Virgil. He's a friend of mine.

– What about her? asked Jocasta. Saint Elfrida, wearing white on the day after her husband's funeral. I haven't heard any note of contrition from her.

Elfrida said : – I am no better than you, and no worse.

– Please, Virgil, said Flapping Eagle. She's not herself.

– That's an improvement, said Madame Jocasta, giving in. Well, come in then, you two wretches, don't just stand there.

Media's smile of welcome more than compensated for Jocasta's reluctant tone.

The room faced the rising mountain, whose occluded peak glowered through its one window. It was not a beautiful room; it would probably have seemed entirely nondescript but for the carvings.

The carvings were hideous.

It was not that they were grotesque, for the grotesque, expertly depicted, becomes beautiful. It was not that their subjects were hideous; even ugly heads can be moving, given the right treatment. The carvings were simply and without any question extremely ugly, seemingly lacking any purpose or aesthetic drive except that of making the world seem vile and hateful. Even that was pitching it too high. The carver had possessed less skill than even Flapping Eagle, who was no artist.

The carvings stared down from the walls and made the room a darker place.

– Liv's room, said Virgil Jones. Hasn't been used since, you know, she left with, er, me. Liv's carvings, I hope you don't mind them, I brought them back when, er, I stayed here some time ago. Before I left K, you know. But never mind that. It's a bed.

One bed, Elfrida Gribb lay down on it at once. A moment later she was sound asleep. No doubt her nerves, on which she had been living ever since Ignatius' death, had finally rebelled and demanded a period of regeneration. Flapping Eagle felt frankly relieved.

Virgil left him alone, saying : – Gather your strength, that's the thing. He moved over to the window, averting his eyes from the misshapen objects on the walls, and looked out at the mountain. A fly settled on his cheek; he brushed it away. It settled on his other cheek; he brushed it away again. The third time, he slapped at it, and it was crushed against his face. He wiped the corpse away.

Despite the ugliness of the carvings, despite the presence of Elfrida Gribb, despite the absence of any sense of direction, Flapping Eagle felt safe here. The brothel air was heavy with the scent of solace. But sanctuary was not for him, or at any rate not for long. If he had failed to achieve stasis – failed, that is, to ingrain himself into the Way of K – he would have to revert once more to kinesis. But that involved knowing what to do, not only with himself, but with Elfrida.

Flapping Eagle stared at the mountain. – You're winning, he said aloud. He turned to the bed and flung himself down beside the sleeping Elfrida, to gaze emptily at the ceiling. Soon he, too, was asleep, tired and asleep.

Media came into the room to watch him dream. Looking at his face, the face that had changed her life, the firm-jawed face with the shadow of a beard and the closed, long-lashed eyes, she began to think heresy. Perhaps it had something to do with being in Liv's room; Liv who had left the brothel and its safety for the sake of a man (hard to imagine now that that man had been Virgil Jones); Liv who had placed herself and her desires above her duties, and seized her moment; but Media, watching the dreaming face, was forming this thought in her mind :

Where he goes, I go.

It was the face that did it.

She spoke softly to the sleeping Eagle :

– What you need is a woman who can cope with you, she said.

Madame Jocasta was pacing the corridors of her realm again; but she was not enjoying it, not listening for the sounds behind the doors, for, at Virgil's request, she had closed the House's doors. Silence everywhere. In her own room, a moody, pensive Virgil; in her predecessor's room, the hidden forms of two people who, she was afraid, would change her small world, too much, far too much. Already Virgil was lost within himself; already Media was afflicted with Flapping Eagle, despite her allotted speciality.

She stood silently outside the door of Liv's room, which was fractionally ajar, and heard Media's voice speak its one sentence. She retreated quietly, her worries redoubled.

But she had given them sanctuary, she thought; she would not, could not break that pledge.

At the head of the mob were Flann O'Toole and One-Track Peckenpaw. There were perhaps a dozen more, all regular customers of the Elbaroom. They carried sticks, stones and a length of rope.

– The House is closed, said Jocasta from the door.

– 'Tis not your women we're afther, said O'Toole in a thick voice, flowing with the fumes of potato-whisky. 'Tis that bastard Eagle.

– We got a harmless little lynching in mind, said Peckenpaw.

– I see, said Jocasta. You want a scapegoat.

– Jesus forbid, grinned Flann O'Toole. But the slightest consideration shows how all our troubles began with his coming. 'Tis entirely logical to speed his going, is it not, now?

– Flann O'Toole, said Madame Jocasta. You know what place this is. When anyone enters the House they leave the world behind. It is a place to escape to; no evil comes here. Flapping Eagle has sanctuary. If you take him by force, the House loses its meaning for you all. You will be hanging a part of your own town. Is that what you want?

The crowd shuffled morosely. Flann O'Toole stopped grinning.

– Now listen, Jocasta, he lurched. What in God's name are you protecting him for? Now you know we wouldn't do a thing like that, violating the sanctity o' the House and all, but that Eagle, he's no friend to you, or your Mr Jones.

— Go away, O'Toole, said Jocasta.

— Okay, said Peckenpaw. Okay, Jocasta. You win. But we'll keep watch right here on your doorstep. And if he shows his pretty face outside, Virgil Jones'll have some more digging to do.

Bestowing a contemptuous look on him, Jocasta closed the door. The look made no impression on One-Track Peckenpaw.

FIFTY

Flapping Eagle sat at Virgil Jones' feet, or, more precisely, sat beside him on the low bed in Jocasta's room as Virgil spoke. There was a satisfaction on Virgil's face and an excitement in his voice, but of a faintly morbid kind, the satisfaction and excitement of a man who senses events are running his way once more, but is highly uncertain of his power to direct them. A spider wove its webs on the ceiling.

— More cases of fever, said Virgil Jones. Certainly there will be more. I'm afraid K is vulnerable now. The Achilles heel exposed. An object lesson in the fragility of the best defences. And make no mistake, the Way of K was a very expert defence. They practised their eyes-to-the-ground life for so long, it became second nature. Hence the confusing illusion of normality you succumbed to, and that entrancing, ethereal quality. They lived here, but they lived *for* their preoccupations, and thus seemed detached, intoxicated, complete. The expertise grew with the power of the Effect, keeping pace, and they might well have resisted it forever. Gribb's death changed all that. Now there are many who find it an effort to keep their minds off Grimus. And they need to, whereas before the deaths they could even joke about him. Hence the determination of the lynch-mob. Hence the attitude of Mrs Gribb. I'm not sure she is so much in love with you. She needs to love, that's more important. It will get worse; for now, the instant they relax, they will be open to the Dimensions. Some of them will die. Which will make the rest even more manic. A gloomy prospect, I'm sure you'll agree.

– Jocasta and her girls don't seem to suffer, said Flapping Eagle.

– Ah, said Virgil. There you have the extraordinary nature of this House in a nutshell. A refuge, you see, from the Effect as well as the mob. Because, as you hazarded earlier, it has become, for them, an end in itself. The only thing that matters to them. Though I fear you may be unsettling dear Media, you know. You do have almost as powerful an effect on women as, as Grimus, ha ha.

– I'm sorry, said Flapping Eagle stupidly.

– The simple fact, said Virgil Jones, is that Grimus is in possession of a stupendous piece of knowledge: that we live in one of an infinity of Dimensions. To accept the nature of the Dimensions involves changing, entirely, our ideas of what we are and what our world is like. Thus rewriting the book of morality and priorities from the beginning. What you must ask yourself is this: is there such a thing as too much knowledge? If a marvellous discovery is made whose effects one cannot control, should one attempt to destroy one's find? Or do the interests of science override even those of society, and, indeed, survival? Is it better to have known, and die, than not to have known at all? A fair number of questions, I'm afraid.

– And you've decided, said Flapping Eagle, that science must yield.

– At this time, in this place, this piece of knowledge is an untenably dangerous thing, said Virgil Jones sadly.

Virgil Jones examined his corns, wiggling his toes. Flapping Eagle sat in silence, watching the spider. Eventually, Virgil spoke again.

– They treat me like an idiot here, he said, because I went through a phase of behaving like one. Just after my . . . disagreement . . . with the Inner Dimensions. And Liv. I ran around town once with my sex hanging out. I dyed my nose blue. I farted into women's faces with my trousers down. Poor forked creature that I was. Am. I had something to prove, then. That they didn't matter to me. That the island didn't matter. That nothing mattered. Trouble was, I didn't believe any of it myself. So the gestures lacked a certain conviction. In the end

I went down the mountain and discovered dignity instead. The clothing of impotence. Until you arrived.

Flapping Eagle burst out: – Virgil, what shall I do? What is there to do?

– Ah, said Virgil, licking frantically around his lips. That's what I've been getting round to. You can choose between withdrawal, inaction and action. No shame in any of them.

– I don't understand, said Flapping Eagle.

– Withdrawal involves walking out there and getting lynched. Not pleasant. Or sneaking out somehow and going back down the mountain to let events take their course. The blinks, the fever, all of it. Leave it behind. Inaction involves staying put right here and waiting to see if Jocasta throws you to the wolves. Action, however, does rather involve doing what I say.

– You chose inaction, said Flapping Eagle. You haven't done much recently.

– Naturally, said Virgil. I can't do anything. You can.

– It's not that the Inner Dimensions burnt my mind out, said Virgil. Or I couldn't have danced the Strongdance successfully. Call it a kind of paralysis. A seized-up gearbox. It worked in extreme need, in the forest. But my little flutter with the Gorf undid that. And now, because I know it would be much easier for you, the need isn't there. I'm not sure the will is either.

– But you said you'd made up your mind?

– Decisions are easy, said Virgil Jones. They're the easy part.

– The field of what I'll call Dimension-Chaos in which we find ourselves, said Virgil, tutorially, and indeed all Grimus' powers, spring from an object called the Stone Rose. As you've probably guessed. This is what must be destroyed.

There is, actually, a considerable risk. It is possible that this Dimension cannot survive without the Rose. What is certain is that no-one will survive here, except for spiders, flies and animals, unless the Rose is broken. So it is a risk we must take.

– Kill or cure, said Flapping Eagle.

– Precisely, said Virgil. How well put.

– Deggle, you know, said Virgil Jones, unintentionally did the only thing that could have turned me against the Rose. When he broke that piece off the Stem, I mean. One has to ascribe both blinks and probably even the Grimus Effect to malfunctions of the mutilated Rose. It was only a small piece, so it went unnoticed. But it has, ah, damaged the dimension.

— If a small piece can create so much havoc, asked Flapping Eagle, wouldn't we inevitably be destroyed if the whole Rose were broken up?

— Not necessarily, said Virgil. Half a loaf is not always better than no bread.

The weight of his guilt and the feeling of futility within him inclined Flapping Eagle towards agreeing to perform the task. His morale had been steadily declining ever since the death of Ignatius Gribb. Now, faced with the grim alternatives Virgil had offered, it was at its nadir. But something held him back from acquiescing, a fragment, perhaps, of the relatively innocent self he had brought to Calf Island; and, thinking about that self, he found a last glimmering of hope.

— I want your word on two scores, he said to Virgil. First, that Grimus possesses some means of undoing my immortality. There's nothing for me on Calf Mountain, and I know eternity palls in my own world.

— So you're back to that, said Virgil.

— Also, Flapping Eagle forged on, I must know that a way back exists: a way back to the place, world, dimension, whatever, that I came from.

— If we're spared, you'd like to return.

— Yes.

— And if I give you my word, you'll go to Grimus.

— If I can.

Virgil Jones smiled sadly.

— As far as I know, he said, the answer to both your questions is that there are no such certain ways and means of achieving either of your aims.

It was like a sentence of death, confirmed, with no appeal. No way back. The aim of centuries, to return to normal life, dashed; his recent aim, to live contentedly here in K, in ruins. Flapping Eagle was an empty man, a Shell without a Form.

— O hell, he said. I'll do it anyway. Why not?

Virgil Jones smiled his sad smile again. It was tinged with triumph.

*   *   *

The time of action obliterates the process of evaluation. Virgil Jones, champion of doubt, had no time for it now. He was planning Flapping Eagle's ascent to Grimus.

– The Gate to Grimus is similar in type to the one through which you entered the Sea of Calf. Though less crude. Impossible to find it unless you know where it is. Which, as it happens, I do. That's where your conquest of the Inner Dimensions will come in handy. They cannot harm you now, so you can concentrate on moving through the Outer ones. It may not be pleasant, though. Grimus will certainly know you're coming; he may well try and close the Gate. In which case you will have quite a battle to break through. He will also resist any attempt to tamper with the Rose. You'll just have to do what you can, wait for the opportunity, you know, strike when the time is ripe and so forth. Remember this : he's only a man.

– The odds do seem to be just slightly against me, said Flapping Eagle.

– About a hundred to one, said Virgil. And even if you get through . . . Grimus can be a very persuasive man.

– Where's the gate? asked Flapping Eagle mechanically.

– Ah yes, the Gate. Now that will involve escaping the mob. And climbing a little further. As far as, as far as, Liv. The black house, you know.

His voice trailed away lamely.

– I know, said Flapping Eagle. I met her. She sends you her regards.

Virgil jerked himself out of an incipient reverie.

– Met her? he said. Are you quite sure?

– No, said Flapping Eagle. She wore a black veil. From head to foot.

– That's her, said Virgil. That's Liv.

Flapping Eagle looked around the room. Creeping plants on the wall. Creeping spider on the ceiling. It was probably one of the last rooms he would ever see. Facing this, he discovered he didn't particularly mind. He was a spent force now, Virgil's tool, no more. Before coming to Calf Island, he had felt a suicidal urge born of desperation. He was not desperate now; he simply saw no particular value in remaining alive.

– Ah well, said Virgil Jones. It will be, ah, pleasant to see Liv again.

FIFTY-ONE

– By all means, said Jocasta. Go, by all means.

Virgil stood before her like an errant schoolboy, wringing his hands, opening and shutting his mouth as though eternally on the verge of producing an acceptable explanation of his misdeeds.

– Go, repeated Jocasta. If the things we have done for you, the things I have done, mean so little, then please go at once. Go back to her. She'll shred you into tiny pieces, that one. This time there will be nothing left for me to patch up. She sits up there and spins her webs and of course you walk right in. Go, go, be done with it, if you have the urge to wound yourself, I will not stop you any more. Perhaps you are a fool. Perhaps you are mad. It is mad, to go back, after the shame she brought upon you, but go. I will not stand in your way.

– I have to, Jocasta, said Virgil, distressed. I must show Flapping Eagle the Gate.

– Flapping Eagle! she cried. Who returned your kindness with betrayal. Who returned my kindness by intoxicating Media. Who has brought nothing but trouble to all who took him in. You'll do anything for *him*.

Virgil Jones said in a very quiet voice:

– It is Flapping Eagle who is doing this for me.

– All of you, burst Jocasta. Go, all of you. Leave me to my House again.

Elfrida Gribb in white lace, her face veiled, a fly crawling unhindered across the veil, standing at the window, carvings to her right, mountain at her back, Flapping Eagle at her left, disaster staring her in the face.

– You will not go, she said. You cannot, after what I did. I love you, Flapping Eagle. My place is at your side.

He closed his eyes and hardened his voice as much as he could.

– I loved you, he said.

Her eyes turned to stone, green marbles of blindness.

– Loved. The word was not a question. It was a bleak statement.

– Everything has changed, he said miserably. I must go.

– A whore, she said. You think I'm a whore. *I do not talk to whores*. You and her. You planned this, to make me love you, to make me jealous, to ruin me.

– No, he said.

– Whore. Elfrida the whore. Yes, why not. Yes, why not. If my love thinks me a whore, I must live up to his idea of me. Yes, why not. I shall be a whore and earn my keep. Yes, why not, why not.

Why not, thought Flapping Eagle, was the phrase of the moment.

Media, eavesdropping, heard the interchange; and was delighted.

In the kitchen of the House of the Rising Son, amid the desolate pots and pans, the man called Stone ate, the only guest of the night, the one who could not be turned away. Virgil Jones saw him, and the escape was planned.

Flapping Eagle left the house by the side door and crawled out on to the Cobble-way, decrepit as his borrowed clothes, stained as the houses, dusty as the streets, and began to count the cobblestones. He greeted them like old friends. Slowly, tattered hat pulled low over stooping face, he made his way down the night road, pail in one hand, cloth in the other, on his knees, mumbling, polishing.

Madame Jocasta lay in her bed, shut into her room, refusing to know what was happening in her house. Media had volunteered to keep the pebble-cleaner occupied, even though it was a breach of House rules; and while Jocasta turned her face to the wall, Media used every scrap of experience at her command to ensnare Stone, her first man in an eternity, long enough for Flapping Eagle to make good his slow, painfully deliberate escape.

Just before dawn, Virgil Jones left the brothel, bowler hat on head, watchless chain around his waist, humming innocently to himself. The mob had dispersed to its bed, for the most part; but the implacable Peckenpaw sat bearlike on the front doorstep. He looked at Virgil angrily, but let him pass. Virgil went humming up the street, and was interested to notice that it bore no crawling figure. Flapping Eagle had either been discovered or had reached his goal.

At the far end of the Cobble-way, at the point where the town of K yielded to the resurgent slopes of Calf Mountain, the forest regained its supremacy. Thick vegetation concealed the the narrow path, more suited to donkeys than men, which led up to the last habitable point, the rock on which Liv's house stood and looked down on K. Here, in the forest, Virgil and Flapping Eagle made their rendezvous.

– Just like old times, said Virgil Jones.

Media, gone. Flapping Eagle's absence was a relief. Virgil's absence she had fortified herself to expect. But to find a man, and a wretched man at that, in Media's bed, and her nowhere to be seen, was almost more than Jocasta could bear. Media, poor, infatuated Media, Media of all her girls.

Gone, but where? To follow Virgil and Eagle, but how far? And had they asked her, and did they want her, and would she come back cowed and crawling and beg forgiveness? Jocasta wanted to think so but she, too, remembered Liv; and she knew Media would not return, not if she could help it, not if she could . . .

Jocasta walked out into the corridor, silent as it was, and was hit by the third blink there, alone.

She gasped when it passed and leant against a wall. Elfrida Gribb came out of her room, tight-faced, controlled.

And put an arm around her.

– Madame, she said. I should like to stay. To stay . . . and work.

Jocasta looked at her vacantly. Anything was possible now.

– Since we have a sudden vacancy, she said, you're hired.

The two bereaved women stayed there a moment, clutching each other; and then Jocasta, eyes red-rimmed, went down to the front door. Peckenpaw stood as she opened it.

– The House of the Rising Son is open for business, said Madame Jocasta.

It was morning.

FIFTY-TWO

Nicholas Deggle was sitting in the rocking-chair among the early chickens, as he had become accustomed to doing. He was thinking about the blinks.

Mrs O'Toole had apparently been entirely unaware of them. Perhaps her wayward mind simply denied their existence, as it denied the evidence of her eyes and enabled her to see and hear him as Virgil Jones. *Nothing changes.*

But, thought Deggle with a tinge of fear, there was another explanation. Grimus. Grimus had acquired this new, devastating power and was trying to get rid of him. Perhaps Deggle had been the only one affected.

Nicholas Deggle rocked between impotence and paranoia, back and forth. Dolores O'Toole came out of the hut holding a knife. Time to assassinate another chicken.

Dolores sat down on the ground. With the knife in her right hand, and with intense concentration, she slit the vein in her left wrist. Then she transferred the knife to that hand and set about slashing the right wrist, equally methodically. Only now did Deggle emerge from his shock and lunge at the knife. She avoided his grasp and held the blade against her neck.

– What do you think you're doing, for godsake? he cried.

– Every night since we made love, she said. Every night you have refused me. It is obvious, Virgil, that you despise my body. I can't live with you hating me so.

Blood spurted on to the ground, creating small specks of red mud.

What does one do to stop a vein bleeding? Deggle looked around him helplessly. – Bandages, he said aloud.

– Leave me alone, she said, and began to sing, weakly.

Whitebeard is all my joy
and whitebeard is my desire, she sang.

Nicholas Deggle pulled his shirt off, over his head. When he could see again, Dolores lay prone on the ground, a second, red mouth grinning bloodily from ear to ear, beneath her chin. She had finished what she set out to do.

Deggle, bare-chested, shirt in hand, watched the blood until it ceased to flow. This thought crossed his mind:
– It is I who will be alone.
The rocking-chair rocked in the early morning breeze.

FIFTY-THREE

The Gorf, being determined to see Calf Island through to the end, had taken refuge from Virgil Jones' successful accusations in the ever stimulating spectator sport of observing other people's lives.

Gorfs, though their bodies move only with great difficulty, can transport themselves instantly from place to place by a process of physical disintegration and reintegration, supervised by their disembodied Selves. Thus the Gorf had eavesdropped with Elfrida at the Elbaroom and sat in her garden watching as she and Irina and Flapping Eagle took turns upon the swing. He had peered through the windows of the Rising Son and watched the travellers depart. He had been intrigued by the blinks and a dispassionate witness to the suicide of Dolores O'Toole.

Now, awaiting the Final Ordering, he returned constantly to the contemplation of the basic anagram which had given rise to so much of the essence of Calf Island – the Re-Ordering which could be made of the name *Grimus*.

This anagram was *Simurg*.

The Gorf looked forward to the imminent clash of the Eagle, prince of earthly birds, and the Simurg, bird of paradise, wielder of the Stone Rose. He found it very pleasing that the names should contain these primordial symbols. It added spice.

PART THREE

GRIMUS

FIFTY-FOUR

It was dark inside the small blackwashed house, a dark chill quiet. Shadows stood everywhere, insubstantial guards over the unseen ugliness. Outside, the shrouds of Calf Mountain's summit hung over the house like a second, thundery ceiling, shielding it from the pale, mist-weak sunlight lying over the plains beneath. Liv's home, blind and without foundation, stood blankly on the cheerless outcrop, its door firmly shut, the only sign of life a single donkey, tethered to the last tree of the climbing forest, munching at the forest's long grass. A bird shrieked.

The unseen ugliness. Behind the shuttered windows lay a scene of cosmic chaos, the debris of a life wrestling and vying for floor-space. Dust lay thickly over the scattered books and plates. A piece of bread, invisible behind its crust of mould, lay on a broken hand-mirror and a spider etched its web between the two. Cloth, paper and crumb alike succumbed to the encasing envelope of dirt. And above the strewn floor, the carvings glared. Carvings which made their ancestors at the Rising Son seem, by comparison, effusions of beauty and joy. The vile, twisted shapes, faces, bodies, truncated limbs, nightmare landscapes, spoke of a deepening passion in their maker, a deepening slough of loathing. If the carver merely extracts from his raw materials the shapes that already lie within it, then the wood must have been made by demons, to contain such hideous forms.

The interior of the small black house was a single room. Hens sat miserably in cages on a shelf. There was a chair, and a bed. And here was a surprise: for these two pieces were as perfectly clean as the rest of the house was filthy. They were dusted and cared for and the bedclothes were washed. They were pieces from another world.

A shadow sat unmoving in the chair.

To re-enter the forested slopes was to relinquish all illusions of normality, to shake off the air of the town, insanely mundane, mundanely insane. The green light of the trees was a kind of purifier for them both. Here Flapping Eagle felt once more the tangible mystery of the mountain and was cleansed of the webs

214

of his own self-deceit. The mountain would not be ignored. Virgil, too, was in good heart, dragging corpulence and corns uncomplainingly up the steep incline, grasping hummocks of earth and tufts of grass to ease his ascent. The air was alive with the hum of insects and the esoteric messages of birds in flight.

– Magister pene monstrat, Virgil Jones quoted, out of nowhere.

They were resting for a moment. Flapping Eagle was obliged to ask for clarification.

– At school, said Virgil Jones in half-embarrassed recollection. An irritating young twerp chalked that up on the blackboard before the lesson. As a joke. The magister in question took it very well. Simply asked why the word penis was in the Ablative rather than the Accusative. Whereupon the young twerp, showing a degree of nerve, stood up and said: – Please sir, it's the Ablative of the End in View.

They resumed their climb. The excitement of the end in view, whatever it might prove to be, had invaded and conquered them both. If the Mountain was to win, Flapping Eagle told himself, at least it would have to fight for its victory. In the excitement of anticipation, he didn't pause to reflect that he knew few of the rules of the battle or of the purposes of his adversary. He was in it now: that was all that mattered.

The scar on his chest itched.

He noticed that Virgil Jones' fingers, when they were not holding on to clumps of grass, were tightly crossed.

A little way behind them, the secret figure of Media followed, keeping her distance, keeping in touch. They didn't hear her, because they didn't expect to be followed. The mind-whine of the Effect, not so much a sound as a feeling, was stronger now, but in their separate ways they were all defended against it: Media by her new obsession, Virgil by his old paralysis, Flapping Eagle by his recent conquest of the fever.

The shadow sat unmoving in the chair and heard the movements outside. Eventually, it would move. Eventually, it would be time to look at the book under the pillow. Eventually, it would be time to wring a pullet's neck, and eat. Eventually, the movements would have to be investigated. But not for the moment. For the moment, sitting here in the dark was enough.

Liv sat like this a great deal, still, stone, statue.

It was cold on the outcrop, cold and damp. The day had moved into late afternoon. Flapping Eagle stood by Liv's donkey, patting it idly, watching Virgil Jones behaving like a schoolboy on a treasure hunt.

(– *No, he had said, let's not bother to see her. Let's get it done.*)

Sixteen paces forward from the edge of the clearing. He turned right. Sixteen paces right. He stopped. The black house was behind him, impassive. – Here, said Virgil Jones. It should be here.

Flapping Eagle closed his eyes and controlled the wild rushing inside him. It was time. He walked across to Virgil, whose tongue flickered in an agony of tension, the blind guide. Being paralysed by the Rose, he could not himself know if it was the right spot. Flapping Eagle had to be the guinea-pig.

– If you stand where I am standing, said Virgil, and concentrate upon the Gate, you should find it. He moved three paces to his left and crossed his fingers anxiously.

Flapping Eagle lunged forwards suddenly and stood upon the spot.

Again, he closed his eyes.

The Gate, he thought fiercely. *This is the Gate. I am passing through the Gate. This is the Gate. I am passing through. This is the Gate . . .*

Over and over, building power in himself as Virgil had instructed, waiting for the Outer Dimensions to claim him and carry him to Grimus.

Was that a change in climate? Was there a breeze where there had been none before? Did the ground feel strange beneath his feet? Cast out those thoughts, they are a distraction. Concentrate, concentrate. The Gate and I am passing through.

Nothing happened.

Virgil's voice, calling: – Think on the Rose. You're going to the Rose.

A rose made out of stone. It is coming to me, I can hold it in my hand. I am going to hold the rose, hold the rose, hold the rose . . .

Nothing.

He opened his eyes. Virgil was staring at him in anguish.

– What is it? he cried. Is it Grimus? Is he fighting you? Can't you get through? Will, will. That's the thing. Where there's a will, there's a Way.

– Virgil, said Flapping Eagle quietly. This isn't the Gate.

– Of course it is, said Virgil. Of course. It always was. I wouldn't forget.

– There was nothing here, said Flapping Eagle in an empty voice.

– You didn't feel the, the power? asked Virgil. Flapping Eagle shook his head. – Didn't you have a sense of being about to be . . . transported? asked Virgil. Again, Flapping Eagle shook his head. He felt drained, voided by the anticlimax.

Virgil Jones subsided to the hard ground and buried his head in his hands.

– He's moved it.

The words came from him like an echo from a hollow cave. Flapping Eagle knew it was the end. They had failed before they had even begun. Bitterness flooded over him.

– Didn't you know? he asked. Didn't you know he could move the Gate?

Virgil looked up, hearing the tinge of frustrated scorn.

– In theory, he said. Yes, in theory. But in practice . . . He must have become infinitely more expert. It took so much hardship to build. So much pain. It isn't an easy thing, you know. Wasn't. I didn't think he would have.

– You didn't think, said Flapping Eagle, adrenalin forcing the insult to his lips. Virgil looked at him, and his eyes were the eyes of a beaten man.

– We'll find it, he said blankly. Can't have gone far. Don't believe he's that expert. Just have to nose around a bit. It's here all right. We'll find it.

– Yes, said Flapping Eagle, turning away, to face the black house.

A figure stood in the doorway, covered from head to foot in a black veil with a window at eye-level.

– I thought you'd come, said Liv in a flat voice.

Virgil Jones was lurching across the small plateau and muttering to himself. Every so often he would stop, squeeze his eyes shut until moisture ran from the corners and stand in a paralysis of thought. Then he would open his eyes, shake his head, and continue on his lurching way. The Gate continued to elude him.

Liv said:

– Does he imagine I have never searched for the Gate? Does he imagine I have lived here for nothing? I have as much reason to hate Grimus as he has. Does he imagine Grimus to be as great a fool as Virgil Jones?

The flat tones were gone now, replaced by a frightening intensity of passion. The venom in her voice would have alarmed a snake.

– Look, Flapping Eagle, she said. Look at Virgil Jones, your guide and my husband, and equally incompetent at both functions. I look at him and see a man as blindly possessed as any man in K. What do you see? I see a man chasing shadows. What do you see? Come inside, Virgil, she called. Perhaps I've hidden your Gate inside. Come and look for it inside.

Virgil Jones continued to squeeze his eyes and lurch from empty ground to empty ground. He might not even have heard her.

– It is time, she said, turning to Flapping Eagle. It is time you knew all about Virgil Jones. High time you knew how great a fool you are to believe in him.

They stood there for a moment, ingrowing, hate-filled Liv and scarred, colourless Eagle, as Virgil muttered and stumbled his shambling way around them, racked by the gulf between attempt and achievement. There were vast spaces between their lives: Flapping Eagle could almost see the holes. And yet, it was those spaces which bound them irrevocably together, weakness, ignorance and hate, united against their will.

Liv wheeled and went indoors. After a moment's hesitation, Flapping Eagle followed her, leaving the shambling Virgil Jones, vulnerable and wounded, to go his muttering way. It was getting darker.

Media, hiding at the end of the wooded slopes, cried tears of sympathy for their failure.

– Did he tell you about Dimension-fever? said Liv. No. I suspect he wanted you to suffer that, because only by conquering it could you become the man he wanted. Did he tell you the danger you would be in, with your face, in K?

– What about my face? asked Flapping Eagle, perplexed.

– He didn't even tell you that, said Liv. The hooded head shook; the voice was disgusted. Twice already he has risked your life. He was ready to do so again. And he didn't even tell you that.

– He saved my life twice, said Flapping Eagle. And he had my agreement for this attempt. But what about my face?

– Poor idiot boy, said Liv, lying back on her bed. Flapping Eagle sat stiffly on the chair amid the accumulated filth.

– Poor idiot boy, she repeated. Your face is as like the face of Grimus as his own reflection. Younger-looking, paler, but so, so similar. Did you not know that was what attracted him to you in the first place? It was not Bird-Dog he was interested in. It was you. Born-From-Dead.

She knew a lot about him . . .

– Sispy, he said. Sispy and Grimus are one and the same? The reclining, hidden figure nodded.

– Then if my face is so like his, said Flapping Eagle, why did Bird-Dog not tell me so? She would have mentioned it . . . we were close then.

– Grimus, said Liv, is a master of disguise. Don't doubt it, poor stupid double. It was your face that fascinated him. But it was Bird-Dog he got.

A cruel laugh. As his thoughts whirled, Flapping Eagle wished he could see the face behind the hood.

– One other thing, said Liv. Grimus is a very attractive man. Does that perhaps explain some things?

Deggle used to call him pretty-face.

Irina saying: – You are not the man you look . . .

Gribb at the foot of the bed, muttering: – Remarkable, remarkable.

The looks of recognition he had received in the Elbaroom, and Peckenpaw saying: – Jones and a stranger, in that loaded voice.

The Spectre of the Stone Rose.

The Spectre of Grimus . . .

That was why Irina Cherkassova had been drawn to him so instantly. That was why Elfrida Gribb had been attracted, too. That was why the girl Media had stared at him so compulsively. That was why Jocasta had disliked him instinctively. He was living behind another man's features, reaping both the rewards and the whirlwind of his personality. That was why.

– I see that it does, said Liv dryly. She stretched lazily on the bed. How fascinating it is to watch the truth at work on people.

– The truth, mumbled Flapping Eagle.

– And now, she said, I shall tell you the truth about me. I shall tell you because you've been starved of truth. This is the truth about Liv : she hates Grimus. She hates Virgil. She hates this infernal mountain.

– But she lives, said Flapping Eagle.

– Hate, said Liv, is the nearest thing on earth to power. One does not give up power easily.

Flapping Eagle was about to speak, but she silenced him.

– It's time to look at the book, she said, and reached under her pillow.

Sitting in this slum of a room, his hopes of redemption shattered by the mumbling failure outside, reduced to the status of a pawn in someone else's game by the truth from this hooded oracle, Flapping Eagle learnt the story of Calf Mountain; learnt it when he believed there was no longer anything he could do about it. As usual, he was wrong about that.

The carvings stared down from the wall as Liv brought the old, old notebook out from under the pillow, wrapped in rough black cloth.

– In those days, she said, Virgil kept a diary. It makes interesting reading.

A hen squawked irrelevantly from the shelf.

– I shall now read from it, she said, and began to recite. Recite, because the room was dark, and getting darker by the second as evening drew on and even the faintest light withdrew. She knew the book by heart.

Wodensday 19th June.
My diaries have always been my friends. The written word is so much more constant than human beings. Honest, too. Holding up a constant mirror to one's own inadequacies, but without malice. There's friendship if you like.

The fact is, my friend, you are going to have to be more understanding today than ever you were. The things I am about to tell you are true, but you could easily be forgiven for disbelieving them. You must not disbelieve.

A tide in the affairs of men which, taken at the flood, leads on to fortune. Dear Brutus. I wonder if he was right. Certainly it is high tide in my affairs. The link between floods and fortune is somewhat tenuous, however. But I am circling round my subject. Perhaps I am reluctant to begin. I shall begin.

My old failures you know: it was sheer laziness, a butterfly quality of the mind, that thwarted my archaeological aspirations. Ironic that idleness should have led so directly to manual labour. But debts must be paid and I do know how to dig. Even if I now inter where once I exhumed. I think of myself as a layer of evidence for future archaeologists. I must; I can see no other dignity in my present labour.

As you further know, Nicholas Deggle arranged for my present employment. He came to see me yesterday. (My apologies for not writing then. Events had me by the scruff of the neck.) I think he came to ridicule. It is his most unfortunate trait. Forgivable perhaps from a creditor. Understandable perhaps when considering my employment.

Not only am I a gravedigger, my friend, but a digger of pets' graves! I have been burying beloved spaniels and lamented moggies by the score. Everyone has to start somewhere, they say. There could scarcely be a more humble beginning.

The pets' section of the cemetery is at its very edge, next to a piece of overgrown woodland. Having consigned my third lap-dog to the soil, I went here to eat my small lunch: two biscuits and a piece of cheese. It was here that I found the Thing.

At first I thought it was a mislaid tombstone. On closer inspection I realized it was not so easily explicable. It is about the height of a man and perfectly carved in stone. It looks like a highly geometric rose, and that is what we now call it: the Stone Rose.

It stood in the middle of a bush. I don't think it was deliberately concealed there. It just *was* there. I cleared a way to it, scratching my hands and tearing my coat-sleeve a fraction.

This is where you must begin to suspend your disbelief, my friend. I touched it and an entirely terrifying thing happened. My head swirled, strange pictures formed before my eyes. I must have fainted. I awoke on the ground by the Rose, dusty and with a couple more scratches. I'm ashamed to say my first instinct was flight. I returned to my duties and buried a few more animals. Then Deggle arrived. It was his condescension that led me back to the Rose. I wanted to see if it had the same effect on him. If it did, he would soon stop sneering.

It did. I was forced to resuscitate him by splashing water over him. I say forced: I must confess I used more than was necessary.

We emerged from the wood, shaken and greatly frightened, to find ourselves being scrutinized by a tallish, fairish man, who somehow gave the appearance of being a good deal older than he was. I suppose he is in his middle fifties and is actually very well-preserved, but he seems older. If that is not too oxymoronic a statement. He had brought us a bird to bury, a highly coloured bird of paradise. He said his name was Grimus; by his accents he is evidently Middle-European, a refugee no doubt.

We must have looked a fright, for he asked us instantly what the matter was. After a brief discussion, during which he looked increasingly interested, we led him into the wood and he tried his hand at the Rose. He staggered away from it, clasping his head; but he did not faint. Which instantly gave him a kind of seniority over us. Perhaps that is why we agreed to keep the Rose a secret for a while, until we understood it better.

He invited us to his home that evening to talk further. Already we seemed to have entered a conspiracy with this man. He returned to the cemetery as I was completing my duties with an empty coffin. Using ropes and sticks, we unearthed the rose and placed it in the coffin without touching it. He had brought his large estate car to the wood and we smuggled our treasure out like three grave-robbers, feeling criminal though we had committed no crime.

Grimus' house is in a dingy suburban terrace in the south-west extreme of the city. It is as dingy inside as out, and cluttered with a quite amazing variegation of objects and books. There are a number of stuffed birds and evidence of wide travel. There are pictures, Oriental I think, everywhere and again the theme is preponderantly ornithological. Grimus is interested in mythical birds and as he talked he seemed curiously bird-like himself, his hands fluttering and his voice a rushing twitter. In my amateur way, I share his interests; moreover he has the quality of interesting others in his own preoccupations, so we were not bored.

It is not his real name, Grimus. He told us so freely. He

changed it from something unpronounceable when he arrived in this country some thirty years ago. True to himself, his adopted name is derived anagrammatically from a mythical bird: the Simurg.

– The Simurg, he told us eagerly, is the Great Bird. It is vast, all-powerful and singular. It is the sum of all other birds. There is a Sufi poem in which thirty birds set out to find the Simurg on the mountain where he lives. When they reach the peak, they find that they themselves are, or rather have become, the Simurg. The name, you see, means Thirty Birds. Si, thirty. Murg, birds. Fascinating. Fascinating. The myth of the Mountain of Kâf.

– Calf? asked Nicholas Deggle.

– Kâf, Grimus enunciated. The Arabic letter K.*

He would have rambled on thus for ages, but Deggle cut him short, reminding him about the Rose.

– Ah yes, he said. The rose. The rose has Power.

– You are an occultist? I asked, depressed. I am always depressed by the occult. It is so cheerless.

– Not exactly, he twittered. Broad-minded. That is what. If the rose has Power, we must learn of what kind.

– Open the coffin, he said to me. I resented the order, but found myself obeying. Grimus moved swiftly to the rose and before we knew what he was doing, grasped it. He cried aloud in pain, but did not release his hold. I saw his eyes dilate and widen.

Then he disappeared. The Rose stayed where it was, but I swear he did not. He softly and silently vanished away.

A few minutes later, he reappeared, beaming and shaking his head.

– Wonderful, he said. Truly wonderful.

I looked at Nicholas Deggle and he at me. – You must both try it, said Grimus. You must.

We both did in the end, after a large measure of Grimus' excellent brandy. We were both scared but I am sure Deggle was

* I should note that the Arabic letter in question has no exact parallel in the Roman alphabet. It is more usually rendered as Q (Qâf) – but it is, in fact, a glottal-stop for which there is no accurate rendering. I have chosen to refer to it as K (Kâf) and risk confusion with the quite distinct letter Kaf, for the simple reason that it is the only way I can pronounce it. A purist would not forgive me, but there it is.

the more so. He had an entire posture of superiority to lose, after all. Deggle is not an humble man.

I cannot describe the planet Thera to you as yet. I must form my opinions of it more completely first. Suffice to say that we have travelled through . . . what? I do not know, and met a life-form vastly superior to our own. The world is suddenly filled with marvellous possibilities.

And it was I who found it!

– I will leave out the next part, said Liv formally. It is an account of other journeys they made.

The room was black now. Eagle listened riveted to the flat recitative.

Moonday 1st July.

Today Grimus made his greatest discovery and propounded his grand design. I must say it enthralls me. Deggle is surly and withdrawn and, I think, disapproves; but the Rose has him gripped as tightly as any of us. Even though he has continued to refuse to use it after that first visit to Thera.

– One has enough problems, he said today, without any of this trickery. He still comes though : comes every evening when we gather around the coffin in Grimus' livingroom to go on the Conceptual Travels which Dota explained to us. He comes to sit and glower as Grimus and I take turns to visit our worlds.

How rapidly I have come to accept a new universe, to sit in an exotic suburban living-room watching a man disappear and reappear and doing so myself! Evidently, like Grimus, I too am (his word) broad-minded. Fortunate. But today the broad-mindedness received a nasty test. Grimus brought something back from his Travel. It is the first time those other universes have entered ours. He brought back two bottles. One filled with yellow liquid. One filled with blue.

– Yellow for eternal life. Blue for eternal death, he says. This is his grand design. In his own words. Or as nearly as I can remember.

– We have now the situation of being able to dispense the gift of life, he said in his feathery Slavonic voice. I propose we accept the responsibility. The necessary first step is that we grant it to ourselves. The necessary second step is the choosing of recipients. I offer some criteria for the choice : those with a pleasure in life. Those with a work to do which eternity would benefit. Those in short who would both benefit from, and seek, a longer span of life. The necessary third step is to provide a place of refuge. A place where those who tire of the world but not of life may come.

– Just a moment, said Nicholas Deggle. How on earth are we to choose these people?

It was at this point that Grimus reached into a pocket of the greatcoat he always wore on his Travels and produced the Watercrystal.

– With this, he said, and with the Rose correctly adjusted, we can see the lives of those we Conceptualize, according to the techniques of Dota. Simply we fix our thoughts upon the selected type of recipient and they appear here like a TV picture. Then with a further adjustment of the Rose we go to them.

– Playing God, said Deggle. Dangerous, don't you think?

– Would you rather we handed our knowledge to the authorities? snapped Grimus. His voice was filled with a bitterness and hatred for authority that must spring from some awful experience in his past, before he became Grimus the birdman. (We never knew his true name.) – Would you rather be locked up in an insane asylum? Or watch as Governments used our gift to make weapons and war? We do it ourselves or not at all. I say only this: to allow knowledge of this magnitude to go unused is more than a crime. It is a sin.

Liv skipped several pages. She made great show of turning to the correct place, though she never glanced at the book in her hand as she spoke.

We have been building a world. Impossible to say whether we *found* the island or *made* it. I incline to the latter, Grimus to the former. He holds that Conceptual Technology merely reveals existences which mirror your concepts. I am not so sure. However, we have made the island and it is a paradise, fertile, lush and green. Grimus has named it. Kâf Island. The mountain is Kâf Mountain. But since neither Deggle nor I are masters either of the glottal-stop or of the flat Arabic vowel, I'm afraid we bastardize the name to Calf. Fatted? Golden? Time will tell.

As for its population: Grimus now spends his entire time at

the Watercrystal. He has made a discovery: each life he sees there comes from a fractionally different dimension, exists in a slightly different *potential present* . . . his phrase. Will there be a problem in assimilating immigrants from these different planets in the one society? Grimus is cheerfully optimistic. The differences are too minute to matter, he says. I trust he is right.

Liv moved on once more.

Calf Island, Day One.
Moonday January 1.

The date is arbitrary. One may as well begin at a beginning. We are all on Calf Island now, at the town called simply K. Grimus has been clever in arranging this beginning: by astute use of the Rose he has engineered that whoever wishes to come to Calf Island (he has kept a careful check on all the Recipients) whenever they do so in their own lives and dimensions, they are brought to K on the same day. – it is a *time-equation* process, says Grimus, and I believe him. He says there has been only one misjudgement. The philosopher Ignatius Gribb and his wife Elfrida's journey has been mistimed; they will not be here for some time yet.

There is an air of joy in K today, as the community meets itself, a sense of paradise. We are the immortals and this is our Olympus. It was a lucky day when I took the job in the pets' graveyard.

Another jump. This time there was a tension in Liv's voice that had not been there before.

Freyday January 26th.

Today's is a tale of two women. For my part, it is a happy tale.

Liv Sylwan is a whore. A very exceptional whore. (Curious, by the way, how many whores chose Calf Island. It must be a very fulfilling job.) Liv rejoices in being beautiful and enjoys working with her body. She is without shame. She is also gifted with command. The brothel became hers instantly. Jocasta, who lies second to her, so to speak, was the only real opposition. I like Jocasta. But Liv is . . . well, Liv is.

I must confess that until the Rose I had never been what you might term a sexual giant. A pigmy would be more accurate for all my bulk. I didn't blame the ladies, dear sweet bebummed betitted things. Who would want to be squashed under me? The Rose gave me confidence. I journeyed to new worlds where fat men were as much in demand as Rubens ladies. The terror of the titties, I. Virgil Jones, a sex-symbol! Remarkable.

I cannot quite believe that Liv Sylwan wants me. She said she did, though, and I must not call her a liar. So she does. But why? In heaven's name, why? She says she will give up her work to keep house for Deggle and Grimus and myself – I cannot understand it. But I will not look the gift horse in the mouth. It is a happy day, when beautiful women want ugly men simply because they *like* them.

We are going to be married. Grimus was apparently a monk once, in his old days, and he will marry us according to the rites of our church, though I am not terribly godly. Ceremonies are fun.

As for Grimus . . . he's an odd bird, to coin a phrase. I've never been one for judging the attractiveness of men, so I'd have said Nicholas Deggle was the best-looking of the three of us. Apparently not. Grimus is the one they all covet, the favourite of the whores (except, of course, my own Liv), the darling of farmer's wife and Russian countess alike. The trouble is he shows no interest in them. It's that monkish background. Trained to celibacy. Perhaps that's the attraction. He's hard to get.

The Axona Indian woman called Bird-Dog is the most per-sistent. As plain a girl as you'll see, she dogs his footsteps as her name suggests she would. He has no time for her, though she fawns on him. She probably sees him as some kind of shaman, and worships him, poor simple child. She'll tire of it.

Interesting fact arising from Bird-Dog's presence here. Grimus became much taken once with the notion of finding his own double. – Logically, he said, in an infinite universe, there must be a precise duplicate of myself. That doesn't interest me. What I'm after is a certain similarity. A likeness to me which is also entirely alien.

He was very pleased when the Axona Plateau loomed up in the Watercrystal. It hasn't worked out as he hoped, though. Bird-Dog's brother hasn't chosen Calf Island yet. Perhaps he will, perhaps he won't.

Perhaps it wasn't really Grimus' hope that he would. One can never be entirely sure with him.

Liv turned several pages, jerkily.

Thorsday April 5th

It's all going wrong. I can feel it. The atmosphere of joy has gone. If that goes then it is no longer worth while. Though Grimus disagrees. — *It is a Great Experiment, he says. It cannot fail.* I am not sure that the force of his will can hold us together. Forever is such a long time.

Besides: the three of us never ran any suitability tests on ourselves. We took it for granted we deserved immortality, and then took it for granted that Calf Island was the place for us. We may have been entirely wrong.

The suicides are doing it. That's what it is. Grimus is furious about them. They should never have come, he says. They should have drunk their blue bottles in peace, somewhere else. Not killed themselves here. Deggle says it's like marriage, agreeing to come to Calf Island. A lot of people will inevitably want a divorce no matter how much in love they were at the time.

The suicides are turning people against us and Deggle is on their side. Is he right? No, he must be wrong. Everyone made a free choice. It's not our fault.

Like a marriage . . . I was blind, of course. Liv doesn't love me. I know that. I knew it then. I thought she liked me, though.

Liv loves power. She loves to be near the centre of power. She loves to be near Grimus. Through me, she is. There's an end to it. An end to paradise. We do not make love. She talks to Grimus incessantly.

I overheard this:

— Your name, said Grimus. LIV. In the Roman numerology that is fifty-four. I was fifty-four when I drank the elixir. The numbers bind us.

I knew Grimus was interested in numerology. But is this simply a monkish, mystic bond? I am becoming a jealous man. Liv says I have nothing to be jealous of. She is right. There is nothing between us.

It's all going wrong.

*   *   *

Mayday, m'aidez. The grand design is broken and so are we. I will try, my friend, to recount events dispassionately, but I may not succeed.

Deggle started it. The violence.

Liv finished it.

But the beginning. Begin at the beginning, go on until you reach the end, then stop. Sound instructions. The beginning, then. Two nights ago. I was awakened by a terrible crash in the Rose Room. I rushed, as rapidly as my bulk permits, to the scene. Grimus was already there, in his ridiculous nightshirt and noddycap, a large, enraged goblin, staring at the disaster.

The Rose lay on the floor, its stem protruding from the coffin, which was overturned on top of the precious thing! And stooping over it, scowling, was Deggle.

I have felt for some time now that all was not well with Deggle, and wondered how much the growing dislike of Grimus and myself in the town was a result of his machinations. We have been passing through disenchanted times in K. Suicides apart (and thank the lord, that phase seems to be over) there have been a number of defections from K. People who have chosen to live elsewhere, in the wooded lower slopes, away from the town. K itself, stultified, discontented. Natural, I suppose, god help us, that they should vent their spleen upon the people responsible for Calf Island. But the violence . . . the whispers about destroying Grimus' infernal machine . . . I had thought we had left violence behind. And the Rose itself . . . I do not even know about that anymore.

Control. Control.

Deggle has been spending much of his time in the Elbaroom. Perhaps he saw himself as a kind of saviour. A popular messiah. A liberator. There has never been much love lost between us. Perhaps the enmity ran deeper than he believed.

At any rate. We found him trying to shatter the Rose! Grimus recovered quickly from the shock and, displaying astonishing strength, hurled him from the room. – It must be tested, he said, and for the rest of the night he was closeted with the Rose, adjusting, permuting, testing. It was dawn before he declared himself satisfied that no damage had been done.

No damage!

– We must not allow this to happen again, he said, with a

229

fierceness in his voice I had heard only once before, in his short diatribe against authority. – The Rose is the most valuable thing on the island, he said. I cannot permit it to be jeopardized. Will you help me?

I was caught up in the fervour of those bright, hooded eyes. – How? I asked.

– By myself I am not sure I can do it, he said. It will take our combined wills. We must expel the vandal from the island. I visited Dota in the night: he has taught me a method. But it is difficult.

I won't bother with the ensuing argument. Suffice to say that we went into the Rose Room, agreed. At once I felt uneasy.

How can I explain it? There was a sensation in the room, like a soft inaudible whine. No, not in the room. *Inside my head.* And it was strongest near the Rose. I asked Grimus what it was, in some anxiety. He dismissed it: it had not affected the Rose's functions in any way. – *It was only a whine,* he said. Dota the Gorf had not been worried about it.

He set the Rose and we fixed our thoughts upon our intentions, repeating this form of words: IXSE SIXITES SIXE IXSETES EXIS EXISTIS. A variant, I supposed, to the SISPI formula for Travel between potential presents.

Deggle has not been seen on Calf Island since. I must presume the expulsion worked. I do not know where we have sent him, but he has gone. No doubt the Watercrystal will spot him should we desire it. I do not desire it. Not now.

I have always thought of uses of the Rose as rites. They are so very unmechanical. So. When the rite was over, it happened. I felt dizzy. I was unwell, I was sure. Grimus was saying: – It is not enough to expel Deggle. We must remove the Rose to a safer place. I have a plan.

I could hardly hear his voice . . . it came and went, and went. (Now, Virgil, dispassion, tell it calmly.)

The whine. It was the whine, somehow, it must have been. Holding the Rose all that time, so close. I wonder why Grimus was not affected . . .

The whine filled my head with shapes and pictures and beasts and terrors. Horrors. *Horrors.* I tried to escape and there was no escape. They were *inside.*

Hallucinations? No, they were too real, they could cause

pain. No, I will not describe them, the infernal scenes I saw and felt, the depths I plumbed. It was as though an army of terrors from the recesses of my own imagination had been released, my inmost fears made flesh. Horrible, most horrible. No, I will say no more about it . . . the Dimension-fever. So Grimus called it.

When I came to my senses, Grimus sat by me solicitously, on the Rose Room floor. He had rescued me, tuning the Rose to my co-ordinates and willing me back from my inner depths. So the Rose can heal as well as hurt. I am more scared of it than I ever was.

Most of all I am scared because I can no longer use it.

Grimus wanted me to master it again, like a fallen mountaineer. He set the Rose for Thera and we grasped it.

I did not Travel! Try as I might, I could not use the Rose.

It is like a paralysis of the mind. It shuts me out from that insidious whine – but it shuts me out, too, from all the countless universes I have not yet seen. Calf Island is all I have now. And a bleak inheritance it is.

I shall be brief now, or else I shall become maudlin.

Grimus, using the Rose for intradimensional Travel for the first time, has removed himself – and it – to the mountain peak. With a great deal of effort, he has succeeded in building a double barrier against the island: a visual barrier of clouds which obscures him perennially from our sight, and a kind of forcefield which we cannot pass. There is one Gate. He showed it me *in case things improved*. They will not improve.

His departure has brought about the end of my – not marriage – cohabitation with Liv. I was obliged to watch the degrading spectacle of my wife pleading, begging Grimus to take her with him. Misogynist that he is, he refused. I found myself feeling angry with him for this, this, *insult* to my wife! Imagine that, my friend. So greatly am I reduced.

Picture Liv's fury, then, when he took the woman Bird-Dog instead of her. An explicable choice. He wants a servant, not a mistress. The doting Axona will be a good servant, I expect. She thinks of him as a demi-god.

Liv's fury, in the absence of Grimus, vented itself on me. She has said a number of cruel things I will not commit to this page. She despises me for not being his equal, though I never claimed I was. And for my paralysis, thanks to which she is barred from his company. She wants nothing to do with me. In her eyes, I am just a fat, weak man. Probably she is right. Yes. Probably she is.

The house where we lived is empty now. Liv has gone up the mountain, to be as near Grimus as possible, no doubt. She does not know the location of the Gate, nor how close she is. And even if she knew, Grimus would not let her pass. He will watch the island with his Watercrystal and defend the Rose, and his privacy. The Rose is all he cares for now.

I am being looked after by Jocasta. She has always been a friend to me. I suspect a rift between her and Liv. Because Liv scorns me, Jocasta adopts me. But I am past questioning motives; I accept companionship where it is offered.

Mayday, indeed.

Saturday September 29th.

I am leaving K. It is a town made mad by a machine. Soldiers, policemen, actors, hunters, whores, drunks, wasters, philosophers, menials, morons, artisans, farmers, shoe-salesmen, artists, united by their common inability to cope with the world they have had imposed upon them. Especially as the whine grows worse, they say. I cannot hear it. It has driven some to distraction. It has led to what they now call the Way of K. Gribb's way. Gribb and Mrs Gribb, who arrived recently. No doubt Grimus had a hand in their arrival, but now they deny him and his Effect. Obsessionalism is their defence. I cannot bear what is happening to K, place of erstwhile joy. If my mind is paralysed, at least my life is not.

Guilt. It must be someone's fault. It is ours. It was our experiment. But the Rose . . . the Rose is a wonderful thing. How has it brought so much grief? It is a terrible thing, so much distortion caused by such a wonder. I must leave. I do not want to watch. The woman Dolores O'Toole is going down the mountain. I shall go with her.

As for you, my friend, I shall take my leave of you as well. I want no friends now. I shall sacrifice you to Liv in propitiation of the gods. I shall take you to her. She will probably rend you limb from limb or toss you casually aside, as she did me. That is your future. It may help me forget my past. It may help me forget K and the horrors that burnt my mind. You will be my means of self-immolation. Greater love hath no friend.

To your destroyer, I will say one last word. There was a

moment, back in that fit-to-be-expunged past, when I thought she wanted me. The excellence of that moment is not dimmed by the discovery of my mistake. I thank her for it. Beginnings are always better than endings. Then, everything was possible. Now, nothing is.

Dark. The book shut, wrapped, replaced. The silent black-veiled woman rising to her feet, standing stiffly before him. A hen clucking, once. Outside, the frenzied padding of the diary's author, searching for a door he knew he could not find or pass. And the hiding whore, crouching by the donkey, behind a tree, watching.

But she did not rend it limb from limb, thought Flapping Eagle.

– Fifty-four, said Liv in a flat, regular voice. He said it was a bond between us. His always-age, my name. He is a man who breaks his bond. I knew how he thought, knew how he felt, knew him. It was a bond beyond breaking and it was broken.

As she spoke she stooped over a group of candles on the floor and lit them with flints. Then she stood erect once more, the light yellowing upwards at her from the floor, casting great shadows on the wall. Flapping Eagle remembered: the goddess Axona had looked like this. *Then. Ago. Before.* And the recollection mingled with the revealed history of the island, losing itself in that gloom.

She had not been speaking to him. Again, the sense of ritual: the book recited, the candles lit, the litany spoken. This was how she lived her life, embalmed in the bitter formaldehyde of old hatreds and betrayals. Flapping Eagle felt sorry for her for an instant; then her eyes focused on him through the grille of her hood.

– Aaaaaah. It was a huge exhalation of air, sobbing out from her lungs.

– Of course, she said. Of course. You have returned. The Spectre of Grimus is here to make good the bond of Grimus. Of course. So it is.

She was different, Flapping Eagle realized. The recitation, the entire rite, had altered her. She spoke slowly now, distantly, as though in some kind of trance. The past had possessed her. And he, Flapping Eagle, had become a part of that past.

– Come, she said, backing towards the bed, beckoning. Come and consecrate your bond.

Flapping Eagle sat immobile in the chair, not knowing how to react.

– Look at my body, Spectre, said Liv. Is it not a suitable altar?

Her hands moved suddenly to the back of her neck, where they undid a fastening. The black robe fell to the floor. She stood unclothed before him, her face still hidden by the black veil, the eyes looking out at him, piercing, perhaps even mocking, the candles casting their upwards yellow glow.

– Look at my body, Spectre, repeated Liv. Flapping Eagle looked.

Liv, ice-peak of perfection. Virgil had overstated nothing.

His eyes described her to his unbelieving mind. The feet, a little too large, stained with intricate henna tracery like an Indian bride; the long, tapered legs, the right bearing her weight and the left relaxed, so that the swaying curve of her hips was accented, sinuously, consciously; the tight curls of hair beneath her navel, unshaven, untrained, pale, nestling curls; the deep, deep navel, a dark pool in the whiteness of her skin; the breasts, small, the right slightly larger than the left, the left nipple tilted a fraction higher than its partner, but both still child-rosy, soft; the narrow, straight shoulders pushed back a fraction to an almost military angle, challenging, confident; the arms hanging straight and loose, palms of the hands facing forwards, third fingers curled beneath the thumbs, a generous hint of hair shadowing the pits of the arms. The rest, the neck and face and head, unseen beneath their hood, only hinted at by those sharply quizzical eyes. He looked at her now in the whole, the black garment lying at her feet, a forgotten shroud, the dancing candles on the floor sending rich shadows to flirt with the naked body, the chaos and filth of the room forgotten in the perfection of this vision. She knew how to display her body, just enough emphasis to heighten its beauty without obtrusion. A headless venus in a slum museum.

– Is it not a suitable altar? she said.

He nodded, wordlessly, and with a sudden movement of the right arm she removed the windowed hood. It fluttered to the floor to join its companion-robe.

He had known she would be beautiful; but he had failed to

234

anticipate how *subjugating* that beauty would be. Flapping Eagle had to wrestle with himself to look into that face without instantly lowering his eyes. It was the loveliness of sun on ice, too brilliant to watch. Blinding, imperious perfection. The firm, long, narrow jaw, set and tilted upwards, and the wide, wide mouth without the vestige of a smile; the nose, short and straight, flanked by cheekbones like blades or sharp white cliffs. A long face, the bones perfectly balanced by those vast lucent pools of eyes, deepest aquamarine, eyes you could almost see through, eyes that saw, effortlessly, through you. And framing the head of the ice-queen, an abundance of waving gold, rising a few inches from a central division and crashing effusively around the glitter-hard face with the sea-soft eyes, a niagara of falling hair. *It was the face that did it.*

Liv lying down on the bed.

– Come, she said. Come and consecrate your bond.

As Virgil Jones stumbled around in the night, Flapping Eagle moved towards the body of his wife, towards the clean bed, past the glowing candles and the spiders and the mould.

She could arouse him as Irina never had. Then, he had been in control, a part of him always detached, choosing his next course of action, watching her come to her peak, deriving most of his satisfaction from the giving of pleasure; now it was he who was driven, uncontrollably, by the touches and movements of her body. She spent a long, slow while discovering his preferences and taboos, whispering all the time : – *Do you like that? Is that nice? Shall I do that harder or softer? Shall I lick or nibble or tickle or scratch? Is my hand good there? Shall I be like this, or this, or this?* The new, quiet gentleness in her voice softened interrogation into intimacy, and it was only later that he realized he had never asked if she, too, liked what he chose.

So that, when she did what she had always intended, it caught him with every defence down, open, helpless.

He lay on his back on the bed. The candles flickered closer to guttering out. The time of exploration was over, and the kissing and stroking and squeezing and she knelt over him, the golden cornucopia covering her face like a lavish thatch, the aqua-marine eyes hidden, the long hands kneading and working at the small tilted breasts, the thighs quivering gently as she descend-ed, and then he was in her. Slowly still, making it last, the living strike of flesh in flesh, slowly, slowly gathering force, building, slowly gathering.

She was groaning now (– *I groan*, she had said) and they were striking hard at each other, near, so near, the shudder growing within him, and the moment had . . .

She wrenched herself off him then, hard and without warning, and stood on the bed looking down at him, composed, unruffled, and the aquamarines were filled with triumph.

– It is Liv who breaks the bond, she said.

Liv's revenge on Grimus, plotted in centuries of darkened, still-seated brooding. Now, possessed, entranced, she had wrought it on his Spectre. It was a very final humiliation, hitting him in the core of his carnal pride, the only pride he had left. He looked up at the towering Valkyrie, staring at him with the full force of her century-festered hate, and helplessly, miserably, his body roused beyond his control, spilt his sterile seed upon the sheets.

Virgil Jones had slept squatting on the outcrop. Flapping Eagle was curled into a foetal ball against the wall of the black house. When they awoke, the damp had seeped into their bones. They shivered.

It was the cry that woke them, a half-frightened, half-elated yell from the wood. Flapping Eagle was awake at once and running in the direction of the voice. Virgil, slower, bulkier, followed him, blinking rapidly.

Media stood at the edge of the wood, her arms trembling but her hands clasped rigidly together.

Trapped between her arms was the surly, draggled figure of Bird-Dog.

Brother and sister stood still a moment, taking stock.

– Tell this stupid woman to let me go, little brother.

Her voice was unfriendly.

– I saw her appear, Flapping Eagle, said Media tremulously. Like a spectre. I saw her appear so I caught her. I thought you'd, you'd want to see her.

It had been a brave thing to do.

Bird-Dog said: – If you saw me appear, don't you think I could just as easily disappear? You'd be left clutching thin air.

Media looked doubtful, but didn't release her hold.

– She's right, Media, said Flapping Eagle. If she's here, it's

236

because she wants to be. Let her go and perhaps we'll find out why.

— I don't want to be here, said Bird-Dog roughly. If he hadn't sent me I would never have come.

— Grimus sent you? It was Virgil's voice, blank, disbelieving.

— Not for you, she said. For him. Little Joe-Sue. It's none of my doing, little brother. Remember that.

Grimus actually wants to see me, thought Flapping Eagle. There will be no battle of wills.

— Why? Again, it was Virgil Jones who spoke Flapping Eagle's thoughts.

— Don't ask me why, said Bird-Dog, shaking herself free of Media's constricting embrace. I have a message to deliver, and then I am to take him back with me.

Media was about to speak, but remained silent. She looked worried.

— Well, then, said Flapping Eagle. Deliver your message.

As Bird-Dog began to speak in a memorized, sing-song voice, a figure in a black robe and hood came out of the black house to listen.

Grimus says: — Thank you all for your efforts. I have derived a great deal of pleasure from watching you. To Virgil, I owe my apologies. I have been playing a game of hide and seek with him. Slightly cruel, possibly, but necessary.

It is to Liv Sylwan Jones that I owe my greatest thanks. She has set the seal on Mr Eagle, who is therefore prepared at last to meet me. He knows about me now, intimately, I think. And more important, he has moved from a state of what I should call self-consciousness to a state of what I would humbly term Grimus-consciousness. That is a good state in which to meet me, and I must once again thank you all: the absent Nicholas Deggle for making the meeting possible, you, Virgil, for leading him so astutely towards a confrontation with me, and you, Liv, for breaking down the last barrier to that meeting: his masculinity. In a sense, Liv, you were the Gate, as far as he is concerned. Now that he has passed you, he may come to me. I am very thrilled: perhaps this is my Perfect Dimension, after all.

Bird-Dog stopped and lowered her head. — Shall we go now? she said. To Flapping Eagle, the sight of this servile Bird-Dog, a grumbling, malcontented but totally subservient menial, was a shock and an upset. This was not the sister who had foraged for his food, who had raised and protected him. This was a shadow of the Bird-Dog he had known. What had Grimus done to her?

Liv raised her hood a small way and spat viciously on the ground before her.

Virgil Jones fussed at Flapping Eagle: – Don't forget. Wait your moment.

But life no longer seemed entirely clear-cut to Flapping Eagle. Curiosity and last night's humiliation were creeping over his resolve.

Media came up to Flapping Eagle and said quietly: – Take me, too.

Flapping Eagle was no longer surprised by anything. – Why, Media? he asked.

She shrugged.

Flapping Eagle found himself saying: – Yes. All right. Come with me. Perhaps it was because he felt the need of a friendly face on the journey into the unknown. Perhaps it was a reaction to the night with Liv, a need to reassure himself. He didn't bother to examine his motives, but he realized he was glad she was coming. As for Media, her face had suddenly broken into sunlight.

Bird-Dog said: – Not her. Just you.

Flapping Eagle found a drop of strength.

– Big sister, he said. You're supposed to lead me to Grimus. Now I'm not coming unless she does. So you'll just have to take us both.

With bad grace, Bird-Dog gave in.

– Follow me, she said.

Flapping Eagle clasped Media's hand, tightly. The returned pressure was even more fierce. – I will think about you, she said, and only you. While I do that, nothing can harm me.

He realized that she was exactly, precisely right.

Bird-Dog walked ahead of them to a spot just behind the first trees. She closed her eyes and muttered: – Sispi, Sispi. She became transparent. She nearly disappeared, but the faintest outline of her moved a step to the right and waited. Media's eyes widened; then she closed them and tightened her lips.

Flapping Eagle led her to the Gate.

Virgil Jones and Liv watched the three faint outlines walk away up the rising slope of the mountain, walking miraculously where there was no path to walk on, until they were lost to sight. They were so slight that it did not take long for this to happen.

Liv turned and went back into the black house, slamming the door.

And Virgil? Virgil knew that there was no longer anything he could do, that after all the Gorf's prophecy had come true. Flapping Eagle had reached Grimus without his help, and who knew what the result would be? There was nothing to be done now.

He started down the mountain, back to the beach, back to Dolores O'Toole and the jigsaws, the rocking-chair and the shreds of his helpless dignity.

FIFTY-FIVE

Flapping Eagle and Media (when she opened her eyes) found themselves on a strangely transmuted Calf Mountain, a Calf Mountain in which Virgil, Liv, Liv's house, even Liv's donkey were reduced to wraith-like wisps, in which the outcrop remained, and the forest, both feeling different though they looked the same. Perhaps the most shocking change, harder to accept even than the ghosts of Virgil and Liv, lay above them. The clouds had vanished from the mountain's summit. Flapping Eagle was surprised to find that the mountain was lower than he had imagined; the cumulus cocoon had made it seem much higher than it was. The summit lay only a few hundred feet above them.

– Grimushome, said Bird-Dog, pointing without turning to face them.

A sprawling house, long and low and castellated, looked down at them. It was a stone house, a miniature fortress. Somewhere in that stone home, thought Flapping Eagle, lies the Stone Rose.

The house was wildly irregular, its walls anything but straight, no corner a right angle, but it was a designed eccentricity, a deliberate folly. The zigzag patterns it wove on the mountaintop were purposeful, reflections of their creator.

Reflections: the house gave them off in all directions, for

every window in its wandering walls was also a mirror. This combination of undulating stone and blind, gleaming windows made the house curiously difficult to focus upon, as if his eyes refused to accept it, as if it was an illusion that would not harden into fact.

Possibly it was a question of size. The house was large, but, in an impossible distortion of scale, it lay in the spreading shade of an inconceivably huge tree, an ash which dwarfed its venerable sibling in the Gribb garden by comparison, as if the swing-bearing tree had been a mere sapling. It was more than gigantic; it inspired awe. Flapping Eagle remembered Virgil Jones' description of the Ash Yggdrasil, the mother-tree which holds the skies in place. And wondered what monsters were gnawing at its roots.

Another shock. Flapping Eagle had a clear memory of the upper slopes of Calf Mountain. They had been steep, more arduous even than the ascent from K to the outcrop, and densely forested. He had had severe doubts about the possibility of scaling these heights without proper equipment. It was stunning, then, to see before him a neatly-cleared passage up the mountain, a whole flight of narrow stone steps sweeping effortlessly to the very door of Grimushome. And yet they were there. They were real. Flapping Eagle shook his head, forced into admiration.

They were climbing the stairs now, Bird-Dog leading, Media bringing up the rear, and the birds swooping and swarming all around them. More birds than Flapping Eagle had seen in his life, birds from every climate and of every imaginable feather, birds as common as crows and birds he had never seen before, with uselessly twisted beaks and strangely contorted shapes, flocking and squawling up the mountain to the peak. Often he had to shield his face against a spread of beating wings. He glanced back at Media; there was fear in her eyes, but she forced a smile.

And the whine was still all around him, loud now and pervasive, but the marvels surrounding them took far more of their attention. Eventually they were near the peak. Bird-Dog had maintained a hostile silence throughout the climb, but now she broke it, whirling to face her brother from her higher position.

– Leave us alone, she cried. Why did you have to come here?

Then, equally suddenly, she turned around once more, and

there was resignation in her steps as she resumed her climb.

For a man at the end of a quest, Flapping Eagle felt extremely unheroic.

Engraved in the stone over the door of Grimushome:
THAT WHICH IS COMPLETE IS ALSO DEAD.

Birds crowded the branches of the giant ash as Flapping Eagle and Media followed the surly Bird-Dog in.

The house was a kind of rough triangular labyrinth, the face which it presented to the ascending steps being the jagged base of the triangle. The main door stood towards the left-hand corner of this base. The two other faces were even more jagged than the front; a sharp protruding sub-triangle stuck out on the left and a blunter but larger sub-triangle distorted the right side.

Inside, Flapping Eagle and Media found a bewildering series of interlocking rooms. First of these was the stone hall in which they found themselves upon entering, a bleak spartan room, lit only by oil-lamps until Bird-Dog flung open a mirrored window. It contained no furniture, but variegated pieces of rock, boulders and two beautifully-detailed erotic sculptures in stone stood lining its walls. Flapping Eagle found it an unfriendly room.

It was roughly square, though it grew narrower at the far end, where a door stood closed against them. Bird-Dog moved towards this door and flung it open. As they followed her, Flapping Eagle heard the creaking for the first time.

A regular, rhythmic creaking. The walls were full of it, but they were stone walls and there was no obvious source for the sound. It seemed to grow louder as he listened; he turned to Media. She, too, was listening. Creak . . . creak . . . creak . . . creak. They hurried into the next room.

And momentarily forgot the creaking at the sight of an army of birds.

– Birdroom, said Bird-Dog curtly and unnecessarily.

This was the room which stuck sharply out from the left side of the building. Through an open window poured the birds, a steady stream of comings and goings. Various feeds stood on small pedestals around the room and a large birdbath was the room's central feature. Peacocks strutted on the floor.

But not all the birds were alive. Stuffed creatures stood in glass-fronted cases all around them, immobilized for ever in typical scenes from their lives : birds eating, birds courting, birds breeding and hatching, birds in flight, birds dying, birds swooping on other birds, in a dazzling series of eternal tableaux.

And on the walls, the portraits of birds, an audubon profusion of feathered heads, some real, some imaginary, serried in ranks around the central picture which took up almost all the wall to Flapping Eagle's right. One look at the glorious particoloured creature depicted there was enough. This was the Roc of Sinbad, the Phoenix of myth : Simurg himself.

The creaking broke through Flapping Eagle's fascination. Bird-Dog was hurrying on through yet another door at the far end of the room. They followed her rapidly through an electrifyingly beautiful dining-room, on whose walls hung ancient tapestries and on whose floor lay ancient carpets. Silver plates and candelabra glinted everywhere. This was the room which stood at the apex of the triangle. Bird-Dog did not pause.

Down the right side now, Flapping Eagle told himself, concentrating on orientation. The fourth room stood in darkness, a number of white shapes looming through the shades. As his eyes accustomed himself to the poor light, he saw that a number of podia were scattered about the room, bearing – what? – *things*, hidden by white, shrouding sheets. These silent ghosts – none large enough to be the Rose – were in some way worrying. And the creaking continued here as in all the previous rooms . . .

This time the door was not in the far wall, but in the wall on their right. Following Bird-Dog, they came into a small room, entirely empty, oil-lamps flickering on the walls, the first room they had been in without an outside wall. On the wall facing them, red against the grey stone, was this shape : ق

– The letter Kâf, said Bird-Dog brusquely.

Flapping Eagle did not understand the purpose of this room, unless it was an anteroom, for their journey was near an end. Bird-Dog went through a door in the wall to their left and they found themselves in a bright, airy, well-furnished room : their room. The large bed wore fresh sheets and had obviously been expecting them. There was a deep, soft divan and an ornate low table inset with ivory squares.

His sense of direction told him there was still an unexplained area on each side of this room. One was rapidly clarified – a door on his left as he stood just inside the entrance from the

Kâf-room led to a bathroom and lavatory; and on the far side of this were Bird-Dog's small, dingy quarters. She had her own door to the outside world, as befits a servant. She was retreating now, into this small shell.

Flapping Eagle called after her: – Where is Grimus?

– Wait, she said, and shut her door. He heard a bolt being shot.

Sounds: a range of unfamiliar, disturbing sounds. The whine, the loud combined conversation of birds, and the creaking.

– Are you all right? he said.

Media lay on the bed, her hands over her ears, trying to shut out this new, frightening world.

She is a resilient woman, thought Flapping Eagle, but very near breaking point.

He was retracing his steps to the main entrance. The unexplained area towards the front face of the house, south of their room, must be Grimus' own quarters, he had decided; but he had seen no doors leading into that area. He went outside and circled the house; but other than the front door and Bird-Dog's back door, there were no entrances; and the windows of Grimus' room were closed and reflecting. Puzzled, he returned to the stone hall.

To find a door where none had been, a swinging slab of stone that now stood open. From the room within came the creaking, the all-pervasive creaking. Flapping Eagle walked slowly towards the sound. The dirty yellow light of oil-lamps glowed through the secret door.

– The acoustics here are somewhat haunting, yes?

Quick, clipped consonants and short, flat vowels. The voice of Grimus.

– I trust you are both comfortable?

The rocking-chair stood with its face to the closed window and its back to Flapping Eagle. He could see the head: a shock of white hair, some of it flowing over the back of the chair.

Creak . . . creak . . . creak as the rocking-chair swayed back and forth; and another, slighter sound, a soft clicking which Flapping Eagle could not understand. He reached the rocking-chair and stood beside the man he had come so far to see.

Grimus was knitting.

*　　　*　　　*

Like, and yet unlike. Yes, their faces were alike, the aquiline nose, the deepset eyes, the firm square jaw; but Grimus was nearer Bird-Dog's olive colouring than the white of Flapping Eagle's sepulchritude. And their eyes spoke differently, Grimus' distant, cool, twinkling while Flapping Eagle's were glaring and hot. Like, and yet unlike.

As though reading his thoughts, Grimus said:

— My pale young shadow. That is you.

Flapping Eagle forced the necessary words past his lips; he was finding it difficult to take up an antagonistic stance in this relaxed, amused presence.

— You know why I am here, he said. Where is the Stone Rose?

— I know why Virgil wanted you to come, said Grimus. That is sad, you know. For Virgil to side with the Nicholas Deggles of this world. But no matter, no matter. I hope you will make up your own mind, Flapping Eagle. You are nobody's tool. *The eyes smiled.*

— Well, then, said Flapping Eagle. Tell me why you sent Bird-Dog for me. And tell me what you have done to make her ... what she has become.

The white eyebrows rose a fraction.

— So fast, said Grimus. Such haste. No, my friend, I will not tell you. Not, at any price, before dinner.

Dinner was vegetarian, like Grimus; but so expertly had Bird-Dog prepared it that Flapping Eagle, a great carnivore, scarcely noticed the absence of meat.

— Man's origins, Grimus was saying, are those of the hunter. Thus the hunt, search or quest is man's oldest, most time-honoured pursuit. You must feel a great sense of accomplishment to have arrived.

Flapping Eagle looked at his sister: crushed, servile, cowering menially in a corner, ignored by her master.

— Perhaps it's better to travel hopefully, he said.

Bird-Dog, who had been waiting on Grimus for an eternity now, an eternity of being ignored. She had stood it, Flapping Eagle surmised, because at least she could feel unique, the sole acolyte of the man she worshipped. At least she was significant. No wonder, then, that she grudged his arrival; she would not want to share Grimus with anyone.

Grimus, for his part, treated her throughout the meal as subhuman, a being beneath contempt; and Flapping Eagle found himself shaping a dislike of the strange secret man.

He was talking to Media. – I must compliment you on your strength, he said. But I fear for you. Flapping Eagle, do you not fear for her? This is not an entirely safe place. The side-effect, I mean.

– She's resisted it perfectly well so far, said Flapping Eagle.

– But one can weaken, said Grimus. My dear, would you be prepared to undergo a little hypnosis? It would make you safe.

Media looking at Flapping Eagle through ill, panicky eyes. He was thinking: Grimus is right: the Effect is strongest here. She could succumb at any moment. So, despite his reluctance to allow Grimus near her, he said: – Perhaps you're right.

– After dinner, then, said Grimus. You will of course be present yourself.

– You like my home? asked Grimus, eagerly.

– Very nice, said Media.

– I have built it to enshrine my favourite things, said Grimus. My favourite ideas. The ash outside. The portraits of birds. It is a great pleasure to a lonely man.

– It's very large, said Media.

– When I lived in K, said Grimus, I was prepared to live as modestly as the rest. But since they have forced me to withdraw, I indulge myself shamelessly.

– Acute of you to recall the Ash Yggdrasil, said Grimus over coffee. Let me tell you of a related matter. The Twilight of the Gods, as it is known. This is an entirely erroneous term, you know. The word *ragnarok*, twilight, only occurs once in the entire Poetic Edda, and is almost certainly a misprint for the word *ragnarak*, which is the one used throughout the songs. The difference is crucial. *Ragnarak*, you see, means fall. Total destruction. A much more final thing than twilight. You see how one letter can warp a mythology?

– How do you get coffee here? asked Media.

Grimus frowned at the irrelevance. – I think, therefore it is, he said.

Flapping Eagle imagined he looked pleased at her confusion.

On their way out of the dining-room, Grimus bumped into Bird-Dog. She dropped the dish she was carrying. He dusted himself down at the place where their bodies had touched, looking disgusted; and said: – Bird-Dog, you are a clumsy fool.

– Yes, Grimus, she said.

Flapping Eagle stifled a surge of anger, remembering Virgil's advice: *Bide your time.*

The hypnosis of Media was completely successful; the post-hypnotic suggestion completely shut out the whine from her head. Flapping Eagle cheered up slightly, then thought: *I wonder how much hypnosis he's used on Bird-Dog?*

Media was asleep. Bird-Dog was concealed in her quarters. Grimus and Flapping Eagle sat in the Bird Room, amid the paintings and the stuffed and sleeping creatures.

– Peaceful beings, said Grimus. Yet they can be trained to fight, like cocks. Simple beings, yet they say the mynah bird can tell fortunes. Amoral beings, yet some are highly moral. The albatross, for instance, is monogamous after performing its mating dance. For the rest of its natural life. Few of us could claim as much.

– Grimus . . . began Flapping Eagle.

– They feed, they breed and they die, said Grimus. All we can do is feed. Which of us do you find the superior?

– I think it's time, said Flapping Eagle.

– Now you yourself, Flapping Eagle, are a strange creature. Once you were nidifugous, fleeing the nest which bore you. But not by choice, so you have once more become nidipetal. Seeking a new nest, eh? Admirable. Most admirable.

Flapping Eagle burst out:

– Grimus, what is this all about?

Grimus looked mildly astonished.

– All about, Mr Eagle? But of course it is all about death. Death, Mr Eagle – that is what life is about.

Flapping Eagle felt suddenly very cold.

– Whose death? he asked, fearfully.

– My dear Flapping Eagle, smiled Grimus. Mine, naturally. Whose did you think? That is who you are: the angel of my death.

– Put these on, said Grimus.

– Why?

– Because it must all be properly done, said Grimus, his hands fluttering in bird-like movements.

So, in the Bird-Room, Flapping Eagle assumed the full ceremonial feathered head-dress and face-paint of an Axona Sham-
Man, slung a bow across a shoulder and a quiver of arrows at his
back, and held a ju-ju stick in his right hand. Grimus, in the
meanwhile, put on a different head-dress, whose colouring
exactly matched the plumage of the great bird in the largest
portrait in the room.

– And now, said Grimus. Shall we dance?

Flapping Eagle sat in Grimus' rocking-chair, listening. There
was not much else he could do; he had seen no sign of the Stone
Rose. And besides, he was curious. His head-dress hung proudly
over the back of the swaying chair and the ju-ju stick lay in his
lap. Grimus circled him, walking in an odd, stilted manner,
bending forward from the waist and sticking out his neck at
every step, his hands at shoulder-height, his fingers moving,
moving ceaselessly. There was an angular rhythm about his
movements that dizzied the eye.

– This is the Dance of Wisdom and Death, said Grimus.
Death, still, watching and listening, biding its time, good. Wisdom, circling, gesturing, revealing itself to its Doom. Good.
This is how I chose to be; it is a man's freedom to choose the
manner of his going. I have chosen a beautiful Death and made
it in my own image.

His voice descended from its high pitch and his manner became conversational.

– Ordinary men, he said, by which I mean mortal men, are
made incomplete by ageing and death. As the years give them
wisdom, their failing faculties make a nonsense of it, so that
when Death claims them they have little to say to it. I chose to
be different. Through longevity I have been able both to grow
wise and to retain the faculties which add potency to wisdom.
To be wise and powerful is to be complete. *That which is complete is also dead.* And so I wish to die. Not the paltry fizzling
of mortal life, but a minutely-planned and satisfying death. An
aesthetic passing on.

The Elixir of Death, the blue release, has no power on Kâf
Mountain. It was thus I conceptualized the island, for in building a life one must be conscious of its end. Who would write a
story without knowing how it finished? All beginnings contain
an end. Unknown to Virgil Jones, unknown to Nicholas Deggle,

I planned Kâf Mountain around my death. Around you. The Elixir of Death would have been too easy, too incomplete. One cannot reveal one's secrets to a drink. And then there is the question of the Phoenician impulse, but more of that later.

The Mountain of Kâf, in short, is a place where death is neither natural nor easy. It must be chosen, and it must be an act of violence against the body. That, after all, is what it always is in truth.

But the Mountain is more than this. It is the Great Experiment. Not in the sense that Virgil Jones understood it; I saw no reason to tell him my true intentions. There is every reason to tell you. You are the Phoenician Death. This is the nature of Kâf : it is an attempt to understand human nature by freeing it from its greatest instinctual drive, the need to preserve the species through reproduction. The Elixir of Life is a beautifully two-edged weapon, removing at a stroke the possibility of re-production by sterilizing Recipients, and also nullifying the need to reproduce by conferring immortality. The island, furthermore, is plentiful and fertile. Scarcity, too, has been removed. All of which necessitates a profound change in human behaviour, a change which I believed would reveal our true natures far more exactly. It is a fine combination, sterile immortals and fertile land. A most rewarding study.

Analysts of the mythical mountain of Kâf have called it a model for the structure and workings of the human mind. Fitting, then, that the actual Mountain should be a structure created to examine the interests (and enable the death) of one human mind.

Though, in a sense, it is not my intention that my mind should die. This is the purpose of revealing my secrets to the chosen instrument of my death. This is the Phoenician impulse.

When I became Grimus, I took the name from a respect for the philosophy contained in the myth of the Simurg, the myth of the Great Bird which contains all other birds and in turn is contained by them. The similarity with the Phoenix myth is self-apparent. Through death, the annihilation of self, the Phoenix passes its selfhood on to its successor. That is what I hope to do with you, Flapping Eagle. Named for the king of earthly birds. You are to be the next stage of the cycle, the next bearer of the flag, Hercules succeeding Atlas. In the midst of death we are in life.

– What if I refuse?

The question came unprompted from Flapping Eagle's scared lips. Megalomania is a frightening thing to be circled by.

– You are the next life of the Phoenix, repeated Grimus. The Phoenician Death.

– How can you refuse? said Grimus after a pause. Consider your life: you will see that I have shaped it to this express purpose. In a sense, Flapping Eagle, I created you, conceptualizing you as you are. Just as I created the island and its dwellers with all the selectivity of any artist.

– We existed before you found us, said Flapping Eagle.

– Surely, said Grimus tolerantly. But by shaping you to my grand design I remade you as completely as if you had been unmade clay.

– I don't believe you, said Flapping Eagle, and Grimus laughed.

– A sceptical Death, he said. Good, good. His voice rose again to its formal high pitch and his fingers fluttered more than ever.

– Do you deny that by selecting you as a Recipient I shaped your life thenceforth? Do you deny that by taking your sister from the Axona I forced your expulsion? Do you deny that by expelling Nicholas Deggle into your continuum I guided you towards Calf Island? Do you deny that by allowing you to wander the world for centuries instead of bringing you here I made you the man you are, chameleon, adaptable, confused? Do you deny that by choosing a man similar in appearance to myself I estimated *exactly* the effect of such a man on Virgil and on the town K? Do you deny that I lured you here with the Spectre of Bird-Dog? Do you deny that I have steered a course between the infinite potential presents and futures in order to make this meeting possible? (And then, dropping his voice:) *Which of your Lord's blessings would you deny?*

Flapping Eagle was shaken but not wholly convinced. He shook his head.

– Since you do not know how to conceptualize the co-ordinates of your Dimension, you cannot leave the island, said Grimus. You cannot stay among Kâf's inhabitants, bearing my face. Your only alternative is suicide, and once I have shown you my marvels you will not wish to do so.

– Show me, said Flapping Eagle.

Flapping Eagle stood in the room he had passed through earlier, the room with veiled objects on podia, wondering what he found most alarming about Grimus. He decided it was the childishness underlying his whole so-called Grand Design, the fulfilment of every half-formed whim, and the strangely infantile rituals he devised to amuse him, like this so-called Dance. Grimus: a baby with a bomb. Or a whole veiled arsenal of bombs. On pedestals.

– The second part of the Dance, Grimus twittered, is a Dance of Veils. In Which Much That Is Wonderful Is Revealed.

He stood by the first podium, a didactic, particoloured owl.

– Beneath personality, he said, is concealed an essence. The Meta-Physicists of Oxyput VII have perfected a tool for the detection of this essence. I acquired one on my travels. It is based upon a simple concept: that Essences are of two kinds: atomic, complete, static on the one hand, or on the other, ionic, incomplete, dynamic. What might be termed Ions in the Soul. (A short laugh.) The device I am about to show you is called an Ion Eye. It can examine and record the particular Ionic structure of any Dynamic Essence. Through centuries of experimentation, the Oxyputians have analysed the meanings of these Ionic patterns. This knowledge is also at my disposal. I used it to aid me in the conceptualization of none other than a certain Flapping Eagle.

He unveiled the Ion Eye. It was a simple black box. On its front face were rows and rows of tiny glass windows.

– Stand in front of it, please.

Flapping Eagle complied and at once lights appeared in the tiny windows, a complex pattern of lights.

– Your Ionic Pattern, said Grimus, is the strongest destructive pattern I have ever seen. If one were superstitious, one could argue that it is this essence that Mrs Cramm spotted in your palm, this essence which caused your people to mistrust you, this essence which lies at the root of your misfortunes on Kâf Island. For my purposes, it made you an eminently suitable angel of death. You and your sister. Though her pattern is rather less well-defined than yours.

Grimus moved to a pair of pedestals, which stood close together at one end of the room. He unveiled one.

Flapping Eagle found himself looking at the Watercrystal.

– I see you recognize this, said Grimus. Virgil's diary. Good, good. It was through this that I found you and then tested you with the Ion Eye, through this that I followed you all the way here. But its companion is almost more interesting. It does not occur in Virgil's diary, because I concealed it from him. It is the Crystal of Potentialities. In it I can examine many potential presents and futures and discover the key moments, the crossroads in time, which guide us down one or the other *line of flux.* If you understand what I mean by that.

Flapping Eagle shook his head – *no* – as he stared at the second, unveiled crystal globe. This was filled, not with water, but with a kind of smoke.

– I'm afraid you always see through a bit of a haze, said Grimus. Ah, but you do not understand. Let me refer to incidents you yourself remember. Twice in the very recent past, you have experienced crossroad-points. For instance. Had I not conceptualized a protective barrier around you, you would no doubt have drowned as you floated in to the island. Obviously I allowed some water to enter your system. Verisimilitude is important. And a second moment: when you unconsciously spoke the name *Elfrina* to La Cherkassova. I'm sure you perceived how that one small moment changed the course of your life. Though it is fair to say that if you hadn't made it so easy for me I'd have had to find another way of detaching you . . . Anyhow. You see what I mean. Crossroad points. I have been husbanding you – and others – along the right road for a very long time now. That is what I mean when I say I have made you. I have been constructing the Perfect Dimension, in which everything goes according to plan.

You will say: it didn't. I didn't anticipate the treachery of Nicholas Deggle. To which I reply: one of the greatest qualities of a well-formed Concept is flexibility. One can turn disadvantages into advantages. Thus Deggle's expulsion became a simple way of drawing you into the net. Thus the K-people's dislike of me helped them to react correctly towards you. (Though by denying them access to the Rose I would have fostered that dislike anyway.)

– You denied them the Rose, said Flapping Eagle.

– Naturally, said Grimus. For one thing, it had nothing to do with their reasons for being here. Immortality was their choice, not exploration. The Rose was mine.

– And Virgil's, said Flapping Eagle. Grimus ignored him.

– This is the Perfect Dimension, he said. In another potential Dimension, you never came to Calf Island. In another, I never found the Stone Rose. In yet another, I continue to live, for ever, prisoner to my own ideas. But here, it must all be as I intended it.

His hands were working feverishly now, his voice was piercingly shrill.

– Supposing I had succumbed to Dimension-fever? asked Flapping Eagle.

– You couldn't possibly, said Grimus. Your Ions were too strong. Notice the means you used to vanquish your monster: Chaos. The true weapon of the destroyer. Your unconscious mind knew exactly what it was doing.

– There was a risk, said Flapping Eagle.

– Nonsense, said Grimus. With Virgil Jones, the Gorf Koax as well as myself looking over your shoulder? Nonsense. You played your hand well, though, I won't deny you that.

Something snapped inside Flapping Eagle at the sight of that face, so much his own and yet so little his own, smiling at him benignly. Or perhaps it would be more exact to say that a number of things fell into place. An old, old memory stirred: the memory of a man searching for a voice in which to speak. Flapping Eagle, in the company of the orchestrator of his life, had finally found such a voice for himself.

– Played my hand well, he repeated with quiet fury. A revealing metaphor, don't you think? The Stone Rose has warped you, Grimus; its knowledge has made you as twisted, as eaten away by power-lust, as its effect has stunted and deformed the lives of the people you brought here. This is a game, isn't it, a game you're enjoying? An infinity of continua, of possibilities both present and future, the free-play of time itself, bent and shaped into a zoo for your personal enjoyment. Yes, you have made me, I grant it. Yes, you have brought me here in the condition you wanted for the lunatic purpose you envisaged. You are so far removed from the pains and tormented of the world you left and the world you made that you can even see death as an academic exercise. You can plan your own death as a kind of perfect game of chess. But in the end it all depends on me, Grimus, in some way which you haven't yet explained. It all hangs on my choice and I tell you now I am not going to play. Virgil asked me to destroy the Stone Rose. I am now convinced he was right. It has already shattered too many lives. Too many possibilities of happiness. I said it to the goddess Axona in my fever and I say it to you: *Grimus, I shall destroy you if I can.*

Grimus applauded gravely.

— Ah, a spirited death, he said. Good. Good.

Flapping Eagle gathered his strength to do — what? — he could not form any plan. He stood helplessly, clutching his ju-ju stick, as Grimus laughed.

— I shall destroy you, repeated Flapping Eagle, but not in the way you want. I will not assume your mantle.

Grimus said: — I think it's almost time to tell you my plan for my death, which is, of course, my plan for you. But before I do, I should like to set at rest certain misapprehensions you appear to be fostering. Please follow me.

He went through the door into the Kâf-room, the empty area with the letter Kâf on a wall. Flapping Eagle followed, seeing no reason not to. He still needed Grimus, needed him to find the Stone Rose.

— You say I am detached from my creation, said Grimus. This room will bear witness I am not. And who do you think it is that watches over K? Do you not think those aged houses would have fallen down by now? Do you not think that much-tilled soil would be exhausted by now? Did you ever wonder why Mr Gribb never ran out of paper or where the metal hinges which held the doors on were made? The truth is, Flapping Eagle, a Conceptual Dimension like Calf Island needs constant fostering and Re-Conceptualizing at regular intervals, in order to preserve its existence. If I am to die without a successor the island will crumble. You have to take my place.

— You said this room was to bear witness, said Flapping Eagle.

— Yes, yes, said Grimus, showing a trace of irritation. Very well. Think of anywhere on the island. Anywhere at all.

— Just think about it? asked Flapping Eagle, wondering what was coming.

— Yes. Think hard.

Flapping Eagle found the picture of Dolores' house forming

in his mind. It would be interesting to see what had become of her . . .

And suddenly they were there. In the cottage. The cottage was here, in the room, in Grimushome. The jigsaw there. The pot of root-tea, there. The rocking-chair, there . . .

In the rocking-chair, Nicholas Deggle.

– He can't see us, said Grimus.

– How are you doing this? Flapping Eagle's voice was unsteady again.

– An adjustment of the Rose. I use it to keep watch on the island when I'm tired of using the Watercrystal. So much more detail here. By the way, Dolores O'Toole is dead.

The scene faded. Once more, an empty room.

– You see, said Grimus. I'm not really out of touch.

No, thought Flapping Eagle. You have reduced all other lives to the same level of unreality as your own. They are fictions now, illusions called up by Conceptualizing and the Rose . . . they cannot move you in this form. They don't affect you. Aloud he said : – I disagree.

Grimus turned and walked from the room in that stylized bird-gait of his.

– The third part of the Dance will now begin, he said. I shall explain the manner of my death.

Flapping Eagle, seated once more in the rocking-chair. Grimus, circling around him once more.

– Grimus, said Flapping Eagle. Some questions.

– Questions? Good. Good.

– Why does the Effect leave you unscathed?

– Good question, said Grimus, and fell silent. It was as though he was thinking of the answer.

Eventually he said : – I was once a prisoner of war. Every day I feared I would be killed. It was that kind of war. I sat in trucks with dozens of others and they drove us to the execution-ground and blindfolded us. We heard soldiers coming, orders to aim . . . the bullets did not come. It was an expert torture. And sometimes, just to keep us believing, they really did shoot people. But it was the torture they liked. Some people died of heart attacks. Not me. I learnt two things about myself : first, that it was a matter of the utmost aportance to me whether my body lived or died. Second, that at some future time, I wanted to be the one to organize my life. Exactly as I wished it.

And so you built your own prison, thought Flapping Eagle.

— Aportance? he said.

— When a thing is neither important nor unimportant, said Grimus, when, in fact the concept of importance ceases to have meaning, you have understood aportance. This is why the Inner Dimensions could not hurt me: I am pliable, willing to believe anything, willing to accept any new horror, any vile truth about myself. I have no secrets from myself. So I can live with the Inner Dimensions. They coexist with my conscious self, continually. Do you see?

— Yes, said Flapping Eagle. I see.

— Another question, said Grimus. One tells one's Death everything.

— Yes. Just one more. (*I'll reserve the blinks for a better moment. There will be a better moment*, he told himself.)

— All the people on the island, he said, seem to come from a time roughly contemporaneous with the time I took the Elixir. So do you, in fact.

— Observant of you, said Grimus. Several reasons, really. One, I didn't want to cause vast social problems by combining cavemen and astronauts. Two, I find my own time a great deal more interesting than either the past or the future. And three, it proved easiest to transport people from parallel dimensions if one fixed upon a constant time. Made the settings easier and so forth. No more questions?

— Yes, said Flapping Eagle, remembering.

Grimus clucked his tongue in admonition. — Such mental imprecision, he said.

— Don't you consider your Experiment to have been a failure since the Effect has changed its course so completely?

He kept his voice deliberately level, abstract.

— Not at all, said Grimus. Good question. Not at all. My, you ask good questions. (*Again, a slight feeling that something had got under his skin.*) It merely changed the nature of the experiment. And helped with the necessary alienation. It is important that K should dislike me. For my Death, you know. For my Death.

— All right, said Flapping Eagle, seeing no alternative.

Tell me about it.   *   *   *

– Simple, said Grimus. I have put Bird-Dog through a course of deep hypnosis. At a given command she will Travel to Liv's house. I shall of course open the Gate. She is instructed to tell Liv she hates me – and for the sake of verisimilitude I have abused her for centuries, so she shouldn't find it too difficult to obey the post-hypnotic suggestion. She hates me and wants me killed. Liv, of course, has had her hate of me (carefully-nurtured by me, might I add) revived recently by her adventure with you. Obviously she knows, now that she is no longer in her trance, that her plan misfired somewhat, her sexual revenge I mean. So she will be very bitter, and will agree. The flux-lines say she will. I have examined them. Free will really is an illusion, you know. People behave according to the flux-lines of their potential futures.

Anyhow. They will attempt to drum up support, being sufficiently in awe of me not to attempt my murder on their own. Here again your mishaps in K were exactly correct. K is now more antagonistic to me than ever. And so we come to my murderers. A fascinating trio. Flann O'Toole is one. The thought of playing Napoleon, of leading an invading army, will be irresistible to him. The second is Peckenpaw. For him it will be a revenge for the death of his friend and a chance to return to the chase, the thrill of the chase. The third is more unlikely, perhaps. Mr Moonshy will join the merry band. He will tell himself it is to free the island from tyranny. Perhaps it will be. Perhaps he is really more interested in Irina Cherkassova than he allows. Those are the three who will come through the Gate, which I shall leave open. Flann O'Toole, as no doubt you noticed, has very powerful hands.

Strangler's hands, remembered Flapping Eagle.

– The key figure in all this, said Grimus equably, is Liv. It is her passion which will drive them. Not Bird-Dog's: she is a Spectre of Grimus. Not their own, for it is tempered with fear. It is Liv who will push them. Thanks to you. Angel of Death. You have prepared the Mountain of Kâf to turn upon the Simurg. And you will be the new master, because I shall have taught you how.

– You really wish to die like that, at the hands of a mob? asked Flapping Eagle.

– Of course, said Grimus with simple insanity. I have

planned it for years. It is both psychologically and symbolically satisfying. The period of stability containing the seeds of its own downfall. The cataclysm being followed by a new and very similar order. It is aesthetic. It is right.

Grimus hopped across the room and pulled on a bellcord. Though it was late at night, Bird-Dog was with them within a minute, panting and out of breath. Again Flapping Eagle felt a helpless rage at seeing his flesh and blood so humbled. Perhaps he, too, was as trapped as Bird-Dog, he thought, and then attempted without success to expunge the thought from his mind.

— Bird-Dog, said Grimus.
— Yes.
— This is my final order to you, said Grimus.
— Yes, said Bird-Dog, starting.
— *The Order is Final*, said Grimus.

Bird-Dog turned and walked towards the door. Flapping Eagle rushed to her and grasped her by the shoulders. — Don't go, he said. Fight your conditioning. Say no.

— I want to go, said Bird-Dog quietly. I want him killed.

Grimus laughed happily in the background as Flapping Eagle released his sister. Who walked out of the room and shut the concealed door behind her.

Violence was all Flapping Eagle had left.

— Grimus, he said. If you don't show me the Stone Rose now I shall happily strangle you myself for what you have done to my sister. Now, before your well-planned death can occur, as you say it will. It will be a miserable, meaningless death, Grimus.

— My, said Grimus. How cross you do get. I was just going to the Rose anyway. I have to set it in order to open the Gate.

He moved to the corner of the room nearest the centre of the house.

And pushed open a second secret door. Inside, at the heart of the house, was the Rose Room.

So that was why the house was such a crazy shape. Its labyrinthine excesses fogged the brain to such an extent that the presence of this small room went completely unnoticed. Flapping Eagle, who had been concentrating on the shape of the house when he arrived, had not even begun to guess at the room's existence.

— Come, said Grimus. This is the last part of the Dance of Wisdom and Death.

The Stone Rose was actually not a rose at all. Flapping Eagle watched as Grimus set it, as it lay in its coffin in the small secret room, and began to understand.

Around the top of a central shaft, or stem, were a series of thin, star-shaped slabs of stone. Flapping Eagle counted seven such slabs. The top two had four points each, the next eight, the next sixteen, and so forth. Each slab rotated independently around the central stem. Setting the Rose appeared to consist of aligning the slabs in different relationships to each other. This is what Grimus was doing now. About halfway down the Stem, at convenient holding-height, was a sort of bulge.

— In some Dimensions, said Grimus, the Object is different. It varies according to the capabilities of the ruling species, you see. There are settings for space-warp, Travel to parallel dimensions, and so forth.

Flapping Eagle spoke.

— I haven't changed my mind, Grimus, he said. I am going to break that thing. You can't control it. It controls you. And then there are the blinks. The Rose is damaged, Grimus. It is dangerous. It has made you dangerous.

Grimus' eyes gleamed for a moment, then went dull.

— Please, he said, and there was a new pleading tone in his voice. I would like to show you just one more discovery of mine. If it does not persuade you of the enormous value of the Rose, of the importance of preserving it and maintaining it when I am dead, then I will allow you to do whatever you wish. Just one discovery.

Flapping Eagle could not deny him. It was a small thing to concede. Now that he had the Rose in his reach, Grimus could not hold him back. After all, Flapping Eagle told himself, he was armed. Not just with bow and arrow, but with a powerful obligation. To Virgil. To his own, destructive past. This time his Ions could be put to good use: if he was a destroyer, let him at least destroy dangerous things.

Grimus had moved to a darkened corner of the small room. He took a cloth off a small object lying there. It was a transparent, spherical shape with a handle on each side. As Grimus picked it up by one of its handles, it began to glow.

— I foresaw I would have great difficulty in getting you to see my point of view, he said. It was for this reason that I conceptualized the Subsumer. If you take the other handle, we can communicate telepathically. Through the medium of this sphere. Are you willing?

Flapping Eagle hesitated for a moment.

— Are you afraid? asked Grimus in a child's sing-song voice.

Flapping Eagle said: — No. He could take anything which Grimus, the ancient infant, could take. He had already proved the strength of his will, after all.

He put down his ju-ju stick on the edge of the Rose's coffin and came up to Grimus. Then, taking a deep breath, he grasped the proffered handle of the — what was it? — the *Subsumer*.

The last thing he remembered as Flapping Eagle was Grimus' high, shrill voice saying delightedly: — *My old mother always told me, you've got to trick people into accepting new ideas.*

(I was Flapping Eagle.)
(I was Grimus.)

Self. My self. Myself and he alone. Myself and his self in the glowing bowl. Yes, it was like that. Myself and himself pouring out of ourselves into the glowing bowl. *Easy does it. You swallow me, I swallow you. Mingle, commingle. Come mingle. Grow together, come. You into me into you.* His thoughts.

Yes, it was like that, Printing. Like printing. Press, his thoughts pressed over mine, under mine, through and into mine, his thoughts mine. Mine his. *The swallow is a graceful bird.* Two swallows, and then one half-eagle-half-him and the other half-him-half-eagle. Yes, it was like that. We were one there in the glowing bowl, two here in the flesh. Yes.

My son. The mind of Grimus rushing to me. You are my son, I give you my life. *I have become you, I have become you are me.* The mind of Grimus, rushing through. The mandarin monk released into me in an orgasm of thinking. The halfbreed, semi-semitic prisoner of war and his contradictions, the aportance of self coexisting with the utter necessity of imparting that self, cruel necessity, ineluctable, the mind of Grimus rushing through. Like a beating of wings his self flying in. *My son, my son, what father fathered a son like this, as I do in my sterility.*

The light faded in the glowing sphere; the transfer was complete. I let go of my handle – my body was mine to command once more. He released his grip as well. The sphere fell.

And shattered on the stone floor.

– Now, he said. Now we are the same. Now you understand.

Mad? What is mad? It would be easy to call him mad, but he is in my head now and I can see his whys. They are not whys which go well into words. The undermining horror of prison camp, the destruction of his human dignity, of his belief in the whole human race; the subsequent burrowing away, away from the world, into books and philosophies and mythologies, until these became his realities, these his friends and companions, and the world was just an awful nightmare; the monkish man finding beauty in birds and stories. And then the Rose and a chance to shape a world and a life and a death exactly as he wanted, and naturally since he had no regard for his species he did not care what he did to them. They had done enough to him. To his birds, he was kind. He gathered them around him and lived out his favourite story, his ornithological myth. Mad? What is mad? To him, ideas were the sole justification for existence; and when he found the knowledge and power to play with his ideas, he could not be stopped. Knowledge corrupts; absolute knowledge corrupts absolutely. Yes, he was mad. But he is in me, and I know him.

There is still an *I*. An *I* within me that is not *him*.

We are at war about the Rose.

– Look, said Grimus. (I was in him as he is in me. The Subsumer works both ways.)

He held up a small mirror, held it against his chest, angled up towards my face.

My hair had become white. It was his face now, his face entirely, his head on my shoulders.

I was Flapping Eagle.

A second secret door, leading into the room where Media slept. This small room, at the very centre of the house, adjoining most of its rooms. Grimus (who was partly Flapping Eagle) led Media by the hand to where I stood, by the coffin which held the Rose.

— Stay here, he said. Look after each other. They will come soon. But even Bird-Dog does not know about this room.

There was fear in his face. I recognized it; it was my fear. It was the *me* which he had imbibed that was scared of dying.

— You will not harm the Rose now, he said. We are the same. And he left.

— He's changed you, she whispered.

Media was looking at me, wide-eyed.

I held her hand. At least she was the same. One constant thing in a transfigured universe.

The Rose. The *him* in me had a will of its own, and it was forcing me to bow to its wishes. The *I* in me was weakened, enfeebled by the shock of subsumation. I stood looking at the Rose for a long, long time. The bump on its stem seemed to acquire a great fascination for me, a magnetic attraction. Perhaps it was the *him* in me which did that.

Suddenly, I grasped the Rose. By the bump. It fitted well into my hand. Then I screamed, and Media screamed. I screamed in pain. She screamed because I disappeared from the room altogether.

I had Travelled.

The pain is caused by one's first experience of the Outer Dimensions. Suddenly the universe dissolves, and for a fraction of time you are simply a small bundle of energy adrift in a sea of unimaginably vast forces. It is a devastating, agonizing piece of knowledge. Then it – the universe – assembled once again.

When the Gorfs created the Objects which linked the infinity of Conceived and Inconceivable Dimensions, they always included one element which beamed directly to the planet Thera. The bump served that function on the Stone Rose.

I was there, on Thera, beneath the star Nus, at the edge of the Yawy Klim galaxy in the Gorf Nirveesu. In a small airbubble, sitting on a wide flat rock. Being observed.

Outside, yellow sun against black sky, and a number of stone monoliths surrounding me.

— They look like frogs, I thought. Huge stone frogs. (I-me

thought it, not I-Grimus. I-Grimus was reserving its powers to fight me over the Rose.)

– *Is it Grimus?* The thought, unspoken, unformed into words, came into my mind. It was followed by a second, a deeper, wiser thought-form.

– *Yes . . . no . . . ah, I see.* I had the sense of being stripped naked. My mind had been scanned.

– Where are you? I shouted, and the I-Grimus within me told me that these monoliths, lumpy, huge and surrounded in a slight haze, were the most intelligent life-form in any Galaxy, and that the second thought-form had been that of the great thinker Dota himself.

– *The non-Grimus element appears to be marginally in command,* came a third thought-form.

– *Good.* Dota again. *Listen,* he thought at me, slightly too loud, like a man dealing with a stupid foreigner. *We are the Gorfs.* There then followed a very rapid series of thought-forms which told me the history of the race and the Objects.

– *We have two great concerns,* thought Dota. *The first is for the Gorf Koax, who has settled irrelevantly in your Endimions. Should you meet him, kindly let him know that his gross Bad Order has led to his being banned from Thera. He is not welcome here. He stands or falls with your Endimions.*

– Ah, I thought.

– *Which leads us to our second concern,* thought Dota. *We are extremely perturbed about Grimus' misuse of the Rose. It was never intended to be a tool for intraendimions travel. Nor a magic box for the production of food. It is a flagrant distortion of Conceptual Technology to use the Rose to Conceptualize a packet of* (he searched for the right form) *coffee.*

Most particularly we are worried about the subendimions he has set up on the mountain-top. Subendimions are Conceptually unsound. A place is either part of an Endimions or it is not. To Conceptualize a place which is both a part of an Endimions and yet secret from it could stretch the Object to disintegration-point. We would like this ridiculous Concept to be dissolved forthwith. That is all. You may return.

I could feel the I-Grimus part of me throbbing angrily at Dota's reproof. Then I realized there were some questions that could be answered here better than anywhere else.

– Dota, I thought.

– *Yes?* The thought was curt, the form of a great mind disturbed.

– Are the blinks in our Dimension a result of the mutilation of the Rose?

– *We don't know,* came the reply. *Yours is the only Object to have been defaced, and the only Endimions which blinks. There may be a cause and effect relationship. There may not. It may be something which should concern you. It may not. We don't know everything, you understand.*

– One more question, I asked. The air in my bubble felt stale. I would have to go soon.

– *Well?*

– Is it possible to Conceptualize a Dimension . . . Endimions . . . which does not contain any Object?

A long pause, in which I felt complex arguments flashing between the assembled Gorfs.

– *We cannot be sure,* said Dota. *For us, the answer would be No, since the very existence of the Endimions relative to us is a function of the Object. But for a dweller in the Endimions . . .* a mental shrug-form followed.

– *Goodbye,* said Dota's lieutenant.

I searched in the I-Grimus and found the technique for returning to the Rose. A moment later I stood in the secret room again.

Media looked very relieved!

Flann O'Toole, wearing his Napoleon hat, right hand concealed in his buttoned greatcoat, face whisky-red, climbing the steps. At his side, One-Track Peckenpaw, raccoon hat jammed on, bearskin coat enveloping his bulk, coiled rope hanging over one shoulder, rifle in hand. And behind them, P. S. Moonshy, a glaring-eyed, unshaven clerk. An unlikely trinity of nemesis nearing its goal.

Grimus stood in the shade of the great ash, beside his home, the particoloured head-dress fluttering in the slight breeze, his birds lining his shoulders, clustered around him on the ground, watching over him from the vast spreading branches. His hands twitched; otherwise he was completely still.

And eventually, the four of them stood facing each other, knowing what had to be done.

Grimus said:

– I have learnt all I wish to learn.

I have been all I wish to be.

I am complete.

I have planned this. It is time.

But in his high, shrill voice was the uncertainty of the sub-sumed Eagle within him, the second self protesting. It had not chosen this death.

Flann O'Toole said: – Where is your machine, Mr Grimus? You kept it a secret from your servant woman, we know that, surely. You'll not keep it from us.

Grimus said nothing.

– One-Track, said O'Toole, try and persuade the gentleman to converse with us.

A few moments later, when Grimus' nose was broken, his eyes closing, his skin bruised, and his lips still sealed, O'Toole said: – Don't kill him, man. Not yet. Peckenpaw released Grimus. Who swayed on his feet as the blood streamed from him, but remained erect. Birds screamed in the tree.

– Search the house, said Flann O'Toole.

One-Track Peckenpaw and P. S. Moonshy went into Grimushome then, but found nothing. They did, however, wreck whatever they could; and when they came out, Grimus' shrouded collection lay around its pedestals in fragments, the shards of a lifetime's Travel. The Crystals, broken. The Ion Eye, trodden on and crushed.

Suddenly, as they emerged into the misty dawn light, the whine stopped. Abruptly, without any warning. It was simply no longer there.

Flann O'Toole was watching Grimus; so he saw the face sag, saw the look of horror in the blackened eyes, saw the exhaustion seep through the pain. He saw it, and smiled.

– You found it, then, he said to Peckenpaw.

– We found a whole lot of things, said Peckenpaw. So we broke them all. I dunno what they were.

– O, you found it, said O'Toole. Mr Grimus here has just this minute told me.

Grimus remained silent.

– One more thing, said Peckenpaw. I want Flapping Eagle. Where is he?

Grimus said nothing.

Flann O'Toole put his hands around the battered man's neck

264

and pressed with his thumbs. – Come now, Mr Grimus, he said. You'll tell us that, now?

Grimus said: – I expelled him from the island. He is no longer here.

– That is the truth, isn't it, now? asked O'Toole.

– Reckon so, said Peckenpaw. Nobody in the house. Nobody out here. Flapping Eagle's a lucky man.

P. S. Moonshy spoke for the first time. – What are we waiting for? he said.

O'Toole favoured him with an amused smile.

– Mr Moonshy is in a hurry, he explained apologetically to Grimus. And now that we have completed our task, there is little point in delaying matters, Mr Grimus. I'd be grateful if you'd stand just here.

He moved Grimus to a position directly under the thickest branch of the tree.

Grimus said: – I have no reason to live. It is planned.

O'Toole smiled. – O, good, he said. Most co-operative of you, Mr Grimus.

Beads of cold sweat mingled with the congealing blood on Grimus' face.

– Why, Mr Grimus, said Flann O'Toole. I do believe you're frightened.

– Not I, said Grimus. Him.

– Is there a fire lit anywhere in the house? asked Flann O'Toole.

– I saw one, said Peckenpaw. In the entrance hall.

– Good, said Flan O'Toole.

As the three assassins moved away, down the stone steps, the great ash blazed behind them, and the body of a man, ridiculously small against the trunk to which it had been tied, grew charred and blackened in the flames. Suddenly it fell, as the fire licked through the rope which held it, and lay on the ground as the blaze grew stronger. Branches crashed in showers of sparks and smoke around and over him, forming an incandescent tomb. And around the column of smoke, a great dark cloud of circling, shrieking birds, swooping and shrieking, pronounced his epitaph.

*   *   *

There was no Gate now. Calf Island was one place again. The steps led down to Liv's house, which was solid, visible. With the end of the whine had come the end of the Sub-dimension. There were no ghosts now.

Bird-Dog sat slumped against the foot of the steps, and stiffened as the three men reached her. They passed her without speaking.

The blackveiled woman came out of her small black house. Bird-Dog watched her speak to the trio, followed O'Toole's pointing arm to the rising pillar of smoke. Liv nodded, quickly, and went indoors. The assassins continued down the Mountain to K.

A moment later, Liv Sylwan Jones emerged once more. She held a knife in her right hand, a knife which had carved innumerable ugly things from the wood of the encroaching trees. She sat down on the ground.

With the knife in her right hand, and with intense concentration, she slit the vein in her left wrist. Then she transferred the knife to that hand and set about slashing the right wrist, equally methodically.

Bird-Dog came over to her and stood in front of her, saying nothing, silently looking on. Liv Sylwan Jones returned her gaze.

– It's done now, she said, jerking her head at the column of smoke.

Like Grimus, Liv had chosen her moment of death. Death on the Mountain of Kâf must be chosen. A selected violence against the body.

With exaggerated care, she drew a red line with the knife, a thin, leaking red mouth, grinning bloodily from ear to ear, beneath her chin.

Bird-Dog watched it drip.

A small mound of disturbed earth, freshly-turned, stood in the forest behind the blackwashed house. A wooden carving lay upon it, a distorted, open-mouthed death's head.

A woman in a black robe, her face hidden behind a black veil, walked away from it, away into the black house, averting her eyes from the rising smoke and sat, perfectly still, upon the one chair, amid the filth and mould, and began to chant an old, half-forgotten, half-remembered Axona hymn to death.

*   *   *

– My God, said Nicholas Deggle.

Virgil Jones turned towards him, slowly.

– The Stem, said Deggle. It's gone. Quite gone.

He began to search desperately around the small, rickety shack. Virgil hauled himself out of his rocking-chair and went outside.

– Well done, he said, looking up the Mountain. Well done.

Deggle came out to join him. – It's nowhere to be found, he said.

– The Rose has been broken, said Virgil Jones.

– What do you mean?

– I mean that Flapping Eagle has succeeded. Brilliantly.

Nicholas Deggle charged into the forest.

A while later, he returned, full of bewildered surprise.

– There's no whine, he said. Nothing. We can go up to K.

– I'm going to the beach, said Virgil Jones.

Mr Virgil Jones, a man devoid of friends and with a tongue rather too large for his mouth, was fond of descending this cliff-path on Tiusday mornings, to indulge his liking for Calf Island's one small beach. Below him, under the shifting grey-silver sands, lay the body of Mrs Dolores O'Toole.

Mr Jones stood, facing away from the sea, looking towards the massive forested rock of Calf Mountain, which occupied most of the island except for the small clearing, directly above the beach, where Mr Jones and Dolores had lived. The body of Mrs O'Toole lay between him and the forested slopes.

– Crestfallen, murmured Mr Jones to himself, with his back to the sea. Crestfallen, the sea today.

Well, well, thought the Gorf Koax. A fascinating new status quo. Flapping Eagle and the girl Media replacing Grimus and Bird-Dog. Bird-Dog replacing Liv. Elfrida Gribb replacing Media. Virgil Jones returned to the foot of the island. And the other, earlier re-orderings: Alexei Cherkassov replacing his father. Mr Moonshy replacing Mr Page.

But most interesting of all is the fate of the Rose. Without it, Flapping Eagle is powerless. He is an exile at the top of the mountain. The peak implies no kind of superiority now.

– What are you going to do? Media had said.

Outside, the assassins faced the feathered Grimus.

Inside, in the secret room, I (I-Eagle) was engaged in a furious battle with the I-Grimus within.

– You must preserve the Rose, said I-Grimus. You need it for the constant re-conceptualization of the island. As I explained. You must preserve the Rose. Relativity holds good even between dimensions. They exist only in conjunction with one another, as functions of one another. Destroy the Rose, and you destroy our link with the Dimension-continua. We cannot survive that.

– Grimus misused the Rose, remembered I-Eagle. The blinks are proof that it is both damaged and being stretched to breaking-point. We cannot continue to use it as Grimus did.

– The Gorfs made the Rose to link the Dimensions, cried I-Grimus inside me. Break it and you break us. Dota could not conceive of a Dimension without an Object.

– But he said that he could conceive of a Dimension-dweller devising such a Concept, said I-Eagle.

Then the I-Grimus ceased to reason with I-Eagle and flooded me with thought-forms. The Rose enables you to travel, said the forms, and showed I-Eagle a thousand beautiful worlds, a thousand universes to explore. The Rose enables you to learn, said the thought-forms, and revealed a hundred new sciences and a hundred new art-forms, the cream of the infinite galaxies. You have one life, said the thought-forms. With the Rose you can enter into, and become, a thousand thousand other people, live an infinity of lives, and acquire the wisdom and power to shape your own. And they showed I-Eagle some of the people Grimus had watched and understood, showed the vicarious joys and agonies of countless lives. And one day, said the thought-forms, when you have done all you wished to do, been all you wished to be, you can pass this supreme gift on to another, choose the moment and manner of your going and give the Phoenix a new life, a new beginning.

But I-Eagle had seen too much on Calf Island and outside it, seen too much of the way I-Grimus had ruined lives for the sake of an idea. To I-Grimus ideas, discoveries, learning, these were all-important. I-Eagle saw the centuries of wretched wandering that preceded my arrival, saw the people of K reduced to a blind philosophy of pure survival, clutching obsessively at the shreds of their individuality, knowing within themselves that they were powerless to alter the circumstances in which they lived. The combined force of unlimited power, un-limited learning, and a rarefied, abstract attitude to life which exalted these two into the greatest goals of humanity, was a force I-Eagle could not bring himself to like. I-Eagle saw its effect on Virgil Jones, on Dolores O'Toole, on Liv Jones, on Bird-Dog, his sister even though they had long been estranged. No, I-Eagle thought, the Rose is not the supreme gift.

Then all discussion, whether rational or thought-formal, ceased, and the I-Grimus within released upon I-Eagle the full force of his formidable will. Media saw me (us) stagger and lurch as the war raged within, and she grasped my hand.

Perhaps that was what turned the tide towards I-Eagle. I was not alone. Media was there. Media, one of the many whose lives he had distorted. Media, one of the many to whom I-Eagle felt responsible. The guilt of recent events was still there. I was fighting for the island. *He* was fighting for himself. And he lost.

Outside, Peckenpaw and Moonshy ransacked the house.

I, I-Eagle, spoke to Media. The I-Grimus had receded with-in me, a throbbing pain in the back of my head.

– I intend to destroy the Rose, I-Eagle said. I won't pretend there is no risk. It could unmake us all.

– Grimus' machine is not worth saving, she said. Do it now. Perhaps it is better to be dead than to live in fear of . . . *this*.

I-Eagle nodded and receded once more into my mind, find-ing the I-Grimus, forcing him to reveal the secrets of the Rose. He was unwilling, knowing why I wanted them, but he was beaten. I found the knowledge within him, and made a setting. Then it was a question of Conceptualization.

First, I-Eagle dismantled the Sub-dimension; that was the easy part. I made a picture grow in my head, a picture of Calf Island as one thing, Grimushome on the peak, the steps leading down to Liv's outcrop. No Gates, no barriers. I knew when it had worked. It was, in a way, like *setting* an Inner Dimension. After a while one knew it was there, fixed, as one had thought it. For a moment I was lost in admiration of this Object, so incredibly complex, so incredibly simple. Then I collected myself and set about the harder task.

I began to re-create Calf Island, exactly as it was, with one difference: it was to contain no Rose. I had decided that this was a better alternative than physically breaking the Rose.

Less risky, in view of what had happened after Deggle's attempt.

It was now that the I-Grimus made its last attempt. It showed me something I had forgotten it knew: the co-ordinates of my Dimension, to which he had expelled Nicholas Deggle so long ago. The meaning was simple: if I chose not to destroy the Rose, I could go back to my own world. I-Grimus preferred to go, with I-Eagle, far away from the Rose, perhaps never to find its counterpart in my Dimension, rather than see it destroyed.

I-Eagle cannot say I was not tempted; but then there was Media again, Media and the rest of them, depending on me.

– O, hell, I said aloud. What would I do there anyway?

And the I-Grimus had no tricks left.

I used him. He had shaped the island in the first place, so he knew it best. I drew his knowledge out of him and used it. It seemed like an eternity, but thought-forms move quicker than anything ever known, so it was actually over very soon.

I stood in the secret room with an awe-struck Media, looking down at the coffin of the Stone Rose.

It was empty.

The Rose had gone, and we had not.

The man who had been Flapping Eagle and was now part-Eagle, part-Grimus, was making love to Media, who had been a whore and was now his mainstay, when the Gorf Koax, who had transported himself to the peak of Calf Mountain, sensed something wrong.

The mists around the island.

The mists which circled and shrouded.

The eternal, unlifting veils.

The mists were growing thicker. Slowly, slowly, they were descending, closing in upon the island on all sides, closer, closer, a dense grey fog now, closing, closing.

And they were not mists.

Deprived of its connection with all relative Dimensions, the world of Calf Mountain was slowly unmaking itself, its molecules and atoms breaking, dissolving, quietly vanishing into primal, unmade energy. The raw material of being was claiming its own.

So that, as Flapping Eagle and Media writhed upon their bed, the Mountain of Grimus danced the Weakdance to the end.